Irish author **Abby Green** en
career in film and TV—whic̲ ̲ ̲ ̲ ̲ ̲ ̲ ̲ ̲ ̲
of a lot of standing in the rain outside actors'
trailers—to pursue her love of romance. After
she'd bombarded Mills & Boon with manuscripts
they kindly accepted one, and an author was born.
She lives in Dublin, Ireland, and loves any excuse
for distraction. Visit abby-green.com or email
abbygreenauthor@gmail.com.

USA TODAY bestselling, RITA®-nominated and
critically acclaimed author **Caitlin Crews** has
written more than 130 books and counting. She
has a Master's and a PhD in English Literature,
thinks everyone should read more category
romance, and is always available to discuss her
beloved alpha heroes. Just ask! She lives in the
Pacific Northwest with her comic book artist
husband, is always planning her next trip, and will
never, ever, read all the books in her to-be-read
pile. Thank goodness.

Also by Abby Green

'I Do' for Revenge
Rush to the Altar

Brazilian Billionaire Brothers miniseries

The Heir Dilemma
On His Bride's Terms

Also by Caitlin Crews

Her Accidental Spanish Heir

Notorious Mediterranean Marriages miniseries

Greek's Enemy Bride
Carrying a Sicilian Secret

Work Wives to Billionaires' Wives collection

Kidnapped for His Revenge

Discover more at millsandboon.co.uk.

GREEK SCANDALS

ABBY GREEN

CAITLIN CREWS

MILLS & BOON

All rights reserved including the right of reproduction in whole or in part in any form. This edition is published by arrangement with Harlequin Enterprises ULC.

This is a work of fiction. Names, characters, places, locations and incidents are purely fictional and bear no relationship to any real life individuals, living or dead, or to any actual places, business establishments, locations, events or incidents. Any resemblance is entirely coincidental.

Without limiting the author's and publisher's exclusive rights, any unauthorised use of this publication to train generative artificial intelligence (AI) technologies is expressly prohibited. HarperCollins also exercise their rights under Article 4(3) of the Digital Single Market Directive 2019/790 and expressly reserve this publication from the text and data mining exception.

® and TM are trademarks owned and used by the trademark owner and/or its licensee. Trademarks marked with ® are registered with the United Kingdom Patent Office and/or the Office for Harmonisation in the Internal Market and in other countries.

First published in Great Britain 2025
by Mills & Boon, an imprint of HarperCollins*Publishers* Ltd,
1 London Bridge Street, London, SE1 9GF

www.harpercollins.co.uk

HarperCollins*Publishers*, Macken House, 39/40 Mayor Street Upper, Dublin 1, D01 C9W8, Ireland

Greek Scandals © 2025 Harlequin Enterprises ULC

Billion-Dollar Baby Shock © 2025 Abby Green

Forbidden Greek Mistress © 2025 Caitlin Crews

ISBN: 978-0-263-34475-2

08/25

This book contains FSC™ certified paper
and other controlled sources to ensure responsible forest management.

For more information visit www.harpercollins.co.uk/green.

Printed and Bound in the UK using 100% Renewable Electricity
at CPI Group (UK) Ltd, Croydon, CR0 4YY

BILLION-DOLLAR BABY SHOCK

ABBY GREEN

MILLS & BOON

PROLOGUE

TARA SIMONS LOOKED at her beloved younger sister Mary and tried to keep the flutter of panic at bay.

'Mary, tell me again what happened.'

Her sister's lip wobbled ominously but she said, 'Can you not put your hands on your hips like that? It's intimidating.'

Tara forced a reassuring smile and took her hands off her hips and held them out. 'Better now?'

Mary nodded. She was pale. Blue eyes huge. Tara couldn't help but be reminded of the day they'd stood by their parents' grave nearly ten years ago. Mary had been only thirteen. Tara, at sixteen, had been the eldest, and had been suddenly thrust into being the matriarch of her four younger siblings.

But the past wasn't the issue here. She was about to put her hands back on her hips when her sister blurted out, 'Your eggs. The eggs you had frozen two years ago. There was a mix-up and they got used to create an embryo with a client's sperm.'

Tara's legs went from under her. Luckily there was a chair right behind her in their family home kitchen. She absorbed what she'd just heard and looked at her sister, who worked as a nurse at the fertility clinic. 'Okay…well, that doesn't necessarily mean that—' She saw her sister's face and stopped talking.

Mary whispered, 'I'm so sorry, Tara. I know you froze your eggs because after bringing us all up you wanted to have your independence and a career and be able to choose the right time to be a mother and now...' She trailed off.

'Now what?' Tara asked, panic surging.

Mary gulped visibly. 'One of the embryos was viable. It was implanted successfully into a surrogate here in Dublin and she went back to the United States to have the baby... for the client. A man.'

'A man,' Tara repeated like a parrot.

Mary nodded. Tara shook her head, struggling to understand what this meant. 'But how...why? Where...?'

'I only just found out when I went to extract eggs for another client. I saw that yours had been disturbed. Tara, I'm so sorry...'

'But...you're telling me that there's...a baby?'

Her sister looked green now. She nodded miserably. Tara stood up so abruptly the kitchen chair fell over behind her. Her sister winced. Tara didn't notice.

She felt light-headed. 'You're telling me that there's a man out there somewhere who now has my baby?'

The fact that she was still a virgin and yet she'd created a baby with some stranger struck her as almost hysterically funny for a second. But it didn't last. Panic returned.

She grabbed her sister by the arm and pulled her up from her chair. 'Ow, Tara, you're hurting me...' Tara didn't listen, she all but dragged her sister out of the house to the battered family car outside.

'Where are we going?' her sister asked nervously.

Even though Tara had made that spur-of-the-moment decision to freeze her eggs—future-proofing her fertility—and had had no desire to become a mother so soon after gaining her own independence, the thought of *her* baby out there somewhere, without her, was anathema to her.

Tara looked at her sister. 'To the clinic. You're going to track down the identity of the man who is the father of my child.'

CHAPTER ONE

DIONYSIOS DIMITRIOU SCANNED the thronged room full of the crème de la crème of Athenian society with a practised eye. It was an annual glamorous charity event—a masked ball held in a private villa with jaw-dropping views over Athens.

Dusk was fading into night beyond the wide-open French doors leading out into landscaped gardens. Lanterns threw golden light over the already glittering crowd. The Acropolis was lit up on a hill in the distance, the ancient monument humbling in its magnificence.

Moments like this never failed to fill Dion with a sense of pride—for how much he'd achieved all on his own.

His gaze skated over tycoons, billionaires, politicians and beautiful women. Each woman was more alluring than the last and yet…nothing. He didn't feel a blip of interest. But in recent months his priorities had shifted quite dramatically so he wasn't unduly surprised.

His phone vibrated from inside his jacket pocket. He pulled it out. There was a message from the nanny.

Nikolau is asleep, the night nanny will be here shortly. See you tomorrow. Elena.

This was the reason why his priorities had shifted. His baby son, born to a surrogate in America six months ago.

Dion was afraid to admit that he'd yet to feel a real sense of connection with the baby but he'd been assured by doctors and experts that this was normal. Sometimes it took fathers a while to connect and he had no experience of babies or children.

It was the most spontaneous thing he'd ever done, pursuing becoming a father. But something had compelled him—a growing sense of wondering what were all of his achievements for if he had no one to share it with or pass it down to?

He'd realised that he had a desire for someone in his life—but not a long-term lover. And certainly not a wife. He wanted a child. A child who he could ensure had a better upbringing than he'd experienced. Which wouldn't be hard as the bar was so low. He wanted a child who could inherit the fortune he'd created and nurtured and continued to grow. He wouldn't turn his back on his child as his parents had done to him.

Dion's mother had had an affair with a rich tycoon who had wanted nothing to do with Dion, because he had already been married with his own family.

It was safe to say that when it came to trusting women with his emotions, Dion didn't. Not after the trauma of being abandoned by the one woman who should have loved him most.

And so almost two years ago, Dion had put his plan into action, selecting a couple of the best fertility clinics in Europe to create embryos with carefully selected egg donors and his sperm. He'd managed to create a viable embryo with an egg from a clinic in Ireland, and then the baby had been born to a surrogate in America.

And now he had his son. Nikolau Dimitriou.

What about love? asked a little voice.

Dion scowled. Love hadn't helped him to where he was today. Anger and pain had. Sheer grit and determination to succeed. His son would receive better things than love: security, respect, support. A father. He didn't need a mother. Dion had survived without his.

He looked up from his phone and took in the crowd again. He spotted a woman making her way towards him and, in spite of her mask, recognised an ex-lover he had no intention of reconnecting with.

He turned on his heel and walked across to the other side of the room where there were tables groaning under lavish displays of finger food and drinks. Flutes of sparkling wine as far as the eye could see. Black-and-white-clad wait staff moving nimbly between guests. A jazz band playing in a corner.

Dion had to hand it to Leo Parnassus and his wife, Angel, the hosts of this charity event. Every year they exceeded themselves. No mean feat in Athens.

And then something caught his eye. Or, some*one*. Standing at the buffet table. He wasn't sure exactly what had caught his eye but he found himself resting a shoulder against one of the marble columns in the massive ballroom and watching.

It was a woman. Above average height. She was wearing a strapless dark green satin dress that had a criss-cross pattern under her breasts and over her midriff before it fell in layers of silk and tulle to the floor.

Her skin was very pale, with freckles that he could discern from a distance. Maybe that was what had drawn his attention? When the skin of most other people in this room ran to carefully cultivated golden tans from exclusive exotic holidays or beauty salons.

She stood out. She had red hair, that very unique Celtic

coppery red. Impossible to replicate. Again, not usual in this environment. It was pulled back in a rough chignon, drawing the eye to her slender neck and shoulders.

She wore a face mask covering the top half of her face with an elaborate feather of some kind. The same colour as the dress.

He found that he was curious to see her up close. See her face. *Touch her skin.* And just like that, awareness pulsed to life in his blood. *Not so uninterested after all.*

As he watched he saw her reach out and choose something from a plate and put it into her mouth. He could see her profile now. Straight nose. Delicate jaw. Her mouth—closing around the…prawn?—looked lush and pink. The awareness in his blood started to sizzle.

And then, she made a face and he saw her pick up a napkin, look around furtively for a moment and then spit what was in her mouth into the napkin. She looked around again.

Dion couldn't help smiling at her actions, believing she was unobserved. She was a total novelty. He hadn't come here to find a lover but now his interest was piqued.

He took a step out of the shadows and her head turned towards him and just before he reached her he could see the flush of pink climb up over her skin and into her face, the part of it not hidden by the mask. He could make out green-blue eyes behind the mask and had another realisation as he drew closer. She was stunning.

Oh, God. Had he seen her spitting the food back out into the napkin? Tara wanted the ground to open up and swallow her whole.

She couldn't believe she'd been allowed into the party in the first place. Her brother Oisín—a tech wizard—had somehow managed to get her on the guest list and, to Tara's surprise, when she'd arrived and said her name, the scarily efficient-looking event people hadn't blinked. They'd just waved her in and her mind hadn't stopped boggling since she'd walked into the most extravagantly glamorous space she'd ever seen in her life.

Not to mention the crowd. She'd never seen so many genetically blessed people in one room. And that had never applied more than right now, to the man who was walking towards her with a half-smile playing around his mouth. *His mouth.* Tara's legs felt a little weak. His mouth looked as if it had been sculpted from living marble. Firm and sensual.

He was tall and dark and intimidatingly gorgeous, obvious even with the black Zorro-style mask covering the upper half of his face. Dressed in a black tuxedo that seemed to be shrink-wrapped to his powerful body, he could have stepped straight out of a movie or fashion magazine.

Maybe he *was* a movie star? Tara was pretty sure she'd already spotted at least one Hollywood megastar as she'd tried to fade into the background along the edges of the room. And then she'd spied the buffet table and remembered she hadn't eaten since she'd left Dublin on a flight at the crack of dawn. And she needed sustenance for what she had to do. Find the father of her baby. A son. She knew that much.

The man was in front of her now and Tara had to tip her head back. She wasn't that small but he still stood almost a foot over her.

'Hello.'

His voice was low and gravelly. Accented. From somewhere Tara found her voice and it came out like a squeak. 'Hi.'

'You're not from around here, are you?'

Tara shook her head, aware of the feather on the mask floating somewhere off to the side of her head. She'd thought it was too much but her little sister Lucy, who was a fashion design student, had insisted. She'd said, 'I've researched this, Tara. You don't want to stand out for the wrong reasons, believe me.'

And, to give her her due, Tara's outfit did seem to blend in pretty well, which wasn't bad considering it was homemade. There were women dressed in a lot less and a lot sparklier and a lot more expensive. If Tara did stand out it was because she was like a milk bottle next to the far more honeyed tones of skin around her.

She said in a more modulated tone, 'I'm from Ireland. Dublin.'

'Nice country, very green. And wet.'

'I can't argue with that.'

He held out his hand, palm facing up, and Tara looked at it. She realised he wanted her to give him the food she'd rolled up in a napkin. She put it into his palm and he coolly handed it over to a server behind the tables, who took it without so much as a flicker of surprise.

Now she was really mortified. Maybe this guy was some kind of special security dressed up like a guest and she was going to be taken out discreetly and turfed out—

'Okay, so what do you like? Not prawns, evidently.'

She blinked. He was holding a plate and a pair of tongs and looking at her. She looked at the food and pointed at skewers of chicken. He picked a couple up and put them on the plate along with some salad.

'Do you like hummus?'

She nodded, totally bemused, and watched as he loaded up her plate with more things. Flatbread, cheese, olives.

He handed her her plate and then filled a plate for himself. He caught a waiter and snagged two glasses of sparkling wine and said, 'Follow me.'

Tara did as she was bid. He was even taller from the back. And broader. She could see that his hair was dark and thick. Longer than she might have thought. Brushing against the edge of his collar.

He brought her outside, where tables had been set up with candles flickering. People were sitting and eating as the sky darkened over Athens and lights illuminated the iconic city. The Acropolis was lit up on a hill nearby. Tara hadn't had time to fully appreciate where she even was, she'd been so desperate to get here.

She had to find Dionysios Dimitriou.

And yet here she was having food with a total stranger.

He pulled out a chair at an empty table on the wide terrace and she sat down, telling herself that she did need to eat and it would be better to meet the father of her child when she didn't feel faint from hunger.

Are you sure it's not the stranger's effect?

He sat down opposite her and Tara took a quick sip of wine to give her some courage. She put the glass back down. 'Thank you. I wasn't sure what the protocol was.'

He speared some meat and put it in his mouth, utterly unfazed by this whole scene. He shook his head, 'No problem at all. You might still have been dithering if I hadn't taken pity.'

She could see the gleam of something wicked in his dark eyes behind the mask and her heart pounded and her skin felt hot. 'I wasn't dithering... I just wasn't sure what to choose.'

He lifted his glass. *'Yamas.'*

Tara lifted hers too and felt a strange unsettling motion as if the earth had just shifted on its axis for a second. 'Cheers.'

She ate to try and stave off the strange feeling but it was still there every time she sneaked a glance at the man across the table. When she'd eaten enough to feel a little less...hollow, she wiped her mouth and sat back.

He'd finished eating. A clean plate. She observed, 'You were hungry too.'

Enigmatically, he said, 'I learnt a long time ago never to leave food behind.'

Before she could fully absorb that or respond he asked, 'So how do you know Leo and Angel Parnassus?'

Tara knew they were the hosts of the party. Her brother had drilled that into her. She said, 'I'm a big fan of Angel Parnassus's jewellery.' She wasn't lying. She'd looked her up online and had immediately coveted the delicate subtle pieces. But there was no way that Tara could possibly ever afford even the tiniest item the woman designed.

The man said, 'Her work is amazing.'

'It is,' Tara agreed, happy she had at least done some research.

He noted, 'And yet you're wearing no jewellery tonight?'

Tara flushed. She hadn't brought any with her. Rookie error. And it wasn't as if she had much jewellery anyway. Her mother's modest collection had been shared between her and her two sisters. She'd got her mother's engagement ring but she hardly ever wore it for fear of losing it.

Before he could totally distract her and before she lost her nerve she leant forward. She saw how the man's eyes dipped to her chest and then back up again. She tried to ignore the effect that had on her, like a hot twisting, melting sensation settling low in her belly. Between her legs.

'Actually I am here to find someone.'

He took a sip of wine and sat back. 'Oh?'

Tara tried not to notice how big his hands were, masculine, and yet he didn't look ridiculous with the delicate glass between his fingers. 'Yes…the thing is that I'm not even sure what he looks like… He's reclusive.' All her brother had been able to find out about industrialist Dionysios Dimitriou online had been intimidating facts and figures about his billion-dollar business that he'd built up from nothing.

There had been grainy photos of a tall and dark man on construction sites. Any pictures from events like this never seemed to capture his face, always the side, or back. Invariably he was with a beautiful woman but never pictured with the same woman twice.

He was an enigma. The press called him a lone wolf. And, when Tara glanced back into the crowd, there seemed to be plenty of men who were tall and dark. How on earth was she going to do this?

Then the man said, 'What's his name? Maybe I can help.'

Tara looked at him. She was a little shocked to find that she was about to tell this man who she was looking for. And she realised that if she told him he might ask more questions and she might find herself spilling why she'd come here to a complete stranger. It was up to her to do her own digging and she was getting distracted.

A waiter appeared at that moment and efficiently cleared their plates. It gave her a second to gather her wits. When they were alone again Tara stood up. 'Thank you, but that won't be necessary. And thank you for...' She trailed off. She'd been about to say *for being nice*, but this man didn't look *nice*. He looked dangerous and dark and was far too distracting.

'I should let you get back to the party. I'm sure you have more exciting things to be doing.'

More beautiful women to talk to.

The man stood too. 'Dance with me before you go?'

He held out a hand. Couples had started dancing inside, swaying to the smooth sensual music. Tara felt torn. On the one hand she'd come here on a mission and yet she'd never expected this whole scene to be so...magical. Or for this man to appear and rewire her brain with an awareness she'd never felt before.

She'd rarely, if ever, taken time out for herself since her parents had died. She'd become mother and father overnight in spite of her aunt and uncle taking over guardianship. They'd been lovely and had been financially supportive, but they hadn't been there in the way she and her siblings had needed. Hands on. Taking care to notice all the little things, like when her youngest brother, Oisín, had started spending too much time in his room on his own, gaming.

It was only since he had recently gone to university that Tara had felt as if her foot had finally come off the accelerator pedal. They were all adults now. And she'd missed out on so much. Not that she would ever, ever, regret it, or feel bitter about it. She'd just done what had to be done.

But now this man was looking at her and asking her to dance. She'd never even gone to her school debutante ball. She was still a virgin at the age of twenty-five. And that realisation made something rebellious move through her. A desire to seize this moment. Because, all of a sudden, Tara wasn't sure if she was fully ready to find the father of her baby, because once that happened, she'd be a mother again, and who knew what would happen once she confronted the father? She might have to fight for access. And as for what would happen after that? She hadn't even really gone there yet…all she knew was that she had no intention of not being involved in her son's life.

So, would it be so bad to postpone things for a little while? *No,* whispered a little voice.

Before she could overthink it, she put her hand in the man's and noticed with a little thrill how small and pale her hand was in his. His fingers curled around hers and she noticed they felt rough. This man was no mere businessman.

He got his hands dirty. An electric current ran through her right to her core as he led her back into the vast ballroom.

He turned to her at the edge of the dance floor and she walked into his embrace, wondering if this was all a dream and she'd wake up in the cramped seat of the budget airline she'd used to fly to Athens from Dublin.

But no, as soon as her body came flush with his and she felt the whipcord steel muscles, and the heat rose within her, she knew this was all too real.

He had one arm around her back and his other hand held hers against his chest in a close embrace. Tara felt as if she were floating. He moved like a dream and all she could do was follow.

He also smelled amazing, like nothing she'd ever encountered before—earthy, musky with a hint of something like an exotic spice. Dark. Masculine.

She'd been staring at a point on his shirt at her eye level and now she looked up and almost lost her footing. He was staring at her so intently it was like a physical touch on her skin. Skin that was prickling with heat all over.

His jaw was hard. She could see where a growth of stubble was appearing and had the most bizarre notion to wonder what it would feel like against the sensitive skin of her inner thighs.

He stopped dancing. Tara went cold. Had she said that out loud? It was quite possible. But then he was taking her hand and leading her off the dance floor and back out onto the terrace. She took a gulp of fresh air but the lingering heat of the day didn't do much to cool her blood down.

He led her over to a secluded corner and turned to face her.

Dion wanted this woman, that was clear. But it wasn't following any kind of pattern he was used to where if he found a woman attractive they would engage in a well-worn dance that both he and the woman understood tacitly. For him it was very much a physical thing to scratch a sexual itch. He never had any desire to prolong the experience beyond bed.

He liked sex. He didn't like the strings that came with it.

And yet, he knew that this woman, this situation, was different. But he couldn't seem to care.

He wanted to see her. He asked, 'May I take off your mask?'

She swallowed and then nodded jerkily, turning around. Her skin was amazing, the most delicate translucent pale. Dotted with those freckles. He untied her mask and resisted the urge to bury his hands in the coppery silken strands of her hair and undo it.

She caught the mask and turned around again. Dion undid his mask and lifted it off. He saw her eyes widen on his face. He knew he was handsome but the knowledge came with no arrogance. He'd inherited his father's looks—the looks that had seduced his feckless mother and so when he looked in the mirror he took no pleasure in his even features. They mocked him.

'Wow,' she breathed. 'You're very handsome.'

Dion smiled. Her lack of guile surprised him and very little surprised him these days. She affected none of the cool nonchalance of the women he was used to. Of course, it probably was an act, but he was enjoying it.

Then she blushed, as if she'd just realised what she'd said. Adorable. He couldn't remember the last time a woman had blushed in his company. They were as cynical as he was. Hardened. And that was fine because he didn't want soft.

Except, maybe he did, in this instance. Because this woman exuded a kind of softness he'd never seen before. Soft curves and a self-effacing warmth that was truly novel.

'You are beautiful,' he said. And she was. In a very refreshingly unmanufactured way. Gorgeous skin. Huge blue-green eyes. Long lashes. Finely etched brows. A straight nose. And that mouth...that made him think of far more debauched things than *soft*.

She made him hard.

He touched her chin with his finger, tipping it up a little. Her eyes widened. He felt her breath against his skin and got even harder. *Theo mou.* He'd barely touched her and he was primed to go off like a firecracker.

She said, 'I don't even know your name.'

He looked at her and suddenly realised that for the first time in a long time, a woman didn't know who he was. He'd never courted the press, but in Greece everyone knew who he was.

She could be lying, of course, but again he found that he was prepared to go along with this fantasy and enjoy the moment of anonymity.

'Names are overrated, don't you think?'

He felt her breathing quicken a little. Maybe she liked the fantasy too. She said, 'I think...you may be right.'

Dion's gaze moved back to her mouth. She bit her lip and his blood spiked. He said in a rough tone, 'I want to kiss you.'

He saw the glistening pink of her tongue. 'I... I think I'd like that.'

He put his hands on her arms, slender but strong, and tugged her towards him. Their bodies touched again and Dion had to grit his jaw against the surge of desire. She was so soft. Her breasts were pressed against his chest.

He lowered his head and fitted his mouth over hers and it was like two jigsaw pieces slotting into place. It was as if they'd kissed before but of course they hadn't. And he'd never ever felt this sensation of the ground shifting on its axis as all of that lushness softened against him and with the slightest encouragement she opened to him and any notions of *soft* or *self-effacement* or *shy* were blown to smithereens.

Dion's hands tightened on her arms as he fell down and down into a cauldron of fiery need, barely even noticing how her hands came to his jacket and clung on as if she too were drowning in the fiery pit.

Tara wasn't even sure if she was still standing. All she could feel was the intoxicating, drugging, electrifying sensation of this man's mouth on hers and his tongue, touching hers, exploring her mouth, enticing her to open up…which she was doing with an eagerness that belied her lack of experience.

It was hands down the most uncharacteristic thing she'd ever done and the most exciting. Every part of her body was tingling, vibrating. Her breasts felt heavy and her nipples were tight. She wanted to press closer against his body, to create a friction that she felt instinctively would be good.

But then he was pulling back, taking his mouth from hers, and it was a struggle to open her eyes and focus on his face. It eventually realigned into its perfect lines.

His cheeks were flushed, some hair flopping forward onto his forehead. He asked, 'Are you okay?'

Tara nodded. Her tongue felt heavy, thick, but she managed to get out, 'I…um, think so.'

She realised she was clinging onto his jacket as if he were stopping her from collapsing. She couldn't seem to unwrap her fingers from the material. He still had his hands on her arms. She heard the faint sounds of the party behind him. Tinkling glasses, laughter, music.

They were in a little cocoon of their own. Tara couldn't

quite wrap her head around what was happening but she wanted him to kiss her again.

So when he said, 'Will you spend the night with me?' she felt no hesitation.

She said, 'Yes.'

She hadn't completely lost the run of herself. She knew why she was here and what was at stake—finding the father of her baby—but at this moment she was on the precipice of that. She hadn't yet found him or confirmed for sure that she *was* the baby's mother with a DNA test.

So, she did the most rebellious thing she'd ever done and she chose something just for her. For now. For tonight. Tomorrow she would worry about everything else.

Her baby's father was here in Athens. She would find him. She had time. Didn't she? Feeling a little desperate, she reached up and pressed her mouth to his again, revelling in the firm texture of his lips. The slight burn of stubble on his jaw.

His body was hard, pressing against her, and it sent a wild euphoria through her. She pulled back and said a little breathlessly, 'Just so you know... I don't normally behave like this.'

His mouth tipped up on one corner. 'I believe you.'

Tara immediately felt insecure. Was it that obvious she was inexperienced? But then he said, 'Let's leave now.'

Her insecurity melted away. 'Okay.'

Their masks were left on a wall behind them as he took her hand and led her through the thronged room and out through a reception hall and then out to the main entrance of the villa.

Within seconds a chauffeur-driven car was pulling up in front of them. The man opened the back door for her and she got in. He went around the other side. Tara knew she should be questioning her sanity but her instinct told her she could trust him.

Even so, as the car swept down the winding drive of the villa and towards the centre of Athens she asked a little shakily, 'You're not a serial killer, are you?'

He turned to her and his face was in shadow in the back of the car. Lights from streets illuminated the car for brief seconds. He looked fierce. Intense. Her heart pounded.

He said, 'No, I'm not, you're safe with me. We won't do anything you're not comfortable with. I don't expect anything from you just because you've agreed to come with me. I mean that.'

Something inside Tara eased a little. Then he took out his mobile phone and conducted a conversation with someone on the other end in rapid and incomprehensible Greek. Even that was sexy.

As he was on the phone he was undoing his bow tie and opening the top button of his shirt. Tara wanted to crawl onto his lap and continue undoing his buttons and press her mouth to his throat.

She turned her head and looked blindly out of the window at the streets of Athens, people sitting outside bars drinking and talking. Normal. What on earth was happening to her? The urge to touch him was so visceral. Primal. As if she'd recognised a mate on a very base level.

She'd never been so aware of herself before and her interest in sex. Because she'd never allowed herself to be free like this. She'd had too much responsibility.

But not any more.

Until you find the father of your child.

That stark reminder dropped into her head just as the man turned to her and said, 'Maybe we should exchange names.'

She shook her head, desperately trying to stave off reality for a little longer. 'No, let's not. One night…that's all this will be, right?'

He reached for her and tugged her towards him. He said, 'One night is all I can offer.'

She looked at his mouth and wound her arms around his neck and breathed, 'That's fine with me.' And pressed her mouth to his. His hands roved over her back and waist and any illusion that she was in control soon dissolved as he masterfully took over the kiss and explored her with a thoroughness that had her squeezing her legs together in a bid to contain the damp heat at her core.

After long, drugging moments he pulled back and said, 'As much as I could take you here right now, I think I know somewhere a little more private and comfortable.'

Tara would have been fine with here and now but she tried to sit up and feign a level of sophistication she really didn't feel. 'Okay.'

She only then clocked that they were at what looked like an airfield. The car swept through gates and all the way up to where a helicopter was standing with pilot waiting.

The man got out of the car and came around to her door, helping her out. The warm Aegean breeze lifted her dress a little and ruffled her hair.

She looked at the helicopter. 'We're going in that?'

He nodded. Tara asked, 'Where?'

'A small island not far from the mainland. I'll have you back just after dawn, I promise.'

Tara swallowed. This evening was definitely taking on a dreamlike aspect. He took her hand again and said, 'Trust me?'

CHAPTER TWO

TARA LOOKED AT HIM. Even though he was intimidatingly gorgeous, sexy and very intense, there was something about him—some kind of vulnerability she sensed that resonated deep inside her. She did trust him.

She nodded. He led her over to the helicopter and she clambered in as elegantly as she could and sat down. He pulled the straps around her and his hands brushed against her breasts. She sucked in a breath. He looked at her and his eyes were fiery gold. He gave her a set of headphones to put on over her ears.

He then went and got into the passenger seat beside the pilot and she was glad because it gave her a chance to regain her breath and a portion of her functioning brain cells.

She'd never been in a helicopter and when it lifted off the ground and wobbled, she gripped the seat on either side of her thighs. The man looked back at her and mouthed, *Okay?* and Tara just gulped and nodded.

Soon they were high in the sky and flying over the ancient city. The Acropolis looked like a toy model on the hill. They were flying over the port with hundreds of boats in their berths. Big ferries. Then they were over the sea. Tara could see islands in the distance, lights like jewels in harbours.

After about thirty minutes the helicopter started to go

lower and Tara could make out an island. There was a string of lights around the coast and further inland. Gradually she could make out that they were landing on a floodlit helipad on what seemed to be lush grounds on a hill overlooking the town at the harbour.

She could see a villa now, a modern minimalist's dream. Flat roof and white lines and lots of glass. There was a pool, glittering under the milky glow of a full moon.

When the helicopter had landed the man jumped out and came around to help Tara, undoing her safety belt. She stepped out onto the ground and felt wobbly on the grass in her high heels. He said something to the pilot over the din of the rotor blades and then he was leading her away. She watched as the small aircraft lifted up again into the sky and banked left before disappearing back towards Athens.

So now she was alone on an island with a total stranger who she'd just agreed to spend the night with. The fact that no one in her family had any idea where she was occurred to her and she felt foolish. She'd spent the best part of ten years making sure she knew where every one of her siblings was at any given moment and now she was behaving like a recalcitrant teenager.

The whirring rhythmic beat of the helicopter was gone and in its place was a dense silence broken only by night insects. But then Tara could make out the faintest sounds of music and laughter and talking. The man said, 'When the wind blows a certain way it's possible to hear sounds from the harbour below.'

Tara found that somewhat comforting. They weren't totally isolated. He took her hand again and led her across the lawn towards the villa. Lights came on as they walked through the garden, presumably solar powered.

There was a sleek terrace by the pool and the water

looked serene and very still. Tara could imagine the view in daylight must be outstanding.

He was at a door now and sliding it open. Tara hung back. 'Don't you need keys?'

He looked at her. 'I have a housekeeper who opens the place up when I'm coming.'

'You'd already planned to come here?' Had he intended on bringing a woman here tonight all along? And she just happened to be the lucky girl? The thought left a sour taste in her mouth.

He faced her. 'No, but I rang her on my way to ask her to open up and bring up some supplies.'

'Oh…' This was so far removed from Tara's existence that she wasn't sure where to start trying to figure everything out.

He walked towards her. 'I wasn't planning this… I'd had every intention of going back to my home in Athens but… after meeting you I wanted to come somewhere very private.'

Something else struck Tara. She looked at his hand but it was bare, and back up to his face. 'Are you married?'

If she didn't see the almost visible shudder go through him she wouldn't have believed it. He said, '*Theos*. No. Absolutely not.'

Tara almost smiled at his reaction. 'Not a fan of the institution, I take it?'

Now he scowled. 'No.'

Tara thought again of letting someone know where she was and said, 'Do you mind if I use your bathroom?'

The scowl disappeared. He slid open the door wide and Tara could see into a vast open space. 'Of course, let me show you where to go.'

He directed her to a sleek and very modern bathroom

stocked full of luxury products. She picked up a hand cream and smelled it and closed her eyes at the gorgeous scent—a mixture of bergamot and something like orange. Who was this guy who could just rustle up a helicopter to bring him to an island and the kind of villa Tara saw only on property shows about millionaires and billionaires?

She pulled her mobile phone out of her evening bag and sent a quick text to her brother, Oisín, dropping a pin to her location and saying,

Hi baby bro, got into the party, just letting you know where I am. I'll check in with you tomorrow. Tara X

She put the phone back in her bag and looked at herself in the mirror and groaned. Her hair was a wild tangle on her head, more resembling a bird's nest than the elegant chignon she'd aimed for earlier at the budget hotel where she was staying.

She pulled out the pins and let her hair fall around her shoulders, doing her best to make it look presentable. Then she pinched her too pale cheeks and washed her hands.

She took a deep breath and came out of the bathroom and made her way back to the main living space that reminded her of an art gallery, especially when she saw the vast canvases on the walls. They surprised her because they were full of colour and passion in contrast with the otherwise very white and stark space.

The man had taken off his jacket and was standing with his back to her at the open French doors, hands in his pockets. Tara's insides clenched. Was he having second thoughts about bringing her here? After all, she was nothing special really, and that had been driven home spectacularly when she'd seen the other women at the party, each one more beautiful and lissom and golden than the last.

Tara had no real fashion sense, not like her sister Lucy. She rarely wore make-up. She never went to the gym so any muscle definition was down to sheer luck and genetics.

He turned around and Tara's whirling thoughts stopped. He'd taken off his bow tie. She gestured to her hair, feeling self-conscious, 'My hair...took a bit of a battering from the helicopter.'

'Sorry about that.'

'Oh, no, it's fine, it wasn't as if I had it done professionally or anything.' Tara mentally closed her eyes and cringed. She had to learn to filter her thoughts. She realised her feet were aching in the high heels, also something she wasn't used to, and lifted one foot, saying, 'Do you mind if I take them off?'

He shook his head. 'Not at all.'

She slipped them off her feet and put them to one side. The marble floor was deliciously cool to the touch.

'Can I get you a drink?'

Tara put her bag down on a table and walked forward. 'Sure, what do you have?'

'Whatever you'd like.' He went over to a panel in the wall and pressed something and it slid back to reveal a well-stocked bar, lit up with golden lights.

Tara made a soft whistling sound. 'Impressive.'

She wrinkled her nose as she looked at the vast array of products and confessed, 'I'm not much of a drinker actually, a water would be fine.'

'If you're sure?'

She nodded. He poured her a sparkling water and added some ice and lemon and handed it to her in a crystal glass.

She hoped she wasn't behaving too gauchely but she knew she wasn't equipped to deal with this situation.

Should she now be lounging seductively on a couch and waiting for him to come and ravish her? Or should she be the one making the first move? Like a strong woman in charge of her sexuality?

In a bid to avoid overthinking, Tara went over to stand in front of one of the big canvases. He came to stand beside her. She looked to her side and up. He was so much taller now she wasn't in heels, but she didn't feel vulnerable. She did trust that if she didn't want anything to happen he wouldn't push it. There was something inherently proud about him.

She asked, 'Did you choose this?'

He glanced at her and seemed slightly wary. 'I did, actually. I like this artist's work. What do you think of it?'

Tara cocked her head to one side. 'There's a lot in it. And yet everything around it is so…white and still.'

'I like the contrast.'

'I get that.' She wondered if it hinted at what she could sense under the suave surface of this man—the same passion that had sprung up between them and this totally spontaneous night. But then…maybe it wasn't all that spontaneous. Maybe this was a well-worn routine. She went a little cold.

He came and stood between her and the painting, eclipsing it. He said, 'I also like something else in here.'

Tara gazed up at him. She had to ask. 'Is this…usual for you? Do you bring women here in some sort of showy gesture?'

He looked at her and she could see that he appeared slightly shocked. Maybe he wasn't used to women questioning him.

But then he shook his head. 'Not at all. You're the first

woman I've ever brought here. This is somewhere I usually come to be alone, take time out.'

Something inside Tara melted even as she castigated herself for needing reassurance—after she'd agreed to spend a night with a total stranger! 'You're not just saying that?'

'No, I wouldn't lie.'

She believed him. The air between them was charged now. Electric. He lifted a hand and traced a finger down her cheek to her jaw, before continuing that line down her throat to the little hollow at the base. Her pulse was pounding, skin drawn tight as a drum. Nipples stinging with need. He took the glass out of her hand and put it down and put his down too.

He asked, 'Okay?'

A sudden realisation of what she was doing gripped Tara and she said, 'If I told you I wanted to leave now would you let me?'

He answered without hesitating. 'Of course, I could have Antonio back here with the helicopter within thirty minutes.'

Then he asked, 'Do you want to leave?'

No. It beat through her. She really, really wanted this night out of her life to claim something for herself.

She shook her head and swallowed. 'No, I don't want to go but it's just good to know that… I could.'

'At any time, no matter what's happening.'

Tara nodded. 'Okay.'

He took her hand and led her out of the living space and through the moonlit villa to a doorway. He pushed it open and they stepped into a vast bedroom with a massive bed.

He let go of her hand to flick on some lights, then opened more sliding doors and the sea breeze, warm and fragrant, whispered over Tara's skin. He turned to face her and walked across the room towards her, slowly.

Tara's breathing became more and more constricted as her chest tightened and her skin prickled all over with anticipation.

He stopped in front of her and reached for her, putting his hands on her waist and tugging her into him. He lowered his head and his mouth covered hers and she sighed in relief to have him kissing her again, stopping her thoughts. She moved closer, wound her arms around his neck.

His hands moved to her back, one hand exploring her upper back and under her hair to cup her head.

This was the most decadently outrageous thing Tara had ever done and it didn't remotely resemble the few fumbling kisses she'd shared with boys while doing her university course.

This was another league. This man was a master. Playing her as if she were a virtuoso's violin. His hands were on the zip at the top of the back of her dress now and Tara broke the kiss to look at him.

Slowly, he pulled the zip down. Tara moved, dislodging his hands but only doing so to turn around and give him her back. She pulled her hair over one shoulder.

He continued pulling the zip down to just above her buttocks. The dress loosened around her chest and Tara held it. She turned around again and he reached for her hands, gently pulling them away.

The dress fell down, exposing her bare breasts. Tara couldn't look at him but she heard his indrawn breath and couldn't quite believe it. Her breasts weren't that amazing. They weren't big and they weren't small. They were just... average.

But he said, '*Theé mou*, you are stunning.'

She looked up. His dark golden gaze was fused to her body. A flush rose up, turning her skin pink. Her nipples were tight, aching.

He reached out and cupped one breast, testing its weight. He brushed a thumb across one nipple and Tara sucked in a breath. The feeling was so exquisite and connected directly to a point between her legs.

Half joking, she said, 'I'm not sure if I can stand.'

He looked at her, cheeks slashed with colour. It made her feel less exposed. He took her over to the bed and said gruffly, 'Lie down.'

She did. Her legs dangling over the edge. He reached for her dress and tugged it over her hips and off. Now all she wore was her underwear. Very plain. She put an arm across her eyes in mortification.

'What are you doing?'

She felt the bed dip beside her. She took her arm down. 'I don't think I'm like the women you are used to…' She made a vague gesture to her underwear.

With seemingly no effort at all, he lifted her further up the bed. He came down on one arm beside her and looked up and down her body.

'You are the most exquisite creature I've ever seen.'

Tara blushed. 'I'm—'

But he bent forward and covered her mouth with his, cutting off her words. She was glad. She didn't want to think. She wanted to *feel*. And he indulged her, as if he could hear her thoughts.

He ran his hands all over her body, over her breasts, squeezing them gently before pinching her nipples. He smoothed a hand down over her belly and to her pants.

With an efficiency born of experience she didn't really

want to think about, he divested her of her underwear and now she was fully naked.

He moved his hand down, over the curls that hid her sex, and with gentle encouragement bid her to open her legs to him. She broke the kiss and looked up. She was on fire. He watched her as he parted her legs and his hand explored down, between her legs to where she was hot and aching with need.

She'd only ever done this to herself before and to have this man touching her was so incendiary that she was afraid she'd explode before he even touched her. But she didn't. His fingers delved between the slick folds of her sex and then into her body.

Tara closed her eyes but he said, 'Look at me,' and she did, helpless as he moved against her and wound her tighter and tighter, making her forget everything, all her inhibitions and insecurities. All the myriad things that had occupied her head for so long.

His fingers were deep inside, moving in a rhythm she couldn't hold out against, and when he bent his head and sucked one nipple deep into the hot cavern of his mouth, tongue swirling and teeth nipping, she lost all control and fell deep into an endless chasm of pleasure, her whole body pulsating against his hand and fingers.

When she could open her eyes again, everything was blurry until she blinked. Her body was suffused with pleasure, ebbing in waves.

He was looking at her and she couldn't speak. As she watched, he moved off the bed. She only realised then that he was still fully dressed.

Within what seemed like seconds, he wasn't. He had removed his clothes with the same scary efficiency with which he'd just tended to her. Tara came up on one elbow to look at him, her gaze devouring the most perfect male form she'd ever seen. Admittedly she hadn't seen that many naked male forms, but she was pretty sure none compared to *this*.

He really was a Greek god. Every inch of him hewn from rock and steel. Not an ounce of spare flesh. And that flesh… dark golden. Broad shoulders and chest, flat belly. Narrow waist. Strong thighs. And between his legs… Her insides quivered at his potency. Long and hard. Pulsing.

As she watched he brought a hand to himself and Tara collapsed back onto the bed, her limbs failing her.

He came back down on the bed beside her and curiosity overcame her lassitude. She sat up. 'Can I touch you?'

He nodded. 'Please, do.'

He lay back and, somewhere very dim, Tara marvelled at how he gave himself over for her delectation.

Reverently she touched his chest and he was so warm. His skin was silky with a smattering of hair. Nipples blunt. She moved her hand down over his belly, watching with fascination as his muscles tensed.

And then down… She stroked a finger along the length of his erection and glanced quickly at his face. 'Is this okay?'

He nodded. 'You might kill me, but yes.'

There was a bead of moisture at the tip and, completely instinctively, Tara put her finger to her mouth, tasting him. He groaned softly and sat up too. 'You *are* killing me. I can't wait…'

Tara lay back down. 'Okay…' It came into her head for a fleeting moment that she should tell him she was a virgin but she couldn't bear it if it put him off. She watched as he reached for something nearby and then he was rolling a protective sheath onto his erection.

She was on the pill so she wasn't unduly worried but at least he was taking care of them both without her having to ask. Not what was usual, from what she'd heard. The men her friends slept with seemed to be all too keen on wearing nothing for the sensation.

He moved over her on the bed, his body massive over hers. Tara widened her legs and he came between them, pushing them even further apart. He stroked the head of his erection against her body and it sent flutters of awareness back into her body.

And then, without taking his eyes off hers, he started to breach her body, slowly. Tara sucked in a breath. He was big. She was just thinking, *This isn't so bad,* when he thrust deeper and the pressure was sharp and intense as her body accommodated him.

He stopped moving, looked at her. Tara felt so full she wasn't sure if she could speak, and it was uncomfortable, but she knew instinctively that he couldn't stop now or she would never know how it could be and she knew he would make it better.

She put her hands on his arms and pushed against him, making him go deeper. 'Please, don't stop.'

She is a virgin. The knowledge reverberated in Dion's head like a klaxon. Every instinct urged him to stop this now, pull back. But his body was embedded in hers and she was so tight around him and every last sane and rational thought was on fire and turning to ash.

He'd prided himself all his life—ever since he'd been abandoned—on having control over himself. Never letting anyone see inside him to where hurt and pain and grief festered, but now he was drowning in two pools of green and blue and he was not in control. The only way he could hope to claw back any kind of control was to keep going.

And so he did, moving out and then back in, each glide

of his body within hers growing easier and slicker until he could feel her body quivering under his and see her eyes lose focus and how her back arched and she wound her legs around his hips and brokenly pleaded with him, *'Don't stop...'* and then he felt her go still, the powerful contractions of her body around his sending him flying far beyond anything he'd ever experienced before.

Before he lost consciousness in a sea of pleasure Dion thought to himself, *She was a virgin, that's why it was so amazing*, and, *I can never see her again.*

When Tara woke she knew exactly where she was and what had happened. But superstitiously she didn't want to open her eyes and find herself in the small windowless room at the Athens hostel and risk realising it had all been a dream.

Her body felt weighted down and languorous. A soft island breeze skated over her skin. She wasn't a virgin any more. She was a woman and her eyes had been opened to a level of sensuality she possessed that she'd never dreamed of. *Her!* Responsible, studious Tara.

She smiled. She ached in secret places and couldn't help but feel a deep thrill. She'd never known it could be like that. So transformative. She felt changed. Altered.

And as for the man...the stranger...the God. What a man. A man who had awoken this fire inside her, a fire that was already hungry again... She turned over and reached out an arm, expecting to find solid warm muscle, but found... nothing.

She cracked open her eyes and squinted at the faint dawn light in the sky beyond the room. She was alone in the bed. The sheet was pulled up over her body.

Where was he?

She sat up slightly and noticed her crumpled dress draped

over a chair. She also noticed a robe at the end of the bed. She got up and pulled it on. She went into the en suite and balked when she saw herself in the mirror. Her hair was a wild tangle around her head and her skin was pink with stubble rash. Her mascara had melted and made her eyes look bruised.

She couldn't see him like this. She let the robe drop and stepped into a shower big enough for at least three people, which only had images of him and other women at the same time flooding her brain.

He'd been so...*sexual*. And easy with it. Confident. Clearly he was experienced and she must have proved very pedestrian to him. He was probably ordering the helicopter back right now.

Tara didn't linger under the hot spray, she got out and dried herself roughly and did the best with her hair, finger-brushing it and leaving it damp. She pulled on the robe again and went out of the bedroom and followed a scent of coffee back into the living space, but she was momentarily distracted by the stunning view outside the open French doors.

She stood by the edge of the pool and watched as dawn made the horizon between sky and sea disappear into a milky pink haze. The water of the pool blended into the sky and sea in an infinite melding of water and sky.

Duh, that's why it's called an infinity pool.

Tara could almost hear her brother's voice in her head. She smiled a little at the thought of him and at herself for behaving so out of character. Who would have thought she'd end up on a Greek island losing her virginity to the sexiest—?

'Coffee?'

Tara whirled around at the sound of his voice. He was standing a few feet away holding a cup. He was dressed.

And looked as if he'd showered. Clean jaw. Wearing dark trousers and a light blue shirt. Different clothes. She felt instantly at a disadvantage in the robe.

Last night suddenly felt like a long time ago. He obviously couldn't wait to get out of the bed.

'Sure,' she said, hoping she came across as nonchalantly as he did.

He walked back inside and she followed to see a sleek kitchen and dining area. He poured coffee into a cup and asked, 'Milk?'

'No, thanks.'

He handed her the cup across the top of the island between them. She noticed he was quick to let go. In case their fingers touched.

He asked, 'How are you this morning?'

Tara took a quick sip of the coffee. 'I'm fine. Thank you.' Clipped. Civil. Cool. Was this really the same man as last night who'd whisked her off to this island to seduce her? *Seduce!* snarked a voice. *There wasn't much seducing going on.*

Then he said, 'You should have told me you were innocent.'

Of course he'd known. It must have been so obvious. Tara felt heat climb into her face. She'd long given up trying to control her emotions appearing on her skin.

He asked, 'Why didn't you tell me?'

Tara lifted her chin, refusing to be embarrassed, even though her face must be beaming like a beacon. 'It wasn't really your business…and… I was afraid you might stop.'

His eyes were dark more than golden today. He sounded grim when he said, 'I wanted to, as soon as I suspected.'

But he couldn't? Was that what he was leaving out?

Then he said, 'I don't sleep with virgins.'

'Well,' Tara pointed out, 'you just did.' And then, 'Why not? How can you even tell?'

His jaw tightened visibly. 'The women I'm used to… meeting…are usually more experienced.'

And a million other things, Tara was sure.

Feeling vulnerable, she said a little testily, 'Well, I don't think it's catching, if that's what you're worried about.'

For a second she thought she saw the flash of surprise in his eyes and a faint smile at the corner of his mouth, but she must have imagined it because he said coolly, 'Last night won't happen again.'

Tara was beginning to wonder what she'd seen in him. *This* man was nothing like the suave seducer of last night. 'We already agreed that.'

'There's a dressing room stocked with clothes in the guest suite opposite my bedroom. There should be some things there in your size. Antonio is on his way to pick us up and bring us back to Athens.'

Tara tensed. 'I thought you said you don't bring other women here.'

'I don't. But the villa is rented out from time to time and having a supply of clothes is practical for the kind of guests who stay here.'

Angry with herself for displaying that moment of insecurity, Tara drank the rest of her coffee and said, 'Thank you, I'll get changed and be ready to go.'

She swept as elegantly as she could from the kitchen in her robe and bare feet. So much for waking in bed with her first lover and indulging in lazy morning sex and a cosy breakfast.

While passing through the living area she spotted her discarded shoes and picked them up, and then noticed her evening bag on a table. She grabbed that too. She found the guest suite and walked into the dressing room, a vast space.

He'd been right. There were racks of clothes in a range of sizes for men and women. Even some children's clothes. She went cold. She'd completely lost track of why she was even in Greece.

She pulled out a pair of navy knee-length tailored shorts and matching short jacket, which she teamed with a white sleeveless silk shirt. She couldn't wear the heels again—her feet were still sore from last night. She found a pair of wedge espadrille sandals and put them on.

She found a plain black carry-all bag to put the shoes into, and also the dress which she retrieved from his bedroom, careful not to look at the bed. She went back into the guest bathroom and did her best with the basic supply of make-up products. At the last second she remembered to check her phone and took it out of the evening bag to see a text-message response from her brother after telling him where she was last night.

She opened it and her blood ran cold as she read.

Nice location, sis. So you found Dionysios Dimitriou then? How did he take it? Are you at his villa to meet the baby? What's he like?

Tara stared at the text message. It didn't make sense. But it also did. But...how? Of all the men at that party last night... It was like some cruel joke. It couldn't be true that she'd slept with the father of her child. Maybe this wasn't his villa—maybe he was one of the guests he'd just spoken of.

Maybe he was trying to impress her by making her believe it was his villa. Maybe that was why he was so eager to get off the island. To get *her* off the island...

Feeling a little numb, Tara left the guest suite and went back to the kitchen where the man—*Dionysios?*—was looking at his own phone. In the distance Tara could hear the faintest *thwack-thwack* of the returning helicopter. He couldn't wait to get rid of her. But that was the least of her worries right now.

He looked up and at her when she came in, his dark gaze sweeping her up and down. She was too numb to care what he thought of her clothes choice.

Somehow she managed to formulate the question, 'Are you Dionysios Dimitriou?'

CHAPTER THREE

'ARE YOU DIONYSIOS DIMITRIOU?'

It took a second for him to realise what she'd just asked because his head was full of a vision of slim pale limbs, copper hair and fresh-faced freckled beauty, memories rushing back from the night before of the way she'd lain down for him and had given herself with such trusting eagerness and responsiveness—

But now the question registered and he tensed all over. 'How do you know my name?'

If possible, her face went even paler, freckles standing out starkly.

'You *are* Dionysios Dimitriou.'

'Yes, yes, I am…' It wasn't such a big deal, was it? Their not exchanging names had been a gimmick, a rare moment of anonymity indulged in, but he'd suspected that she'd had to know. He might be relatively reclusive compared to his peers but he was certainly not unknown.

'Why does it matter?'

A cynical voice answered him, *Because now she knows you're a billionaire and she'll inevitably want to foster some sort of intimacy.*

She swallowed. 'It matters because you were the man I was looking for last night…at the party.'

Dion had a vague memory of her saying something about

finding someone—he'd even offered to help her. A sense of unease prickled down his neck. He frowned. 'Why were you looking for me?'

She looked stricken. 'There's something I need to tell you.'

'What?'

'I...' she started and then stopped. 'It's hard to just come out with... It's a lot.'

Dion was growing frustrated. The helicopter was so close now that it was hovering over the villa, making conversation all but inaudible. Dion spoke over the din. 'Can this conversation wait till we get back to Athens?'

She shook her head. Dion cursed silently. What on earth could she possibly have to say to him? He'd never met her before.

But now you know her intimately.

A flash of heat went through his body at the reminder and a sense of exposure made his skin prickle.

He said, 'Wait here, I'll tell Antonio to stand by.' He went outside and spoke to the pilot when he'd landed. Then he went back inside. All was silent again. It felt ominous.

She was pacing back and forth and stopped when he appeared. She said, 'My name is Tara. Tara Simons.'

'Okay. Now we know each other's names.'

'You know I'm from Dublin.'

Dion thought of his son, Niko, who would undoubtedly be waking up now. He wanted to be home to see him before work took over. 'Yes...look, I have meetings and things to—'

But Tara interrupted him. 'The thing is that I'm the mother of your baby, or at least I'm pretty sure I am. Your son. He's my son too.'

Dion looked at her. Something cold in his gut started to

spread outwards, turning his blood to ice. 'It's not common knowledge yet that I even have a son. How do you know?' Protective hackles he hadn't felt before rose to the surface.

'Because it was *my* egg that was used.'

Dion shook his head as if he might be able to clear it. 'But you're not... I chose someone who was as close a match to me as possible.'

She gestured at herself. Pale skin. Red hair. 'I'm aware that's not me.'

Dion thought of his son's eyes. Light. Blue-green. Someone had told him they changed colour after a few months but he was six months old now and they were still light.

But she'd been a virgin.

His mind couldn't compute what she was saying. Of course, she hadn't given birth to the baby, his surrogate had. It had been an egg donor. Chosen by him.

As if hearing his thoughts, she said, 'There was a mix-up. My egg was used instead of the one you'd chosen.'

Dion scrambled to try and find meaning in this. And he seized on something. 'You knew who I was all along, didn't you?'

She shook her head, those bright copper strands moving over her shoulders distracting him. Dion cursed his weakness. He should have known last night was too good to be true. That such a woman couldn't exist.

'This was all a set-up, wasn't it? You knew who I was and you set out to trap me and, lucky for you, I found you attractive.'

Now she looked green. Dion had to applaud her acting skills, because he was certain now that she'd somehow found out about his son and was using the opportunity to feather her nest. It was what his own mother had done.

'No, that's not it at all. I arrived in Athens yesterday and all I knew was your name and that you were due to be at the party. I wasn't even sure what you looked like.'

Dion usually took pride in the fact that he managed to stay out of the public eye as much as possible. But that hadn't stopped this woman. He recalled the way he'd first seen her. Engaging in her cute act at the buffet. Had she tracked his progress through the party? Staged that for his benefit?

He folded his arms. 'The virginal act was particularly effective.'

Her mouth dropped open and now she went from green to red in the face. If he weren't so blindsided he'd have to admit that he could watch reactions crossing her face all day.

'How dare you even suggest such a thing?' she hissed. 'I was a virgin actually.'

Dion snorted. 'You expect me to believe that a woman of…how old are you anyway?'

She folded her arms. 'None of your business.'

'I think that horse has bolted by now. Your age.'

She looked mutinous for a second but then she dropped her arms and said, 'Twenty-five.'

Dion's eyes widened. 'You really expect me to believe a woman of your age was still an innocent? Of everything you've said so far that's the most outrageous.'

Now her face was burning. 'It's true and I had my reasons and they are *not* your business because you are hateful and, I agree, last night was a mistake.'

'I never said last night was a mistake. I might regret it now because I was duped by a beautiful face but I can't deny it was enjoyable.'

Dion had to admit that he didn't really believe she'd been faking her innocence. He'd felt the tightness of her body, how she'd resisted and then the exquisite mind-bending pleasure of her body accommodating him. Massaging his length. His body responded now and he cursed himself.

At that moment the pilot knocked discreetly on the outer door. Dion turned and they had a short conversation. He turned back to Tara. 'We have to leave now. The winds are picking up.'

'Duped by a beautiful face!' And... *'It was enjoyable.'* Tara felt as if she were going to explode. For her last night had been life-altering. But then, she'd been a novice and he didn't even believe that now.

Even more disturbingly she couldn't get out of her head that he'd thought her *beautiful*. She'd never felt beautiful in her life and she hated that in spite of everything she wanted to ask, *You really think I'm beautiful?*

She said as coolly as she could, 'I'll get my things.' She turned on her heel and went and got the holdall with her shoes and dress, and her handbag. Even though she'd got a shock to find out who she was with, at least she had found him. Not that he seemed to be remotely inclined to believe her or listen to her.

When she returned he briskly ushered her out of the villa and over to the helicopter, and inside. This time he didn't help strap her in. She did it herself. Soon they were lifting into the air and off the island. Tara was too distracted to take in the beauty of the white houses strung along the coast and the sparkling sea. Empty beaches.

Before long the mainland coast came into sight and then, the sprawling city of Athens. They landed in an airfield at a small airport, presumably the same one as last night. Tara could see a yellow Athens taxi waiting, alongside a much sleeker SUV. Dionysios's chauffeur-driven car. It seemed as though he had no intention of giving her any special treatment any more.

When they were on the tarmac Dionysios turned to her and said, 'I don't believe for a second that you're the mother of my child. I think somehow you found out and you're an opportunist who sought me out.'

Tara strove for calm. 'I *am* almost certain that I am the biological mother of your son, and I should be given a chance to prove it with a DNA test, because if he is my son then we have a lot to discuss. For starters, why were you with me last night and not him?'

His face darkened. 'Not that it's any of your business but he is perfectly fine—' He broke off to look at his phone and frowned. He looked up again. 'I don't have time for this. I have to go. You have no grounds to demand a DNA test. If you have anything further to communicate you can do so via my legal team. Their contact information is on my company website, which shouldn't be hard for you to track down, considering your sleuth work in tracking me down.'

He gestured to the taxi, waiting. 'This taxi will take you wherever you want to go. The fare is paid. Goodbye, Miss Simons.'

He turned on his heel and disappeared into the back of his car. Tara just stared as it smoothly glided out of the airfield. Before it disappeared through the gates she sprang into action. She wrenched open the back door of the taxi and got in and said to the driver, 'Can you follow that car, please?'

Dionysios Dimitriou might be done with her, but she was not done with him.

The taxi managed to follow his car through the city and up into the leafy hills where Tara caught glimpses of vast villas behind high walls of greenery and steel fences. Much like the villa where the party had been held—only last night? It felt like a lifetime ago.

Eventually his car slowed and turned into a particularly formidable set of gates, bracketed by high stone walls on either side. There was a security guard outside. Refusing to be daunted, Tara told the taxi driver he could let her out at the side of the road.

Tara waited until the taxi was gone and Dionysios's car had disappeared into the grounds. She crossed the road to the high wall. No way was she getting in via the security guard, not once Dionysios knew who was there. And she had no idea who she could pretend to be.

She started to look at the wall and could see that it wasn't perfectly even. It wasn't meant to be. She spotted a couple of bricks where she might gain a foothold. The handles of the carry-all bag were long enough to put over her head and go under one arm. She set to climbing the wall but realised pretty quickly that she'd have to do it barefoot.

She slipped off the wedges, left them in the grass and tried again, and, forcing herself not to think about what she was doing, and focusing on climbing, she managed to get to the top and swing her legs over.

She was sweating but euphoric. Now all she had to do was drop the nine feet or so into what looked like impenetrable bushes and she'd be in. She groaned softly. What was she doing? But she'd come too far to stop now so she turned around and started to scale her way down the other side of the wall, finding small footholds until she could jump down into the tiny space between the bush and the wall.

She sidled along between the bush and the wall until she saw a gap. Breathing a sigh of relief, she made her way through the tangle of leaves, wincing a little as her feet crunched on earth and branches, until finally she popped out onto a lush smooth lawn and could see the imposing shape of a majestic villa in the distance.

Breathing a sigh of relief, she took a step forward and stopped suddenly, her knee lifted in the air, when she heard a soft but menacing growl and a voice said something in Greek.

She looked to her right and saw a man dressed in a security uniform holding a big dog on a lead. The dog wasn't growling now, and was clearly under control, but Tara wasn't taking any chances. She put her foot down and smiled weakly. She'd just ruined any chance of Dionysios taking her seriously.

But to her surprise, when the guard indicated for her to precede him, it wasn't back to the main gate and out onto the road, it was up towards the villa. All the way to the front door. Which was open. And filled with the sight of Dionysios Dimitriou. But he wasn't alone. He was holding a baby in his arms.

The most adorably cherubic baby she'd ever seen. Thick glossy dark hair. Olive skin. Light eyes. Huge eyes. Green-blue. *Her* eyes. Something inside her melted and dissolved into a pool of what she could only describe as love at first sight. She didn't need a DNA test to tell her they were related.

Her son looked at her and she looked at him but then he opened his mouth and screamed. She noticed then that his eyes were red and his cheeks were red.

She looked up into a set of much darker eyes. Angry eyes. Not golden any more. He said over the squalls of the baby, 'I thought I told you I didn't want to see you again.'

'We need to talk about this.' Tara gestured at her son, who was becoming inconsolable. Sobs coming in gasping gulps.

'What's wrong with him?' she asked.

Dionysios jiggled him inexpertly in his arm and Tara had to curb the urge to reach out. Looking extremely reluctant, he finally said, 'My day nanny, Elena, just walked out, a family crisis. It's a feast day and so the rest of my staff have a day off, including my housekeeper. The night nanny won't be here until five p.m.'

Two nannies! She pushed that aside for now and looked at the baby. 'He's teething, his cheeks are red.' A smell hit her nostrils and she wrinkled her nose. 'And he needs a nappy change. When was he last fed?'

Dionysios stared back at her nonplussed. She guessed in a second that he didn't know the answers to any of what she'd just said and also she'd wager that he'd never changed a nappy. Anger rose and a strong maternal instinct to pluck her baby out of his arms. She forced herself to say calmly, 'You look like you need help.'

The baby's screams went up a notch as if in agreement. Dionysios didn't move though. Concerned for her son, Tara said, 'You can't claim that I orchestrated this! At least let me help settle him. He's upset!'

'Do you know what to do?'

'I have four younger siblings and I used to help out in a nursery to make extra money. I think I know more than you do right now.'

Still looking very reluctant, Dionysios eventually stood back and said, 'Fine, come in.'

Tara stepped into the cool marble interior of the villa's reception hall. She only remembered then she was in bare feet. She looked down and back up to see Dionysios staring at her feet too. Weakly she explained, 'I had to take the shoes off to climb the wall.'

The bag was still across her body and she lifted it off.

He arched a brow. 'You couldn't have just asked Security to contact me?'

Tara arched a brow back. 'And you would have just let me in?'

He scowled and then he said, 'You can leave your things on the chair,' before handing her the baby. Tara did as he instructed and lifted the baby into her chest. He was heavy, solid. The surprise of being handed over to someone else made him stop crying for a few seconds, but she could see that he was working up to a new round of crying if she didn't move fast.

'Where's the nursery?'

'This way.' Dionysios led her out of the entrance hall and up a central staircase to the first floor. Tara's bare feet sank into the plush carpet. He walked down a long corridor to a door at the end and opened it to reveal a lovely suite of rooms, kitted out for a baby. She could see instantly that no expense had been spared.

She saw the changing table and went over and laid him down and thought of something. 'What's his name?'

'Nikolau... Niko for short.'

The baby was looking up at Tara, her own eyes mirrored back to her. A gush of emotion filled her chest as she said, 'Hi, Niko...it's nice to meet you.' She stroked a finger down one chubby cheek and he kicked his legs and smiled.

But then she could see him register his hunger, wet nappy, tiredness or any other manner of things again and his little face scrunched up before he let out a renewed massive wail.

Tara deftly started taking off his clothes to get to the nappy and said to Dionysios, 'Can you get him a bottle? I'm sure the nanny will have left some pre-prepared.'

Dionysios started to walk from the room and Tara called out, 'Make sure it's warm.'

He nodded and kept going. Tara busied herself changing her son and tried not to let that fact—*her son!*—overwhelm her too much. She managed to find clean clothes—there were enough clothes for ten babies. She also found a teething ring and when she gave it to him he promptly put it straight in his mouth, confirming her suspicion.

She was just picking him up again—freshly changed and dressed—when she heard a sound behind her and turned to see a slightly flustered-looking Dionysios holding a bottle of milk. He said, 'I think this is it. They were in the fridge.'

Tara took it. 'I'll give him a feed and see if he'll go down afterwards. I think he's tired.'

She saw a rocking chair and went and sat down, positioning Niko in the crook of her arm. She tested the milk's temperature and it was fine. As soon as she put the teat into Niko's mouth his little hands grabbed the bottle and he drank as if he hadn't been fed in hours, eyes glued to hers as if she held all the secrets in the universe. In that moment she was barely aware of the powerful figure of the man in the doorway watching them both warily.

She was enraptured with her son and knew there and then that she would lay down her life for him.

Dion looked at the woman in the rocking chair with the baby in her arm, feeding him, little pudgy legs kicking happily, hands clamped on the bottle.

The jarring juxtaposition of what he and she had been doing just hours ago and what he was looking at right now was too much for him to try and unpick. It made him feel very off-centre. As did their intense absorption in each other—his son and this woman. Ridiculously it made him feel excluded in a way that he hadn't felt before when the nannies had tended to Niko.

Maybe she's telling the truth?

No, Dion assured himself. He was too cynical to be taken in so easily.

She was an opportunist who had somehow found out what the press didn't even know yet. That he'd had a son. And she was using the information to get something out of him.

But he couldn't deny, as peace reigned again and the only sound that could be heard was the rhythmic sucking of the baby on the bottle, that he needed her for now.

Dion left the charming but disturbing tableau and went back down to the kitchen, making himself a strong coffee. It had been mayhem as soon as he'd arrived at the villa, with the nanny crying and all but shoving his son into his arms saying something about her mother in hospital. Dion hadn't even had time to offer assistance before she'd been gone.

He had to admit uncomfortably that he hadn't quite given due thought to the reality of having a baby in the house. Elena had travelled to the States with him to collect Nikolau after he'd been born, and he'd been so tiny that Dion had been justifiably terrified of doing anything to harm him—so he'd been quite happy to let the nanny take charge.

And since then, not much had changed. He'd held his son but as soon as he felt that little body tensing, or squirming and stiffening and arching away from him as if he knew instinctively that Dion couldn't provide what he needed, a kind of terror would take over and he'd hand him back.

When Elena had left earlier, he'd looked at his son in his arms and had suddenly become aware of just how fragile he was. And that he was now looking to Dion to fulfil needs that Dion had no idea how to fulfil. And then Niko had gone from zero to full-on meltdown and then his security guard had informed him they'd found an intruder, and *she'd* appeared.

Dion didn't like to admit it to himself, especially now, but, before she'd dropped her bombshell, he had been toying with the idea of seeing her again, in spite of everything—her innocence, and the fact that he rarely saw the same woman twice.

But thankfully he hadn't exposed himself. She'd got to him and she'd exposed a weak link in his defences and that was unforgivable.

There was a small sound from behind him and then a voice. 'He's down. He's exhausted, the poor mite.'

Dion turned around. Tara was standing a few feet away. Still in bare feet. Long legs slim and pale under the shorts. She'd taken off the jacket and now wore just the sleeveless silk shirt. There were stains on her clothes, evidence of her clambering through his bushes. Her hair was loose and wild, reminding him of how it had looked spread out over the pillow as he'd joined their bodies.

The memory made his voice sharp. 'Shouldn't you be with my son?'

She held up a white plastic device with different colours going up and down along a display. 'It's a baby monitor. He's asleep. He's fine. I'll hear if he wakes up. And speaking of which, shouldn't you have been with him last night?'

'His nanny was with him.' Dion's conscience pricked. The truth was that even if he'd been here he would have deferred to the nanny's care. The gaps in his knowledge about how to bond and handle his own son were becoming glaringly apparent and he didn't welcome the sense of exposure in front of this woman who seemed to be able to see through him in a very disconcerting way.

'He's got the best of care, around the clock.'

She shook her head. 'Who does that? Acquires a baby and then hands it over to staff?'

Dion gritted his jaw. No one spoke to him like this. 'You have no right to judge my reasons for having a son. He will want for nothing.'

'Except a mother?'

Dion's patience snapped. 'My mother had me purely to extort money out of her rich lover. When the money ran out she dumped me on the steps of an orphanage and walked away. I survived and thrived. I'm proof that perhaps mothers don't always know best.'

He saw how the woman in front of him went pale. Her eyes widened. He immediately regretted blurting out his sad story but it was too late.

'I'm so sorry that happened to you, that's...*awful*. Where was your father?'

Dion spoke around the almost physical sensation of a stone in his chest. 'He was a married man with his own family, no interest.'

'Dionysios... I'm so sorry, that's just...no child should experience such cruelty.'

To his fascination and horror, Tara's eyes shimmered with emotion and that stone in his chest got even bigger. Curtly he said, 'Don't call me Dionysios—that's what she used to call me. It's Dion.'

Tara blinked and, to Dion's intense relief, the shimmering emotion went away. She said, 'I'm sorry, Dion, it is.' Hearing her speak his name had a direct effect on his body, like a little electric charge.

His conscience nudged him to acknowledge what she'd done. 'I should say thank you for settling Niko.'

'And also,' he had to add, 'for showing up a weakness in my security system.'

She grimaced. 'I really didn't think you'd let me in.'

'You were good with him... Niko,' he also had to admit

grudgingly. It wasn't usual for Dion to feel redundant and he didn't like it. He vowed to get over his fear of tending his own son.

She shrugged a little. 'Babies are pretty straightforward. They eat, sleep, poop and once those needs are met they're usually content.' She looked at him and Dion felt momentarily breathless under that aquamarine gaze.

She said, 'I know he's my son. He even looks a little like one of my brothers when he was a baby. Daniel. He's the only dark-haired one in our family. We always used to joke that he was the postman's.'

She blushed a little. 'Sorry, sometimes I don't know when to stop talking.'

Dion tried to curb the way he felt a softening in his chest. Until he knew for sure what was going on she was an unknown quantity. He could see some logic now in keeping her close, at least until he knew he could get rid of her for good.

But you wanted to see her again. Last night was amazing.

Dion scowled at his rogue thoughts but before he could say anything else she asked, 'Would you mind if I had a glass of water, or something?'

Now Dion felt embarrassed. He was forgetting his manners. No matter who she was. 'Of course, you must be hungry.' He thought of how he'd all but hustled her off the island and despatched her in the taxi.

He pulled out the tray of breakfast items that the housekeeper had left prepared for him in the fridge. Fruit, granola, yoghurts. He found a plate and cutlery and a napkin.

'Take a seat.' He gestured to the other side of the island. She came closer and put the baby monitor down. He caught her scent, clean and flowery with a hint of musk, and instantly he could taste her skin in his mouth, the slight salt of her perspiration as she'd climaxed around his body.

Theos. He gritted his jaw and found where the pastries were kept and put some on a plate and pushed the tray and plate towards her. 'Would you like some coffee?'

She nodded as she picked up a mini croissant and put it straight into her mouth. She spoke with her hand over her mouth. 'Yes, please. Thanks.'

Dion poured her some coffee. She took a sip. 'Thank you.' Then she said, 'You mentioned no one knows about Niko yet…why?'

Dion felt like telling her it was none of her business but he'd already spilled his sorry life story. 'I haven't gone out of my way *not* to tell people. I just haven't made an announcement. I wanted time to let him settle before a media frenzy is unleashed.'

'I don't think a six-month-old is going to be all that aware of a frenzy.'

Dion felt like scowling. She'd hit a nerve because maybe he was avoiding the glare of media attention and all the inevitable questions about why he'd choose to have a baby on his own, questions that could lead back to his less than ideal start in life.

People knew he'd come from nothing, from the streets, but no one knew the grittier details of his very early life and that was how he wanted to keep it. He didn't need his personal humiliation to be made public.

In a bid to try and divert her attention from him he asked, 'Do you have a job?'

She shook her head. 'I just graduated from university.'

Dion frowned. 'But you're twenty-five?' She struck him as bright. Bright enough to get his attention. He wanted to scowl again and schooled his features.

Her face flushed again, and Dion felt as though he'd never get used to the way emotions played across her face so easily. She swallowed what she was eating and wiped her mouth with the napkin. 'I did it over five years, part-time. That's why it took longer than most degrees.'

'A degree in what?'

'Quantity surveying.'

Dion's eyes widened. He hadn't expected that. 'How did you get into that?'

'My father was an architect. I used to go on site visits with him when I was small and I was always fascinated by the QS, who seemed to be the one who really had the full picture of the build. I loved the way they managed to merge the creative with the practical.'

Dion was a little flabbergasted. He too had always had an appreciation for those in the business who had the practical measure of things.

'You mentioned siblings…four?'

She nodded and lifted a hand, ticking off fingers. 'Daniel, Mary, Lucy and Oisín.'

'Osheen?'

'It's Irish. It means little deer, as in, a fawn.'

'That's a big family.' Dion couldn't even imagine such a thing. It had been him and his mother, until it hadn't. As it was, he barely remembered those years with her because she'd routinely left him alone to fend for himself.

'I guess so.'

'Why did you become an egg donor? Was it for the money?'

CHAPTER FOUR

TARA'S EYES WIDENED. 'No, it wasn't like that. My eggs were there for my future use, not to be used as donor eggs for someone else.'

The man opposite her frowned, drawing his gorgeous dark features into an expression of incomprehension. 'Then…how did they end up being used to make an embryo? That's *if* what you're saying is true.'

Tara had to stop herself from saying something she might regret. She'd lambasted him for leaving his, *her*, son alone and he'd taken the fire out of her anger by revealing his truly awful experience at the hands of his parents. His decision to have a child alone wasn't so easy to judge now. She hadn't been able to help her soft heart from aching at the thought of him as a small child, bewildered and neglected. Dumped like an unwanted dog. She couldn't get her head around how a mother could do that to her own child.

Dion arched a brow. Waiting.

'Do you have issues with your fertility?' he asked before she could figure out how to formulate her response.

She shook her head. 'No, I don't have any issues…or at least, not that I know of.'

'So…why?'

Now *she* was under the spotlight. She felt defensive. 'Lots of women freeze their eggs now. It gives us choice and options for the future. Unlike men, we don't have an unlimited amount of time to procreate.'

His jaw tightened, a muscle twitched. Tara wanted to put her mouth there. She focused on his eyes, which weren't any less provocative. He had incredibly long lashes and yet they did nothing to detract from his sizzling masculinity. He said tautly, 'I am aware of that.'

Tara sighed. If she was going to be embarking on some kind of long-term arrangement with this man to have a relationship with her son, then she'd be wise not to completely alienate him.

Or give him the impression that you're a total sl—

'My parents both died when I was sixteen,' she blurted out, before any more intrusive thoughts could throw her off. 'In a car crash. A drunk driver on the wrong side of the road.'

Dion responded, 'That's…very rough. I'm sorry.'

'It was the worst thing. But…after they died, as the eldest, I had to step into their roles.'

He frowned. 'Was that allowed?'

'Technically, no, but my mother's sister and her husband became our guardians. They lived really close by and so we continued living in our own house and I took care of the day-to-day stuff while they supervised us and made sure we had enough money for everything.'

'While you were still at school?'

Tara nodded. 'Yes, I had two years left. But that's why it took me so long to get my degree. I took a couple of years out after school to stay at home while working part-time so I could be there for my brothers and sisters who were still in school.'

He looked at her and Tara could see that he didn't quite know what to make of this information. Eventually he said, 'That was admirable.'

She could almost hear the unspoken words, *If you're telling the truth*. He was so cynical. 'I had no choice, but that didn't matter. Even if I had had a choice, I would do it again. I love my brothers and sisters and they needed consistency and our routine to stay the same.'

He made a sound. 'Believe me, you had a choice but you chose not to shirk your responsibility.'

'I guess so.' It had never occurred to Tara that she would do anything else. They'd all been in pain and grieving. She'd needed her brothers and sisters as much as they'd needed her.

She said, 'That's why I froze my eggs. My sister was working in the clinic and she put the idea in my head. I liked knowing that if I froze them, I'd have options if I wanted to delay having children. I'd been mother and father to my siblings since I was sixteen. I never intended on having children young. I know how hard it is. I wanted to study and have my career.'

Dion's mouth had thinned into a line of disapproval. 'Your sister works at this clinic?'

Tara nodded, wondering where he was going with this.

'Was it her fault the wrong eggs were used?'

Tara sat up straight. 'No, not at all. She just noticed that my eggs had been disturbed.'

'But, if what you're saying is true, then this clinic has made a massive error.'

Tara's insides clenched. 'Well, yes, but there's not much we can do about it now.'

'I could sue them.'

Tara's blood drained south. She put a hand on the counter to hold onto something. 'You can't. My sister would lose her job. They help hundreds of couples.'

'They've been negligent. How many more errors have they made? They can't be allowed to stay open.'

Panic gripped Tara. She put out a hand in a pleading gesture. 'Until we do a DNA test and establish that Niko is my son, we don't know for sure that there *was* any negligence.' She put her hand down and looked him dead in the eye. 'And now that I've met him, I'm not leaving Athens until you agree to a DNA test. Surely you want to know for certain too?'

That muscle was twitching in his jaw again. She could tell that he would love to say *no*, that he couldn't care less. But could he live with the doubt of not knowing?

At that moment there was a snuffle on the baby monitor. Tara held her breath but it went quiet again. But Niko would be waking soon. She looked at Dion. 'I can stay here with Niko and take care of him today. If you want.'

He looked as if he wanted anything but that, but clearly he was not in a position to negotiate. 'Fine. Where are your things? Where are you staying?'

She named the hotel and his eyes widened marginally, no doubt because it wasn't exactly a salubrious area. He said, 'I have my assistant lining up a search for a new day nanny, until Elena can come back, but it probably makes sense for you to have your things brought here. There is plenty of space for you to stay and if you're going to be taking care of the baby in the meantime then it'll be more practical.'

Tara felt a jolt of relief that he wasn't sending her away. Even if it was only because he needed her.

She got off the stool. 'I can call a taxi to take me into town to pick up my things?'

He shook his head. 'No, you need to stay here for Niko. I'll have someone go to the hotel and collect your things if you give me your room number.'

'But I'm booked in for a few days. I didn't know how long I'd be here.'

He waved a hand. 'I'll take care of it.'

Pride stiffened Tara's spine. 'There's no need. I have money.'

'Call it payment for helping me with Niko.'

Tara couldn't argue with that. 'And the DNA test?'

'Your presence has created enough of a doubt for me to require it now for myself, if not just to prove that you're on the make. I'll arrange to have someone from my doctor's office come to do the test.'

Even as she was relieved to hear he would allow a test, Tara's hands clenched to fists. 'I am not on the make. I have better things to be doing, like looking for a job. I did not intend on becoming a mother so soon after seeing my youngest sibling settled into university. This is the last thing I wanted.'

Dion looked insultingly relieved. 'So you'll leave even if Niko *is* your son?'

Tara shook her head, frustrated at the way he was so quick to jump to conclusions. 'No, that's not what I meant. If he is my son, then there is no way I will be turning my back on him.' Especially not now she knew that his father barely knew how to hold him and had palmed him off on nannies.

Tara's conscience pricked. He had his reasons for having a child and it must be hard to bond with a baby with no natural bonding hormones to help. Still, she wouldn't be abandoning her child.

Dion made a scoffing sound and said, 'I'll believe that when I see it.'

Tara forced out the sympathy she felt when she thought of his experiences and just said, 'I have no intention of leaving my son.'

He just looked at her but then he was asking for her hotel details and at the same time a cry came from the baby monitor. Niko was waking up. Tara gave him the details and said, 'I'll go and tend to Niko.'

Dion said, with a warning tone that Tara really didn't appreciate, 'I'll be here, working from the home office. Needless to say I won't be leaving you alone with my son.'

Tara curbed the urge to say something in response, but in truth she wasn't sure what she would say because in that moment she was also realising the full extent of just how much her life was about to change, *if* Niko was hers. And so she lifted her chin and walked out with as much dignity as she could muster in her bare feet.

A couple of hours later, after Dion had made some calls and had a couple of online meetings with his team, he went looking for Tara and Niko. He'd alerted Security to make sure that she didn't try to escape or do anything foolish with the baby.

That conversation with her, earlier, hadn't been what he'd expected at all. Of course, he couldn't trust a word out of her mouth, but, even if she'd made it all up, it was a compelling story.

He had to concede that he could see her stepping in to take responsibility for her family. She gave off an air of practical capability, as evidenced by her reaction earlier and initiative in taking the baby to settle him.

He stopped in his tracks when he heard the sound of the baby laughing. He walked to the door of the baby's suite of rooms and stopped again at the sight in front of him.

Tara had pulled up her hair into a loose knot that sat slightly askew on top of her head with tendrils falling down around her face. She sat on the floor with legs spread out and

Niko was in between them and she was bending down and blowing raspberries on his belly and then playing with his legs, pumping them up and down, before blowing more raspberries. He was ecstatic, laughing and gurgling, a big grin on his face. Pudgy arms flailing about, eyes glued to Tara.

As were Dion's eyes. Taking in those pale arms and legs. He could see tantalising glimpses of the curves of her breasts under the shirt as she moved and it made him think of how they'd felt in his hands, under his tongue.

At that moment she looked up and saw him, as if hearing his thoughts. He couldn't help but scowl in response and he saw how her own expression became wary.

The baby obviously noticed a change too and his head came around, two huge eyes looking at Dion. Mirror images of *her* eyes. He couldn't unsee that now. The laughter had stopped and he felt unaccountably guilty.

She scooped Niko up and stood up gracefully in one movement. 'We were just playing. I hope we didn't disturb you?'

Now he felt even guiltier. He had a memory flash of his mother—who he'd realised in later years was probably an alcoholic—shouting at him to stop making noise because she had a headache.

'No, my office is the other side of the villa, but it's after lunchtime, you must be hungry and I'm not sure what Niko's eating routine is. Will you come to the kitchen?'

At that moment Tara's stomach made a noise and she blushed. 'Okay, food would be good. I can check out Niko's bottle and food situation. The nannies might have started him on solids by now.'

They went back to the kitchen and Dion pulled out some prepared food the housekeeper had left. Salads and cold meats. Bread. He directed Tara to where Niko's supplies were kept and she had a look, returning with a container. She held it up and it had a sticker on the side. 'Puréed vegetables, made yesterday. We can try this and I'll give him a bottle and put him down after.'

Dion looked at his watch. 'The night nanny will be here in a couple of hours. She said she'd come early to help out.'

After warming the baby food in a microwave, Tara set Niko up in a high chair by the dining table and sat down to feed him. Dion came over with two plates loaded up with food and put one down for her nearby. He sat down too. She thanked him and fed Niko, who seemed to love the food, smacking his hands on the high-chair table, inevitably spraying some purée everywhere.

Onto Dion's shirt. Tara looked at him and he could see her struggle to keep in a laugh as she said, 'Sorry, they're not the tidiest of eaters.'

Dion had a sense that she saw him as being stuffy or uptight and didn't like it. He wiped his shirt with a napkin. 'It's fine. It's true that I leave most of his care to his nannies, but I don't have any previous experience with babies.'

Tara took a bite from her own plate in between feeding Niko. She seemed to be totally at ease with everything that—admittedly—had been thrown at her since she'd arrived.

Since last night...the most spontaneous and responsive lover you've ever had.

Then she asked, 'So...why embark on having a child on your own?'

Dion once again lamented divulging so much to her earlier. He wiped his mouth with his napkin and shrugged minutely and said, 'I've created a very successful business and I would like to hand it on to someone.'

I don't want to be alone.

That rogue thought entered his head and made his blood run cold for a second before he crushed it ruthlessly. Not wanting to be alone was not an admission of anything other than realising no man was an island, no matter how he might have played it up to now.

Oblivious to his thoughts, she went on, 'But don't you want a partner? A mother for your child?'

'I have no desire to be in a relationship.'

Tara's eyes went wide. She was holding the spoon of food for Niko just inches from his mouth and he let out a frustrated shriek at her distraction and she hurriedly put the spoon in his mouth and then looked back to Dion.

'Do you not like women? Because of your mother?'

Dion had a flash of last night, how it had felt to join their bodies. He wanted to unsettle her as much as she unsettled him. 'Did it feel to you like I don't like women last night?'

She immediately blushed, but, contrary to a sense of triumph, all Dion could think about was that encounter and how erotic it had been.

Before she could say anything he responded, 'I have nothing but respect for women, but when it comes to personal relationships I decided a long time ago not to go there. I fully intend for Niko to grow up feeling secure and wanted and respected. He won't be rejected by one parent and abandoned by another.'

Tara was looking at him and opened her mouth to say something but, just then, Niko let out a little cry and rubbed his eyes, getting some puréed food onto his face. She deftly wiped him clean and said, 'He's tired. I'll take him up for a change and give him a bottle and put him down.'

Dion stood up feeling redundant as Tara unhooked Niko from the high chair and lifted him into her arms. She pressed a kiss to Niko's chubby cheek and he gave her a gummy smile and Dion felt as if the earth were shifting under his feet. Again.

She was still in her bare feet and the clothes from the villa that morning. It struck Dion that she hadn't made a murmur of complaint at having to take over minding a baby that might or might not be any relation to her. But he noticed the faint circles under her eyes now and that guilt was back.

He said, 'Your things have been collected and delivered from the hotel. They're in a suite near to Niko's room. I've left the door open so you can find it. And a nurse from my doctor's office will be here this evening to take swabs from you and Niko.'

'Wow, okay, that's fast. Thank you.'

'Feel free to relax when Niko is napping. You must be tired.'

She blushed again and avoided his eye. Dion hated to admit he found her reactions utterly disarming. Niko regarded him with huge eyes over her shoulder as they left. *Her eyes.* As if mocking him for the way she had got under his skin so easily.

If Tara was a fake and a hustler he'd have her on the next plane out of Athens so fast her head would be spinning. And if she was the mother of his child then…it was even more imperative that he figure out exactly what her agenda was and make sure he was in control.

The woman was too disturbing to his equilibrium, and he hadn't clawed his way out of abandonment and rejection to unbelievable success and respect only to risk it all because he couldn't control his hormones.

When Niko was sleeping again, his lashes long on his plump cheeks, Tara crept out of his room, pulling the door half shut and taking the baby monitor with her. She went down the corridor and found an open door, as Dion had told her.

The room was vast. Light and bright. Gorgeous soft greys and blues and silver trim. Chinoiserie wallpaper.

She had an en suite bathroom decked out in cool white tiles, shelves stocked with exclusive products. And there was a dressing room, where she spotted her bag. She pounced on it and pulled out the few of her own clothes that she'd brought, changing into a soft pair of jeans and a T-shirt. She laid the clothes she'd worn from the villa on top of what looked like the laundry basket. They were pretty creased and dirty after her hauling herself over the wall and hours of interacting with a six-month-old.

She felt a bit more like herself in her own clothes and then a wave of weariness came over her. The bed, dressed in cool linen, looked so inviting. She sat down on the edge of the bed and tried to get her head around everything. In a matter of hours her life had been turned on its head.

She'd known she had a son, and that she had to find his father, but she hadn't expected to have her son in her arms within twenty-four hours of landing in Athens.

Or to sleep with his father? snarked a little voice.

Definitely not that. But could Tara regret it? *No.* Shamefully. Last night had been…earth-shattering. Life-altering. Literally.

And now…a sense of resolve filled her. She would get confirmation that she was Niko's mother and, when she had that, Dion would have to acknowledge her place in Niko's life.

She could understand why he might feel a mother wasn't necessary. But her mother had been wonderful and loving and kind and Tara felt sorry for him that he obviously hadn't had that experience.

Her life was now going to look very different and it wasn't what she'd intended for herself, but she'd fallen in love with her son. She would make Dion see that *his* vision for a future with just him and his son would have to accommodate her. She felt a frisson of trepidation. Dion wasn't going to make it easy. But she would do anything to make it work.

Tara glanced back at the bed. It looked too inviting, and soft. She scooted up to the pillows and lay down again, and told herself she'd close her eyes for just a minute.

'Tara?'

Tara sat up straight, disorientated. Dion was standing at the end of the bed. It all came rushing back.

'Niko,' she breathed, looking for the monitor and not seeing it where she left it. 'Where's Niko? Did I not hear him?'

She was aware of Dion giving her a look but then he said, 'He's fine. Maria, the nanny, is here. He's with her downstairs.'

Tara immediately felt a sense of possessiveness and had to remind herself that she wasn't yet confirmed as Niko's mother. She got off the bed. 'Sorry, I fell asleep.' She was conscious of her jeans and T-shirt. Messy hair.

'The nurse is here from my doctor's office to take a swab. He's already done Niko.'

The DNA test.

'Of course.' Tara slipped her feet into her sneakers and followed Dion out of the bedroom and into the main part of the villa. She could hear the sounds of Niko from the kitchen and longed to go to him but this was obviously important.

They went through the impressive reception hall and into one of the corridors leading off the hall. Then they were in a suite of rooms. His home office. She followed him into the inner room and saw a young man in what looked like a hospital uniform of dark blue scrubs.

Tara sat down and let the nurse swab inside her mouth. Dion stood in the corner looking brooding, arms folded across his chest. The nurse bagged up the swab and spoke to Dion in Greek before nodding at Tara and leaving.

Dion stayed standing in the corner of the room. 'We'll have the results tomorrow.'

'That fast?'

He nodded. Then he looked at his watch and said, 'I have an event to go to this evening. Feel free to help yourself to food from the fridge. The housekeeper will have left something ready to heat. I mostly eat out.'

'Even since Niko?'

He looked at her and his jaw clenched. He obviously didn't like her implication. 'I have sole custody of my son. How I choose to bring him up is not up for discussion.'

Tara stood up. 'When it's proven that I'm his mother I will have rights, Dion.'

'We'll cross that bridge when we come to it.'

Clearly he still expected that this DNA test would come back negative and he could be shot of her, and this was all a reminder that he didn't want her here. The atmosphere between them couldn't be more different from the previous evening, when she'd grown dizzy under the full impact of his charm and seduction. He hadn't even had to seduce her all that much. One blistering-hot kiss and she'd been ready to get onto a helicopter and let him take her anywhere.

'I'll go and introduce myself to Maria.'

She turned and left the room before he could see the humiliation she felt for being so...easy. She found the nanny, a perfectly pleasant dark-haired young woman, in the kitchen with Niko and did her best to push out of her mind that tomorrow she would be embarking on a very different life path.

When Dion returned from the event he felt restless and irritable. He undid his bow tie and opened it and the top button of his shirt, feeling constricted. All evening he'd been distracted. Thinking of *her* and how she'd been like such a breath of fresh air when he'd spotted her last night.

She was a Trojan horse, not a breath of fresh air. She was here, under his roof, and she couldn't have planned it better.

But when he got near to the bedrooms he heard the cry of a baby and saw a shadowy figure pushing open the door to Niko's room. He knew it wasn't Maria. Because he knew the figure in those soft jeans and T-shirt intimately.

And he wanted to know her again.

At that moment a sleepy Maria appeared in the corridor, belting her robe over pyjamas. Then both women saw Dion and startled. Dion put out a hand. 'Sorry, I didn't mean to scare you.'

Tara was framed in Niko's doorway. She said, 'It's okay, Maria, I was up watching a movie. Why don't I check on him and you go back to bed?'

The nanny shot Dion a worried glance, clearly not used to having to answer to anyone else, but after a moment's hesitation he just nodded and said, 'It's fine, go back to bed, Maria, thank you.'

Dion followed Tara into the baby's bedroom illuminated only by a low light. She went over to the cot and lifted Niko out. He looked sleepy and Dion had that sense again of not knowing what he should do, but hating himself for this fear of interaction.

Tara turned around. 'I was in the lounge watching something on TV. I hope that was okay?'

Dion was disconcerted by how natural it felt to see her here in this milieu and how much she'd occupied his thoughts all evening. She didn't look like a Trojan Horse at all now. She looked utterly innocent. And he couldn't trust it for a second.

'It's fine,' he dismissed. Tomorrow she would be gone, once they knew for a fact she was an opportunist.

Tara cut into his thoughts. 'Have you ever changed a nappy?'

Dion shook his head. He hadn't been expecting that.

'Want to try?'

For a man who regularly faced down adversaries in boardrooms and negotiated deals worth billions of euros, he suddenly felt a spike of terror. But that galvanised him.

He walked forward. 'Sure, it would be useful to know.'

In case you have another emergency like today? prompted a sly voice, reminding him of how Tara had stepped into the breach.

She had Niko lying on his back on a high table and she was getting him out of his sleep suit explaining as she went. A pungent smell hit Dion's nostrils and his face screwed up. Niko was looking at him and laughed, gurgling.

'He thinks you're funny,' Tara said.

A little glow of warmth settled in Dion's chest. He moved closer. Niko kept staring at him. Tara was deftly undoing the nappy and wiping Niko. She said, 'Here, your turn.'

She kept a hand on Niko's belly as she moved aside and handed Dion a fresh nappy. 'Open it out…like that, yes… the sticky ties will be at the top, hold his feet together and then lift…like that, and slide the nappy under his back… pull through his legs…and up over his tummy and then secure it…perfect.'

As if sensing he was being used in a lesson, Niko didn't make a sound. Dion looked at the baby, fresh nappy in place.

'Here's a clean sleepsuit.'

And now Tara was handing him something that looked as if it had a hundred arms and legs. She lifted Niko to sit up and helped Dion get him into it, saying, 'They're really not that fragile. Don't be afraid to handle him.'

Their fingers touched and it threatened to derail Dion's focus but he somehow managed to get Niko buttoned up.

'Why don't you hold him while I get a bottle in the kitchen?'

Tara was already handing Niko to Dion and he had to take him. Then she was gone. He was holding Niko awkwardly and he struggled to recall how the nannies and Tara did it—effortlessly.

Experimentally he lifted him up against his chest and to his surprise Niko curled against him and put his head into the crook between Dion's shoulder and neck. Dion went very still. One hand was on Niko's back and he had an arm under his little bottom, cradling him.

He moved his hand up and down. He'd never held Niko like this before. Felt his little sturdy body curling into him so trustingly. For him, deciding to have a son and going about it—even since Niko had come home—had felt like a more abstract or existential thing, not an actual physical reality.

But now it felt very real and he had a sense of his son's vulnerability. And now Dion felt ashamed, because it was very belatedly coming home to him that Niko was a tiny human being who would need a lot more than nannies doing shift work while he got on with building his empire.

With uncanny timing Tara returned to the room with a bottle in her hand. She held the bottle out to Dion. 'Do you want to try feeding him?'

Dion was reeling with the revelation he'd just had and Tara's eyes were far too incisive. He'd been exposed enough for one night. He lifted Niko away from his shoulder and he made a little snuffling sound that almost had Dion clutching him back. But he said, 'I'll leave that to you. I don't want to upset him.'

Tara deftly took Niko back into her arms and said, 'He seemed very happy just now. He's half asleep again anyway, he probably won't even drink any of this.'

'We'll have the DNA results first thing in the morning.'

She sat down in a rocking chair with Niko and looked up at Dion. 'Good, then we can know how to proceed.'

Dion hated to admit it, but every sense in his body was telling him that the news they would get tomorrow would not be conducive to restoring his sense of control or equilibrium. Quite the opposite.

CHAPTER FIVE

'I HAVE THE results here—shall I go ahead?'

Tara was sitting on the edge of a chair in Dion's office, tense. He was standing facing away from her, looking out of the window, hands behind his back. The doctor's disembodied voice, coming from the phone on the desk, hung in the air.

As if startled out of a reverie, Dion turned around and said, 'Yes, please do.'

The doctor coughed a little and then said, 'Well, the test is ninety-nine point nine per cent conclusive that Tara Simons is Niko's mother.'

Tara felt a surge of emotion and looked at Dion, who was looking at the phone, his expression unreadable. Then he said, 'Is there any possibility it's not correct?'

Tara absorbed that like a blow to her belly.

The doctor said, 'Of course, we can run the test again, or you could go elsewhere, but I think you'll find that—'

'No, that's fine, thank you for your time.' Dion came over and reached forward and pressed a button, cutting off the doctor.

Reeling a little with the confirmation she *was* Niko's mother, Tara said jokily to hide her hurt, 'You really don't want me to be Niko's mother, do you?'

He looked at her and his eyes were dark. No hint of gold today. 'It's nothing personal.' He waved a hand. 'This is not how I expected things to go. I had never intended having any kind of relationship with the mother.'

Still feeling hurt and defensive now, Tara said, 'For what it's worth, I'm glad Niko will have a mother. He has a whole family in Ireland, aunts, uncles…presumably cousins one day. Did you consider that?'

To Tara's eye, Dion went a little pale. 'No,' he admitted. 'But you're assuming a lot to think Niko's life will intersect with theirs.'

Tara stood up. '*Intersect?* He's not a Venn diagram.'

They stared at one another across the space. And then Dion said, 'You'll probably want to make arrangements to go home now, I can organise that for you.'

'Why would I want to leave? My son is here!'

'You have a career to get back to. Your family.'

'I hadn't actually got a job placement yet and for the first time in my life my family don't depend on me for everything. They're all adults now.'

'Well, what are you proposing?'

Tara felt cornered, under pressure. 'I don't know yet. But all I know is that I don't want to leave Niko.' *Or you.* It sneaked into her head even as she was wondering what she'd ever first seen in this man. Had he ever been charming? Right now he couldn't be more closed-off, cold. And yet something about him called to her—beyond the physical—deep inside in some emotional place that she couldn't deny. She'd felt it the first time they'd met.

'You froze your eggs in a bid to control when you'd have children after becoming a mother too young. How long will it take before you start to resent Niko for taking your freedom again?'

Tara shook her head. 'I did that because the option was available to me and it seemed to make sense for lots of reasons, not least of which is because I can't take for granted that getting pregnant would be easy for me.'

Dion pointed out, 'You have four siblings. I doubt fertility will be an issue.'

Tara lifted her chin, 'It still could be, in spite of family history, and that's a luxury women don't have—endless time to wait and have children.'

He had the grace to look slightly sheepish. 'Fair point.' His expression hardened again. 'That still doesn't assure me that you'd not end up resenting Niko and ultimately abandoning him to take up your life again.'

Tara put her hands out, 'This isn't what I'd planned but, as I've learnt, life doesn't always go according to plan. My parents shouldn't have died so young, but they did. But they left us with a legacy of unconditional love and endless encouragement. I have a son now, and I will give him the same as my parents gave me. My life is with Niko and I will never resent him for that. And if that means taking up work here, and living here to be near him, then so be it. Only time and my commitment to my son will prove that to you.'

His gaze narrowed on her now and she felt a frisson of trepidation. He said, 'The clinic messed up. Badly. I should be taking legal action against them.'

Tara's insides curdled. 'You can't. This wasn't Mary's fault but it could ruin them. She'd lose her job.'

'But how many other people might have been affected by someone's shoddy work ethic?'

Tara swallowed uncomfortably. She couldn't answer that. 'Maybe there's a way to let them know about the mistake without going as far as suing them. I'll do anything.' She crossed her fingers behind her back because she wasn't going to leave Athens. Not even for this. Not now she knew Niko was hers. She felt a very primal urge to stay close to him.

Dion looked at her for a long moment and Tara, who'd never really given her appearance much thought, was suddenly acutely aware of her bed hair roughly pulled back and up into a knot. The same jeans as yesterday, albeit with a fresh T-shirt. She must look like a messy student.

'Maria is doing a double shift, as you know.'

Tara nodded. When she'd got up this morning expecting to relieve Maria, the other woman had told her she'd agreed to stay until this evening because Elena was due to come back.

Dion continued, 'Before you came in here to get the results, I talked to Elena. She was due to return to work later but she's actually resigned. She realised it wasn't going to work out.'

'Oh.'

'So I'm stuck.'

'I'm his mother, Dion. You're not stuck.'

His jaw clenched at that. 'If I agree to let you stay here, for now, until I get a replacement for Elena, maybe it'll give you the opportunity to re-evaluate your priorities.'

Tara gritted out, 'They don't need re-evaluating.'

As if she'd said nothing, Dion said, 'I'll pay you, of course.'

Tara was immediately incensed. 'You'll do no such thing. I'm his mother. I don't expect payment to watch my own son.'

Dion shrugged. 'Fine.'

She could stay. For now. Be Niko's mother. Let it sink in. She sat back down again as the enormity of it all washed over her.

'Are you okay?'

Tara looked at Dion and a tremulous smile she couldn't stop rose up with the emotion inside her. 'I just... I'm so happy that he's mine.' And now he would have at least one parent who would lavish him with love and not hold him at arm's length.

But then Tara thought of the previous night and how she'd seen such vulnerability in the way Dion had changed Niko's nappy. And how he'd been holding him when she'd come back into the room. As naturally as if he'd been doing it all along. Father and son were already changing.

Dion said, 'I have to go to the office today. Feel free to make yourself at home. Thea, my housekeeper, and the rest of the staff are back today. She'll provide whatever you need. I'll be out this evening again.'

He went over to the desk and scrawled something down on a piece of paper and handed it to her, 'My personal mobile phone number in case you need to contact me.'

Tara took it and felt an absurd urge to giggle. She'd already slept with this man and they were parents to a six-month-old baby boy and they were only now exchanging numbers.

'What's funny about that?' he asked sharply.

Tara shook her head and swallowed down the giggles. 'Nothing...' Before she left the room she looked at Dion and said, 'You know, it mightn't be the worst thing in the world for Niko to have his mother.' And then she left before Dion could sour her mood with his own. She was going to spend time getting to know her son and try to ignore the fact that his father actively wanted her gone from their lives.

You know, it mightn't be the worst thing in the world for Niko to have his mother...

Dion scowled at the words that had reverberated in his head all day and evening as his car stopped outside the villa later that night. The business dinner he'd just endured had been interminable. He'd felt restless to get back home and check on Tara and Niko.

She was Niko's mother.

As improbable as that might be. He had to admit uncomfortably that her story did stack up. She'd come to Athens looking for him and hadn't known who he was at that party, not helped by them agreeing to remain anonymous. And yet, would he have given up that night—the most erotic of his life—for having known who she was earlier?

His body answered him emphatically: *no*.

The fact that he still wanted her was inconvenient in the extreme. As much as her words had dominated his thoughts all day and evening, so had the image of her. That lithe body, dressed in just jeans and a T-shirt. Hair messy. No make-up. Pale skin. Tantalising freckles. He already had a sense of regret for not taking more time that first night…for not spending hours exploring her body with single-minded dedication. Maybe if he had, he would have exorcised her from his system.

Dion's head was so full of Tara as he walked through the darkened silent villa to his bedroom that when he saw her coming out of Niko's room and pulling the door behind her, he almost wasn't surprised. After all, she was filling in for Maria, after the other woman's double shift. But that wasn't the reason. Somehow, he expected to see her now. *Wanted to see her.*

His gaze devoured her. She was wearing a short robe and her long legs were bare. Hair down her back and a little wild and messy. Copper, even in this light.

Annoyed for noticing her before thinking of his son, he asked in a low voice, 'Is Niko okay?'

Tara whirled around. She glared at him. 'Would you stop doing that?'

He noticed she was holding the baby monitor in her hand. But that was not all he noticed now. Her robe was partially open and he could see she was wearing a vest top. The firm swells of her breasts visible under the fabric.

He leant a shoulder against the wall, something illicit and dangerous fizzing in his veins. Lust. The urge to throw caution to the wind, in spite of everything that had transpired over the last couple of days, was overwhelming. He needed to connect with this woman again on a level that he could understand when so much was veering wildly out of his control.

Then she said, 'He's fine. I just changed him and fed him and he's asleep again. He's the most—' She stopped and then asked a little breathlessly, 'Why are you looking at me like that?'

It had never been in Dion's nature to be coy or disingenuous. One of the reasons he'd done so well in business was because he was straightforward.

'Because I still want you.'

Tara's mouth opened and closed again. 'I...well, I was not expecting you to say that.'

'The truth is that the other night was...unprecedented for me. I told you it wouldn't happen again but I was lying to myself. I would have wanted to see you again.'

That admission caught at Tara somewhere vulnerable. The shock of seeing him in the dimly lit corridor was receding and she couldn't help but take in his tall, powerful form in a grey suit and white shirt, open at his throat.

There was stubble on his jaw. *He still wanted her.* She hadn't considered for a second that that night had been anything but a passing diversion for him.

'But...we can't.' The elephant was literally sleeping in the room behind her, legs and arms splayed out like a starfish.

'Why not? We're two consenting adults who want each other.'

'Until this moment I was pretty certain it was just a one-night thing.'

He shook his head and all Tara could see was that thick hair and the hard angles and planes of his face. She wanted to go over and put her hands on his face, soften the edges for him.

The truth was that she didn't just *want* him, he'd caught her on a much more profound level where her emotions lived. And she knew—because of her family—that when she loved, she loved fiercely and unequivocally. Like the way she already loved Niko. And to be thinking of Dion in the same vein was not a little terrifying.

'Not true,' he said. 'I want you more than I've ever wanted a woman.'

It was also scary for Tara to acknowledge that, even after knowing him for only a couple of days, she trusted him enough to know that wasn't a line. Her heart thumped and she went against every cell in her body when she said, 'I don't think it's a good idea. There's too much…stuff between us.'

Like a baby. Their son. And what would happen.

'I think we can keep the two separate. You know I'm not remotely interested in a relationship.'

A half-laugh came out of Tara's mouth. She put her hand to it and then let it drop, saying, 'You've made that more than clear by choosing to become a single father.'

'So…we know where we stand.'

He made it sound so simple but Tara knew it wasn't. For her. And yet…she really, really wanted to repeat what had happened that first night. Before the world had imploded around them with the bombshell of discovering who he was.

And something else struck her then, a very earthy primal feeling of connection. This was her baby's father. And they might not have conceived him in a conventional way but the fact that there was this chemistry between them—completely unexpected—was an unbelievable aphrodisiac. The fact that in some alternate universe, they *could* have created him together.

He pointed out, 'You've said yourself you're not planning on leaving.'

Now Tara shook her head. 'No, I want to be with my son.'

'Then why don't we let this…mutual chemistry run its course? At least then, when we go our separate ways, we won't have any loose ends.'

Tara chafed at that. 'I'd call Niko a pretty permanent loose end.'

'We'll come to an arrangement—I don't intend to stop you being in his life, Tara. You have a point about his needing a mother.'

Tara had a strong suspicion he was just humouring her and that he didn't trust for a second that she'd stay in Niko's life, but he'd soon learn.

'I know I have rights. There's no question I'll be in his life as his mother, for ever.'

'For ever is a long way away. Why don't we focus on the present moment?'

In spite of everything and Dion's clear doubt that she would stay the course as Niko's mother, her blood was hot and her heart was thumping erratically. She wanted to alternately kiss Dion and then slap him for being so arrogantly cynical. And then that made her think of how his own parents had treated him and her heart ached.

'You want me, Tara.'

How she longed to dent that arrogant self-assurance. But

it was hard to do when she was literally weak at the knees and already imagining what it might be like to have his mouth on her again.

'Niko...' she said weakly.

'Niko is asleep, we have a baby monitor and we're literally next door.'

We. Any paltry resistance dissolved. Dion straightened up from the wall and held out his hand. Before she could overthink it, Tara stepped forward and put her hand in Dion's. His fingers curled around hers and he led her back down the corridor a little and into his bedroom.

Inside, there were some low lamps sending out golden pools of light. Tara could see the bed, massive. Dion pushed the door almost closed but not quite. He let her hand go and took the baby monitor, putting it on top of a chest of drawers. He asked, 'Is it turned right up?'

Tara nodded. The bare flicker of lights on the monitor indicated that Niko was still fast asleep.

'Come here.'

He was standing at the end of the bed. He'd taken off his jacket and was undoing the buttons on his shirt. She lamented the fact that she wasn't wearing some silky filmy negligée as she walked towards him. He pulled off his shirt, revealing his broad, hard-muscled chest. It truly was a sight to behold.

Instinctively, Tara reached out and her put hand on it, splaying her fingers, feeling the soft springiness of his chest hair, the warmth of his skin. The hard nubs of his nipples, making him suck in a breath.

She looked up. He was staring down at her. 'I need to taste you.' He cupped her face in his hands and urged her closer while lifting her face to his. Tara's mouth opened on a sigh just as his covered it and their breaths mingled and tongues touched, tentatively at first and then with more intensity, exploring and tasting...

Dion's hands moved down, fingers undoing her robe and pushing it from her shoulders, down her arms and off her body. He drew back and looked at her. All she was wearing was a flimsy vest and sleep-shorts. Plain and unadorned. At least the first night they'd met she'd been wearing the evening gown. She ducked her head but he tipped her chin up and shook his head and said with a rough quality to his voice, 'Don't do that. You are beautiful.'

How could he say things like this to her and make her feel like the most precious thing, and then also be the man who had acquired a baby like an accessory to his life?

But she didn't have time to think about that because he was lifting her vest from the bottom and she lifted her arms to allow him to pull it up and off completely.

Now she wore only panties. While he was still half dressed. As if he were reading her mind, Dion's hands went to his trousers and he undid them and pushed them off his hips, taking his underwear too, stepping out of his clothes. Now he was naked. Skin gleaming in the half-light. A Greek statue brought to life.

He caught her by the arms and tugged her into him again so that their bodies were touching. The tips of her breasts against his lower torso, his rising erection against her belly.

She moved closer, trapping him against her, and moved delicately.

He caught her hair and pulled gently, tugging her head back, 'You little cat.'

Tara felt like purring. She came up on her tiptoes then and wound her arms around Dion's neck, finding his mouth and pressing hers against it in a desperate kiss, silently asking him to take control so she wouldn't have to think about anything but these wondrous sensations that he sparked to life in her.

For someone who'd spent the last decade worrying about everyone else, it felt beyond decadent to indulge herself like this.

Dion obliged. He ducked a little and caught Tara under her legs, lifting her up and carrying her to the bed. It made Tara feel emotional—just this small act—because it made her feel cared for, when she'd been the one who had done all the caring. *Dangerous.* She had to push notions like this out of her head because it was an illusion. This was just about *sex*. And she was catching up on lost time.

He laid her down on the bed and put his hands to her underwear, tugging it off. She lifted her hips. Now she was naked too. But she didn't feel self-conscious. She felt hungry.

Dion was standing, looking at her, that dark gaze roving all over her body, making her tingle.

'Dion...please...'

'What, *gattina*?'

'What does that mean?'

'Little cat. Do you want me to touch you?'

Tara liked that, too much. She nodded. 'Yes, please.'

Dion smiled and it was wicked. 'So polite. How can I refuse?'

He came down on the bed beside her, all six feet plus of rippling muscles and long powerful limbs. He put a hand on her belly, splayed. She sucked in a breath. And then he lowered his head and their mouths connected again in a deep and explicit kiss, as his hand left her belly and ventured down, over the curls between her legs.

Tacitly she opened her legs, giving him permission, and he explored her there with long fingers, finding where she was hot and achy. Wet for him. He stroked into her and Tara broke the kiss, back arching as he found the centre of her body.

He brought his mouth to her breasts, finding those stinging points and biting, licking, sucking them into even tighter peaks of need. Tara bucked against his hand and those wicked, clever fingers and within seconds she was shattering against him in a climax that winded her with its force.

When she could breathe again she opened her eyes. Dion was looking down at her, eyes glittering. 'You are unbelievably responsive. It's the sexiest thing I've ever encountered.'

Tara opened her mouth to say something but she couldn't speak. He'd rendered her speechless. She watched as he reached for protection and rolled it onto his erection, her eyes widening. She'd forgotten how majestic he was. And only for the fact that they'd already slept together, she didn't feel intimidated.

He came up over her and, with one smooth thrust, seated himself in her body. Tara sucked in a deep breath at the way he stretched her, to the point of almost pain, but not quite.

'Okay?'

She nodded and shifted a little under him, and the pressure eased. He started to move in and out and Tara kept her eyes glued to his, as if somehow that could keep her anchored when, with every slide of his body in and out of hers, she was being wound higher and higher.

She put her hands on his shoulders. They were so wide. As the tension built, she wrapped her legs around his hips and he went even deeper. He cursed a little and Tara felt a spurt of momentary delight that she had some power over him. But it faded quickly when he took control again, and touched her so deep that she gasped.

An urgency gripped them both as they strained to reach

the pinnacle. Skin slick with perspiration, desperation mounting.

'Come for me, Tara… I need you…' Dion said brokenly. He put his hand between them and touched her where their bodies were joined in this age-old dance and before she knew what was happening she was flying over the edge with nothing to hang onto, her body convulsing in waves of pleasure, over and over again, barely aware of Dion's muffled shout as his body went still and then jerked against her as he found his own release.

He collapsed on top of her and Tara bound her arms and legs around him. After a few minutes he lifted his head and said, 'I'm sorry… I had planned to take more time…'

A wave of tenderness washed through Tara before she could stop it. She shook her head and brought up a hand to push back a lock of hair that had fallen over his forehead. He looked so much younger right now.

'Don't be sorry, it was…amazing.' Then, feeling shy, she asked, 'Is it always like this?'

She felt a tension come into Dion's body and then he gently extricated himself from her embrace. He got up and disappeared into the bathroom for a few seconds and then re-emerged, lying back down on the bed, unselfconscious in his nakedness. Tara pulled the sheet up over her chest, suddenly a little cold.

She thought he wasn't going to answer her question but then he said, 'It would be easy to lie and say, *yes, it's always like this,* but the truth is no, it's not. It's usually something far less…intense. Pleasurable, yes, if you're doing it right, and hopefully for both partners, but not like this.'

He turned then to face her and came up on one elbow. 'It won't last, Tara, it never does. It'll burn out…'

He touched her hot cheek with a knuckle and dragged it

down to her jaw. Her skin tingled. He continued, 'But what I propose is that we make the most of it while it lasts.'

Tara forced herself to say, 'Aren't things complicated enough?' As if she were somehow the sane adult in the room.

Dion smiled. His hand went down and found the sheet she'd pulled up. He dragged it back down again, exposing her chest. He looked at her and she saw how his eyes flared and his cheeks darkened with colour. Her insides went on fire, again.

He dragged his gaze back up and said, 'Wouldn't it be so much more complicated to try and ignore this?'

Weakly she said nothing. Not even when he bent towards her and touched his mouth to hers. Softly. In a question. The only answer Tara could give was to press her mouth against his and move closer until her chest was touching his. Dion whipped the sheet aside and he pushed a thigh between her legs and Tara gave herself over to Dion's very persuasive brand of logic.

When Dion woke it was dawn. It took him a minute to orient himself, which was disconcerting because he always woke with absolute clarity and knew exactly where he was.

Tara. Hearts pounding in unison, straining to reach a higher pinnacle of pleasure than he'd thought was possible. He lifted his head but he already knew he was alone. For a crazy second he wondered if it had all been a dream but when he put an arm out to the other side of the bed he could feel faint lingering warmth. And her scent tickled his nostrils, along with something much earthier. *Sex.*

Then he heard a sound. Screeching. Splashing? *Niko.* Awake. Dion got out of bed and had a rapid shower, pulling on jeans and a polo shirt. He followed the sounds of his son to find Tara in the bathroom with him, giving him a bath. She was supporting him in the water and he was splashing with enthusiasm, spraying everything within a large radius. Including Dion. And including Tara, Dion noticed when she looked up and saw him. She'd got dressed into shorts and a loose white shirt, which was pretty transparent by now, showing a white bra.

Dion looked away quickly because he could already feel his body responding.

She said, 'I thought he could do with a bath when he woke up a while ago.'

Dion realised that he didn't like not being the one who generally knew everything about everything. He had no idea how often babies should be bathed.

Tara grabbed a towel from nearby and stood up, lifting Niko out of the water and wrapping him in the towel.

'Can I do anything?' Dion heard himself asking before he'd even intended saying anything.

Tara looked at him. 'Sure, you could put him down on his playmat and dry him off, let him kick his legs and arms a bit before we dress him again. I can clean up in here.'

'Thea's staff can do that.'

Tara smiled at him in a way that Dion felt was a kind of reproach. She said, 'I'm sure Thea and her staff have enough to do. It'll only take me a minute.'

She handed Niko over to Dion and he took him, for the first time not feeling as though he were handling an explosive object. Niko looked up at Dion and then he smiled and tapped Dion on the cheek with his pudgy hand. A swooping sensation caught at Dion in the gut.

CHAPTER SIX

Tara was still trembling a little after she'd cleaned the bathroom and gathered Niko's clothes up to put in the laundry basket. She caught sight of her reflection in the mirror and groaned lightly. Her shirt was wet through and clearly showing her underwear. Her hair was up in a damp topknot after her shower. There was the faintest pink on her jaw, stubble rash from Dion's kisses. She also had it on her thighs. She blushed.

She went to the door of the bathroom and looked into Niko's suite. Dion was on the floor, with Niko on his back on his playmat, legs and arms kicking happily. Dion was staring at him as if he'd never seen him before, but also not doing much to interact with him.

Tara went into the room, forgetting for a moment about her déshabillé. She came down on her knees and pulled over the frame with things hanging off it that could sit over where Niko lay, allowing him to play with the various things.

She said, 'This is a good way to let him interact with shapes and toys.'

Niko reached up and grabbed a soft toy and yanked it, making it squeak. He gurgled happily. 'He's a contented baby.'

Dion sent her a side-eyed glance. 'Considering he's had nannies as mothers for the first six months of his life?'

Tara flushed. 'I didn't mean it as a dig. He's obviously

had very good care. Maria is great and I'm sure Elena was too. They just need consistency...obviously a mother is ideal but not everyone is lucky enough to have that.'

'I had that—I can't blame my mother for not being there initially but I'd question how good the care was.'

While Niko seemed happily content to play with the mobile, Tara asked a little hesitantly, 'What happened after your mother left you at the orphanage?'

For a long moment he said nothing, he just kept looking at Niko. Tara was about to apologise for asking such a personal question when he looked at her and said, 'Nothing good, that's what happened. It was run by a particularly stern sect of nuns who viewed us as somehow defective. I ran away when I was sixteen.'

Tara said nothing. He went on, 'I was on the streets for a while but then I went to my father and demanded he give me the money he should have been paying for basic maintenance. It wasn't even that much, but it was enough. I knew I had to get off the streets.'

Tara's eyes went wide. 'And he did?'

Dion nodded. 'I didn't say it but I let him think I would go to the press and tell them who I was. It would have ruined his precious reputation and undoubtedly his marriage. Within a year I'd paid him back every cent he gave me, plus interest, because it had almost killed me to go to him, but my need to survive was greater than my pride.'

'That took guts.'

Dion shrugged. 'It was survival, pure and simple.'

He was so proud. It was visible in the line of his noble profile. But he wasn't too proud to demand what he was due.

Tara could imagine that he might already be regretting revealing so much and she said, 'I should dress Niko and give him his breakfast.'

Dion reached down and scooped him up, already displaying more ease with his son. 'Let me try with the nappy.'

Tara stood up too. 'Be my guest. Everything is on the changing table. I'll get him some clothes.'

Dion went over and laid Niko down, still kicking his legs energetically and gurgling in that baby talk. Tara busied herself picking out clothes for Niko and tried not to let the fact that Dion seemed inclined to want to be more involved make her chest swell up too much.

She came back over with the clothes just as Dion was taking out a nappy and unfolding it, and just as Niko went very still and unleashed a perfect arc of urine straight onto Dion's lower belly.

Tara froze and looked at Dion, who had also frozen. She held her breath, terrified that this would scupper the very fragile link growing between him and Niko, but then, to her surprise, he smiled and let out a bark of laughter. Niko smiled gummily back at his father, showing the whites of his emerging first teeth.

Dion bent down towards Niko and put a hand on his belly. 'You are the only person who is allowed to display such insolence. Next time I better be quicker, hm?'

Niko gurgled in agreement. Tara watched, a little dumbfounded, as Dion found the wet wipes, cleaned Niko up and the surrounding area and then went back to arranging the nappy and putting it on the baby. Perfectly, of course. Tara could appreciate that the man had become a billionaire because he was extremely ambitious and had an eye for detail that most didn't.

She moved forward when he'd secured the nappy and said, 'Not bad for a novice.'

He glanced at her and looked a little shamefaced before admitting, 'I might have watched some videos on YouTube.'

Tara's insides melted at that admission. Before he could see the softness she was feeling—especially after his revealing how he'd been treated after his mother had abandoned him—Tara said, 'Why don't you get changed and I'll finish dressing him and get him downstairs?'

Dion was looking at Niko. 'Are all babies as clever as him?'

Tara's insides melted even more. 'No way. He's special.' She spoke the truth of biased parents everywhere.

Dion took a step back from the changing table and Tara started to deftly dress Niko in a cute romper suit.

Before Dion left, though, he said, 'It's Saturday today.'

Tara had completely lost all track of what day it was. Or how long she'd been here. Days? A week? This was her world now.

'Do you have to work?' she asked.

'Normally I would but maybe we could do something together.'

Tara shrugged. It wasn't as if she had plans! And the more time Dion wanted to spend with his son, the better.

'Sure. Did you have anything in mind?'

'We could go to the island villa until tomorrow night. I have meetings in Paris next week.'

Tara's heart thumped unevenly when she thought of the villa. It felt like an age ago when she'd been there with her anonymous lover. Not so anonymous now.

She remembered the stark clean lines and the infinity pool. She frowned, 'That sounds lovely but is it set up for Niko?'

Dion said nothing and she looked at him. He said, 'It doesn't need to be set up for Niko. It'll just be us.'

Tara stopped halfway down buttoning Niko's romper suit

and looked at Dion. She shook her head. 'I don't want to leave Niko behind.'

'But Maria will be here. She'll be well compensated for extra hours.'

So much for imagining those burgeoning moments of bonding between father and son. He still had Niko compartmentalised somewhere in his life but not in the centre of it.

'No,' she said. 'If you want me to come then Niko comes too. Maria can be there if you feel she's required.'

Dion looked at her for a moment as if he couldn't understand what she'd just said and she realised that Dion most likely never had anyone talk back to him or refuse him. Well, tough.

Niko started to crib, clearly hungry by now. Tara said, 'I'm not going anywhere without Niko, take it or leave it.' She walked out of the room and avoided checking Dion's expression, imagining it would be nuclear.

It took a minute for Dion to realise that Tara had just issued him an ultimatum and then walked away from him. With his son.

Her son too, reminded a little voice.

He also realised that it wasn't altogether...as irritating as he might have found it if it had been anyone else.

Much like getting peed upon, by his son. He looked down at the almost perfectly symmetrical wet stain on his polo shirt.

Something had just shifted in this room. Something seismic. Dion wasn't the sole authority over his son any more. And perhaps Tara was right. Would he have felt totally comfortable leaving Niko behind? He had before...but that had been when Niko was still very much an unknown quantity.

More of an abstract idea than a flesh and blood little person with an emerging personality.

But could he take Tara to the island and do the things to her that he wanted to with Niko there too?

It didn't stop you last night, pointed out that voice, again.

The alternative—not having Tara in his bed—was not an option. Especially after last night, which had blown the first night out of the water. So he would just do whatever it took to make this work. And as soon as he had exorcised her from his system they could draw up a plan and get on with living separate lives.

In any case, he doubted it would even come to that.

Dion had a moment of crystal-clear realisation—Tara was a woman who had devoted herself admirably to her family at the expense of her own needs and freedom. Once she realised she could have anything she wanted *and* her freedom, she'd be gone. All Dion had to do was to take every opportunity to show Tara what she had been missing and then not stand in her way when she was ready to leave.

What if you're not ready to let her go?

Dion ignored the voice. He would be ready, of that he had no doubt.

Tara knew she shouldn't have been surprised by the speed and efficiency with which they were all, including Maria—who'd come to an agreement with Dion to work more fluid hours than she had before—despatched to the villa on the island. It was even more impressive in the daylight, all sleek white lines and glass. It was fine for Niko now, as he couldn't move around much, but would be an absolute deathtrap once he was more mobile.

Maria now knew that Tara was Niko's mother and she was already deferring to her and Tara had had to reassure her, saying, 'You still know him better than me, so please don't feel like anything much has changed.'

But of course it had, and Tara was still trying to get her own head around it all, together with the fact that she and Dion were...conducting this...affair? Co-parenting with benefits? She didn't know what it was, but she did know that she was fast becoming obsessed with the man.

He was outside on the patio of the villa now, near the pool. Wearing the same jeans as earlier and a fresh polo shirt, in cream, that showed off his olive skin and defined musculature. He was holding his phone to his ear and the muscles bunching in his arm were more suited to a prize fighter than an industrialist.

His success was all the more remarkable now that she knew of his adverse upbringing. To go from being on the streets, totally abandoned by any family, to where he was today, was so impressive. And she could understand why he was such a lone wolf.

As if he could hear her thinking about him, he turned around. He was wearing shades and they made him look like a movie star. He took the phone down from his ear. It was too late to try and pretend she hadn't been ogling him so Tara just kept looking at him as he walked into the living area.

He asked, 'Where's Maria and Niko?'

'She's changing him and unpacking his things in the nursery.' When they'd arrived, the housekeeper, a friendly older woman called Daphne, had been supervising a team of people who had set up a nursery in one of the spare rooms.

'Can I take you for lunch?'

'What about Maria and Niko?'

At that moment Daphne appeared and Dion spoke to her in rapid Greek. Tara realised then she'd have to start taking lessons, especially if her life was now going to be in Greece. Her insides lurched a little at that. Her whole life had been sent spinning off its axis but she had to admit it wasn't fear or resentment she was feeling, it was something more like excitement.

He turned back to Tara. 'Daphne is going to relieve Maria and give her a break while we're out.'

Daphne said something to Dion and smiled at Tara. She could only smile back without having a clue what had just been said. Dion translated helpfully, 'Daphne has seven grandchildren so Niko will be in good hands.'

Tara nodded and smiled and tried to convey her gratitude before Dion put his hand on her elbow and urged her out of the villa and down the steps to an open-top four-wheel drive.

He stopped and looked at her for a second. 'Do you have sunscreen on?'

Tara was still wearing the same shirt and shorts as she'd worn earlier. She felt unkempt now next to Dion's suave gorgeousness. But it wasn't as if this were a date really...was it? There was nothing remotely conventional about what was happening here. She pushed aside the dangerously tempting daydream of what it might have been like to be properly seduced and wooed by someone like Dion.

She put out her arms. 'Yes, factor fifty.' As a pale redhead from Ireland, she knew the importance of sunscreen.

'Good. You'll need a hat. We'll make a stop.'

But before Tara could ask *Stop where?* he was opening her door and she had to get in. He got behind the wheel and they were driving down the driveway, lush plants either side, and through a set of gates.

It was only as they drove along a winding coastal road with spectacular views of the sea and other islands in the distance that Tara realised she hadn't really taken a breath since she'd got to Athens. So much had happened.

The air was salty from the ocean and the scents of fresh flowers and herbs tickled her nostrils. 'It's beautiful here,' she couldn't help observing.

'Yes, it is.'

Dion drove with confident assurance. Not showy. Relaxed.

'Why this island?' Tara asked.

Dion kept his gaze on the road. He took a while to answer, which made Tara curious. She could see the tension in his shoulders and jaw. 'If it's too personal—'

'It's where my father's family came from. He owned some land here and his business hadn't been doing well, so I bought it for a knock-off price. Under a company name he wouldn't recognise. It wasn't as if I wanted to gloat over his misfortune.'

'But it would have been understandable.' Who could have resisted crowing over their success with a father who had rejected them? Not many.

He glanced at her and then back to the road. 'Maybe. But the truth is that a part of me was tempted by something I can't even explain…to own the land that was a link to my ancestors, even though they're all gone. There are no people belonging to my father's family here any more. They all went to the mainland for work and didn't return. Probably after the Second World War.'

'We're all pretty tribal when it comes down to it.'

'Yes, but I hate my father. I hate that I felt compelled to take ownership of something that should have been mine by right.'

'You're human, Dion. We behave in ways that aren't always logical. And now you own a piece of this island where maybe you had ancestors who wouldn't have shut you out.'

He slid her another look but his eyes were hidden behind shades. 'You believe in fairy tales.'

Tara's insides clenched. 'I stopped believing in fairy tales when my parents died and left a whole family orphaned. I believe we make our own luck and fortune.'

'So do I.'

They were silent for a long moment, and Tara absorbed this unexpected sense of affinity. Even though, deep down, she knew guiltily that she had just been harbouring a little fairy-tale dream of being seduced by Dion.

She could see a town in the distance, and the harbour.

Dion's voice broke into her thoughts. 'This is the main town…the only town at the moment. Nisos. That's the name of the island too.'

Tara was glad of the diversion. Maybe she was getting sunstroke—she could feel it beating down on her head. The town was very pretty. A big main square with an old church. Dion parked and they got out.

She followed him into cobbled streets, white buildings with bright blue painted trim. Profusions of flowers bursting out of boxes on window sills. There were lots of artisanal shops with crafts and art.

People saw him and called out greetings. Tara realised he must be something of a celebrity with his impressive villa and buying up land on the island.

He stopped outside a boutique. Tara looked in the window where a mannequin was wearing a glittering iridescent midnight-blue sheath of an evening gown.

To her shock, Dion caught her hand and tugged her towards the shop. She didn't have time to ask what he was doing before he was bringing her inside the cool interior and a very elegant woman looked up and greeted Dion as warmly as everyone else had.

He was speaking in Greek to the woman, who was looking at Tara with a critical expression, taking her in from head to toe. Tara's toes curled inwards in her scuffed sneakers. Now she felt even more dusty and unkempt and self-conscious. Why hadn't she changed earlier?

Into what? Another pair of shorts, or jeans?

The woman stepped forward, impossibly cool-looking in cream trousers and a matching silk shirt.

In accentless English she said, 'Hello, Tara. My name is Michaela. Please, come with me, let's see what we have.'

Tara shot Dion an expressive look as she was led into the back of the fragrant boutique but he just said, 'I'll book us a table for lunch and come back for you.'

A very bemused Tara found herself being measured and then given a stack of clothes and shown into a dressing room.

'Was I embarrassing you, or something? I know I'm not the most put-together person on the planet but I didn't look *too* out of place, did I?'

Dion sat on the other side of the table in the restaurant they'd come to after he'd collected her from the boutique just a short while before. She had to admit though that the loose linen trousers and matching waistcoat, worn as a top, together with the wedge espadrille sandals and simple gold jewellery, did help her to feel a little less conspicuous among the very well-heeled clientele of the restaurant.

When Tara had asked Michaela where her own clothes were, after trying on a seemingly endless array of clothes—including evening wear, which Tara had had no choice but to try on because Michaela would disappear before she could object—the woman had given her an arch look and said, 'I'll bag them up for you if you really think you want to keep them.'

Tara had muttered something like, *No, that's okay.* She imagined they were already on a bonfire for sub-par clothes.

Dion said now, 'No, you weren't embarrassing me, at all. But I'm aware that you only came to Greece with limited supplies and I'm simply making sure you have enough clothes to get by.'

'She made me try on evening dresses. She wouldn't listen when I tried to tell her they weren't necessary.'

'Was it really that traumatic?'

Tara rolled her eyes. 'No, of course not, but I can buy my own clothes. These must have cost a fortune. I'll pay you back.'

He waved a hand. 'No, you won't. You're the mother of my child, Tara. You've been helping to care for him since you arrived. It's the least I can do. When was the last time someone took care of you?'

Those last words impacted her like a soft punch to the gut. 'What do you mean?'

Dion shrugged, his eyes hidden behind his shades. 'Just that…when was the last time someone checked if you had all you needed? Took you for lunch?'

A slew of images kaleidoscoped through Tara's head of times when she'd made a fuss over her siblings' birthdays or cheered one or another up with a trip to the cinema or made their favourite food when they were down. And it wasn't as if they'd not done nice things for her, but they hadn't had to worry about her… They'd taken her for granted, not that she'd ever admit it, or admit that sometimes it had hurt.

'Not for a long time, I guess.' To her shock and horror, emotion rose up, making her eyes prickle ominously. She reached for the very cool sunglasses Michaela had furnished her with and put them on before Dion could see how his words had affected her.

Luckily he hadn't seemed to notice. He said then, 'By the way, I've had my legal team contact the clinic about the mix-up.'

Tara took off the glasses and looked at him. She could feel the blood draining south—she hadn't even warned her sister Mary. 'I asked you not to.'

'I had to. Their negligence could have affected people who were using their own sperm and eggs to create a baby. But I'm not suing. I've told them I won't, if they conduct a thorough investigation and give me a report on measures they'll take to ensure it doesn't happen again.'

Relief swept through Tara. 'Thank you. And you're right, they should have to answer for their negligence.'

The waiter arrived with their starters, light seasonal salad with zesty feta cheese that melted on Tara's tongue. She decided to put the emotion, the clinic and boutique incident out of her head, for now, and enjoy the surroundings.

And Dion, whispered a sly voice.

Her gaze kept straying to him like a magnet. Even sitting down and while engaged in the very civilised activity of enjoying food at a clearly sophisticated restaurant, he still oozed a very masculine, sexual energy. So much so that Tara couldn't help but find herself responding, watching his hands, and those long fingers, imagining him gripping her, squeezing her flesh—

'Tara?'

She looked at him, feeling a little dazed. Maybe she really did have sunstroke. The very chic straw sunhat that Michaela had given her was on the table nearby and Tara planted it on her head.

'Are you okay?'

She nodded. 'Fine, I'm sorry…so, apart from the villa, are you doing anything with the land you bought?'

'Actually, yes, I'm building a luxury eco-friendly fully sustainable hotel and spa resort on the other coast. And I'm involved in trying to resurrect the old and disused farming industry here—they have vines, olives, lemons...but it's all died out. If we can get it going again the island has a chance of year-round employment, instead of seasonal.'

No wonder he'd been treated so warmly by the locals. Their mains were delivered now—a tasting board of different Greek specialities. Dion explained what the different foods were. Tara found herself unwinding even more as she indulged in the food and crisp white Greek wine.

Impulsively she asked, 'Is the eco resort you're building far from here?'

Dion shook his head. 'Not far, no, about thirty minutes. Would you like to see it?'

Tara felt shy. 'If you didn't mind? Projects with sustainability at the core of their genesis are the ones I'm most interested in working on.'

'Sure... I was planning on going to see it tomorrow but now is as good a time as any. There won't be any workers at the weekend so it'll be quiet.'

After lunch Dion drove them out of the small harbour town and this time they cut through the middle of the island. He pointed out the old olive and lemon groves. Where the vineyards had been. It all looked sad and overgrown and neglected but Tara could envisage it thriving again. It was an ambitious project but she had no doubt Dion could pull it off.

After a while Tara could see the glitter of the sea appearing again, and when they crested the brow of a hill they were suddenly looking down at a vast area all along a stretch of the coastline with waves crashing along a pristine beach. Behind a tall chain-link fence, Tara could make out low-rise stone buildings and little pathways between them. One larger, slightly domed building, which presumably would be the hub of the resort. It all faded into the landscape beautifully.

Dion stopped the car and said, 'It's laid out over twenty-five acres. We're building stand-alone suites among the hills and sand dunes. There's a private beach. Each suite will have its own private pool. There'll be a spa with every kind of wellness therapy you can think of.'

'Wow.' Tara was surprised to feel a little emotional. She confided, 'You know, I haven't been on holiday since my parents died and I've never been to a spa…' She continued hurriedly, 'It's not that I'm sore about it, I just never had the chance, but this sounds amazing. Maybe when it's open I'll treat myself.'

Dion looked at Tara with a funny expression but she didn't see it. He put the car back into gear and kept going to where a security guard came out of a little hut. He greeted Dion with a little salute and opened the gate to let them through.

He parked up near the big main building with its slightly domed roof and they got out. Tara kept the hat on her head. It was later now though, so the sun's rays weren't as merciless.

He brought her through the half-finished buildings and she could already make out the vision of how it would all seamlessly fade into the background and yet provide a luxurious setting.

They came out at the other side, near where a path went directly down to the beach. Feeling the need to cool off a little, Tara made her way down the path and then onto the sand. It was gorgeous. Empty. Peaceful. Only the sound of the waves lapping against the shore. Some trees along the shoreline provided shade.

She slipped off the sandals and left them on the beach as she went towards the water.

Dion called from behind her, 'What are you doing?'

She threw back over her shoulder, 'Going for a paddle!'

She lifted the trousers and stepped into the water and it was gorgeously cool and refreshing. She closed her eyes and let the scents and sounds wash over her. It had been so long since she'd experienced quiet like this.

And then she opened her eyes again and the ocean seemed to be calling to her. Asking her to be audacious. She turned back to Dion, who was standing where the beach met the path. Something about that made her feel reckless. She walked out of the water and took off her hat and let it fall to the sand, then she undid the buttons on her waistcoat and took it off.

She could see Dion frowning over his glasses. 'Tara?'

She had her hands on the button of her trousers and was pulling down the zip. Dion started walking towards her, his face tight. She pushed the trousers down and stepped out of them. Now she wore only her underwear. Plain and very *un*-sexy. White.

Now he was close enough for her to see his jaw twitch. He took off his glasses and that dark gaze looked suspiciously golden. He gritted out, 'What are you doing?'

Tara put out her arms. 'There's no one here. I'm going for a swim. You can join me if you like.'

She turned around and all she heard was, 'You can't just—' before she walked into the water and, as soon as she was deep enough, she dived under an oncoming wave.

CHAPTER SEVEN

DION WAS STILL grappling with the effect on his body of watching Tara taking off her clothes, stripping down to her underwear. Those slim pale limbs. The curves of her breasts, waist and hips. That copper hair falling over her shoulder. The sassiness in her stance. As if goading him.

He felt tight all over. Since when had he become so tight? And where the hell was Tara? He was waiting for her distinctive red hair to pop up above the water.

Just when he felt as if he might explode, she appeared, popping above the water line. A long way out. She turned back towards the shore and waved and that made something inside Dion snap.

For the second time in the space of a mere week, he gave into spontaneity and stripped down to his underwear and waded into the sea. It was still a bit of a novelty to him—he hadn't grown up indulging in the luxury of beach holidays. Or any kind of holiday. Like Tara, albeit for very different reasons.

He dived under the water and swam out into the sea, the initial shock of the cold fading as the water turned silken around his body. He got to where Tara was treading water, a big grin on her face. He was pretty sure there were more freckles across her nose than there had been a few days ago.

'What are you doing?' he asked, noticing that he didn't feel so tight any more.

'Testing out your private ocean, what does it look like?'

Dion couldn't help but smile at her infectious sunniness. 'And what's the verdict?'

Tara cocked her head, pretending to think for a moment. 'I think we'll be giving it a ten out of ten, for accessibility, freshness and aesthetic beauty.'

Dion swam closer until their legs touched. He saw a flare of colour in her cheeks. Her eyes widened. They matched the sky perfectly at that moment, bright blue. He said mock seriously, 'Thank you for that. I'll be sure to let the team know.'

Tara wound her arms and legs around Dion. She was lighter than air, the buoyancy of the water holding them up. Her breasts were pressed against his chest, the sharp stab of her nipples sending his blood soaring.

She looked at him for a moment before touching her mouth to his. It was such a fleeting and sweet gesture that it loosened something else inside Dion. Something hard and obdurate. He slid his arms around her back and turned the kiss into something much less hesitant and sweet.

They treaded water, kissing for a long moment, the water lapping around their bodies. Dion pulled back. Tara's hair was slicked back, a dark red. Her mouth was pink and plump and he needed her now. Blood was surging to his groin and all he wanted was to slip them free of their clothes and slide into her right there and then.

As if hearing his thoughts, or maybe he'd spoken out loud, Tara said, 'Can we?'

Dion huffed a tortured-sounding laugh. 'As much as I'd love to, believe me, I don't think it's anatomically possible without drowning.'

Tara groaned. 'Breathing is so overrated.'

Dion huffed a laugh, surprising himself. Women-lovers didn't make him laugh. He lay on his back, pulling Tara over him, and kicked his way back to shore. They lay in the shallows, limbs entwined, mouths fused together.

But then Dion pulled back and said, 'The sun...your skin.'

'I'm fine,' Tara said breathlessly, rubbing her leg between his. He looked down at her and almost groaned. Her underwear was completely see-through by now. Hard nipples, pink, pushing against the wet fabric. He could see the coppery red of the curls between her legs.

But that delicate pale skin was a little pink. He stood up, pulling her up with him, and led her up the beach to where trees overhung, providing shade.

He'd grabbed his shirt and laid it down on the soft sand. 'Lie down,' he instructed. Tara did, looking up at him. He almost spilled there and then, she looked so innocent but knowing all at once.

He went to strip off his underwear but stopped. She came up on an elbow. 'What is it?'

He muttered, 'Protection.'

Relief crossed her face. 'I'm on the pill.'

He looked at her, the fire in his blood raging with his brain urging caution. Her gaze narrowed on him. 'I froze my eggs, remember? I was hardly going to risk pregnancy after going through all that effort.'

The fire burned away Dion's functioning brain cells. He took off his underwear and saw how Tara's gaze fell on him and the way her eyes widened with a naked feminine appreciation he'd never noticed before. Or had never taken time to notice.

He came down on his knees and, first, pulled down her underwear and dispensed with it. Then he pushed her legs apart. He could see the glistening folds between her legs and leant forward, stroking a finger along her body, making her gasp and twitch.

'Dion,' she said a little brokenly, reaching for him. He came forward then, and guided his body to the entrance of hers. He pulled down the cups of her bra, and lavished each peak with attention, sucking and flicking and nipping at the taut peaks. She was urging her hips towards him but he kept pulling back slightly, torturing her, torturing them both.

Eventually, Tara dug her hands into his hair and pulled his head up. She glared at him, cheeks on fire with need, eyes burning like two aquamarine gems.

'I need you, *now*,' she growled, and it was the sexiest thing Dion had ever heard.

He stopped torturing them both and entered her with a smooth thrust, watching how she sucked in a breath and her eyes glazed over. Had any woman ever turned him on this much? *No.* He pushed that disturbing revelation aside and focused on the tension building between them until they were feverish with it, both straining to reach the peak, and as much as Dion would have loved to hold out as long as possible, he couldn't.

He barely managed to wait until he felt Tara's body tighten around his before the contractions of her orgasm pushed him over the edge and he fell too, down and down and down to a place where nothing much mattered but *this*.

Tara had never felt such a sense of deep peace. The air was the perfect temperature, warm without being oppressive. The shade protected her from the sun. The sound of little insects stopped and started again. The scent of the earth and pines and sea and…*sex* filled her nostrils.

She was lying on the sand, spent. Limbs heavy with a delicious languor. Dion was lying beside her. They were naked. Or, mostly. Her bra was somehow miraculously still on.

Dion's eyes were closed, his lashes long on his cheek.

Tara's heart clenched because she couldn't help but imagine him as an adorable young boy, full of potential and love and then to have it so cruelly crushed by his neglectful mother and his absent father.

At least Niko wouldn't suffer the same fate. No matter what happened between her and Dion, Niko would have two parents who adored him. Tara knew it was a difficult concept for Dion to get used to, and that he probably hadn't really thought through the reality of having a son, but she could see how he was starting to bond with Niko and it was lovely.

The sun was lower in the sky now and Tara became aware of sand in places where it shouldn't be. She realised there was a trail of clothes from the seashore to where they were.

Had they really just made love on the beach? Dion sat up. 'We should get back.'

Niko. Tara immediately felt guilty. 'Yes, Maria will need a break.'

Dion stood up in an enviably fluid motion, and, totally unselfconsciously, he walked back to their clothes and picked them up. Tara drank in his tall, powerful form, still not quite able to believe that she held interest for a man like him. She also felt ridiculously shy as he handed her her trousers and the waistcoat. Crazy, after what they'd just done.

Contorting herself, she tried to dress without displaying too much flesh, which was next to impossible. When she was fully clothed she stood up and saw her pants on the sand nearby. Face flaming, she picked them up and put them in her pocket.

She grabbed the discarded hat too, and felt thoroughly sandblasted and more dishevelled than ever as she followed Dion back up to where her shoes lay. She picked them up and slipped them on and they walked back through the main building.

They got back into his car and Tara clamped the hat on her head to try and hide her face from the security guard who let them out. She felt sure that it must be emblazoned onto her forehead what they'd been doing.

Dion was quiet on the journey back and the lines in his body were tense. Tara asked a little hesitantly, 'Is everything okay?'

He glanced at her and back to the road. 'Fine, I just hadn't planned on taking you on the sand like some sort of…animal.'

Tara could see that pride in the line of his jaw. It obviously mattered to him that he behaved with decorum…to counteract his upbringing? Prove he wasn't unsophisticated?

'You can blame me if you want. I led you astray.' When he didn't respond right away, she said, 'I enjoyed it.'

The line in his jaw relaxed a little. 'I *let* you lead me astray. My control seems to vanish when I'm around you.'

It won't last. His voice in her head.

She said lightly, 'Just as well this kind of thing doesn't last for ever?'

'It doesn't.' He sounded determined.

When they got back to the villa they heard the sound of Niko crying. Dion had stopped the car and was out and walking into the villa before Tara could catch up.

She saw Maria, walking up and down with an inconsolable Niko, and watched as Dion reached for his son, taking him into his arms. Niko stopped crying almost immediately, his little head falling into the crook between Dion's head and shoulder. It almost took Tara's breath away—so much had begun to change between father and son in the space of days.

She walked in and Maria looked at her, clearly upset too. 'I couldn't settle him. I don't know why—'

Tara put her hand on Maria's arm and hoped the debauchery of the last few hours wasn't evident in her creased and sandy clothes. 'I'm sure it's just his teething and he's probably overtired. I'll shower and change quickly and I'll take over, okay? You could do with a break.'

The young woman smiled gratefully. 'I'll get a bottle ready. He had some food earlier.'

Tara looked at Dion, who was rubbing Niko's back. 'I'll be back in a few minutes.'

Dion looked tense. 'It's my fault, isn't it? Because he's had too many different people looking after him. I thought I could do this on my own but it was arrogant and short-sighted.'

Tara shook her head, her heart going out to him. 'Niko is fine. He's a happy baby and he's surrounded by people who love him and want the best for him. You can't ask for much more than that.'

'Except a mother,' noted Dion a little bitterly.

'I'm here now. He has a mother.'

A moment passed between them, something very delicate and shimmering, but then Niko let out a little wail again and it was broken. He settled again but Tara moved fast, going to the bedroom and undressing before stepping into the shower and sloughing away the sand and Dion's touch. She lamented that.

Towel-drying her hair, she put on a robe and went into the dressing room and realised that the clothes from the boutique had already been sent to the villa and were hanging up or folded neatly into drawers. There was even underwear.

She also spotted the stunning midnight-blue evening gown that had been hanging in the window of the shop. She hadn't even tried that dress on, but it was in her size.

But she didn't have time to ruminate on that. She found a

pair of super-soft sweatpants and put on a bra and vest top and twisted her damp hair up into a loose knot and went back out to where Niko had started cribbing again.

He saw Tara and leant out of Dion's arms, reaching for her. She couldn't help but feel a surge of maternal emotion at his recognition of her. She took him into her arms just as Maria reappeared with a bottle. 'Thanks, Maria. I'll stick with him in case he wakes during the night.' Tara knew she needed some space to try and gather her wits.

The girl looked a bit panicked. 'But I'm happy to do the night-shift.'

Tara shook her head. 'You've been working all afternoon. I don't mind. He's obviously teething a lot.'

A little reluctantly the girl said, 'If you're sure?'

Tara smiled, 'Positive. I know the hours are a lot different than before but you shouldn't have to do double shifts. We'll work it out as we go along, if that's ok?'

Maria relaxed and smiled a little, 'Ok, thanks.'

Maria left and Tara noticed an expression on Dion's face. 'What?'

He noted dryly, 'I'm the one who pays Maria's wages.'

'And I'm Niko's mother, I'm entitled to have a say.'

For a moment he was silent and then he said a little grudgingly, 'You are. To a point.'

The point where he expected her to leave her son? wondered Tara. She shut out that thought and said, 'I'll take him to his room to feed him and try to get him down afterwards.'

'Daphne has probably left some food. I can prepare it.'

At that moment Tara's tummy rumbled so she couldn't very well feign lack of hunger. She cursed her healthy appetite. 'Okay, thanks.'

After Niko had been fed and changed, he went down easily enough, obviously exhausted from his crying jag earlier.

Tara stroked a downy cheek. She took the baby monitor and grabbed a loose cashmere cardigan from the clothes in her dressing room and went back to the main part of the villa.

When she went into the kitchen she saw Dion at the cooker, stirring something. He'd obviously showered and changed too, like her, into sweats and a clean T-shirt. He looked around and her heart skipped a beat.

'Is he okay?'

Tara nodded and tried to get her rampant hormones under control. 'He's asleep.'

'Daphne left some stew.'

'Sounds lovely. Can I do anything?'

'There's bread and salad and wine on the counter. We'll eat outside.'

Tara saw the table on the terrace near the pool. The sun had set but the sky wasn't totally dark yet. It was a deep lavender. She brought the things out to the table. A candle was flickering. She hated the way she wanted to read something into the romantic setting.

When Dion came out with the plates of stew she said, 'You didn't have to go to this trouble. We could have eaten inside.'

Dion sat down and poured wine into their glasses. 'It's no trouble.'

Tara took a mouthful of stew and almost moaned aloud. 'This is so good.'

Dion made a similar sound. 'Daphne is renowned on the island for her cooking skills.'

After a few more mouthfuls of food, Tara said, 'The clothes from the boutique... There are too many, Dion. I don't need all those clothes and they sent over the evening dress too.'

He put down his cutlery and sat back, picking up his glass of wine. Tara wondered a little churlishly how he could look so suave in just a T-shirt.

'I asked her to include the dress.'

'Oh...but why?'

'Because I've been considering some things and the fact that it's bound to come out sooner rather than later that I have a son. The interest will be intense.'

'And what does this have to do with me?'

'Well, as you're his mother, I'd imagine people are going to want to know who you are.'

Tara felt a shiver go down her spine. Her life was not remotely in the media spotlight and she liked it that way. 'Can we avoid it?'

'I can do my best but generally it's better to give out some information rather than have people go digging for it. There's nothing worse than a vacuum of information.'

While Tara was absorbing this, Dion said, 'There's a party I've been invited to on another island near here, tomorrow night. It's a gala opera performance with proceeds going to charity. I think we should go together, be photographed, and then when I release a statement about Niko I can name you as his mother and mention a relationship.'

'A relationship?' Tara said, aware that she was focusing on that and not on the fact that Dion was prepared to name her as Niko's mother, which was obviously huge.

He nodded, totally sanguine about all of this. 'They'll be interested for a bit but, if there's nothing more to it, the interest will soon die down.'

'What if they find out how Niko was conceived?'

'They won't.'

Feeling agitated, and her appetite fading fast, Tara stood up and paced away from the table. The moonlight rippled over the calm water of the pool.

'What are you thinking?' Dion asked.

Tara turned around and admitted, 'I hadn't considered

this part of it…the fact that you're…*you* and that people might be interested in who I am.' She looked at Dion. 'I'm not cut out for any kind of attention. I'll embarrass you.'

'Nonsense,' dismissed Dion.

'And what happens when…this is over?'

Dion shrugged, unflustered. 'Then we'll issue another statement saying something about co-parenting amicably.'

After a moment, Dion said, 'You do have a choice here, Tara. You could go home.'

It took a second for what he'd said to sink in and it caught at her on lots of levels. The main one being that he *still* didn't really want her around. Or, expect her to stick around, as his little comment had alluded to earlier. She was Niko's mother, *to a point*. And, that perhaps, in spite of their passionate moment on the beach earlier, his desire was not as all-encompassing as hers felt. It made her feel hurt and vulnerable. And defensive.

She folded her arms. 'I told you, Dion, I'm not leaving.'

'You will one day.' He said this with such absolute surety that it almost took her breath away. Confirmation, if she'd needed it, on how little he trusted her. She knew what lay behind it, she could even understand it, but she still wanted to go over and slap that cynical assurance off his face. And she was not remotely violent.

She went over and picked up the baby monitor and said, 'I'm tired. I'll sleep in Niko's room tonight in case he wakes.'

She went to leave but from behind her Dion said, 'Tomorrow night?'

Tara turned around. 'I will do whatever it takes to be a part of Niko's life.' She turned and walked away.

Dion watched Tara leave, every line in her body tense. He could still see the emotions that had crossed her face when he'd told her she could go home. Even though every cell in his body had protested at that notion.

He wasn't ready to let her go.

She'd looked wounded.

But that only firmed his resolve now, to put some boundaries down. Lines were getting blurred. Today, at the beach, was unprecedented. He'd…lost control. Taken her like a callow teenager on the sand. Without protection. The memory of that made his blood run cold.

He still didn't know that he could trust Tara Simons. And yet he'd trusted her in that moment.

He'd forged his way to success by maintaining absolute control and never letting his hormones or emotions get the better of him. Even deciding to have a baby had been a decision made with cool logic and a desire to pass his legacy on and give a child a better life than he'd experienced.

Tara had to know that he *knew* that she would go. And that that was okay. They'd establish her as Niko's mother, they would exorcise this chemistry that burned between them and Dion would make sure that Tara knew she could have a very good life—free of all responsibility.

Obviously if she wanted to maintain contact with Niko he would facilitate that but it would be on his terms. She wouldn't have the power to derail Niko's life.

Or yours, you mean? asked a little voice.

Dion scowled and stood up and went over to the spot where Tara had been standing, dressed in nothing special, just sweatpants and a vest top, and yet he'd had to focus hard to not get distracted by memories of that afternoon and how hot it had been.

The magnitude of how much Tara had infiltrated his life so comprehensively since that first night was sinking in. He was glad that he'd said something to make her walk away this evening. He'd almost forgotten that he needed to focus on whatever means necessary to make sure his son was kept from all harm or hurt.

Was that love?

Dion was ashamed to admit he didn't know what love felt like, but he did know that he would do anything to protect him and make him happy.

The following late afternoon Tara looked at herself in the mirror. Maria said from behind her, 'You look very beautiful.'

Tara smiled weakly, feeling the woman was being overgenerous. 'Thank you, and thanks for helping me to get ready.'

'No problem.' Maria went over and scooped up Niko, who had been amusing himself on his front on the playmat in Tara's dressing room while she got ready for this…strategic date night with Dion.

She'd not seen much of him all day. He'd been in his office making calls. She'd tried not to take it personally, especially after what had happened the previous day. Maybe he regretted the spontaneous swimming and making love on the beach. He'd certainly seemed tense afterwards. And then, he'd reminded her last night of how nothing had really changed between them.

He expected her to flit off as soon as she got bored. Which only made her more determined to prove that she was here to stay. So she'd used the time today to spend it with Niko, letting Maria go down to the harbour town for a few hours, because Maria would be working tonight.

Tara was wearing the midnight-blue dress from the boutique window. It was deceptively simple—strapless and falling in a straight elegant line to the floor—but that was just an outer layer of chiffon and the dress itself was moulded to every curve of Tara's body and so when she moved the chiffon, which was overlaid with thousands of tiny light-catching crystal beads, moved and clung to the dress, revealing the shape underneath.

Maria had blown out her hair into smooth waves and caught it back on one side with a diamanté clip that had also come from the boutique.

And then, she'd encouraged Tara to wear a simple diamond necklace and matching bracelet. Diamond drop earrings. She'd painted Tara's nails red and they kept catching her eye now, making her feel like some kind of a fraud or someone playing dress-up.

There was a knock on the door and Tara tensed. She said, 'Come in?'

Dion pushed the door open and Niko immediately gabbled a greeting, one arm stuck out. But Dion was looking at Tara, his dark golden gaze moving up and down. He said, 'The helicopter is en route.'

Tara tried not to feel insecure about the fact that he'd said nothing about how she looked. He, meanwhile, looked breathtakingly gorgeous in a classic black tuxedo.

'I'll wait for you on the terrace.'

Tara nodded. He was gone. Maria sighed from behind her. 'It's so romantic.'

Tara looked at her and the young woman had a dreamy look on her face. A little sharply, she said, 'What is?'

'The way he looks at you.'

Tara's skin prickled. She was still feeling a little raw after the previous evening and Dion's stubborn cynicism. She hadn't seen anything in his look right now. For all she knew, he'd decided that *this* was over between them. The madness on the beach might have told him he didn't want to indulge their desire any more.

'How…how was it exactly?' She felt so exposed for asking but…

'Like he wants to grab you and take you away. Like he's never seen a woman before.'

Tara let out a slightly nervous laugh. 'I'm sure you're imagining things.'

Maria winked at her. 'I know what I saw and I hope I find a man who looks at me like that some day.'

Niko gurgled, as if in agreement, and Tara wanted to give him a kiss but her mouth was slicked in flesh-coloured lipstick.

Maria backed away saying, 'I have to finish packing to get Niko and I ready for Athens.'

Tara frowned. 'What do you mean?'

'The boss wants us to go back ahead of you this evening. He said something about going to Paris?'

The faint *thwack-thwack* sound of a helicopter came from outside and with a little wave Maria disappeared with Niko and left Tara standing with her mouth hanging open.

Suddenly totally unconcerned with anything else, Tara went out to the terrace where Dion was waiting, hands in his pockets, back broad…and distracting even now. Annoyed with herself for being so easily dazzled, she came around and stood in front of him.

'Why are you sending Maria and Niko back to Athens?'

He was wearing dark shades, which made him look remote. She saw him grit his jaw before he said, 'Because I can. He's my son. I decide where he goes.'

Now Tara gritted *her* jaw. 'And I'm his mother, Dion, I have a say too. I thought the point was that we're here together.'

'We're not here as a family, Tara.'

Tara's insides swooped and she went cold. Had she somehow forgotten for a moment what was really happening here? Where the power lay?

'So what is this, then?'

Dion cocked his head to one side as if he was regarding her from behind his shades. She wanted to rip them off and see his eyes. He said, 'It's…a temporary arrangement while we adjust to you being a part of Niko's life.'

'An arrangement with benefits?' she asked a little tartly.

'That's one way of looking at it.'

Tara caught up her dress in one hand and tipped up her chin. 'Well, if you're going to make me choose who I prioritise in this *arrangement*, that's easy. I choose Niko. I'll go back to Athens with him and Maria.'

She set off towards the villa but Dion caught her hand and stopped her. She turned back, a little shocked at how upset she was. She avoided his eye. The helicopter was closer now. He tugged her towards him and tipped up her chin. She strove to look as impassive as possible.

He took off his shades but his expression was still enigmatic. He said, 'I'm sorry. I was blunt last night but only because I need to be absolutely clear about the fact that I don't expect anything from you.'

She hadn't been expecting an apology, but the hurt from last night lingered. 'You do expect something of me—the worst possible outcome.' And yet, knowing about his past, she couldn't exactly blame him.

He said, 'I'm not used to being in this situation. Being answerable to anyone.'

'Because you've avoided relationships.'

He didn't even have to acknowledge the truth of that. 'I wasn't ever expecting to meet Niko's mother. And I certainly wasn't expecting to have to accommodate her into our lives. I can't say I'm comfortable with that, but I do agree that I think it can only benefit him to at least know who his mother is.'

'He'll *more* than know who I am, Dion. He'll have me in his life from now on.'

A muscle twitched in Dion's jaw and Tara waited for him to refute what she'd said but instead he responded, 'You're also in *my* life, in my bed, in a way I don't think either of us expected.'

Tara prickled at that. 'I certainly didn't. I came to Athens looking for the father of my child, nothing more than that.'

Then she said, 'You're not accusing me of seducing you any more?'

Dion shook his head. Tara wasn't sure if she should take that as a compliment or not. Maybe she was so woefully inexperienced he'd had to concede that she couldn't have possibly come here to seduce him.

The helicopter was close enough now to make conversation inaudible. Dion still had Tara's hand in his. Their gazes were locked and it became something of a battle of wills. Tara refused to be the one to look away.

But as they waited for the helicopter's engine to cut off, Dion tangled his fingers with hers, turning it into a much more intimate embrace. Tara's insides got hot. He knew exactly what he was doing. He was the master. She was the novice.

When they could be heard again, Dion said, 'Come with me to the event tonight. You'll be established as Niko's mother. That's what you want, isn't it?'

Tara nodded. She couldn't deny that.

'And then,' he said, 'I'm going to fly directly to Paris after the event, for my meetings tomorrow. Come with me. The more time we spend together, the sooner this will burn out. And we still need to get to know each other. Especially if we're going to be in each other's lives.'

Tara felt torn and was a little ashamed of how much she wanted to cleave to Dion and let him whisk her off to Paris to *burn this out* and *get to know each other*.

'What about Niko?'

'He's survived six months without you, I don't think a couple of days will do any harm.'

'But Maria—'

He cut her off. 'Will be very well compensated for her time and Thea will be there to help her. We are mere hours away if we need to come back.'

And then, 'You're not on your own with this, Tara. It's not like when you took responsibility for your siblings.'

Tara cursed him silently. It was as if he knew right where she was most vulnerable.

Then he undid her completely. 'By the way, I should have told you how beautiful you look, and you really do. Stunning. Please, come with me.'

Tara melted inside. She couldn't even pretend to feign reluctance. She was his and she feared it was becoming fatal and yet she knew she couldn't do anything to save herself. The pull to be with him was too strong.

She pulled her hand free of his and saw how a flash of uncertainty came into his eyes. That small hint that he wasn't totally sure of her mollified her slightly. She said, 'Very well, but let me say goodbye to Niko.'

CHAPTER EIGHT

AFTER A FIFTEEN-MINUTE journey across the Aegean Sea, they landed on a much bigger island on a small airfield beside an airport. A car was waiting to take them to the venue and Tara sat in the back, glad she and the dress and her hair were still relatively intact.

The driver put up the privacy division, cocooning them in the back of the car. She was still feeling guilty at walking away from her son but Dion's words reverberated in her head.

'You're not on your own with this.'

No, she wasn't. And it was taking some getting used to. The fact that she could take time for herself. *Indulge herself.*

Tara sensed Dion's eyes on her and her skin got hot. She looked at him and his gaze was golden. He was looking at her with such nakedly explicit desire that her insides liquefied. *He did still want her.* The relief was a little shameful. He said, 'I'm glad you came. It would have been an awful waste of a dress.' His gaze moved down and then back up again. He said, '*Gattina*...you're killing me.'

Gattina. Tara couldn't breathe.

He had so much control over her body it made her feel vulnerable enough for a moment to try and inject something of the outside world back into this cocoon. She wasn't quite ready to succumb to his raw magnetism without letting him know she was still focused on her son. 'Have you thought about what you'll do when I don't leave?'

He said nothing for a long moment, then finally, 'I'm sure we'll make it work.'

Tara tried to envisage that. With her living and working in Athens to stay close to her son. In the same city as Dion. Possibly seeing him out and about with other women. And what if he did meet someone one day who managed to break through that impenetrable wall he'd built around himself? A woman who he would marry. Niko would have a stepmother.

Tara suddenly felt quite alone at that prospect and it shook her to her core because, not only had finding out she had a son turned her world upside down, but his father had too. Making her rethink everything she'd believed she wanted for her life, after years of sacrificing her own wishes and dreams for her siblings.

She'd believed her freedom would come from no longer feeling responsible for her siblings, but she realised that would never go. And now she had a new responsibility: Niko. But he didn't feel like a responsibility. He felt like opportunity and possibility and things Tara had never considered she might feel.

Excitement, for the future. *Love, desire.* She looked at Dion in shock as those words struck her. Love and desire.

He caught her eye and frowned. 'What is it? You've gone pale. Are you all right?'

Somehow Tara shook her head and garbled something unintelligible. 'Fine, just fine.' She hurriedly looked out of her own window unseeingly as that revelation resounded through her head and body. She knew she was in thrall to him physically, but was she really falling for Dion? A man she'd met mere…days ago, and yet she felt as if she'd known him for ever. And who she would know for ever, no matter what. Their lives were bound together by Niko. But Dion had made it very clear that they wouldn't be *together*. She would be at a remove somewhere.

The thing that was keeping them together, this crackling electricity, was finite. As Dion had also pointed out. Maybe he thought—hoped?—that a couple of days in Paris would rid him of any desire for her.

Feeling a little desperate, Tara wondered if it might rid her of this notion that she was falling for him. And rid her of her desire for him. It wasn't exactly a complication she relished either!

It was a far cry from what she'd originally imagined might happen when she met Niko's father. If she did love him, how would she cope if anything happened to him, or Niko? She went cold all over. She knew the devastation of loss. How had she not even considered this until now?

Her breathing became short and fast and she could feel her chest tightening. She hadn't had a panic attack in years but she was afraid she was on her way to one right now. But then Dion took her hand. 'Tara, look at me.'

She turned her head and concentrated on Dion's eyes. The lines of his face. His hand, warm on hers. She managed to get her breathing under control. The tightness in her chest eased.

'Are you nervous about this evening?'

She shook her head. 'No, I'm okay now.' Which was just as well, because the car was pulling to a smooth stop outside the venue. All Tara could see were huge stone walls and lots of people being disgorged from cars onto a red carpet.

Dion let her hand go and stepped out of the car and came around, opening her door to let her out. She sucked in fresh air. He took her hand again and she clung on as they walked over to the red carpet. A veritable wall of photographers was on one side. Dion bent his head towards her. 'Just follow my lead, okay? Normally I wouldn't stop but we'll let them take some pictures.'

Tara had no choice but to follow Dion as they stepped up in front of the bank of photographers. She even heard one say to another, 'Dimitriou is stopping—he never stops!'

And then it went crazy, a million flashes of light. Dion bent his head again. 'Just smile, a couple more seconds.'

Tara fixed a rictus grin on her face and, somehow, endured the ordeal and then Dion was leading her up the carpet and into the venue. Tara's heart was clamouring. Dion turned to her, 'Okay?'

She half nodded. 'That was…intense. Is it always like that?'

He nodded. He looked grim. 'Sorry, I should have warned you.'

Tara waved a hand. 'It's fine, but I think I might need a drink.'

Dion snagged two glasses of sparkling wine from a passing waiter and handed her one. Tara took a gulp and wrinkled her nose at the fizz. Dion was looking at her.

She said, 'What?'

He shook his head. 'Nothing.'

She didn't have time to probe further because he was accosted by someone, who was followed by someone else. It gave Tara time to get her breath back and take in their impressive surroundings. She could glimpse an amphitheatre where an orchestra was set up, people milling about. It was more than impressive, the location was stunning, against a backdrop of ancient ruins and with the vast sky and sea beyond.

They were gradually encouraged into the amphitheatre and Dion had seats near the front and right of the stage. As the crowd settled, the music started and the opera singers' voices swelled and filled the entire space. Tara was swept away. The fact that it was outside in the balmy air, with the moon rising in the sky behind the ruins...it was magical. She'd never experienced anything like it, and soaked it all up, rapt.

When it was over she looked at Dion, who was regarding her with an indecipherable expression on his face. He said, 'You really loved that, didn't you?'

She felt emotional. 'It was the most beautiful thing I've ever seen or heard.'

There was a wry touch to Dion's mouth. 'Now you're making me feel jaded.'

'Good,' Tara responded tartly. 'If you've lost the ability to appreciate such beauty then I fear for your soul.'

'My soul was lost a long time ago.'

Tara looked at him. 'No, it's still there, it's just buried under layers and layers of self-protection and cynicism.'

Dion might have argued with Tara but she excused herself to go to the bathroom before they left and he found himself waiting for her as the guests made their way back out of the venue. Night had fallen now and Dion had to admit that he couldn't really have argued with Tara because she was right.

She was also the only person he could imagine saying something so blunt to him. *Self-protection and cynicism.* The fact that she *saw* him was both disturbing and exposing. He'd told her so much. Spilled his guts to her, practically from the moment he'd met her.

He knew he was cynical. He couldn't remember a time when he hadn't been cynical. As for self-protection...wasn't that just what everyone did? Otherwise how could you function in the world? You wouldn't last two minutes before being crushed under the pain and disappointment meted out by people.

She'd been in his life for mere days. Another reminder of what was at stake here. Falling under her spell and forgetting the devastation she could cause.

He'd looked out of his office window earlier that day and he'd seen Tara in the pool with Niko, holding him high before lowering him into the water. He'd been squealing with joy, arms flapping at the water. They'd been wearing sunhats. Niko in a sunsuit and Tara in a one-piece that might as well have been a string bikini for the effect it had had on him.

It had been a perfectly pedestrian domestic scene, a mother playing with her son, and yet it had caught at Dion in a million jagged places deep inside him. He'd felt a sense of poignant loss for something he'd never experienced. But he was also ashamed to admit that he'd felt a spurt of something that had felt suspiciously like jealousy. An emotion he'd never really encountered before. Certainly not for a woman. But he'd felt jealous of Tara too, and her easy accord with Niko, and how she'd slotted so seamlessly into their lives.

The overwhelming sensation it had left Dion with was one of dread. He knew not to trust such a benign image. He knew the only things he could trust were himself and his son. They were a unit and they would be a unit long after Tara had decided to move on. And that was okay. He'd left her under no illusions that he expected anything else.

Her voice came into his head. *'You do expect something of me—the worst possible outcome.'*

Yes, he did. Because he'd lived it. And he would do whatever it took to ensure he protected Niko from ever feeling as abandoned as he had. So this trip with Tara would mark the start of establishing some very necessary boundaries.

In your bed? asked a mocking voice.

Dion shut it out. He was in control here. Tara would stay well within the boundaries he was going to set for her. In his bed until such time as he no longer wanted her, and at a remove from the far too cosy domestic idyll they'd been enjoying since she'd appeared in his life.

Tara had never been to Paris. There had been a trip in her last year of school but she hadn't gone because her younger sister hadn't been well. The Eiffel Tower sparkled now under a clear starlit sky like an ornament, instantly recognisable. The streets were wide and tree-lined. Sophisticated bars with people sitting outside around tables, drinking wine and eating.

Tall, beautifully designed buildings soared high into the sky, windows lit up giving glimpses into high-ceilinged apartments, full no doubt of elegant people sitting around tables talking about all sorts of intellectual things.

Another poignant reminder of all she'd missed and another reminder of the man who was opening up her world in so many ways.

They'd taken a flight from the airport on the island and Tara had found a bag packed with an array of clothes and her personal items on board. She'd looked at Dion. 'How do you *do* this?' She hadn't even thought about the fact that they were flying to another country. Not that the staff in Paris had checked her documents. They'd been waved through to Dion's car like VIPs.

He'd said, 'Magic.'

Tara had snorted to hide how seductive it all was, being

in Dion's life where things materialised and getting from A to B *was* like magic.

And now this, driving through the streets of Paris in a chauffeur-driven sleek SUV. Dion had been on his phone for most of the flight and was on his phone again, speaking in Italian. Tara couldn't deny she was so impressed with the way he had single-handedly formed himself into this formidable titan of industry. No wonder he wanted to pass it down to someone, but she wondered if he'd even considered that perhaps he was hungering for more than that. That he'd wanted to create a family for himself.

She couldn't help her insides knotting a little at that provocative thought. That perhaps Dion could be persuaded to think of *her* as part of that family.

And create an even bigger family?

A mixture of excitement and trepidation washed through Tara. Was she really ready to contemplate raising another family?

Yes, because this was vastly different.

This would be born out of love and commitment, not grief and pain.

'Tara?'

Tara's head swung around so fast she almost got whiplash. Dion had stopped talking on the phone and was looking at her. She went red. If he had any idea how far her thoughts had just strayed—*love!* She went cold at the thought. The man didn't want a family. How many times had he told her that? And he certainly didn't feel anything for her apart from this wild chemistry. He wanted rid of her as soon as that burnt out. She couldn't afford to forget that.

She forced a smile. 'Yes?'

'We're here.'

Tara's gaze moved beyond Dion to the name on the hotel

where they'd stopped. Her eyes widened. It was an iconic and instantly recognisable name.

Dion was saying, 'I have an apartment here.' He got out of the car and came around to her door. Tara felt very self-conscious now in the jeans she'd changed into. At least she was wearing a silk top and a smart jacket. And flat brogue-style shoes. And her hair was still relatively tidy from the event earlier.

Dion took her hand to lead her into the hotel. A distinctive scent teased her nostrils in the plush lobby and Tara realised it must be one of those signature scents.

A manager met them, bowing to Dion, and led them straight to an elevator, where they were whisked smoothly upwards to the top level and down a corridor to a room on the end.

Dion's apartment was on a corner with views over what seemed to be all of Paris. The Eiffel Tower in the distance. There was a terrace. The manager exchanged a few words with Dion and then left.

Tara turned around and around, taking it all in. Too stunned to speak.

'It's just an apartment.'

Tara stopped and looked at Dion. 'If you think this is *just* an apartment then maybe you really have lost your soul.'

Dion stalked towards her. He'd changed too, into dark trousers and a long-sleeved polo shirt. Light leather jacket. He looked suave and dark and unbelievably sexy.

He backed her up against a door and put one hand over her head, and, with his other, he found her waist and hip. He bent his head and kissed her and she pressed her body against his.

He pulled back for a moment to say, 'Don't think you can save my soul, Tara. You'll only get hurt.'

Tara looked up at him, and said bravely, 'I have no intention of getting hurt, Dion. Don't flatter yourself.'

He smiled. 'Good.'

Feeling a little overwhelmed with how many emotions Dion was evoking within her, Tara moved her hips against him suggestively, shamelessly focusing on the physical.

Dion arched a brow and smiled, and his smile made Tara's heart turn over. He looked so much younger and less brooding when he smiled. She could catch a glimpse of the young boy and man that he could have been if given half a chance. The rush of emotion when she thought of that was so huge that she stretched up and put her mouth to his to try and defuse it.

Thankfully he seemed equally inclined to focus on the physical and Tara felt herself getting weightless as Dion scooped her up into his arms and carried her through the apartment to the bedroom.

Dion had specifically initiated bringing Tara with him to Paris so they could indulge themselves and burn this thing out. It astounded him to think that they'd only met less than a week ago and yet he couldn't seem to remember what his life had been like without her in it.

But as he sat here now in front of a boardroom of his employees, the last thing on his mind was work. He was remembering waking at dawn and how Tara's arm and leg were flung over him and holding him down and how his first reaction to that hadn't been one of rejection or claustrophobia. It had been to pull her closer.

When he'd realised that, he'd extricated himself so fast he'd been light-headed. She hadn't woken, just moved slightly, giving him an even more tantalising view of her naked body.

Before he could stop himself or give into the urge to wake her and continue what they'd been doing hours before, he'd scooped her up and taken her over to the guest room.

Sex, *yes*. Anything more intimate? *No way*.

And yet, as Dion sat here now with his team, who were discussing the hugely exciting project of managing the reconstruction of one of Paris's most iconic art deco buildings, all he could see was her face as she'd appeared looking sexily dishevelled and sleepy, in a robe, just before he'd left that morning.

A couple of hours earlier...

When Tara woke she knew she was alone. The bed felt cold around her. She cracked open her eyes and it wasn't Dion's room with its soft brown and dark gold furnishings. Not that she had taken all that much detail in last night. She'd been embarrassingly eager to get naked and lie back and let Dion use her body like an instrument that only he could play.

And he had obliged her. Over and over again. Showing Tara that, contrary to her view of herself as being quite boring and responsible, she had a capacity for sensualism that astounded her.

But there was nothing sensual about finding herself naked, in another bed, with the covers pulled up to her chin. She tried not to let the hurt in. The hurt that Dion was so expressly making the point that he didn't want her near him unless they were making love.

Having sex, she amended.

And then she told herself she should be grateful. If she'd woken wrapped around him like a limpet, she might not have been able to hide her emotions.

Then she heard a noise out in the apartment and a little rogue devil inside her made her jump out of bed and pull on the robe that had been left on a chair nearby. Along with her clothes. That little detail made the hurt dissolve to be replaced by something else more volatile.

She went out into the apartment and stopped at the doorway leading into the dining room, her recent surge of adrenalin fading a little when confronted by the sight of Dion's broad back. A blue shirt tucked into dark trousers. Hair still damp.

Then he turned around and Tara wasn't even sure she remembered her own name. He was clean-shaven, hair swept back. Breathtakingly gorgeous.

'Hi,' she managed to crack out.

'Morning.' He gestured to the table that was full of breakfast things that smelled delicious, especially the coffee. 'Help yourself. I have to leave in a couple of minutes.'

Tara felt bereft already and that reminded her. She lifted her chin. 'You could have woken me last night. I would have gone to the other room. You didn't have to carry me.'

Like a sack of potatoes.

It was galling to think she'd been so out of it after the pleasure he'd wrung from her body that she hadn't even noticed being moved.

A small cup of coffee was halfway to his mouth. Tara could have sworn she saw a twinkle of amusement in his eye, which made her emotions surge again.

He said, 'It was no problem. I didn't want to disturb you.'

Tara held back the waspish response, *It's a bit late for that*.

Then he said, 'There's an event this evening, a charity banquet to raise funds for different charities.'

'And this is relevant because...?'

'We should go together. News is already trickling out online about us after yesterday evening at the opera, so it'll shore up our position. I think news of Niko is going to break any day now. Apparently someone, somewhere, has leaked it. To be honest I'm surprised he's been a secret for this long.'

The thought of Niko being subjected to a barrage of cameras like Tara had experienced earlier made her go cold. But as Dion said, it was inevitable.

As lightly as she could, Tara asked, 'And what happens when we're no longer...a thing to *shore up*?'

Dion's face was impassive. 'We'll issue a brief announcement stating that we're no longer in a relationship but we'll continue to co-parent our son.'

Co-parent. It sounded so...reasonable. And perhaps it would be possible. If Tara could ever come to look at Dion and not be filled with desire and those tumultuous emotions.

Surely, she thought a little desperately, this couldn't be it? Her first lover, ruining her for all other men?

'What will you do today?' he asked, clearly taking her silence as acquiescence to go to the event with him.

Tara blinked. She hadn't even thought of that and she suddenly had a feeling of weightlessness. She was in one of the most beautiful cities in the world with all the time to explore it. Her spirits sank a little. On her own.

She forced a bright smile. 'I've always wanted to see the *Mona Lisa* painting so maybe I'll do that.'

'Sounds good. It's definitely worth it.'

'You've seen it already?'

A look Tara couldn't decipher crossed Dion's face and he just nodded. 'Years ago.'

He put down his cup and said, 'I've arranged for a team to come and help you get ready for the event from four p.m. I'll meet you there. I won't have time to come back here first.'

Tara immediately thought of the photographers but Dion said, 'Don't worry, I'll meet you at the car.'

Tara's trepidation eased a little. 'Okay.'

When Dion had left, Tara hated the hollow feeling his absence evoked and went and got her phone. She would video-call Maria and Niko and check in with her family. By the time she'd done that it was mid-morning and she rushed to get ready to head out to sightsee, pushing all intrusive thought of one very tall, very handsome and very disturbing Greek man out of her head for as long as she could.

That evening Dion waited near the start of the red carpet where the cars were stopping to let their passengers out. He'd changed into a tuxedo at his offices. He knew Tara was almost there—she'd been texting him. He felt unaccountably nervous. All day he'd thought of how she'd looked a little crestfallen as he'd left the apartment and then he hadn't been able to stop thinking about her wandering around Paris, on her own.

He'd wanted to drop everything and go find her. He wanted to see her reaction to things.

He'd missed her.

No. That was unconscionable. It was just the sex effect. Dion did not miss people, or things.

He'd missed Niko.

That was his son. That was understandable. And it surprised him, how much he was missing him. He'd bonded with his son more in the last week than he had in the last six months. The fact that it was the arrival of Niko's mother that had precipitated that bonding was something Dion couldn't continue to deny.

And on that thought, a car pulled up beside him and he saw the flash of bright red hair and pale skin and gold. He stepped forward and opened the door before the driver could do it.

Dion put his hand out and Tara's hand slipped into his. An electric jolt went straight to his groin. He gritted his jaw. She stepped out and the breath left his body as he took her in. Her hair was pulled back and up in an elegant chignon. Smooth. She wore a strapless gold dress, fitted bodice and then falling in layers of tulle over silk to the ground.

She looked like a princess. Dion felt strangely humbled.

Tara's eyes went wide. 'What is it? Is it the gold? I thought it might be too garish but the stylist insisted.'

From somewhere Dion found the capacity to move and shook his head. 'No...you are utterly perfect.'

A flush came into her cheeks. 'Thank you.' She looked at him, and then said a little shyly, 'You scrub up pretty well, too.'

Dion had taken his physical looks for granted for so long. He was surprised at the little glow of pride to bask in her approval.

He was really losing it. He took her hand. 'We should go in.'

Tara took a deep breath. 'Okay, I'm ready.' Her fingers gripped his tight and as they proceeded along the red carpet he had to battle with the urge to just bundle her up and run back to the car and drive far away from here, just the two of them.

Paris was veering way out of his control and there didn't seem to be much Dion could do about it. He assured himself that when they got back to Athens, he would be able to put the necessary distance between them. He had to.

Tara had thought she'd seen it all, at that party in Athens, where she'd met Dion first. And then the open-air opera amidst centuries-old ruins. But this...blew her mind. The Grand Palais, built over a hundred years ago for an exhibition, was a vast open space designed like a nave with an intricate glass roof, thronged with possibly the most beautiful people in the world.

After being served aperitif cocktails while being serenaded by a small orchestra playing classical music with a modern twist, they were directed to where a long banquet table was laid out with gold cutlery and crystal glasses. A centrepiece of wildflowers ran down the centre, and as the sun set outside the Grand Palais, candles were lit, imbuing the surroundings with an even more magical glow.

Tara was afraid to touch the food, it looked so perfect. She was also afraid she'd drop something on the exquisite dress, so she took just a couple of mouthfuls.

Dion was talking to someone on his left but then he turned to her. 'So how was the *Mona Lisa*?'

Tara couldn't hide the lingering disappointment. 'I'm sure it's amazing but I'm afraid I couldn't get near her. It was too packed and everyone was so tall. The guards were moving people along and by the time I went past, all I caught was a tiny glimpse. I didn't realise how small the canvas was.'

And then, afraid she must sound unbearably ungrateful, she said, 'But just to be near it was amazing. And I saw a lot of other exhibits. Maybe I'll go back when it's less busy.'

Dion looked at her for a moment and then his attention was taken by the person on his left again. He apologised before turning away. The person on Tara's right touched her arm lightly and she turned to them, smiling, grateful for the distraction. So what if she'd wished Dion had been with her earlier? This trip to Paris wasn't a date trip.

CHAPTER NINE

'READY TO GO?' Dion asked, a couple of hours later.

Tara nodded. After the dinner there had been a lavish and eye-wateringly extravagant auction, with all proceeds going to the different charities. There'd even been a date auctioned with a well-known Hollywood star who had appeared on the podium.

Now, Tara's feet were screaming at her. But she forced herself to say, 'You don't have to stay and network?'

Dion shook his head. 'All networked out.'

Tara couldn't help feeling relieved. And then Dion said, 'There's somewhere else we have to go.'

She hoped the disappointment she felt didn't show. 'Oh? Okay, great.'

Dion chuckled. 'Don't worry, it's not a social event.'

Tara winced. 'Sorry, was it that obvious? I mean, this was lovely and amazing but—'

'After the initial sheen wears off and everyone has got whatever they wanted out of whoever they wanted it from, it's tedious and boring.'

She shook her head. 'So cynical. Why do you come, then?'

He shrugged. 'Because it's good to be seen and there are always networking opportunities.'

Tara mimed yawning and rolled her eyes.

They were outside now and the car pulled up. The driver

hopped out and opened the door for Tara. She got in with a little sigh of relief and slipped off her shoes, wriggling her toes.

Dion got in on the other side and gave instructions to the driver in French and saw Tara's bare feet. She winced again. 'Sorry, I'm not used to wearing high heels.'

Dion reached down and grasped her feet and pulled them up onto his lap and started massaging them. Tara's pulse-rate tripled in seconds and her skin flushed all over. And then she groaned out loud when his big hands and long fingers expertly massaged the aching balls of her feet. She could be very grateful now for the pedicure she'd received earlier from the beautician and her team that had appeared with the stylist.

'Thank you for earlier, by the way.'

'For what?'

Tara indicated to the dress. 'This, and the team... I've never had any beauty treatments before. My brothers and sisters used to buy me vouchers for a place but the vouchers always ran out before I could use them.'

The car was pulling up outside a department store and Dion asked Tara what her shoe size was. Bemused, she told him and the driver got out of the car and disappeared into the store. He came back out minutes later with a couple of bags and got back into the car.

Nothing else was said, and Tara was finding it hard to focus anyway, while Dion's hands were on her feet. One hand was creeping up to circle her calf, and behind her knee.

Little fires were racing across her skin now. She couldn't look away from his dark golden gaze, as that hand crept higher, above her knee, to her thigh. Tacitly, she parted her legs and Dion's fingers traced patterns on the delicate skin of her inner thigh, almost within touching distance of—

'*Nous sommes arrivées,* Monsieur Dimitriou.'

Tara looked out of the window and frowned. The car had pulled in at the side of the road. Dion's hand left its provocative place on her inner thigh. Tara could see the shining illuminated glass pyramids in the square outside the Louvre. She'd been here hours ago.

She sat up, vaguely aware of Dion pulling her dress back down and getting out of the car. He came around to her side and opened the door. He was standing in front of her, holding out two pairs of sneakers fresh from boxes. That was what the driver had been doing.

One of the pairs was white and gold. She looked at the driver, who blushed and said, 'I have daughters. I know how important it is to…how do you say…*go together*?'

Tara was beyond touched by Dion's instruction to the driver and the driver's gesture. She nodded and pointed at the pair with gold stripes. 'They're perfect.' She felt ridiculously emotional as Dion bent down and put the shoes on her feet, and laced them up, as if she were a child. *Or Cinderella.*

When the shoes were on he took her hand and pulled her up to standing. Still not sure what was happening, Tara let him lead her towards the massive iconic art museum. Under the moonlight it all felt a little surreal. She held the dress up a little in one hand to protect it from the ground.

As they drew closer, she could see an open door and a woman in a dark suit waiting for them. She greeted Dion with huge deference and welcomed them in as if this were all entirely normal.

As they followed her into the building, which was completely empty and hushed when only hours ago it had been thronged with tourists, Tara squeezed his hand and whispered, 'What are we doing here?' She couldn't wrap her head around what was happening.

Dion merely put a finger to his mouth and they kept walking. They passed by the statue of the *Venus de Milo* and Tara nearly tripped. Dion steadied her.

Eventually, their guide stopped at an entrance to one of the rooms and stood back. She put out a hand and said, 'Please, enjoy.'

They walked in and Tara realised that they were in the room of the *Mona Lisa*. It was all the way at the other end and Dion walked her towards it. Tara wasn't sure how her feet were even moving.

They stopped at the barrier a couple of feet back from the painting. No crowds. No jostling. No craning to see past tall people. Just them, and arguably the most famous painting of a woman, in the world. With her enigmatic smile. Looking at Tara as if to say, *Back again?*

Her vision started blurring and she furiously blinked to keep it at bay. When she felt she could speak she looked at Dion, who was staring at the painting. 'How…? When…?'

He looked down at her. She noticed that he'd undone his bow tie and it hung loose around his neck. Top button undone.

He said, 'When you were in the bathroom earlier, I made a call.'

Tara shook her head. 'This must be costing a fortune.'

Dion's mouth twitched. 'It's crude to talk about money.'

She wanted to say, *Please tell me you haven't done this for anyone else,* but she didn't have the nerve. And maybe it was better not to know.

Then he said, 'In case you're wondering, I happen to know someone who was involved with renovations here recently. They put in the call for me. I don't have the Louvre on speed dial for such occasions.'

Relief swamped Tara. She feigned unconcern. 'It hadn't even occurred to me.'

She heard a soft, 'Liar,' beside her and restrained herself from elbowing Dion in the ribs. Instead she focused on this moment and this painting and soaked it in.

When she finally let out a deep breath and tore her eyes off the painting, she looked to see Dion standing in front of another painting. She went over and nudged into him with her shoulder. He glanced down at her. That emotion bubbled again. She forced it down.

'Thank you so much… I can't tell you how special this is. To be here, like this.'

'You're welcome.'

Tara was trying really, really hard not to read anything into this extraordinary gesture. As they made their way back out of the huge room, she said, 'You mentioned that you'd seen the painting years ago.'

'Yes, I took it upon myself to educate myself and I went around Europe to all of the major tourist sites and museums and galleries. So that I'd be ready to be accepted into a section of society that had never been meant for me.'

Tara was deeply touched at the thought of a studious Dion making up for the lack of his education like that. Striving to earn his place among his peers. Learning about all the cultural reference points. She stopped him by putting a hand on his arm and said a little huskily, 'You have as much of a right as any of those people we were with earlier to be in their space.'

Dion looked at Tara and her kind eyes and words were making something completely alien fill his chest. It was expanding and breaking down years-old hardness. Protection. Leaving him exposed. Vulnerable.

In a bid to negate it, defuse it, he stepped up to Tara and put a hand around the back of her neck and tugged her to him, slanting his mouth across hers. She was smaller in the flat shoes and it made him feel protective. She'd looked like some kind of a New Age sprite in that dress, standing on tiptoe leaning on the rail to see the picture better. Tendrils of hair coming loose from the chignon, falling down to her shoulders and around her face.

He'd made the decision to come here on a whim because she'd looked so disappointed and he'd wanted to make her happy. It hadn't been an extravagant billionaire's gesture to woo a woman. It had been much more prosaic. And dangerous. Because he'd seen her eyes, suspiciously bright. The way her throat had worked.

He pulled back from kissing her and she took a moment to open her eyes. Swirling blue and green. Oceans of emotion. Dion said, 'This is all that matters, Tara, and it will burn out.'

Her eyes became guarded. She tensed. Dion hated how he automatically wanted to kiss her again to undo that change.

'Don't worry,' she said. 'I know exactly what's happening here.'

She was pulling away, walking ahead, through the vast empty halls of the Louvre, her back as straight as a dancer's, her bearing as regal as a queen, and Dion felt as if he'd just ruined something very special, and yet he'd had to do it.

Tara refused to let Dion's reminder not to read too much into his gesture bring her down. She wouldn't let it ruin the most precious and amazing thing anyone had ever done for her.

They were silent on the journey back to the hotel. When they got up to the apartment Dion turned to Tara and started saying, 'Look, I'm sorry but I—'

She walked up to him and put her hand over his mouth. Then she took it down and said, 'I know. It's okay, Dion.'

She reached up and pressed her mouth to his, infusing her kiss with all the things she couldn't say, that he didn't want to hear. It turned molten in seconds, an urgency gripping them as they made their way to the bedroom, shedding clothes as they went.

By the time they reached Dion's bed, Tara's hair was completely undone and falling around her shoulders. The sneakers had been kicked off. Dion was wearing just his trousers, chest bare. They were both breathing harshly.

And then it became something else. Slow and languorous, as Dion made her turn around and pulled down the zip, baring her back.

The dress loosened around her chest and then fell. Tara shimmied her hips to make it fall to the floor. She pulled down her underwear and stepped out of it. Naked, she turned again and faced Dion. She put her hands to his trousers and undid them, pulling down the zip, her knuckles brushing his erection. She saw how his cheeks flared with colour.

She pulled his trousers down and he stepped out of them, and his underwear. Now he was naked too. There was something very elemental about facing him like this with nothing in between.

Acting on an instinct as old as time, Tara dropped to her knees before Dion. She desperately wanted to do something for him but also push him to the edge of his control. He reached out a hand saying, 'Tara, you don't—'

But he stopped talking when she took him in her hand, circling the hard length of him, squeezing gently, moving her hand up and down. She was fascinated by the steely strength encased in delicate silken flesh.

Then she leant forward and put her mouth around his

flesh and heard his sharp indrawn breath. His hand came to her head, fingers tangling in her hair, as if he wanted to pull her back but couldn't.

She was sure her touch had to be gauche, inexpert, but Dion's hips were jerking and suddenly she was being hauled up in front of him and he was wild-eyed. 'I need...to be inside you. Now.'

Tara lay down on the bed, beyond excited by Dion's desperate intensity. He pushed her legs apart and came between them and then he was thrusting deep inside her, taking her breath away and making her back arch, hands gripping the cover. He found her hands and caught them, putting them up and over her head, catching them with one of his.

He pulled her closer with his other arm and kept up a remorseless steady and devastating rhythm that had her arching higher against him, wrapping her legs around his waist, begging, pleading for him to take mercy on her. He bent his head and found her breast and sucked her nipple deep into his mouth and that sent her soaring higher than she'd ever been before. Waves of pleasure wracking her body as Dion found his own release and slumped over her, head buried in her neck.

'I think you should go back to Athens. I'll be stuck in meetings until late this evening.'

Dion had said that to Tara just hours before, when she'd found him, much like the previous morning, dressed and ready for work. None of the signs of the previous night on him, whereas Tara felt as if she wore his lovemaking like a brand. Permanently altered.

She'd woken during the night, curled into Dion, his arm around her. She'd revelled in that for a moment before extricating herself and picking up her things and going back to her bedroom. She didn't want to wake again as she had the previous morning.

She hadn't argued with him about leaving Paris. In a way she'd welcomed the bursting of the bubble. Not that Dion hadn't already burst it a little with his reminding her not to read anything into...*anything*.

And, as his driver pulled up to the Athens villa now, she couldn't wait to see Niko. She had to remember that Niko was the centre of all of this. Niko would endure, Tara and Dion wouldn't.

Dion wasn't losing sight of what was important to him. She shouldn't either. The only problem was that, for Tara, what she'd believed to be important to her had undergone a seismic change since coming to Athens mere days ago.

Far from wanting to spend the next few years carving out a career and enjoying her independence, she now still yearned for a career, but also to create a family with the man she loved, and her son. She wanted it all, and she didn't need anyone to point out that having it all was about as impossible as finding a way into Dion's well-guarded heart.

A day later, when Dion returned to the villa, he didn't like to admit to the level of anticipation he felt. And it wasn't just about Niko. He realised that he'd never had a sense of *coming home* before. To someone.

Since Tara had returned to Athens, she'd been sending Dion pictures and videos of Niko. Now, he felt as if he'd been away for a month and was vowing never to go away for longer than twenty-four hours again.

The car pulled to a stop outside the main steps and the door opened as Dion got out of the car. Tara appeared with Niko in her arms and Niko squealed and put out his arms when he saw Dion.

This image tore something apart inside Dion. It made him think of how, when he'd woken up yesterday morning, he'd been alone in his bed. Tara had gone back to her bedroom. And relief had been the last thing he'd felt. He'd wanted her there, close.

Need warred with the urge not only to self-protect but also to protect Niko. He closed off the part of himself that wanted to melt into this image and take it at face value.

He couldn't keep letting Tara cloud his brain.

He forced himself to move and went over and lifted Niko into his arms, holding him close. It felt like second nature now to hold his son.

'Hi,' she said.

Dion looked at her and steeled himself against the reaction that it was becoming harder and harder to believe might fade. Damn her. She shouldn't even be affecting him, dressed in cut-off shorts and a sleeveless shirt tied at her waist. Hair up. Bare feet. No make-up.

He had to start setting the boundaries.

'Dion? Are you okay?'

Tara's heart was still thumping to see Dion. It felt as if she hadn't seen him in a week. But it had been only the previous day. She'd been so happy just now to see him returning. Her heart expanding in her chest. A big silly grin on her face. But he'd just looked at her and then he'd come and plucked Niko out of her arms and was holding him now as if she might try to take him back.

He blinked and the intensity in his face cleared. 'I'm fine, but we do need to talk.'

He went inside, still holding Niko. Tara followed, her insides going into freefall. Was it happening already? Dion had had enough and this…was over? As she followed him and Niko back inside, she felt like an interloper, for the first time since she'd scaled that wall to get onto his property.

'Thea has prepared some food, if you're hungry?'

He turned to face her. 'I ate on the plane. Can you meet me in my office in an hour? I'll stay with Niko for a bit.'

Tara swallowed. 'Sure, no problem.'

An hour later, Maria was putting Niko down for the evening and then she was heading home. Tara couldn't put off the moment any longer. She went and knocked on Dion's door, feeling as though they were right back where they'd started when she was coming for the DNA test results.

'Come in.'

Tara took a breath and pushed the door open. Dion was behind his desk. He looked up. 'Please, sit.'

Tara did, perching on the edge of a chair across from him. He looked serious but a piece of hair was flopping onto his forehead and Tara wanted to go and push it back, sit in his lap—

He stood up. 'So, I think it's time to talk about making arrangements.'

'Arrangements,' Tara echoed faintly.

He nodded and went over to the huge window, his back to her. 'Yes,' he said. 'Arrangements for a more permanent solution.'

'I…' Tara wasn't sure what to say. 'What do you mean exactly?'

He turned around. 'Well, it's not as if this was ever more than a temporary situation, was it?'

Tara felt winded. Was he as brutal with all of his lovers? 'No, I knew that.' But she'd hoped…

'You can't stay here. It won't be good for Niko. He'll get used to you.'

Tara stood up, fire in her belly. 'I won't be cast out of Niko's life.' *Or yours,* wailed a little voice.

'You won't be cast out of Niko's life, but you will be at a more appropriate…distance.'

Tara frowned as something became more clear. 'You're talking about living arrangements.'

Dion looked at her. 'Yes, of course.'

Tara sat back down, legs suddenly wobbly. She hated herself for asking, but she said, 'And what about…us?'

'We'll continue to see each other until such time as the desire fades.'

Tara felt light-headed. It wasn't over. Yet. Desperate to feel some kind of control in this situation when she felt very much adrift on the currents of Dion's whims, she lifted her chin and said, 'What if I'm already over it?'

He stalked over to her before she could take another breath and pulled her up out of the chair, close to his body. She felt his heat and strength and her insides predictably melted into a pool of lust. She was so not over it.

'You're saying you don't want me any more?'

Her gaze roved over his face, the lean lines, the intense expression. She wanted to make him laugh. *She loved him.* She reached up and touched his face, tracing his hard jaw.

She shook her head. 'No, I was just…saying nonsense.'

He speared a hand in her hair and pulled her head back. His gaze went to her mouth and lingered there. He said something in Greek. Tara imagined he was cursing her for this crackling chemistry between them. Well, tough. It wasn't her fault that it wasn't burning out.

He lowered his head and took her mouth in an open kiss, explicit, immediately sexual, and she welcomed it, meeting him with equal hunger and passion.

The fire was raging between them in seconds, no words

spoken as Dion pulled open her shirt and palmed her breasts, finding those hard peaks and pinching them gently, making Tara moan. She was leaning back against Dion's desk and reached for his shirt. She pulled it apart too and thought she heard ripping, buttons popping, but she didn't care.

He opened her shorts and pulled them down, taking her underwear with them. He lifted her, sitting her on the edge of his desk. 'Open your legs.'

She did, feeling like a goddess as Dion fumbled with his clothes. His face was flushed. She reached up and pushed that lock of hair back and for a moment he looked at her, but then he was moving into her and then filling her with his hard body, making her back arch. She put her hands behind her, head thrown back as Dion caught her up against him and moved in and out, taking them higher and higher. It was fast and explosive. Over in minutes. Both gasping for air, skin slick. Clothes half on, half off.

Tara clung to Dion and thought to herself, *As long as we have this...there's hope.*

But that hope felt very elusive the following day when Tara stood, with Niko in her arms, in a vast penthouse apartment in an exclusive suburb of Athens. Not far from Dion's villa.

She turned around, taking in the huge open-plan living-dining area. There was also a separate living room with full media centre.

There was a state-of-the-art kitchen. Three bedrooms, all en-suite. The master suite had a dressing room and small private sitting room. There was an outdoor terrace. A gym. A home office. It was stunningly modern and sleek and impressive and… Tara turned to Dion. 'Why are you showing me this?'

'I bought it for you.'

Tara nearly dropped Niko. She had to tighten her grip on him and he squirmed a little, reaching out for Dion, who took him easily, perching him high against his chest. The little boy snuggled in. Traitor.

'You bought it, for me,' Tara echoed flatly.

Dion nodded. 'This is one of Athens' newest developments. Easy access to the city. Parks nearby. Lots of cafés and restaurants. There's a concierge downstairs.'

All that she could possibly need for her independent life once Dion cut her loose. She looked around, feeling a little bewildered. She noted, 'It's not very child-safe.'

'I'll have people come in to make sure it's safe, but it shouldn't cause problems in the short term. Niko is barely crawling.'

No, he was pretty stationary. Tara looked at Dion again. 'You didn't have to buy this… I could have rented for a while, bought my own place eventually.'

'You're the mother of my child, Tara. I will provide for you. It's in your name, yours to do with as you wish.'

Her gaze narrowed. 'You mean I could sell it?'

He shrugged minutely. 'If you wished, of course.'

Because, on some level, Tara was sure that Dion still believed her capable of disappearing. Maybe this was a test, to see how she would react? She forced a smile. 'Well, it's lovely, and far too generous. But thank you. When is it available?'

Dion held up a key. 'It's yours as of now.'

Tara blanched. She hadn't been expecting that. In the normal world people didn't just move into new houses or apartments the minute they saw them.

Dion went on, 'I've arranged for your things to be packed and moved over tomorrow.'

Tara felt winded again. 'And how…how will we do this?'

'You'll be living here, you can come and see Niko as often as you like, or have him here if and when it suits, maybe when I'm away, working.'

'And you'll be in your villa.'

His gaze got darker, golden, igniting every nerve-end in Tara's body. He said, 'I'll visit you here.'

'I can't see you at the villa?'

'I think it would be best for Niko to minimise that association, of you and me together in his domestic sphere.'

'But what if he's here and you come here and we…?'

'I don't really envisage that happening. Not in the long term.'

Because it would be over. She really did need him to spell it out for her, didn't she? She castigated herself—this development was unexpected but not inevitable. It wasn't as if she could continue living with Dion, she knew that. But to be faced with it so abruptly was jarring.

Things moved swiftly after that. They went back to the villa and Thea gave Tara a sad look—she obviously knew.

Dion disappeared to work and sent a text later.

I'll be back late, don't wait up.

Tara packed up her meagre belongings. It seemed like aeons ago that she'd travelled from Dublin to Athens to find the father of her baby. She had, and she'd found so much more.

Maria had been due to do the night-shift but Tara told her she could go home—she wanted to spend as much time with Niko as possible. They agreed that Maria would work the following day while Tara moved out.

The next day, movers appeared in the morning and she rode with them in the van to the apartment. When she got to the apartment, she was surprised to see that the dressing room had already been filled with the clothes from the island and also new clothes.

After the movers left, Tara was standing alone in the huge sleek space, feeling hollow inside. She heard the melodic chime of the bell. Her heart started pounding. Maybe Dion had come to tell her it was all a mistake and that she could stay with them at the villa, even though she knew that wasn't really— She pulled open the heavy door, a tentative smile on her face, which faded as she took in three women, one older and two about her age.

An efficient-looking blonde stepped forward, hand out. '*Kalimera*, Miss Simons, I'm Athena, Mr Dimitriou's executive assistant.' Tara shook her hand a little dumbly. The woman indicated the older woman on her left. 'This is Sara, she will be your housekeeper and you can give her instructions on your wishes, and this—' she indicated the other woman, an attractive brunette with a nice smile '—is Georgia, she's an interior designer and will have a consultation with you about how you'd like to do up the apartment.'

Tara felt an absurd urge to giggle. The apartment couldn't be more 'done'.

Georgia said, in an American accent, 'Apparently you need to baby-proof the place?'

Tara's urge to giggle faded to be replaced by something much sadder as the full enormity of her new life here hit her squarely in the solar plexus. She nodded and stood back. 'Please, come in. I'm afraid I don't have anything to offer in the way of drinks yet.'

Sara smiled and said, 'That's my job. I'll see what's here and arrange for shopping to be done.' She bustled off in the direction of the kitchen.

Athena said to Tara, 'Do you have a driver's licence?'

Tara nodded. 'Somewhere... I'll have a look.' She went to her bag and dug it out and handed it to Athena, who said, 'Thank you, I'll be back soon.'

Tara forced a smile at Georgia, who was taking in the apartment with a low whistle of appreciation. 'Wow, this is some place.' She turned to Tara. 'So, what do you envisage exactly?'

Tara knew exactly what she envisaged but it had nothing to do with soft furnishings and everything to do with a life with the man she loved and her son.

CHAPTER TEN

LATER THAT DAY, Tara was looking into her fully stocked fridge. She shook her head at how money could just conjure up things.

She took an apple out of the fruit basket and bit into it as she wandered through the apartment, stopping at one of the guest bedroom doors. She and Georgia had designated that this room would be Niko's as one of the doors opened into the master bedroom—Georgia, who had a young child of her own, about Niko's age—was going to come back with some drawings based on their discussion of how to do it up.

The doorbell chimed. Tara's heart stuttered even though she didn't expect it would be Dion. But when she opened the door, he filled the space. She drank him in.

'Can I come in?'

Tara stood back and swallowed the piece of apple in her mouth before she choked on it. 'Of course.'

He was wearing a suit, tie slightly undone, top button open.

'How's Niko?'

'He's fine. He's with Maria, she's agreed to live in until we hire a second nanny, which hopefully won't be too long. I've lined up interviews at the villa tomorrow. You're welcome to sit in.'

A knife twisted inside Tara. She felt like pointing out that if she could be Niko's full-time mother, he wouldn't need to hire two nannies. But her being Niko's full-time mother wasn't an option.

'Thank you,' she said.

'I've got something for you, downstairs.'

Tara took the key from the bowl inside the door and followed him into the elevator. It was only then that she realised what a state she was, her image reflected in the steel wall of the elevator. Wearing jeans, flip-flops and a loose shirt, hair pulled up haphazardly. No make-up.

But then the doors opened and she realised they were in the basement garage. He walked over to a small black SUV. Sleek and stylish. Roomy but not intimidatingly large. He zapped it and opened the doors. The interior was as stylish as the exterior, enough controls to launch a space rocket. And it was automatic. She looked at Dion, not comprehending. He handed her the key. 'You'll need something to get around. My drivers are at your disposal, of course, but I know you value your independence.'

She looked into the back. 'There's no baby seat.'

'I'd prefer if you used my drivers if you want to go anywhere with Niko.'

Tara looked at Dion. 'Millions of mothers the world over are successfully driving their children around in cars without incident.'

A muscle twitched in Dion's jaw. 'I would prefer it for now. At least until you get used to driving in Athens. The traffic can be a bit nuts.'

Something melted inside Tara to think he was genuinely just concerned for their safety. She looked at the key in her hand and back to him. 'I don't know what to say... You really didn't have to do...any of this.'

* * *

Dion kept waiting for some kind of sense of relief to wash over him. He was literally handing Tara her freedom and independence and yet when he'd shown her the apartment yesterday, it had felt all...wrong.

Far from relief, it was something much more complicated. He pushed the conflicting emotions aside for now and said, 'Why don't you take it for a spin now? You can bring me up to the villa and have dinner. There's something I need to show you.'

Tara looked wary. 'More?'

Dion shook his head and also pushed aside the revelation that any other woman he'd ever been with would be ecstatic to be given gifts. And he knew it wasn't that Tara wasn't appreciative, she just wasn't remotely materialistic.

She couldn't be less like your mother, pointed out a little voice. It jarred inside Dion.

He refocused. 'Not as in a thing, it's stuff online. The pictures of us together from the opera event and Paris. And news has broken about Niko. I've prepared a statement to go out that will hopefully take fire out of the story. I'd like you to see it before we send it out.'

Tara went pale, her freckles standing out. She could have passed for an art student right now but Dion had never wanted a woman more.

She looked at the car. 'Drive up to the villa now?'

'Might as well start to get used to it.'

'I've never driven on the other side of the road before.'

'I'll guide you.'

But again, in the car, as Dion fought not to get distracted by her pale hands on the wheel and the way her thighs looked under the snug jeans, and as he instructed her where to turn and which side of the road to stay on, he felt that this was all wrong—not Tara driving, but the fact that he was handing her a tool to stay separate from him. *From them.*

The following morning, it took Tara a long time to figure out that she was in a new bed. In a new room. In a new apartment. She turned her head. The bed was dented slightly beside her. So she hadn't dreamt that Dion had been here. He'd insisted on accompanying her back to the apartment in her car, after dinner and after Niko had gone to bed.

He'd leaned against the door with one shoulder and had said, 'Want me to tuck you in?'

Tara had longed to be able to say, *No, thanks,* and shut the door that he had put between them in his face, but after spending the evening with him and Niko all of her defences had been toast. She'd grabbed his shirt and pulled him to her saying, 'Damn you, Dion Dimitriou,' before kissing him and kicking the door closed at the same time.

But now he was gone and Tara could feel the silence of the apartment settle around her. It was unnerving. After growing up with four siblings, she was used to people being around, barging into rooms. Coming and going. The villa had been busy with staff.

But after last night she had an unnerving suspicion that this could become a pattern. Her mobile phone pinged and she looked at it. A text from Dion.

Interviews with nannies start at midday. I can send a driver for you?

Tara scowled at the phone and responded.

No, thanks, I'll drive.

She threw the phone down and lay back on the bed. And then she picked up the phone again and did a search online and saw the headlines: *Dimitriou introduces his baby mama to the world. Have they set a date?*

Tara almost laughed at that one but she stopped laughing when she saw, *Who is Tara Simons, the unknown woman who snagged one of the world's richest men with the oldest trick in the book?*

She threw the phone down again and groaned. She was well and truly a public entity now. But at least she could glean some comfort in the fact that she'd been established as Niko's mother.

Later that day at the villa, Dion said, 'There's an event on Friday night. I think we should go. It'll give us another opportunity to be seen together.'

They had just chosen the second nanny, together with Maria, who had also sat in on the interviews, while Thea had given Niko lunch.

Now Tara was sitting on the floor in Niko's room, encouraging him to crawl towards her. She looked up at Dion. 'Okay, sure.'

'I'll arrange for a team to come to your apartment to help you get ready.'

Tara opened her mouth to object but then closed it again. Who was she kidding? She needed help. 'Okay.'

Dion looked at his watch. 'I have to go into the office now... I'll see you later?'

Tara caught Niko's hands and he gurgled at her. She knew what Dion meant. That he would come to her for one thing only. And then steal away again. Like last night, she longed to be able to say, *Actually, that doesn't suit,* but a part of her didn't want to be all alone in that apartment.

She looked at him and sold a little more of her soul. 'Okay.'

* * *

On the Friday evening, Tara was nervous. The team Dion had arranged had just left. Once again Tara could hardly recognise herself in the mirror. Hair sleek and pulled back and over one shoulder. A plain black silk gown, off the shoulder. It oozed the kind of elegance that only a household-name designer could manufacture.

Tara took a selfie in the mirror and sent it to her fashion-designer sister, Lucy.

Not bad, hmm?

Two seconds later, a response.

OMG, is that really a—?

The doorbell chimed. Tara nearly dropped the phone and ignored her sister's message, stuffing the phone in her bag. Dion was on the other side, in a classic tuxedo, but this time with a white jacket.

Tara wondered if he would ever not take her breath away. His eyes moved from her head to her toes and back up again. 'You look...stunning.'

She felt shy. Ridiculous. Especially when she thought of how bold and insatiable she'd been the previous night, as if doing all she could to ensure Dion stayed. But when she'd woken, she'd been alone. Again.

'My driver is waiting.'

Tara came out and closed the door. The journey to the venue—one of Athens' most exclusive hotels—was short. When the paparazzi realised it was Dion and Tara, they went crazy. Screaming, shouting. Tara was trembling by the time they got inside and Dion pulled her to him. 'I'm sorry, I should have realised it'd be worse, but they will lose interest, I promise.'

Tara didn't say it, but she thought it—they'd definitely lose interest when she was no longer by his side and relegated to being his *baby mama* with no other status.

Tara moved through the crowd with Dion but she couldn't help but feel increasingly as if she were behind a glass wall. The separation between her and Dion had started with him sequestering her in her own apartment. Even though his arm was around her back, he might as well also be pushing her away.

At one point Tara slipped free and went and stood at the roof-terrace wall. The ancient city was laid out before her and she felt all at once excited but incredibly lonely at the thought of forging a new life for herself here.

It was also painful knowing that she'd be so close to her son, but so far. Kept at a remove.

Not to mention his father, pointed out a little voice.

She would have to look into her legal rights as his biological mother, maybe even demand joint custody—

'Okay?'

Tara's thoughts scattered instantly. She carefully composed her expression before turning to him. He handed her a glass of champagne. She took it. *'Efharisto.'*

Dion raised a brow. 'Learning Greek?'

Tara nodded. 'I am, actually. I signed up for classes today, at a language school in the city. I start next Monday.'

'I could have arranged a tutor for you.'

Tara shook her head. 'No, this is going to be my home. I need to make friends and meet people. Not to mention start looking for work.'

Dion was silent for a long moment and when Tara glanced

at him he was looking at her with a slightly taken-aback expression.

'What is it?'

He shook his head. 'Nothing. I can arrange for you to interview with the team working on the eco resort on Nisos. They're working on other projects there too.'

'I'd appreciate that, as long as they don't feel like they have to hire me because I'm...' She faltered, because what was she?

'They won't, don't worry. It'll be purely merit based.'

'That's good.'

The sun was almost disappearing behind the Acropolis and Dion said, 'Ready to go?'

Tara looked around. The crowd had thinned out. She nodded and tried not to feel dispirited at the thought of going back to her palatial but very empty apartment.

In the car on the way back to the apartment Tara said, 'Interior decorators are coming tomorrow to start work on turning the guest bedroom into a nursery for Niko.'

Dion seemed tense. 'That sounds good.'

Something occurred to Tara and she said, 'Imagine when he's a lanky teenager and he's going to have all his friends around watching movies or playing computer games.' She nudged Dion. 'Maybe my apartment will be the *fun place* to hang out.'

Dion looked at her as if she'd just spoken a foreign language.

'They do grow up, you know,' Tara pointed out gently. 'But luckily I have a vast amount of experience in dealing with moody teenagers.'

She could swear he went pale in the dim light of the back of the car. Concerned, she asked, 'What is it? What did I say?'

* * *

'Nothing…nothing.' Dion got out, sounding a little strangled. But she'd just said everything. She'd given Dion a glimpse into the future—his son growing up, becoming a young man. Having the kind of normal life that Dion had never experienced. Which was exactly what Dion had wanted for his son. But somehow he'd never factored Tara into this picture and he could see her now, in another fifteen years, even more beautiful. Vibrant. Sexy. Rounded. Mature.

He'd never factored her in because he'd been fully sure she would be gone. And yet she was starting Greek lessons. Looking for a job. Getting on with her life. *Without him.*

Which was exactly what he wanted. So why did he feel as if a massive weight were pressing on his chest? At the thought of their son floating between the villa and the apartment. Spending time with his mother. Who could well be in another relationship by then. Perhaps not living in the apartment any more but another place. With more children.

Dion nearly stopped breathing. His mind blanked into a red haze. His car pulled up outside the apartment block now and Tara put a hand on his arm, saying lightly, 'You don't need to come up. I'm fine. I'm quite tired this evening.'

Dion was frozen into a kind of paralysis, watching as his driver jumped out to help Tara out of the car. Something he should be doing but couldn't. He watched her go in, greeting the concierge, who smiled back.

She disappeared into the elevator, the doors closed. The driver got back in and Dion was suddenly moving, out of the car, and through the doors. Only for the fact that the concierge knew who he was, he didn't stop him.

He was outside Tara's door, pressing the bell. It opened and she was there, smaller, because she'd obviously kicked off the shoes.

'Dion?'

He saw the way colour flared into her cheeks. The pulse at the base of her neck under her pale skin. The future was the future. *Now* was all he needed to worry about.

'I want you.'

She bit her lip.

'I said I was tired.'

'You did, and I won't come in unless you invite me.'

She didn't look tired. She looked glorious. Like a fiery queen. He asked himself why he had put this door here. Why had it been such a good idea? Because now it felt like a very bad one. Lust was clouding his brain.

And then just when he thought she was going to close the door in his face, she stood back and relief mixed with triumph pounded through his veins.

When Tara woke the next morning her body was heavy from an overload of pleasure. She didn't have to open her eyes to know Dion wasn't there. She could see it now so clearly. How he'd neatly excised her from their lives. She could visit Niko in the villa during the day, invariably when Dion was at work. And then he would spend the evening here. As if he was having an affair but not betraying a partner, betraying their son.

She'd been congratulating herself last night for walking away, for showing him she didn't need him, but as soon as he'd turned up at her door, looking wild and slightly crazed, she'd had no will to turn him away. She had no idea how long he would want her. She would never stop wanting him. She did need him.

This desire between them only seemed to be burning brighter. She knew it frustrated Dion. She could feel it in the desperation of their lovemaking. And she could sense the turmoil within him. She knew that he'd never had any intention of having a family, but surely even he could see that it was worth trying? For Niko's sake?

She couldn't go on like this, living like a mistress, in this lonely apartment. And if he was doing this to try and drive her away, she would double down on her determination to make a life in Athens work.

At the very least she wanted to ensure, not only that the public knew her now as Niko's mother, but that she'd be recognised legally and have equal rights to her son.

'He's gone to the office this morning, something about a meeting on Monday,' Maria told Tara.

Tara had arrived at the villa in her car a short while before. She'd spotted one of Dion's drivers standing by, presumably in case Maria needed him. The new nanny was due to start the following week so Maria was still living in, for now. Niko was sitting up against a cushion and playing with a soft toy. He'd smiled gummily at Tara, showing his emerging baby teeth, when she'd arrived. That had only made her even more determined to assert herself now.

For all Niko knew, she was just another nanny. She said to Maria, 'Why don't you take the day off? I want to talk to Dion. I'll take Niko with me for a little trip.'

Maria looked worried. 'Are you sure?'

Tara nodded. 'Totally. We'll call you if anything comes up.'

When Maria had left, Tara dressed Niko, grabbed some supplies and asked Dion's driver to take them to his office. Tara hadn't been there before. It was an imposing modern building in the centre of Athens, surrounded by much older buildings. She liked it. It was like a statement of intent from

Dion, demanding to be seen, after a life of being abandoned by those who should have loved him the most.

That made her feel emotional though and she had to push it down. She strapped Niko into his pram and went into the building. The receptionist brought her to a private elevator and said, 'I'll let Mr Dimitriou know you're coming up.'

Tara's belly erupted into butterflies as the elevator ascended. When the doors opened Dion was standing there, in trousers and a shirt, sleeves rolled up, frowning. 'What are you doing here?'

He looked at the pram. 'Is Niko okay?'

'He's fine. I wanted to talk to you.'

'Where's Maria?'

'I told her to take the day off.'

'She answers to me.'

Tara's spine straightened. This is why she was here. 'She should have to answer to me too. I'm Niko's mother.'

Dion looked at Tara for a long moment before he seemed to realise that she wasn't leaving. He took the pram and pushed it down the hall to an office at the end. She followed. There were lots of empty offices, all visible behind glass walls.

And an empty anteroom outside Dion's office, presumably where his assistant worked.

Dion's office was vast and impressive. Windows on all sides, giving amazing views of the city. 'This is really cool,' Tara breathed, standing at one of the windows.

'Would you like something to drink? Coffee?'

Tara turned around to see Dion at a sideboard that contained very futuristic-looking tea and coffee facilities.

'Yes, please, black is fine.'

Tara went and checked on Niko. He was sleeping. He'd

been due a nap anyway. She pulled a muslin net over the pram to shield him from the sun coming in the windows.

Dion handed her a small cup. She took a fortifying sip. Dion had a cup in his hand. He leaned back against his desk. 'You wanted to talk?'

Tara swallowed. She could see how daunting it might be to face up to Dion. He was formidable. She had to try and remember that only hours ago their naked limbs had been entwined, skin slick, hearts racing...

Not helpful, Tara.

She cursed her imagination and had every intention of launching into a demand to be recognised legally as Niko's mother, but instead heard herself blurting out emotionally, 'I want us to try and be a family. I'm lonely in the apartment.'

Dion was like stone. But she knew he was flesh and blood.

'You know that's not what I want.' His voice was like steel. Unyielding.

'This chemistry doesn't seem to be fading. You said it would burn out.' Tara couldn't help but sound accusing.

'It will.'

'What if it doesn't?'

Dion's eyes flashed. 'Not possible.'

'I think you had Niko because deep down you want a family, not just an heir.'

'I told you why I had Niko and you know why I won't go down the road of risking him being abandoned by his mother.'

'I'm not going anywhere, Dion. I'm not your mother.'

'You just said you're lonely.'

Tara gripped the coffee cup. 'Yes, but that's because I'm used to being around a lot of people. I have four siblings. Just because I'm lonely doesn't mean I'm going to walk away. I know I'll build a community here.

'But,' she said, 'I think we owe it to Niko to try and see if we can make it work.'

'And when it doesn't? And he's devastated?'

'And what if it does, and he's not devastated?'

Tara's phone had been vibrating in her back pocket for the last few minutes and she couldn't keep ignoring it. She took it out and looked at the screen. Thirteen missed calls. Her stomach tightened. She looked at Dion. 'Sorry, I have to answer this. It's my sister Mary. Something must be wrong.'

Tara put down the cup and answered, walking away a little. Then she stopped dead. 'Okay, Mary, calm down… just tell me what happened.'

She listened to her sister, her blood running cold. 'I'll get a flight home as soon as I can.'

She turned around to face Dion. 'That was my sister. My brother Daniel has just come back from backpacking in Asia, and he was taken ill. They think it's a tropical bug. He's in Intensive Care in a hospital in Dublin. I have to go to him.'

Dion stood up straight. 'Of course, I'll arrange it.'

'Will you and Niko come with me? Please?'

He hesitated for one second and then said, 'Of course. Let's go.'

Dublin was humid under grey skies. Tara was in knots. Even though, since she and Dion and Niko had left Athens, her brother had apparently woken up and was responding to treatment. They'd moved him out of ICU to a less acute bed. She still needed to see him.

Dion had organised a private flight and a car had been waiting to take them straight to the hospital. They were directed to the room and Dion stayed in the waiting room with Niko while she went and had an emotional reunion with her sister Mary, who was waiting for her.

'He's okay, Tara, he's out of Intensive Care. He's awake and talking.'

Tara nodded, tears filling her eyes. She felt guilty for having left them all and having been so focused on Dion and Niko.

As if reading her mind, Mary said, 'Do *not* take this on yourself. Daniel is twenty-three and he ate street-food insects on his last night in Bangkok. It's entirely his fault.'

Tara let out a half-laugh of relief and then went in to see her brother. The doctor assured her that he would be fine, it was a tropical bug but they'd treated it in time.

After assuring herself her brother was ok, Daniel said, 'So can I meet my nephew now? Apparently he takes after me, the lucky kid.'

Tara rolled her eyes, but went to get Dion and Niko. Mary's eyes went wide as saucers when she saw Dion, and Tara couldn't blame her. Here, against this very sterile backdrop, he looked almost other-worldly, in dark trousers and a long-sleeved light top.

Niko was in a pram and Tara lifted him out. Mary got teary-eyed when she saw her nephew, taking him from Tara. She looked at Dion. 'I'm so sorry, Mr Dimitriou, about the mix-up…but now that he's here I can't say I'm *that* sorry.'

Tara gave her a dig in the ribs and Mary said, '*Ow*, what?'

Tara just shook her head. She'd saved Mary's skin but Dion was smiling and he said, 'I think I'd have to agree with you.'

See? said Mary in a look to Tara. And then she was off, taking her nephew, who seemed to be completely content in his aunt's arms, in to meet his uncle.

'Sorry,' Tara offered as she and Dion walked to the room. 'My brothers and sisters are a rambunctious lot.'

* * *

Dion was still reeling from the speed at which they'd dropped everything and run to Dublin. The whole way over on the flight, he hadn't been able to get that last conversation with Tara out of his head. She wanted to try and be a family. She'd admitted she was lonely but that it wouldn't make her leave. He'd isolated her and yet he couldn't stay away from her.

He'd told her over and over again he didn't want a family. He wouldn't take the risk. The risk of harming Niko.

Or the risk of harming yourself? asked a little voice.

And now, he was dealing with double vision. Mary, Tara's sister, shared her red hair and colouring. But she had blue eyes. Not blue-green. She'd helped herself so easily to his son, as if it were second nature to claim him. It disturbed and heartened Dion in equal measure.

He was at the door of the hospital room and looking at a young man with dark hair in the bed. Presumably Daniel. He was talking to Niko, who was still in Mary's arms with Tara hovering nearby.

'Hey, kiddo, welcome to the family. I'm the most fun out of everyone so just you wait until I'm on my feet again and we'll go out on the town, okay?'

Niko babbled happily, kicking his legs and arms.

Then from behind Dion someone else slipped into the room. A younger woman, her hair more strawberry blonde than red. She stopped at the bottom of the bed and said, 'You're not dead? Ah, pity, I'd picked out the best suit for you to wear at your wake.'

Daniel made a face. 'Ha-ha, Lucy, I know you'd be devastated if anything happened to me because I know you still fancy Stephen.'

'Shut up, I do not!'

A kind of chaos ensued that Dion had no idea how to comprehend because he'd never seen anything like it before. Lucy spotted Tara and squealed and then spotted Niko and started crying, taking him into her arms and saying, 'Oh, my God, you're so gorgeous.'

And then she saw Dion in the doorway and went pink. Mary came and stood beside him. 'This is Dion, our…sister's…baby daddy.'

Lucy said, 'I'm so sorry, I just assumed you were a doctor.'

'Not a doctor, an industrialist, one of the most innovative in the world.'

Dion looked around to see yet another member of the family. More red hair. A slightly nerdy-looking young man in glasses. He put out a hand. 'Oisín, I presume?'

Tara's youngest brother flushed with pride and shook Dion's hand. 'Yes, although that was probably just a matter of deduction.'

'You helped your sister hack her way into a party.'

'Yes, I did. But it was worth it, I think?'

Dion looked at Tara, who was hugging Lucy who was still holding Niko. He couldn't deny it had been worth it. He was now seeing the true breadth and wealth of what he'd missed out on his whole life. A family. Tight-knit and loving. Already forming a sort of cocoon around Niko as he was passed around and cooed over.

Dion felt as if he were behind a glass wall. Observing this unit. Something rose within him, something he hadn't felt in a long time. Envy. A sense of loss. And more, as he observed his son basking in this outpouring of love and attention from his aunts and uncles. Something much darker. Guilt. *Shame*.

And then Niko started to grizzle. He hadn't eaten since

the plane and Dion could smell something suspicious. Mary took him back from Lucy and said, 'I'll change him. I think it's the least I can do after everything.' Tara gave her the bag of supplies and Mary took him into the bathroom.

Tara came over to Dion. 'He's getting cranky. He needs to be fed and probably put down for a nap. My family home isn't far from here—we could go there, if that's okay?'

Dion's chest was tight. This scene represented too much. And it was washing over him and through him like a tidal wave. The thought of going to the family home was suddenly too much. He stepped back from the room. 'You go, with Niko. Spend the night with your family. I'll go to the hotel.'

Tara seemed to sense his reluctance. 'If you're sure?'

'Will you come to my hotel in the morning? I'll send my driver for you.'

'Of course.'

Dion turned and walked away. But even as he walked away, he wanted to turn around and grab Niko and take him away from here. From this place where there was so much potential for pain.

But Dion kept walking, because he knew that, as of this moment, everything had changed. He couldn't *unsee* what he'd just seen. And he couldn't stop the walls he'd spent years erecting to protect himself from crumbling to pieces.

CHAPTER ELEVEN

THE NEXT MORNING, early, Tara and Niko arrived at Dion's plush city-centre hotel. Dion appeared in the lobby, freshly shaved and dressed, hair damp. Effortlessly suave in dark trousers and a shirt. He took Niko into his arms and the baby smiled at his father.

'I was having breakfast. Have you eaten?'

'No, but Niko has.'

Dion led the way to his room, at the top of the hotel with stunning views of the city. Tara barely noticed. Dion gave Niko back to her and rang for some fresh breakfast things and more coffee.

Tara settled Niko into a safe spot on the couch surrounded by cushions. He played happily with his stuffed toy, alternating between trying to pull it apart and eat it.

The room attendant arrived with a tray of food and fresh coffee. Dion thanked him and let him out.

Tara sat down but her appetite had fled. She poured some coffee and looked at Dion, who was staring broodingly at Niko. There was something different about him but she couldn't put her finger on it. She felt unaccountably nervous. 'Why do I feel like you're going to tell me something?'

He surprised her by saying, 'I hope you don't mind but I took the liberty of using my connections to get your brother checked by another consultant, just to be sure he's getting the best treatment. I've been assured he'll be absolutely fine.'

Tara swallowed a sudden lump in her throat. 'Thank you. You didn't have to do that, but thank you.'

'Your family mean everything to you, don't they?'

She wasn't sure where Dion was going with this but she said, 'Yes, of course. I love them. But...we're all moving on with our lives now.'

'Yet you didn't hesitate to run when they needed you.'

Tara's hackles rose. She stood up. 'Dion, if you're going to use this as some sort of reason to not trust that I'll—'

He cut her off. 'I think you should have full custody of Niko.'

Tara realised belatedly that Dion looked pale. She must have misheard him. 'Sorry, what did you just say?'

She glanced at Niko quickly to check him and saw that he was falling asleep. She went over and put him lying down, bolstered by the cushions to stop him rolling off. Dion handed her a throw and she put it over him. As she was doing this she was telling herself she must have—

'I said,' Dion said in a low voice from behind her, 'that I think you should have full custody of Niko.'

Tara stood up and turned around. When she could get a word out, it made no sense. 'But... I...you can't... I can't...'

Dion was shaking his head. 'Do you know that I've never seen a family, at close hand like that?'

Tara's insides sank. 'I knew it—it was traumatic.' Clearly, because he'd lost his mind.

But he shook his head. 'No, it was amazing. The shorthand between you. The incredible bond. The *love*. The support.'

'I...yes, I'm very lucky.'

Dion looked at her. 'You lost your parents, you suffered a massive tragedy but you used it to forge something strong and durable and amazing. I know, even after only meeting your siblings for a brief time, that they would do anything for you. And for Niko.'

'You're included in that now. You're family too, even if we're not together…' She trailed off ineffectually.

But Dion was shaking his head. 'No, I'm not your family. I don't have any family.'

Tara's heart broke for Dion. 'You have Niko. You have me.'

Dion turned away from her as if he couldn't bear her to look at him. He said, 'What I did—having a child on my own—it was the most arrogant and selfish thing I've ever done. I would have subjected Niko to a half-life with just me. Seeing him with you and your family last night, how can I deny him a family who will adore him and care for him?'

He turned to face her again. 'How can I deny him a mother who is willing to move to another country and set up a life there in order to be with her son?'

'How can you deny him his father?'

'A selfish father. How could I offer Niko a family when I don't even know what it is?'

'It wasn't selfish to want to create a life. People do it with a lot less consideration than you.'

He seemed determined not to hear her. 'I'm no better than my mother. I'm worse.'

Tara gasped. 'That is not true, for one second. You *love* Niko.'

His eyes blazed. 'I would lay down my life for him but how do I know if that's love? I've never felt it, how can I show it? You and your family have that… Niko deserves that. He should stay here with you.'

Tara shook her head. 'My life is not here any more. It's in Athens, with you and Niko.'

Dion said, 'I'm going back to Athens today. You're staying here with Niko.'

'So, you're repeating history after all?'

Dion frowned. 'How?'

'By abandoning your baby.'

He went pale. 'I would never.'

'That's exactly what you're doing, if you leave him behind.'

'But he'll be with you.'

'He needs *you*.'

Dion started to pace back and forth. Tara glanced at Niko. He was still fast asleep. She looked back at Dion. He stopped pacing. 'I'll end up hurting him. He'll resent me for not giving him a family.'

Tara couldn't help saying, 'So give him a family.'

'Not this again, Tara.'

She tried not to be dissuaded. 'We already have a son. We could have more children...maybe not right away...but in a few years...'

Dion was shaking his head. 'But why would you...? You're already sacrificing so much...'

'It's not a sacrifice when you love someone.'

Her words hung in the air for a long moment, Dion staring at her. Then he said, 'You don't love me. You can't. It's pity...or your overdeveloped sense of responsibility. You love Niko so much you'd sacrifice your ultimate freedom to give him what he needs.'

'This isn't about what he needs. Well, I mean, of course it is...but it's my needs too. Selfishly, *I* need you. I love you, Dion, and I would like to create a life with you and Niko.'

What Tara was saying simply didn't make sense. 'But how can you? I'm not...lovable.'

Tara walked over to him and stood in front of him, looking up. Dion felt as if he were falling. 'Yes,' she said, 'you are. Eminently lovable. No matter what happened to you.'

All Dion felt, though, was shame. He turned away from Tara's gaze. She was searing all the way through to where there was something so deeply bad inside him that it had caused his mother to abandon him and his father to reject him. It had made him acquire a child so that he might feel love.

She put a hand on his arm and turned him back to face her. He'd never felt so exposed. Vulnerable. Undone.

'Maybe take it from me, then, because I was lucky enough to know what it felt like to be loved.' She lifted a hand and touched his jaw. 'And I can tell you that I do truly love you, Dionysios Dimitriou. Not just for your looks and amazing body and the way you make me feel…' she blushed but went on '…but because you've got integrity and you're kind and you went against everything you knew to create a family, even though you told yourself it was for more practical reasons. You love your son. You did it because you were looking for love.'

Tara's words hit a chord inside him even though his first instinct was to deny it. She'd said she was lonely in that apartment. But he'd been lonely too. There was no real need for him to pass down his business—he didn't even come from that kind of background. And he knew he couldn't care less if Niko wanted to inherit it. He wanted his son to be happy. He wanted more for his son than he'd ever had. To be *loved*?

What about you? prompted a little voice.

The thought of giving voice or a name to the swirling mass of tangled emotions inside him didn't bear thinking about. That way lay annihilation.

He assured himself that she was wrong. He'd been Tara's first lover. She thought she loved him. She was confusing lust with love. He was profoundly damaged. And yet he still wanted her. It beat through him now like a life force. Not fading. Getting stronger.

Maybe he could meet her halfway.

He shook his head. 'I'm sorry. I can't tell you what you want to hear... I think after some time has passed you'll realise that what you're feeling isn't actually that deep...'

That blue-green gaze narrowed on him. Her hair was down. She was wearing a denim button-down dress. Bare legs. Sandals. And Dion ached from wanting her.

She folded her arms across her chest. 'Do not patronise me, Dion. I know how I feel, and I want you, body, heart and soul. Nothing less.'

She was like a warrior. Dion had the strangest urge to go to his knees before her and beg for mercy. He had a sudden fear that he would drive her away and that sent a shard of ice into his gut. He felt panicky.

'I can't offer you that, but I could offer you a marriage... That way we'd be together and you'd have legal custody of Niko, for ever.' And he could have her in his life and not think too much about how she made him feel. About her words.

Tara's eyes widened. 'You'd offer me marriage, like some sort of compensation for not being able to tell me you love me. We'd exist in a slightly less dysfunctional situation than we currently do.'

'Tara... I wish I could give you more...but I just can't...'

'Can't, or won't?'

He couldn't answer. It was as if a massive stone were lodged high in his chest. The past was all around him, whispering at him to protect himself at all costs.

Tara just said, 'Right, I have to get something. Wait here, I'll be back.' And then as Dion watched, she picked up her bag and left the suite, the door closing behind her.

As if sensing his mother was gone, Niko woke with a

little cry. Dion went over and picked him up, cradling him against his chest.

Dion felt cold inside. Tara had said she would be back but he knew he'd driven her away, exactly as he'd planned to do all along. But of course he didn't feel remotely triumphant or relieved. He felt bereft. He was a coward. She'd offered herself to him and what had he done? Nothing. Offered her half a marriage in a moment of panic at the thought of not having her in his life.

He smelled a familiar pungent smell and looked at Niko, who was regarding him warily with huge eyes. His mother's eyes. He brought him into the bathroom with his bag of supplies and set about changing his nappy.

Niko freshly cleaned and changed, Dion went back into the main living area. No sign of Tara.

Damn it. Had he really driven her away? *No.* Dion refused to believe it for a second. That woman was the bravest woman he knew. She'd told him she loved him. And he loved her. Of course he did! It surged through him now, like an unstoppable cleansing force. He had nothing left to hold it back. Deny it.

He did know love.

He had felt love before—for his mother—but after what she'd done, he'd buried it so deep that it had calcified and become hard and impenetrable. Unrecognisable.

Niko had started changing that. And then Tara had burst into his life and completed the process. And her wild family. Wild with love and fierce loyalty. He'd seen it in that hospital room and it had made him run. The fear of rejection too much to bear. He was a coward.

Panicking, Dion quickly loaded Niko into his pram and left the suite, taking the elevator down to the lobby. He was almost out of the door with no idea where to start looking for Tara when he heard her voice. 'Dion!'

He turned around. She'd come in another door. He went straight over to her and cupped her face in his hands, words tripping over themselves. 'I'm so sorry, I'm such an idiot, of course I love you, I think I've loved you since that first night when you blew my world wide open and me and how could I have not seen it? But I'm a coward and I was afraid of *you* abandoning me, but I hid behind Niko and I'm just…' He drew a breath. He could see her eyes shimmering, a smile on her mouth. He looked up and down again, trying to control his own emotions. 'I just love you, and you could walk away right now and I'd still love you and—'

She shook her head. 'I'm not going anywhere. I have something to ask you.'

She slipped out of his hands and suddenly she was on one knee at his feet. Niko squealed happily to see his mama. Tara quickly leaned over to kiss him, and then took something out of her back pocket. A small velvet box. She opened it and Dion saw a golden band. Plain, simple.

She said, 'The only marriage I'm interested in is one based on love… I was going to say that if you really didn't feel the same, I'd settle for legal custody but that we couldn't continue to be lovers—'

Before she'd stopped talking, Dion reached for her and pulled her up, covering her mouth with his. She'd said enough. He wanted her for love. They were oblivious to the small crowd around them who clapped and cheered. He pulled back and said, 'Yes, yes, yes. You are the only woman I want to ever marry.'

Tara was laughing and crying. She took the ring and put it onto Dion's finger. He felt its weight and relished it. The weight of love. He said, 'We'll have to go out again.'

Tara leaned against him, arms around his neck. 'Why?'

'Because I want to get you a ring.'

Her eyes were bright. 'You don't have to.'

'Yes, I do.'

'Okay, and then can we come back, and maybe when Niko is napping we could—?'

'Oh, yes, we're not leaving this hotel for at least a couple of days.'

They went out of the main door, arms wrapped around each other, Dion pushing the buggy that held their beloved son in one hand.

Much later, while Niko slept in a cot in a little anteroom beside their room, Dion and Tara lay entwined together. On her finger sparkled a ring, an emerald-cut aquamarine stone, with two smaller white diamonds on either side.

Niko vowed never to remove his gold band. Well, apart from on their wedding day. But they were in no rush to get married.

In fact, the marriage wouldn't happen for another three years, when Tara was pregnant with Niko's little sister, Lexie, and they both realised they should probably regularise their situation. Because they'd been too busy living and loving and becoming a family. And working together. Tara had undergone a rigorous interview process and had found work with the eco resort project on Nisos, and had loved every second of being involved with the project.

She was almost fluent in Greek, helped by the fact that she was in love with her very attentive tutor.

So, now, at five months pregnant, with her bump just starting to pop under the loose empire line of her stunning cream wedding dress, with her hair piled high and a bouquet of flowers from the villa garden in her hands, Tara walked down the aisle of the Greek church in Athens, to Dion, with Niko in front of her flinging rose petals with abandon.

All of her family were there—Daniel had come back

from working in Australia to give her away, thankfully not with a tropical bug this time. Mary and Lucy were her maids of honour, and Oisín, who had since moved to Athens too, to work for Dion's company in its tech section, was Dion's best man. He was the new resident of Tara's apartment.

Needless to say, even with the apartment, the villa in Athens had become a frequent port of call for everyone and Dion had got used to returning home to find any number of the Simons family in residence. And he loved it. His life now didn't remotely resemble his life before and he gave thanks every day for the mishap that had brought him and Tara together. Not that he'd ever admit that to Mary, of course. But she knew.

Tara reached Dion at the top of the church. Daniel melted away. One of the aunts took Niko and his rose petals to the pews. Tara faced Dion, smiling. Joy bubbling up. Love tangible between them.

He lifted a hand and touched her face and said simply, 'Thank you.'

She shook her head. 'I did nothing. I just fell in love with you.'

'You brought me back to life. You gave me a life.'

'You are my life.'

'Gattina...'

Tara blushed.

Someone—probably Daniel—whispered loudly, 'Sheesh, get a room, guys.'

Tara giggled. Dion grinned. He looked so much younger.

The priest cleared his throat and they got on with the business of getting married. And living happily ever after.

* * * * *

FORBIDDEN GREEK MISTRESS

CAITLIN CREWS

MILLS & BOON

CHAPTER ONE

THANASIS ZACHARIAS WALKED into his father's tasteless monstrosity of a villa that took over the entire north side of a relatively obscure island in the Aegean—as his equally tasteless monstrosity of a father had commanded—and saw a ghost.

Had he been anywhere else, he would have rushed to her. He would have crossed the marble floors, heedless and wild with the need to touch her. He would have got his hands upon her, immediately, to feel the warmth of her skin beneath his palms. He would have crushed his mouth to hers—anything to prove that it was truly her.

That she was alive. That this wasn't yet another one of the dreams that had haunted him relentlessly for five long years. That she was really and truly *here*—

It was the *here* that was a problem.

What was his resurrected lost love doing *here?*

Thanasis had grown up in this villa. This was the place where he had learned entirely too much about his father's delight in hurting others, causing pain and sorrow wherever he could, and lifelong commitment to his own selfish ego. It was, at best, a place of smoke and mirrors. Lies upon lies upon lies.

He had learned long ago to keep his reactions to

himself, not to mention any inconvenient emotions that might present themselves at the worst possible moment.

The consequences for not doing so had always been dire.

Here, now, there was an impossible ghost standing there beneath the glittering light of the chandeliers in the villa's great hall, and he did not dare approach her.

Not when he could not be certain how he would act.

Or what he would reveal.

Thanasis forced himself to look away from her, though it caused him actual, physical pain. He had to do it in stages, looking back to make sure he wasn't seeing things, then going through entire stages of grief again to make himself tear his gaze away once more. He had to be careful. He had to monitor his stampeding heart and the blood surging through him, not to mention the expression he feared was on his face. The face he had only ever showed *her*—

He looked around, assessing the situation with the cool calculation that had made him such a success in business, despite his father's appalling antics and reputation for drama.

No one had seen him enter. He had come late, deliberately. It was clear at a glance that he had missed nothing, just the usual chaos of a typical Zacharias family event. He could see three of his five half siblings from his place by the ostentatious marble arches in the entryway, though he had no doubt that the others were somewhere about. They always were. They circled like sharks, because that's what they were. Forever jockeying for favor and position, when surely they should have known better by now.

Thanasis was the heir to all of this. This excessive bacchanal. This abominable offense against architecture and all the vanity cluttered within it. This enduring mess his father took such delight in making, knowing that one day he would simply leave it behind him, and better yet, in Thanasis's lap.

Not for Pavlos Zacharias the questionable charms of actual parenting or maintaining healthy relationships with the children he'd fathered indiscriminately, all while remaining married to Thanasis's mother. Not for him some sort of acknowledgment that he had created these lives that now depended so heavily on his own. Then again, he didn't seem to care overmuch what sort of relationship he had with Thanasis, either, legitimate or not.

Pavlos delighted in torture. Not the rack or the stocks. No thumbscrews or bamboo beneath any fingernails. Those things took effort and Pavlos was too lazy. Why bother making that sort of effort when it was easier by far to simply behave like the depraved monster he was and watch the ripples of that behavior spread out before him?

That was why Thanasis could not trust his eyes. Maybe it wasn't a ghost, stood here before him in the grand hall. Maybe it was simply a woman who *looked like* his lost, adored Saskia.

Obviously, he told himself sternly, it could not be anything else.

Not here in this funhouse mirror of a place, where nothing was as it seemed, unless, that was, it seemed like hell.

He stayed where he was. He let himself look at her,

then forced himself to look away. Again. When that was something he had never been any good at. That had not changed, no matter who this woman really was.

Thanasis could not allow his hunger to show on his face. He could not allow anyone here to see any hint of the things he actually felt inside. He could not allow them to imagine that he had any emotions at all, for that matter. Pavlos's infamously depraved villa was a festering sore, not any kind of home, and anything found within it was a weapon.

He had learned that when he was still small.

Thanasis smelled what he was certain was a whiff of sulfur, and then there beside him was the half sibling he liked the least—a difficult distinction, but hers all the same. The venal and vain Marissa was a product of Pavlos's widely publicized affair with a sharp-edged Parisian model who was as famous for her spitefulness as her cheekbones.

"I thought you no longer adhered to the old man's commands," Marissa said in that cut glass voice of hers, sharp and vicious. She did not bother to speak Greek, though they were both in Greece tonight. She preferred her native French and did not care at all if she was understood. The venom came through, loud and clear, no matter what language she used.

Thanasis allowed himself another glance at his beautiful ghost, currently standing across the hall with a wineglass clutched in her fingers, her head tilted slightly to one side, an expression he recognized on her face. A baffled sort of curiosity that, once, had been a precursor to laughter—

But it couldn't be. It couldn't.

What he recognized was a memory, nothing more, and this woman before him had nothing to do with it.

Because this woman was not Saskia. Saskia was dead.

It had taken him every moment of the past five years to be able to accept that simple statement of fact.

He couldn't allow himself to linger, not even with a gaze from across a great hall. Not with this ghoul at his elbow, more than prepared to leap on him like a carrion crow.

Hoping he would give her the opportunity, more like.

"I accepted my father's invitation, if that is what you mean," he replied. With a certain cool neutrality that he had perfected over the years, because it drove every member of his family into paroxysms of temper and rage.

Marissa sneered. "I keep waiting for him to announce that he's changed his will. Perhaps then you wouldn't be quite so high and mighty, eh?"

Normally, Thanasis played this game when he was here. If he had allowed himself to be enticed or ordered back to the villa, there was no point attempting to avoid the unpleasantness as he otherwise preferred to do from afar. He allowed these conversations. He leaned into them. And he was not averse to crossing a sword or two when he encountered his father's by-blows.

But everything was different tonight.

Because *she* was here, whoever she was.

And until he knew who she *actually* was—or, more importantly, who she *wasn't*—he found he had no stomach at all for the games he usually lowered himself to play in this place.

"I cannot understand how you have reached your thirties without understanding that he will never do anything of the kind," he told his venomous half sister, impatiently. "I do not want to be his heir, and therefore, he will make certain that I am. You, by contrast, have debased yourself for the whole of your life in the hopes that he will give it all to you instead, and so he never will. It is really that simple, Marissa, and I have no idea why you cannot grasp it."

She bared her teeth at him and he broke away, too aware that he could not afford to let her or anyone else here goad him into revealing things he shouldn't.

Not that he had. Not yet. But he didn't like that it felt *precarious*.

He had always hated his father. This was a natural consequence of watching how the old man treated Thanasis's stoic, heartbroken, stubborn-to-her-own-detriment mother. When she'd died, when Thanasis was in his twenties, he hadn't known whether to cheer her escape or mourn her passing. And the vile old man had bloomed in the face of his son and heir's disgust, entertaining himself by dragging Thanasis into the family business no matter how he'd tried to break away.

Those dreams had crumbled after university, when Thanasis had finally understood that no matter what he did or where he went, his name went with him and the specter of his father hung over him like the sword of Damocles. He had been forced to surrender to the inevitable, and so he had—but he had done it on his own terms.

It had taken him years to demonstrate that there were two Zacharias shipping concerns under the same corporate name. One catered entirely to his father's whims, grudges, reversals, and lies. The other was Thanasis's domain.

Pavlos made headlines. Thanasis made deals. And one day, he would wash his hands entirely of the problems his father made for him.

He dreamed of that day all the time.

The only other thing he ever dreamed about appeared to be standing here, in this very same room, with music wrapping itself around her and light finding her as she breathed, but he told himself—again—that this was impossible. This woman *resembled* his Saskia, that was all. He needed to stop imagining it could be otherwise.

He had spent years trying to imagine her back to life.

If it was possible, he would have done it already.

The usual twisted, vacuous socialites flooded about as he moved along the outskirts of the crowd, knowing better than to get in his way. The paparazzi, forever being fed stories by his bitter half siblings, called Thanasis the boardroom bully. Or the real Zacharias monster. They took great pleasure in shredding him apart in their pages.

But if the goal was to isolate or shame him, it didn't work, because he was entirely too competent at his job.

All his half siblings' efforts had brought him was entirely too much female attention, little as he wanted it. The idea of a demanding man with too much money on his hands was apparently catnip to some. Yet though they flocked to him, they rarely stayed near him. He cut through small talk like a blade. He was too intense, too certain, too opposed to the usual nonsense.

And most importantly, he had yet to get over Saskia.

In this world where everything was brightly colored, airy, and insubstantial until it drew blood, Thanasis—according to his father—dressed like an undertaker. Always all in black, he carved his way through parties like a hearse.

These frilly, frivolous people fluttered around him like he was the king of the underworld himself.

Sometimes he even enjoyed it, but not tonight.

Thanasis didn't trust himself to drink, not when what he really wanted was to take a whole bottle of whatever was on offer and toss it back. Not when he generally allowed these people to think he was drearily sober, because it made them hate him more.

And certainly not when he couldn't be certain how he would react if alcohol hit all the yearning and need and cruel hope inside him.

He skirted the edges of the vapid crush, listening to them bray and shriek, and got a different vantage point of this woman before him who could not possibly exist.

Saskia. Her name was a song inside of him. Saskia, whose lovely, perfect body had never been found. He had grudgingly come to accept that she had died in that train derailment, because surely no one could hide for five whole years. Not from a man like him with so many resources at his fingertips.

He had monitored her bank. Her credit cards. She'd never returned to the flat he'd set up for her in London and he knew she had nowhere else to go. She had been an orphan, in London for her studies and focusing on art history, of all pointless things. She had been quick and bright, intense and in love, and he had never wished to be parted from her. Then, after a night he wished he could do over again—oh, how he had wished it a thousand times—she had boarded that train in the morning and he'd never seen her again.

He'd been left with nothing.

And Thanasis had quickly discovered that without this woman he had hid away from the world, he was a stranger to himself.

It was possible that he had become used to that stranger. Or anyway, he'd learned to accept him, because it wasn't as if he had another option.

But here, tonight, he was staring at her doppelgänger.

And he felt very much like the him he had lost that terrible day...

He cautioned himself against too much hope. He had acquainted himself with all the various stages of grief and then some, more than once, and nothing had changed the truth. There was no reason to suppose that would change now, either. Everyone had a twin, wasn't that what they said? Everyone had a double.

Thanasis told himself that this woman here tonight resembled the woman he'd lost, that was all. She wasn't—she *couldn't be* his Saskia. Just someone who looked so much like her that it was almost as if she had come back from the dead.

Obviously, that was impossible.

Obviously.

Still, he maneuvered himself closer. She wasn't speaking to anyone, though she stood in a loose group of guests. She wore a pretty dress and a smile on her face and looked as if she couldn't quite believe what she was hearing from the people standing around her. Given that those people included Pavlos himself and

Thanasis's half brother, Johannes—who could best be described as two-faced and vengeful, and that on a good day—this was not a surprise.

She didn't look like Saskia, Thanasis assured himself. Or rather, she looked different than *his* Saskia. Older, perhaps.

She wore her hair differently, longer now, tumbling down her back in glossy waves that made his fingers ache with the memory of running a shorter version of those thick waves between them.

He knew how she would smell, like bergamot and flowers, and he only realized he'd clenched his hands into fists when his knuckles began to ache.

This woman, who could not possibly be Saskia because Saskia was dead, had the same perfect oval of a face. The same clever, dancing eyes like steeped tea run through with the brightest sunshine. She had the same delicate nose and the same high cheekbones, both of which he had traced again and again with his fingers. His mouth.

And that was *her* mouth, just as he remembered it. A sensual affair that made her look as if she was pouting when all she was doing was thinking. That mouth that he had felt all over his body, then lush and hot on his cock.

God help him, but he could feel himself stirring even here. In this squalid place where sex was merely one more commodity.

He stared at her so hard that it must have disturbed the air around her, because she looked up. And he braced himself, waiting for that clash of recognition when her gaze met his. That punch of understanding and electricity that had changed his life completely when he'd encountered her by chance in the Tate Modern in Central London.

But though she looked at him, and held his gaze, he saw nothing in the dark brown depths of hers save the mildest interest.

As if he really was nothing but a stranger.

This only proved that she wasn't Saskia, he assured himself—but everything in him rejected it.

Emphatically.

Thanasis could feel it like a blow, a kind of terrible seizure rolling through him and churning him up, leaving nothing but destruction in its wake.

He gritted his teeth. And it took him a lot longer than it should have to make sure that no matter what devastating implosions were happening inside him— and there were too many to count tonight—his face betrayed nothing.

When there was movement beside him again, he found the sly and ever chemically impaired Telemachus beside him, another half brother. This one so dissolute that it was never clear if he knew who Thanasis was or if he thought that he was involved in some sort of extended drug-addled experience in his own otherwise empty head.

"Have to admit it," Telemachus slurred at Thanasis as if picking up a conversation. "The old goat has always had good taste in women."

"I'm aware of only one woman who fits that description," Thanasis replied frigidly. "My sainted mother, may she rest in peace. The one and only wife he ever took."

"My mother was a whore," Telemachus said cheerfully, as if in agreement. "She'd have been the first to admit it if she was still alive. Not just admit it, but defend it. That doesn't change the fact that she was beautiful."

"I have asked you repeatedly not to speak to me in public," Thanasis reminded Telemachus, who likely forgot that again the moment he said it. He moved away, growing more impatient with each step.

Though impatient for what, he could not have said.

He was too aware of the ghost of Saskia, there in the center of this room, as if this entire party was about her. For him, of course, it was.

Thanasis could not manage to think past it. He could not make any sense of it.

He could feel his father looking at him, but he didn't move toward the old man. He refused to give him the satisfaction.

You must come to the villa, Pavlos had told him, hijacking a business call to make this demand.

I need to do no such thing, and won't, Thanasis had replied, mildly enough.

It had been years since he'd darkened the marble arches of the villa with his presence. He preferred to avoid it altogether. Refusing to return to the island meant he only had to interact with his father in Athens, where they could keep it in the office and talk some semblance of business, though he kept that to a minimum too.

Handling his father was much easier from afar.

Pavlos stayed in Greece, flitting in and out of the office in Athens as it suited his sense of importance.

Thanasis remained in London, where he could run the business with the focused ruthlessness that had made him a billionaire in his own right before the age of thirty.

As the years passed, fewer and far between were these visits home. If he had his way, he would see to it that there was no crossover between Pavlos's vanity projects and the actual concerns of the shipping business that had been in the family for generations, but that Thanasis had turned into a multinational conglomerate.

You must come, Pavlos had said merrily, sounding wholly undeterred, as ever. *I have an announcement to make of supreme importance.*

Are you terminally ill? Thanasis had asked dryly.

Pavlos had laughed. *You wish, my boy. Soon enough, all this will be your problem to solve. But in the meantime, I require your presence at the villa.*

If I refuse this invitation, will you finally cut me out of your will? Thanasis asked.

But the old man only laughed again, and rang off.

If Thanasis had thought that Pavlos really would disinherit him, he might have stayed back in London the way he'd wanted to do. But everything with his father came down to weighing the options. Deciding what was worse at any given time—or what would become worse in the future if ignored—and acting accordingly.

At the end of the day, it cost him relatively little to turn up, appear to dance attendance on the old man's whims, gather what intelligence he could, and then leave.

Not that there was ever much intelligence on display, of course.

Now, fully in his glory and with all of his children in attendance, Pavlos tapped his glass with one of the signet rings he wore on his thick fingers. He kept going until he claimed the attention of everyone in the room.

It was perhaps more true than Thanasis wanted to admit that his father had excellent taste in women. But what they saw in Pavlos in return was his wealth. His power. His status and fame. A woman who dated Pavlos Zacharias could be certain she would find herself infamous almost at once. Some of his mistresses had parlayed that notoriety into something resembling a career, depending on a person's definition of that term, but one thing remained certain.

Not a single one of them could possibly have dated the old man for his looks. Not in decades, anyway.

Because Pavlos had once been tall and commanding. Thanasis had seen the pictures. But he was not a handsome man. All of his features were bold and arresting, and he had been called *exciting* and *powerful* in his heyday. Those same bold and arresting features coupled with a lifetime of dissolution and excess, however, meant that these days he resembled nothing so much as a goblin.

Something Thanasis had told him once, though it had done nothing but make the old man howl with laughter.

Jealous, are you? Pavlos had asked when he stopped laughing. *A goblin I might be, my boy, and yet still the whole world finds me magnetic beyond reason.*

You pronounced rich *incorrectly,* Thanasis had replied in his usual dry way, but that had only made his father laugh more.

Someday you will understand that these things are

the same, the old man had said. *Or you will be poor and forgotten.*

Thanasis liked to think that he would be neither, thank you.

Pavlos, ever attuned to the shifting sands of attention and admiration, waited until everyone was staring at him. He smiled broadly. He looked beside him, and took the hand of Saskia's ghost.

His Saskia's ghost, Thanasis thought.

And something inside him...detonated.

He had kept her hidden away from any and all prying eyes, his Saskia. He had protected her when she was his. He had kept her a secret from everyone who knew him, the paparazzi, the world. She had come to think that he was ashamed of her, but nothing could be further from the truth.

What he had never wanted was this. His corrosive father anywhere near her—

But he shook himself.

Saskia was dead. This woman was an imitation, not the real thing.

And still, he didn't like his father touching her. It crawled all over him like something sick.

"I have invited everyone here to celebrate with me," Pavlos boomed out, smiling fatuously in all directions. "I have asked this beautiful woman, my lovely and innocent Selwen, to marry me. Better yet, she has accepted."

He beamed at Saskia. Thanasis thought he might actually have died himself.

But Pavlos wasn't done. "And she has graciously accepted," he continued. "And who can say, perhaps she will be the making of me. Isn't that wonderful?"

The crowd burst into the expected applause. The band began to play something saccharine.

And Thanasis stared at the ghost of his lost mistress and vowed, then and there, that she would marry his degenerate of a father—apparition or no—over his dead body.

CHAPTER TWO

SELWEN SHOULD HAVE known that this night was going to be overwhelming. Over-the-top, outrageous, and excessive in all ways.

All of the things that Pavlos was that she had decided to accept, because surely he exemplified all of the things she had decided she wanted for this odd little life of hers. He was *exorbitant* and she was trying her best to aim for extravagance in every possible aspect of her life. She was saying *yes*.

To everything.

Ffion had demanded this of her before she died. And Selwen, who would have promised the older woman anything at all, anything she'd asked, had solemnly vowed that she would do her best to find it. No matter what it looked like.

Until the extravagance is me, Selwen had promised. It had become the little mantra she whispered to herself in moments of need. It was the engine that had gotten her out of Wales and into the shocking bright blue of Greece.

Still, nothing could have prepared her for the reality of this party tonight.

It had been one thing to spend time in the villa with

Pavlos alone. He was an odd man, she'd decided, given to long-winded speeches only partially in English and many broad gestures as if she was to look for hints to his personality in the furnishings. She wasn't certain that she understood what he was on about at any given time, but then, she didn't need to.

All of this was about Ffion. And the promise she had made the older woman, her best and only friend in the world. Ffion had lain there on her deathbed, clutching Selwen's hands in hers, and she had asked only one thing.

Extravagance.

And because she knew Selwen too well, and rightly expected that Selwen's idea of extravagance might default to an extra bit of beans on her toast one night, she had thoughtfully prepared a list. Then had raspily declared that Selwen was to do her very best to go down that list and do each and every thing on it.

At first, Selwen hadn't done anything of the sort. There had been the usual grim, tedious, grief-laden details of the death to handle first. Ffion had left Selwen everything, which still made her misty-eyed each time she thought about it. Ffion had told everyone that Selwen was her niece, up from London, and by the time she died, everyone had believed it.

Even Selwen forgot, from moment to moment, that Ffion *wasn't* actually a family member. But then, Selwen believed, on a deep emotional level, that finding Ffion had been fate, not an accident.

Or anyway, she'd come to think that it had been fated, her coming to know Ffion the way she had. The sweet old woman who had taken her in when she was literally a stranger on the street and who Selwen had taken care of in return when the time came, because neither of them had anyone else.

And, more importantly, because she had come to love Ffion as if they really were family. To Selwen, that was exactly what they were.

She'd carefully disposed of all of Ffion's things in accordance with her wishes. She'd sold the sweet old house in Pembrokeshire. And the ancient motorcar that had been sat in the shed for years. She'd given the money that Ffion had set aside to the various charities that she had stalwartly supported during her life.

And then she'd turned her attention to the *life list* the old woman had created for her unofficially adopted niece. It was a list aimed at forcing Selwen to live the grand life Ffion had fretted over, thinking it was how Selwen ought to have been living instead of caring for an old woman in her final years. No matter how many times Selwen had told her that there was nothing she would have preferred to do than care for Ffion, her friend wouldn't hear of it.

There is nothing extravagant or special about a terraced cottage, love, Ffion had said.

You are in it, Selwen had replied, every time.

But Ffion had furnished her list all the same, in her spidery cursive that made Selwen think of all the years her friend had seen. The demands were simple, really. Grow out her hair. Dress to look pretty, not to hide. Ride a train to Europe. Dance on a Greek island. Watch the sun come up with a man she was in love with, preferably from a well-tested bed.

They had laughed about that last one, but Ffion, who

had been widowed after many years of marriage to her beloved Alun, held firm.

Love is meant to be extravagant, she had said.

These were all things the two of them had discussed over the years they'd spent together as companions, usually when Ffion would read about some exotic foreign location in the paper and start making noises that Selwen should hare off and *find herself* there.

Once Ffion was gone, there was no more reason for Selwen to scoff, and no reason to stay in Wales anyway.

The hair had been easy enough. For as long as she could remember, Selwen had kept her hair short. It was the first thing she'd done after Ffion had found her. She'd woken up that next morning and cut it all off, and couldn't explain to her new friend why she'd done it. Then she'd kept it in a short cut, but as Ffion grew more and more ill, she hadn't bothered with her hair at all.

So by the time that Ffion died, it had already been mostly grown out. And by the time she'd finished handling the funeral and getting rid of the property and all the rest of it, it was good and long.

You would have loved this, she'd told her friend in her head when she'd actually taken her hair down from the twist she'd kept it in for at least the last year and had a proper look at it. *You always loved long hair.*

The dressing part had been easy, too. Selwen had always dressed herself with an eye toward practicality, that was all. Ffion liked to make up stories about the things Selwen wore because *she* had been quite stylish in her youth, but there was nothing mysterious about her choices. A life in blustery Wales, as quiet as it was damp, didn't lend itself to slinking about in whatever was fashionable these days. She preferred jeans and hooded sweatshirts and waterproof shoes.

Still, she did her duty to Ffion. Once she left Wales she took the Eurostar to Paris, which she decided was enough training about through Europe. In Paris, she bought herself the sort of impractical things that she knew her friend would have approved of, heartily. Then she'd done the truly fun part and had gone off to the Greek islands. She'd toured about through the crowded, famous places, then she'd started poking around the lesser-known destinations too. And she was certain that somewhere in her travels she would stumble across someone to fall in love with, because wasn't that what people did? They went off into Mediterranean climates, found themselves, and fell in love. Sunrises with said lovers were soon to follow.

But it hadn't gone that way.

Because even with her hair long and wearing lovely, completely impractical garments that caught male attention wherever she went, Selwen found herself entirely indifferent to men.

Precisely the same way she'd felt plodding about in ugly boots and her raincoat back in Pembrokeshire.

She could read lovely, spicy books about falling in love with men. She could watch admittedly dreadful movies starring terrible men who saved the day and won the heart of the heroine. Both of these enterprises could make her feel dreamy and a bit short of breath, in all the nicest ways.

But real men? She didn't really see the point.

Ffion had left Selwen a bit of money along with the rest. And while it certainly wouldn't last a lifetime, it allowed Selwen to enjoy the Greek islands. She went wherever the wind took her. She wandered where she pleased across the islands, soaking in the culture, the colors, the astonishing views. She sketched and painted, because she could hardly keep her brushes and pencils out of her hands.

And every night, wherever she was, she would dutifully present herself at one taverna or another.

She danced with men. She laughed. She ate good food, and she drank good wine and better *ouzo*, and she always went home alone. She had fun, but none of the men ever made any kind of impression on her.

Until Pavlos.

Now, standing in his overwhelmingly over-the-top villa that could probably sleep the whole island and then some, she tried—not for the first time—to figure out what it was about this man that she found intriguing.

She had never had the slightest urge to kiss him, which Ffion had always assured her was the very base level of what a woman should feel in the presence of a potential lover. Ffion, by her telling, had lived a wild and beautiful life with lovers in every port before she took one look at her Alun and settled down. She had known what she was talking about.

Passion is the entire purpose of life, she would pronounce grandly over tea. *I have tasted passion in its many flavors and I want the same for you.*

No matter how many times Selwen told her that she didn't think she was a passionate sort of person, Ffion would scoff.

There's no such thing as an un-passionate person,

she would say. *There's only a person who hasn't met their match.*

Selwen had tried rather diligently to convince herself that Pavlos was her passion, but she knew better. He was *intriguing,* was the thing. That was the word she kept coming back to when she tried to explain all this to the Ffion she carried about in her head.

There was something about him that made her… take notice. There was something about his features and how they worked together that almost made her feel as if she was haunted.

It had been that way from the start. She'd walked into the *taverna* here and had felt drawn to him, though he was the sort of man she usually avoided. Too loud. Too sure of himself. Too cold through the eyes.

But she'd found herself searching his face, like she was trying to find someone else there.

She couldn't make any sense of it. It was the strangest sensation, it only seemed to get worse the more time she spent with him, and she doubted very much that he was having a similar experience.

Really, it was hard to tell if Pavlos felt much about anything.

Selwen knew who he was. She hadn't recognized him, but she'd known his name when he'd given it to her. The night they'd met, she'd gone back to her hotel and had looked him up. She'd seen headlines upon headlines, all of them about his wealth and his womanizing, and she hadn't bothered to read further.

Intrigued or not, she expected him to irritate her. She hadn't spent any time with men as far as she knew, but Ffion had always commented on the fact that she'd always seemed to particularly avoid the men in the village who had reputations for putting it about.

But he hadn't been like any of them, lairy and red-faced with drink. He had taken walks with her. He had showed her his olive groves, which she had half expected to be euphemistic but had, in fact, been a grove of lovely olive trees. They had wandered together on this quiet island, far from the frenzy of a Santorini or Crete.

They had talked—or rather, *he* had talked—and she had gotten the vague impression of a man who felt his mortality pressing in on him and wanted something different from his last few years. She'd felt enormously sympathetic to that, having just witnessed Ffion move through that same, last period of life.

And when Pavlos had asked her to marry him, quite unexpectedly, he delivered a long and rambling speech that had led her to believe that he considered her... Religious, perhaps? Innocent, certainly.

Things she wanted to argue about, but didn't, since she couldn't remember having ever been near god or man and didn't particularly want to discuss that.

Will you accept me? Pavlos had asked, but not in the way of a man who was truly worried about her answer.

She had told him she needed to think about it. And she had, sitting in her narrow bed in that hotel in the village with nothing but sea outside her window. What she kept coming back to was that he didn't seem to want much from her. He had promised her an art studio. He had promised her a lifetime of all the art supplies she could ever want. He'd reminded her that he owned an art gallery or two, should she ever have work she wished to present.

And the thing about it was that Selwen had always been the practical one. Ffion had pretended to be practical, but at her heart, she was a dreamer. She was all about the *what if* and the imagination.

Selwen had loved that about her friend—but she couldn't spend the rest of her life dancing around on Greek islands. She couldn't go back to Wales, and not only because Ffion had forbidden it. But because she'd sold the house, and now that she'd experienced the Greek sunshine, she wasn't at all certain that she could tolerate the Welsh rain again.

And given that she was largely indifferent to all nonfictional men, she thought…why not?

Pavlos had always been kind to her. He did not speak of love, or passion, or anything that might have been alarming. Besides, he was quite old. And not in the greatest health, and no, she didn't think that was mercenary. It couldn't be, because he already had a will, and he'd told her that he would never change it. She would have to sign documents when they married, but since she didn't have an emotional investment in him, what did she care?

She could indulge the true passion of her life, her art.

And when she thought that, something seemed to shift inside her, like she was finally finding her way home. Like she was finally on the right path. Surely that was the kind of thing she ought to pay attention to.

Really, Pavlos felt like a happy, sunny place to land.

The only thing she had asked of him was that she be allowed to stay private. She didn't wish to go with him to all those grand balls where he was always photographed. She didn't want any part of his fame.

She wanted this. A Greek island where there was dancing and there was sunshine and where Ffion would have enjoyed herself tremendously. She wanted her art, quiet walks on the beach, and lazy wanders through Pavlos's estate, in and out of the olive groves.

A sweet little life to replace the sweet little life she'd lost.

Because sweet little lives were all she had. Her memory stopped where Ffion started, and Selwen had given up trying to push through that. She'd read loads of books on the topic and had come to the conclusion that whatever lurked behind that wall of her memory was something she didn't want to know.

So she was dedicated to keeping her life as sweet as possible.

Though that was difficult to remember now, surrounded by all these people with avarice in their gazes, and worse still than all the fluttery ones and the glittery ones and the giggling ones…was him.

She had seen him the moment he came in. There in that operatic archway, festooned with bougainvillea as if it was outside.

It was like her entire attention had been suddenly slammed straight to him, like a rope snapping taut.

She didn't know what it was about him. He…disturbed her.

He disturbed everyone, she'd seen in an instant. She saw the way people moved away from him. The way he cut a swath through this party, dressed all in black and with a certain menace on his face, like a memory.

Selwen felt something like dizzy, but then again, she'd allowed herself to drink a little too much of the bubbly stuff. This was supposed to be a celebration, after all.

Maybe she wasn't all that dizzy, because she had no trouble tracking him as he prowled across the floor, the guests who crowded her and Pavlos falling away from him like he was some kind of wild predator.

It took her a long moment to realize she was breathless. It was the strangest thing.

It was *him*.

He was entirely too tall. He wore a dark, obviously bespoke suit that clung to his body in ways that should have been illegal. His shoulders were wide, and every part of his torso was hard as it narrowed down to his hips. There was not an ounce of extra flesh on his frame, but that was only half of it.

It was more the way he moved.

He was sheer ruthlessness as he navigated his way through the crowd. She watched as whoever stepped up to talk to him fell away from him as if he'd struck them down with his gaze alone.

He was causing a commotion and it was clear he didn't care and wasn't trying.

When he moved closer, Selwen could see that his hair really was that black. His gaze was even blacker. He should have looked like a devil.

And she supposed he did, insofar as the devil was an angel fallen from grace.

Because this man terrified her. She could feel that terror inside her, like her own overheated blood. He was also the most beautiful man she'd ever seen.

She wanted to draw him. She *ached* to draw him. To capture, somehow, the powerful lines of his body, the power that seemed to emanate from him like a fact that no one dared deny, and the starkly sensual presentation of that face of his.

Selwen thought he would haunt her forever. She felt as if he already did.

All this, and he was looking at her with something like grief on that unbelievably perfect face of his, carved from stone and marble and yet very clearly made of flesh.

She had to look away from him then, because the announcement had been made. And Pavlos was standing beside her, accepting congratulations from his flock, none of whom looked as if they were actually all that happy for him.

They congratulated her, too, and she could see the sharp way they regarded her and was certain that if she didn't pay closer attention, she might just get a talon in the back. More reason to not have parties like this, she thought.

"How extraordinary," seethed a woman who she thought was his daughter, and who also seemed deadly. "To think of my father, marrying again after all this time. You do know, of course, that he treated his first wife shabbily. One mistress after the next, and never a care for her feelings."

"Thank you," Selwen murmured. "I'm sure we will be very happy."

And for a while, she was lost in all these poisonous exchanges. The snide comments, the sharp little barbs.

None of which felt particularly sweet, it had to be said, so she thought about her art instead.

She thought about that man's astonishing, addictive face, and how she could use a charcoal to best exemplify the way those lines of his jaw—

"We must dance!" Pavlos cried from beside her.

He drew her out into the middle of the floor and then there was dancing, for a while. This was better than verbal barbs, by a long shot. Dancing was lovely, as it was always possible to drift off in the music and ignore everything else around her—though that wasn't quite what happened. Not tonight. Not when, look though she might, Selwen couldn't seem to find that younger man anywhere in the watching crowd.

After the dancing was done, and women who very clearly wanted to tear her hair out cooed over the ring that Pavlos had put on her finger, Selwen stole away the first moment she could and left Pavlos to his minions.

It had gotten late. She had been too anxious—*excited,* she had told herself repeatedly, though it hadn't taken—to eat anything in the party. Her stomach grumbled as she moved through the maze that was this villa, winding her way around and around in what she thought was the right direction if she was headed to the kitchens.

But when she drew close, she realized her error. There was a party going on, after all. She was supposed to be the guest of honor, according to Pavlos, so she could hardly hide away in the kitchens and expect that none of his staff would rat her out.

She changed direction just in time, because she could hear footsteps approaching, and darted out the nearest door. Once outside, she breathed in deep as the soft Aegean air pressed in all around her.

It was cool tonight, but it felt marvelous against her skin after all that time in the ballroom. Too many people. Too much heat.

Selwen crossed her arms, wishing she'd thought to bring a wrap, but not enough to turn around and go find one. Instead, she followed the path that led away from the villa and out to the stairs carved into the hillside that led down to the beach. She could hear the sea. She could see the waves toss themselves against the sand and leave their lingering caresses on the way back.

She didn't think. She didn't glance behind her. She kicked off her notably impractical shoes and then she ran all the way to the bottom of the stairs. Then she crossed the beach, pulling up her dress to keep the hem safe, and stuck her feet in that gloriously warm sea, nothing at all like cold Watch House Bay.

All that before thinking to look around and see who else was there.

Because one moment she could have sworn she was alone with the moon and the waves.

And the next, when she turned, he was there.

The moonlight made him gleam, obsidian straight through, staring straight at her as if he wanted to eat her alive.

For a wild, wondrous, terrifying moment, she thought that she could think of nothing better than to sacrifice herself to this man's appetites—

What was *wrong* with her?

"What the hell are you doing?" he growled at her, and it felt, uncomfortably, as if he was reading her mind.

That same breathless, dizzy feeling surged through her.

"Yes," she managed to say, the same way she had all night. "Thank you. I'm sure we'll be very happy together. Is that what you want to hear?"

She could see his face too clearly, though the night pressed in all around. It was that moonlight pouring over him, making it impossible to look away, obsidian covered in silver. And so she saw the look that moved over his face.

It felt like fire when it echoed inside of her.

"What game is this?" he gritted out.

"It's not a game," she replied. Something in the way he looked at her, as if betrayed, made her want to shiver, though it felt more like exhilaration than anything else. "It's an engagement party."

He said a word that didn't make sense. *Saskia.*

And Selwen realized, then, that he had spoken to her in English though he was very clearly Greek. Maybe everybody knew that Pavlos Zacharias's new fiancée was English. Or spoke English, anyway. She couldn't really speak to her nationality. It said she was Welsh on her passport—or that she had been born there, anyway. She didn't like to think how Ffion had gone about getting her one of those, mostly by leaning on her long relationship with the officials in the little town, who Ffion had minded when they were children.

Best not to ask, her friend had said when she'd presented the passport. So she hadn't.

"Come out of the water," the man ordered her.

And the oddest thing was, she did.

Not only that, she *wanted* to obey him. She felt it

move all over her, molten hot and sweet, as if her whole body was shivering into a different level of awareness—

Though this made no sense.

Just as it made no sense that she could feel that shivering deep between her legs, like a heartbeat all its own.

She moved toward him because she couldn't seem to talk herself out of it. When she stood before him, her bare feet in the sand, she thought he would…*do* something. Grab her, maybe. *Say* something. Anything.

There was something almost exultant inside of her, as if she wanted all of the above. As if she just wanted him to—

But instead, he reached over and wrapped her hair around his fingers. He didn't tug on it as she half expected, instead, he lifted those fingers to his nose with the hair wrapped round and inhaled.

Selwen watched as his eyes went unfocused. She watched his nostrils flare. And she was close enough that she heard that low, growling noise he made.

She *felt* it in that pulsing, hot place between her legs.

And she was transfixed as he leaned closer and took another deep breath, as if he was trying to inhale her skin.

She really shouldn't have been allowing this. She didn't know what this was, but it clearly wasn't all right. She needed to say something.

But she didn't.

He took another breath. He made another growling noise.

Between her legs, that shivering pulse got deeper. Lusher, somehow.

"I really—" she began.

But his hand shot out, and wrapped itself around the line of her jaw and her cheek. He hissed in a breath, a lot like he felt that same wild spark that jumped in her, too.

A spark that too quickly began to blaze.

"How is this possible?" he whispered. "How can this be?"

She didn't know what he meant and she wasn't even sure he was speaking to her, but his hand seemed to fit there, against her face. It was like she was being electrocuted. That odd sensation poured through her, lighting her up until she felt as if she was being filled up from the inside out with too much sunshine to bear.

"Where have you been?" he gritted out, a stark demand. "Where the hell have you *been?*"

And then, impossibly, he bent his head to hers, and claimed her mouth with his.

Selwen had never been kissed. She couldn't remember it. Either way, she had to believe that the anodyne impression she had of what kissing was couldn't possibly be anything like this *thing* that he was doing.

This bold, brilliant, impossible storm between them.

She could feel everything that he was doing, the way he angled his mouth against hers, the side of his tongue, the press of his lips. He kissed her like he knew her, like he'd kissed her just like this a thousand times before.

He kissed her like she was his.

He kissed her and more astonishingly, she kissed him back, and when she felt his hands move down the length of her torso she leaned in closer to get more of that friction, that pressure.

Selwen thought she would do anything to keep feeling *just like this*.

She leaned in and his hand was beneath her dress. She felt that lick of hard heat along her thigh and her body was doing things all on its own, leaning back, arching into him, like she was welcoming him home. Then his hand was between her legs, and still he was kissing her and kissing her, and she was making noises she had never heard before, not from her—

"Saskia," he said, his mouth against hers, "damn you, I thought you were dead."

And when the storm broke over his hard hand and the way she clamped down to keep it where it was, she broke with it.

CHAPTER THREE

THANASIS FELT THAT crash and tug inside of him, and he couldn't tell if it was the sound of the sea against the sand, or simply his reaction to the feel of her clenching tight on his fingers. Or the quivering that took over her whole body and left her sighing.

She made that noise he knew better than he knew his own name, slightly high-pitched and in the back of her throat. There was a time he had lived for that sound—that incontrovertible evidence that she came apart in his hands so easily.

That together they were fire and magic, no matter what might happen in the world outside the space they kept together.

He had no idea how he had lived this long without it. Without *her*.

What Thanasis knew—the way he also knew his heart pumped, his lungs breathed, and his bones held him upright—was that he had no intention of ever doing so again.

Whatever this situation was, and he did not pretend to understand it, there was no possibility that he would end up without her again. She was alive.

Saskia was *alive* and that was the beginning and end of everything that mattered to him.

Now it was simply a matter of sorting out the details. And what had happened over the last five years.

Not to mention, the fact she seemed to think she was marrying his father.

But first there was the sweet weight of her, limp in his arms. He could hear her breath coming in fast. He stroked her hair, still not entirely sure he wasn't dreaming, which would mean he might wake at any moment. He didn't think, this time, that he could bear it.

She straightened then, pushing herself upright while he took his time disengaging from her. When he stood, he found her eyes on him. And he could have sworn there was something very nearly accusatory there in those steeped tea depths, though he found he was not in the least apologetic.

He watched her swallow, hard. And there were many things he could have said. There were conversations to be had and he was fairly certain they wouldn't be pleasant.

But this was. He decided to stay with *this*, then. Thanasis lifted his hand and without shifting his gaze from hers, he licked his fingers clean.

And had the distinct pleasure of watching her react to that. Her cheeks flooded with a bright red flush. Her lovely eyes went wide and something like stunned.

The heat between them seemed to *hum*.

It reminded him of when he'd first met her, in those early days when she was still so innocent and he had still been able to shock her. It reminded him of the pleasure he'd taken in that, in her, in the way she gave herself to him simply because she'd loved him.

Oh, how she'd loved him, in such a fast rush of utter certainty that he'd felt duty-bound to warn her against it. He'd been the worldly, sophisticated one. He'd tried to protect her from herself—

I don't need your help, thank you, she'd told him, sitting astride his lap while the mercurial English sun teased its way through the windows of their flat in Chelsea. *I will love you no matter how terribly you treat me, as important men of the world are wont to do.*

She had been teasing him, then. She had laughed, and then she'd kissed him.

He remembered that too well because she hadn't been laughing two years later. She hadn't been laughing at all that last night.

But he forgot about that, because her taste was flooding through him again. Tart and sweet, it was quintessentially Saskia, and it removed any lingering doubts he might have had about who she was.

This was *her.* This was *his Saskia,* at last.

The taste of her made that abundantly clear. It also made him so hard it actually hurt, but he ignored that.

This was the woman he had lost five years ago. This was the woman he had believed he would never see again. He could taste her. He could smell her. He could touch her, and he had.

"Saskia," he said urgently, "you must tell me what this is all about. What happened to you? Where were you going on that train and why have you hidden yourself away all these years?"

Her eyes widened even further. The flush in her

cheeks faded as she blinked, then she shook her head as if she was trying to clear it. He thought she looked a bit pale, suddenly. "I have no idea what you're talking about."

"Saskia—"

"Stop calling me that." Her voice sounded strangled, unwell and uneasy. She stepped back and looked around wildly, as if she expected to find attackers on all sides.

It took him too long to understand that her reaction meant that she felt *he* was an attacker, too.

He took a step back himself.

"My name is Selwen," she told him, very carefully, as if the name itself was made of glass. "I don't know who you are. I think you have me confused with someone else."

He might have thought so earlier. He had *hoped so* earlier, even.

But he had hoped for this more, and for much, much longer.

"I am Thanasis Zacharias," he told her, the way he had once before, long ago. There in an echoing chamber of the Tate where modern art he could not pretend to understand cavorted about shapelessly on the walls all around them, somehow making her eyes seem brighter. He couldn't recall what the exhibit had been or what he'd been meant to take from the viewing of it. Because she had been there and that had been that. "You know me, no matter what you call yourself these days."

"Zacharias?" she echoed. "But that's…?"

"Pavlos is my father," Thanasis growled. "And you must know you cannot marry him."

"I'm not who you think I am!" She threw that at him, her voice close to a scream, and then she ran.

And almost everything in him roared at him to chase her, to keep her with him, to never let her out of his sight again—

But there was another part. The part that had seen the confusion on her face and something like fear in her eyes.

And this was the woman he loved. This was the woman who he had thought for five years had died thinking he was ashamed of her. That he didn't truly love her in return.

He could not also be the man who scared her. He could not live with that version of himself.

And so Thanasis made himself stand still in the moonlight. And he forbade himself from turning around to see what became of her.

Then again, he didn't need to look. He knew.

It was as if he could see her through someone else's eyes. As if she was once again a part of him the way she'd been back then.

Whatever it was, he knew that she ran up the stairs, scrabbled for the shoes he'd watched her kick off, and then stopped. He knew—and he was sure that he knew it, that it wasn't merely another a wish—that she turned back and looked at him, still breathing too heavily. Still, he was certain, filled with the clamor inside her body thanks to his mouth and his fingers.

He could feel his spine prickle, and the urge to look was almost too much—

But he didn't.

Instead, Thanasis waited on the beach as the moon

took a leisurely turn across the heavens. He waited there, letting his mind do what it did best. He let it go running down pathways, making new connections, trying to figure out how his adored and cherished mistress had turned into a woman with a different name, here on an island he avoided, looking at him as if they'd never met before.

He didn't know how long he stood there, but eventually he'd had enough of brooding at the sea. Thanasis stripped off his clothes and waded in, letting the Aegean perform its magic all over him. Letting the water make him new again.

Letting the salt and the tide do what it needed to do so he was ready to stop playing with ghosts, so he could figure out how to remind his Saskia who she really was.

He swam and swam, let the current play with him, and found himself deeply grateful that he'd learned how to swim off this very same shore. He was not afraid of the currents or the waves, and besides, there was always all the blazing light from his father's villa there to beckon him back to dry land.

When he'd been a young boy, he'd swum out too far and there had been no one to watch him, much less save him. His father had been with one of his mistresses. His mother had been performing her furious piety in the local church.

He had choked and flailed. But he had survived.

Some might have stayed away from the water after that.

Thanasis had always been made of sterner stuff. He'd made himself swim every day, refusing to fear the water that was everywhere on an island like this. Refusing to fear anything, except the one thing in his life that he couldn't change.

The one person who could always be counted upon to do his worst, deliberately.

It occurred to Thanasis then that this was something his father would absolutely do, deliberately. Hunt down his own son's mistress, secrete her away for the express purpose of causing pain, and then marry her. Simply because he could.

But that didn't explain the memory issue.

He floated on his back with the moon up high, and glared at the stars as if they might give him some clarity. When the truth was, he knew better. They had never done a damned thing but shine.

Thanasis thought through every possibility, but it all came back to the same thing.

He was tempted to think that she was only pretending she didn't know him, but he couldn't really make himself believe that. Saskia was no actress. No liar. He'd seen genuine emotion on her face. He had to believe she truly didn't know who he was, however impossible he found that.

Once she remembered him, he had no doubt, he would have no need to convince her to leave his father. She would do it herself. With bells on.

That was who she was.

So what he had to do was figure out how to introduce her to herself, before it was too late.

The next morning, Thanasis tended to business matters abroad and then, when afternoon threatened, he went and found his father.

On the rare occasions he came to the villa, Thanasis

stayed in one of the cottages set apart from the main house. He enjoyed the walk, and the privacy, and there was something in him that no number of years in gray and rainy London could repress. That something that loved without reservation the brightness of a Greek day. The scent of sweet flowers on the breeze, and the silvery olive leaves as they took in the sun.

And, always, that gleaming sea that waited in the distance no matter where he looked. That wild Aegean blue, forever *just there, just* out of reach.

As he walked, he could pretend that there was nothing to worry about but this. The weight of a summer afternoon. The songs of the birds in the trees. The endless blue sky above and the whitewashed walls of all the buildings that seem to beckon the blue closer, then bring it deeper.

But soon enough, all he could see was the sprawl of his father's pet project. The original villa that had stood on the site dated back to a time when the Zachariases were little more than goat herders. It was Thanasis's great-grandfather who had started the business and had renovated the cottage that had always stood here to better reflect his new station in life.

It had been his grandfather who had made the villa a showpiece in its time, a restrained bit of Greek beauty.

And then had come Pavlos who had decided that he could command architecture the way he did his minions. He had thrown up a wing here and a bristling collection of roofs and structures there, connecting them all by breezeways and archways so that it all resembled balled-up pieces of discarded paper.

Though not in any sort of Frank Gehry sense.

The place was, truly, a vulgarity.

Though today Thanasis found that he felt more sanguine about the place than he normally did. He had detested living here, that was true. His childhood had not been a happy one, and while he knew it was not the house to blame for that, the house was where most of his childhood had occurred.

It was where he'd come to understand exactly who his father was.

But today all he could think about was the resurrection of his beautiful Saskia, and so he didn't have it in him to condemn the massive display of more wealth than taste outright.

It was possible, he allowed as he drew closer, that there was a certain charm to it all. It was so over-the-top, so outrageous, that there was nothing to do but surrender to it. That was why he'd hated it all his life, perhaps.

He found he minded it less, today.

Inside, the staff was still sorting out the mess from last night. Thanasis picked his way through the front hall and made his way deep into the center of the sprawling building, where, if he knew his father, Pavlos would be nursing a tender head in his personal spa.

And sure enough, that was where the old man was. He was stretched out on a massage table next to his private pool, enjoying the ministrations of a masseuse who looked far prettier than she did physically capable, which only made Thanasis grit his teeth.

It had always been this way. His father did not consider women his weakness, but his right. This take of his had been the bane of his mother's existence, Thanasis knew too well.

For this and a hundred other reasons, he could not allow the same fate to befall his Saskia.

His father looked up and smiled, smugly, when he saw Thanasis standing there. "I thought you ran off before dawn, as usual. Didn't you once promise me that the sun would never fall upon your face on this island again?"

"I think you have me confused with one of your other children," Thanasis said calmly. "One of the more theatrical ones, I would wager."

Pavlos waved his lovely masseuse away and then sat up, sparing no apparent thought for the sheet that had barely covered him. He stood, stretched luxuriously, and then took his time settling his waiting robe back over his shoulders and belting it around his waist.

He had greeted company in precisely this way whenever possible, as Thanasis recalled. Especially if they had been there to see his mother and, preferably, knew her through the church.

The old man liked nothing more than making everyone around him uncomfortable.

Thanasis, obviously, refused to give his father the satisfaction of seeing any kind of reaction. What he did instead was wait there, one brow raised in vague distaste, until his father finished peacocking about and sat down in a chair beneath an overwhelmingly bright canopy of bougainvillea.

Pavlos lifted a hand and servants rushed from inside the house to present him with a tray of drinks and food, all calculated to settle his stomach and ease the pressure in his head.

Thanasis only took a seat when his father made a

grand production of waving him into the one beside his, after acting as if he didn't realize that Thanasis intended to stay.

"To what do I owe the pleasure of this unusual, extended visit?" the old man asked as he settled back in his chair, then began to sample the food before him. With a certain laziness that would have befit a king.

"I decided to stay a while," Thanasis said mildly. "It's been too long."

Pavlos gazed at him, challenge in his dark eyes. "You hate it here."

Thanasis gazed back, impassively. "There are things I dislike about the place, certainly. I think you'll find that most people have complicated feelings regarding their childhood home. I presume you must also, or you wouldn't keep changing the shape of it."

He knew that he'd struck a nerve when the old man sniffed, and took his time with his *dolmades*.

"And what do you think of my bride-to-be?" Pavlos asked. He smiled. "Soon enough your new stepmother?"

Thanasis thought too many things to name. It was like a wretched kaleidoscope winching this way and that in his head, clogging his throat, and making everything in him tense up immediately.

But he made himself smile. "She's not really your type, is she?"

"Do I have a type?" Pavlos sniffed again, though this time he frowned at his son, not his tray of food. "I am merely a slave to beauty, my boy. It is a curse."

"Most of your paramours are already famous in their own right," Thanasis said, almost offhandedly. As if he was reading an article about his father. He knew that it was important that he never seem *too* interested in anything. It only fueled the old man's vindictiveness. "Marissa's mother is still a model. Telemachus's mother was an actress of some renown."

Pavlos laughed, and not nicely. "That is one word for what she did, hopping from one yacht to another in the unforgiving glare of the Côte d'Azur."

Thanasis ignored that. Even if it were true, which he was not certain it could be, that suggested only that his father was the sort of man who took part in the kind of squalid parties that Thanasis had assiduously avoided his whole life. Because the only way to enjoy such events, or pastimes, was to forget that the women there were *people*.

That had never been a possibility for him.

"This choice of yours seems different, that's all," he said, with a careless shrug.

The old man looked at him for a dark, brooding sort of moment, then returned his attention to a bit of hair of the dog. He threw back a small measure of *ouzo,* then followed it with a few plump grapes.

"I am not the young man I once was," Pavlos pronounced after a moment. And it was tempting to imagine that he could hear something like humanity in his father's voice in that...but Thanasis had fallen for such tricks before. "Perhaps I would like a bit of sweetness and ease as my time here dwindles."

"I'm surprised to hear that." When Pavlos's thick brows shot up, Thanasis shrugged. "I have never heard you entertain the faintest thought that you could be anything but immortal."

Pavlos shook his head. "You don't think much of me. Most of the time, I don't care. You must dance to my tune no matter what you think, and that entertains me. But at the end of the day, Thanasis, every man must die alone." He eyed his eldest son. "Even me."

He stared at Thanasis as if he expected an argument. But when Thanasis only regarded him in the same deliberately impassive way, he grunted. "It is no secret to you, of all people, that marriage did not suit me. I did it because it was expected and, no matter what else I might have done, I always did what was necessary to honor the Zacharias name."

Thanasis couldn't help the laugh of disbelief that came out of him, then. "Did you? When was this, exactly?"

His father sneered at him, and the sad part was that Thanasis found that more recognizable than whatever the rest of this was. This…unburdening of a twisted soul, unsolicited and unwanted though it was.

"You think your mother is some kind of holy creature," Pavlos growled at him. "But I set her free almost immediately. *She* chose to stay. *She* wanted to suffer. Remember that the next time you think to accuse me of anything. Martyrs tend to light their own fires, Thanasis. How better to burn?"

Any other time, Thanasis might have walked off at that, because he would not tolerate his father's take on his mother. Not after the way she had been treated here.

But there was Saskia to consider now. There was more at stake here than his mother's memory, and in any case, he had the sneaking, unwelcome suspicion that his father was not entirely wrong.

"You, of course," he said, and he forced himself to sound lazy and unbothered, "never threw any accelerant on that fire, I suppose. It simply burned and burned of its own volition. Nothing to do with you at all."

Pavlos inclined his head, giving him the point. "I never pretended to be a good man. And I don't really care what you think of me. But I will tell you this. That girl makes me imagine that I could be a different man altogether. And at my age, after my life? That is a gift."

Thanasis studied at his father for a long while.

Oddly enough, he felt something like sympathy for this version of the old man, when he had never felt anything like it before. But that was Saskia. That was what she did. He knew exactly what it was like to look at her, to fall into those dark, clever eyes of hers, and imagine himself redeemed.

He wasn't at all surprised that this was not a unique experience, given only to him. He supposed something in him would grieve that, later.

But here, sitting in the shade with the mean old man he had been so determined to hide Saskia from five years ago, he couldn't help but feel something else instead. Some measure of distant regret, almost, that he could not allow his father to experiment with that redemption. That he could not countenance the marriage between Saskia, no matter who she thought she was, and this man who could never, ever, appreciate her.

Hadn't he spent the two years he had with Saskia going out of his way to keep her as far away from the reach of his family as it was possible to get? Wasn't that why she'd left him that night?

She had imagined that he was embarrassed by her.

When the opposite was true. He was embarrassed by all of this. By this mess he came from and carried with him.

And now, all he felt was a sadness mixed with determination, because he could not allow this wedding to take place.

He could not permit his father to get any closer to Saskia than he already had—and Thanasis discovered that he could not allow himself to think about that closeness, not now. Perhaps not ever.

Perhaps that was something to simply decide, here and now, he would never consider too closely. For his own sanity.

His father was not, really, the man he wanted to be with Saskia. Just as Saskia was not the woman she thought she was, with no memory of her actual life.

Thanasis was the only one who knew the truth. About both of them.

And the only way he could think to make certain this abomination never happened was to remind her of that truth. To find a way, somehow, for her to remember what she really felt. And who she really was.

So what he did was smile at his father, until the old man narrowed his eyes with suspicion.

"I think I'll stay a while," Thanasis said, and it wasn't a question, or request. It was a statement of intent. He could see that his father knew it. "It's been far too long since I enjoyed the particular pleasures of the family nest, don't you think?"

Pavlos sneered at him again. "Careful, boy. You wouldn't want to wear out your welcome in this nest of vipers."

"How could I?" Thanasis replied. He lifted a hand. "After all, all of this will be mine someday. Isn't that your plan? To bludgeon me with all of this once you're gone?"

He smiled wider when his father grunted and said, "I hope it is a killing blow, you arrogant—"

Thanasis cut him off, pleased that he'd provoked him into temper. It meant he'd won, and he could tell the old man knew it.

"Congratulations, *Patéras,*" he said smoothly. "How very mythical of you. Like Kronos himself. I believe that is a certain kind of immortality, after all."

CHAPTER FOUR

Selwen spent the next two days hiding out in her room. She told the staff she had a migraine, and they left her to it. They left trays of food by her door and took them away again without bothering her when she left them largely untouched. She kept the shades shut tight and all the lights out. She lay in her bed, watched the ceiling fan rotate again and again, and asked herself what in the name of God she'd been thinking.

She went over every single detail of every moment that she'd spent in the presence of the overwhelming, disturbing Thanasis in forensic detail—over and over again—but she still couldn't explain to her own satisfaction how she'd allowed…any of *that* to happen. She had danced with too many men to count in too many *tavernas* to name. She had laughingly brushed off their advances, such as they were, and gone on her merry way. It hadn't even required thought.

And yet she had kissed that man in the moonlight as if she been starving for the taste of him all her life.

She could still feel that kiss all over her, and worse, like some kind of muscle-deep memory within.

Just as she could feel those hard, blunt fingers deep inside her, claiming her and shattering her with a certain confident insistence that made her breathless to recall. More disconcerting by far, she could remember the way she'd clamped his hand between her thighs and ridden him as if that was the only possible response she could have given.

As if she'd done the same thing a thousand times before. As if her body knew him, and wanted him, and was desperate to welcome him.

The implications of that…frightened her.

Or rather, overwhelmed her, because she didn't want to think through those implications. She didn't want to think about all the things her responses could mean. Or the way he'd spoken to her. Or that disconcerting way he looked at her, as if he was waiting for her to recognize him.

Selwen preferred that her life remain blank before Ffion. She had grown used to it. She *liked* it that way.

On the third day, she snuck out of her room in the early morning. Because she thought it was high time she moved her body a little bit, lest she become welded to the bed. She might not have *actually* had a migraine, but that wasn't to say she felt good. Because she didn't.

That terrible feeling, something like anxiety and vulnerability mixed through with shame, sat on her hard.

She walked down to the beach again in the sweet morning light. Once she walked down the steps, the breeze playing with her hair and tugging at her clothes, she frowned at the gleaming white sand as if it had personally betrayed her. Then she blew out a breath—wishing she could blow away her memories of the other night as easily—stuck her hands in her pockets, and walked along the shore with no particular aim or direction as she tried to come to terms with this terrible thing she'd done.

Because it was terrible, wasn't it? On the very night that her engagement to one man had been announced she had been out in the darkness, losing herself in the arms of another.

Not just any other man, for that matter. *His son.*

"It's like you're starring in your very own soap opera," she muttered to herself as she walked, because that was what she would have said to Ffion if she'd been here. Ffion, who had always maintained a deep attachment to her nightly soaps, would have been pleased with any extravagance but would have taken a dim view of any melodramatic behavior in her adopted niece.

Life is not the telly, she'd liked to say.

And she had strongly discouraged any telly-like behavior in her daily life.

The notion that she'd let Ffion down, even in death, made Selwen want to sob. Her eyes watered and she wiped at them furiously, because surely she didn't deserve to cry when nothing had happened to her. She'd participated all on her own. That was the real problem.

That was what she was going to have to sit with.

She walked and walked, and only when she could no longer see the big villa on the hill from the waterline did she turn back around. She cut inland then, up and over a different set of stairs cut into the bluff. On the other side she found herself on what passed for a road on this island, an old dirt track better suited for carts and goats.

Now as she walked she could feel the sea all around, but could only glimpse it here and there, between the trees. She knew she was back on Pavlos's estate when she began to see the outbuildings and little cottages, scattered here and there. Then the villa once more, taking over the horizon as she moved toward it.

She picked up her pace, happy that the walk had done its work and was making her feel a bit more like herself again—

But then she stopped dead.

Because there on the porch of the cottage directly before her, he was there.

Thanasis.

His name danced inside her like the breeze. Like a song.

She told herself it was a warning.

Selwen had the near-overwhelming urge to run. The same way she'd done that night. She could feel the adrenaline flood through her and she almost turned and set off, but something stopped her.

This was Pavlos's son. His *son,* damn it. She couldn't avoid him forever.

So instead of running, she squared her shoulders and marched straight toward him, instead.

She kept going until she reached the edge of his porch and then stopped there. Then glared at him as he sat there and did nothing but…*look* at her.

There was nothing to do but return the favor.

The moonlight, it turned out, had told no lies about this man.

Today he was dressed more casually. Still in black, she noticed, and she approved because *she* certainly felt like some level of mourning was called for. This morning it was a black T-shirt over a pair of casual trousers in the same onyx shade. He was not wearing shoes. He looked wildly, impossibly Greek, all that black hair and those impossibly dark eyes.

And he still looked at her in that same hot, insolent manner.

He was a fallen angel. There was no doubt about it. Selwen could think of no other explanation for how compelling he was, how breathtaking, when she knew exactly how dangerous he really was.

In the sunshine, the shocking beauty of his features was even more unpalatable than she'd recalled in the dark of her bedchamber. It was like her eyes rejected what she was seeing, out here in all this tumbling sunshine, because it didn't make sense. It shouldn't have been possible. How could he be very nearly *pretty,* yet so ruthlessly masculine that she could feel the adrenaline inside her become a long, slow shiver. And then that shiver wound its way down between her legs, there where she stood before him, and bloomed—insistently—into a soft yet pressing heat.

"You owe me an apology," she told him, because she was afraid that if she didn't speak, she would simply...melt.

"I cannot imagine for what."

He did not sound apologetic. He was lounging there in a chair, a laptop closed beside him on a small table. She felt unwieldy and strange in her own body and so made a small production of looking behind her, like she thought he must be staring at someone else.

But it wasn't helpful. When she turned back, Thanasis merely lifted a dark brow.

And she now understood that he had seen her coming

from a long way off. Something about that made that shivering heat inside her glow all the brighter.

"I decided not to tell your father what you did," she said, though she had actually come to no such conclusion. She didn't even know where those words came from. They simply exited her mouth without warning and then she was standing there, arms crossed and chin tilted up—belligerently, she could feel it—as she regarded this man before her.

Her beautiful nemesis.

"What makes you think that I didn't tell him myself?" he replied, almost carelessly.

All of Selwen's breath left her, as if he'd punched her, hard, in the stomach. She heard it go out of her in a rush, and the world spun a little, and then he was moving. He rose from his seat with an unnerving display of speed and grace and she didn't know what he meant to do—

But she didn't resist as he guided her up and onto his porch with him, then sat her down in the chair facing his.

When she could breathe again, Selwen found herself noticeably profoundly disappointed that guiding her to a seat was all he'd done.

And didn't that tell her harsh truths about herself she didn't wish to know?

"I didn't tell him anything," Thanasis told her after another moment—long or short, she couldn't tell, because she was lost in that dark gaze. And now his voice seemed to match. "I only told him that I intended to stay here a while. And I do, Saskia. You and I have some history to work out."

"That's where you're wrong." When his eyes flashed, she thought he might say something else, so she hurried on. "I don't have any history. That's the thing. There's nothing to talk about."

Thanasis regarded her for a long moment. She had the same feeling she'd had in the grand hall the other night, and then again on the beach. It was the disconcerting notion that he could see straight through her, when she couldn't even see into herself. It was more than simply disconcerting. It made her skin feel like it no longer fit. It made her want to jump to her feet. Explode.

Run.

"I can see that you don't remember me," he said, in a voice that was too low. Too even. Selwen got the distinct impression that the words cost him. But she didn't want to think about the possibility that this was hard for *him*.

It made something inside her turn over, uncomfortably.

"You're right," she said quietly, and not quite as evenly. "I don't."

But that wasn't the truth. Not precisely. She didn't remember him, that was true. But she had spent the past two days lying in her bed in the gloom of the closed shades, staring at her ceiling and wondering if that thing she'd recognized in Pavlos from the start… was Thanasis.

Every time she'd thought such a thing she'd backed away from it, and quickly, because it seemed to settle in her so strangely. It had made her feel wired and odd and like she might, at any moment, break into pieces.

The trouble was, she'd been waiting for *someone* to

recognize her for years. She and Ffion had talked about the possibility of this, again and again, from the start.

The past has a way of turning up, this I promise you, her old friend had said. *Sooner or later, you must expect that someone will know something about you, whether you can remember it or not.*

Maybe I don't want to remember, Selwen had said.

Ffion had nodded. *Then enjoy the stories you hear about a stranger, let them entertain you, and move on. This is how I treat stories from my youth anyway, and I imagine I could remember, if I fancied mucking about in all that ancient history.*

Ffion had possessed the gift of always managing to make things better, even if nothing really *was* better.

In the early days, Selwen had been on guard for any stray hint that someone might know something about her that she didn't. She'd been on guard, even in Ffion's tiny, picturesque village. She had been ready for people to come leaping out of the shops, or to stop her on the streets. But it had never happened.

She'd begun to think it never would.

And as tempting as it was to simply tell Thanasis that he was mad, that he didn't know her, that she couldn't be the *Saskia* he kept mentioning, she had to face a few unpleasant facts that she'd been avoiding as she lay about in that bedroom. Out here with all the wild Greek sunshine dancing between them and his dark gaze on her like he was still lost somewhere in that kiss, there was no hiding from it.

She could, in fact, be his Saskia, whoever that was. She could be anyone.

Selwen didn't *know,* was the thing.

Another problem was that while she found Thanasis overwhelming in every regard, what she didn't think—much as she'd like to—was that he was particularly mad. No matter what Pavlos's other children had tried to insinuate about him. What they always came back to was that Thanasis was the only one among them who was, in almost every regard, entirely his own man.

Not to mention, apparently, a spectacularly successful businessman in his own right. Even Pavlos had said so on the rare occasions he mentioned Thanasis, preferring—always—to focus on what was directly before him.

What Thanasis was or wasn't was one thing. She could research the man if she liked. But what Selwen couldn't deny was the fact that, however odd it was to her, he was the only man in the last five years that she'd ever had any kind of real reaction to.

Whatever that might mean, she certainly couldn't investigate it without talking to the man himself. Or without finding out what it was he thought he knew about her.

"Why don't you tell me about this Saskia of yours," she said, when it seemed that he was prepared to sit there and gaze at her forever. "You said you thought she was dead. Why?"

The sunlight was just as bright. The calls of the sea birds, wheeling about in the distance, was as plaintive and lovely as before. But there on the porch, with climbing vines winding their way around the posts that held up the roof and the flowers bright and happy, it was as if a storm cloud rolled in.

Selwen had to repress the urge to shiver.

Thanasis settled back in his chair and regarded her with that fathomless black gaze of his. She felt a different sort of shiver creep over her as she remembered all the little scraps of things she'd heard Pavlos and his various children say about Thanasis. They didn't like him, that was clear. Or perhaps they wished that he liked them—it was hard to say. She had gotten the impression that he was some sort of demon, out there ruining lives but doing it in such a way that he fooled everyone into imagining him a great power.

The implication had always been that he was not. That it was all smoke and mirrors.

But she could see, now, that the truth was he was all of that and more. He wasn't anything like his siblings. She had met them all during this little whirlwind she was swept up in. They frolicked in and out of the villa, vying for Pavlos's attention, positive or negative. They didn't care much for Selwen, but then, they also didn't care much for each other. They all had different mothers, they all had inflated senses of their own importance, and they were more than happy to cause trouble. They did so, often.

And meanwhile, despite all their carrying on about Thanasis, it was obvious at a glance—it had been obvious from across the hall last night—that he was nothing like them. That he did not gossip and flutter, nor flaunt himself about, nor cause whatever trouble he could.

It was obvious now, as he looked at her as if he could see deep inside her. As if his gaze was doing the same work his fingers had, finding their way deep within her, tearing her apart, making her cry out to the sky above—

She had to lift her fingers to her own mouth to make certain that her lips were shut tight. That her mouth wasn't wide open.

And she couldn't shake the impression that he knew exactly what she was doing. While she was doing it.

"I met *this Saskia of mine,* as you put it, in an art museum in London," he said, and once again she had the sense that he was being very, very careful. That he had chosen his words with precision.

"Do you spend a lot of your free time swanning about art installations?" she asked, a bit tartly, because she couldn't imagine it. This dark, broodingly powerful presence, prowling into whitewashed rooms empty of anything but a few canvases? It would be like welcoming a storm cloud into the middle of a priceless art collection. It would be unthinkable.

"I had a business meeting in the area." And there was a certain gleam in that dark gaze of his that suggested he knew exactly what she was thinking. "I would not, as it happens, consider myself a great patron of the arts, but then, I also am not given to *swanning* anywhere. And I'm not certain that blobs of paint on a canvas convinced me otherwise. But you were there."

"*She* was there," Selwen corrected him, because that seemed of paramount importance. She had to make some distinction between who she was and whoever this Saskia was to him. Even if it turned out they were the same person, they weren't. They couldn't be, because she couldn't remember him, or Saskia, or anything about an art museum in London.

She felt her own nails prick her palms, because she needed to hold on to *her.* Selwen. Ffion's niece. A proper Welsh girl who cared for her aunt and kept herself to herself.

Nothing on earth could get her to surrender that girl, especially to a man like this. *Nothing.*

"There was something about her," Thanasis said then, with only the faintest inflection on *her*. So faint that, really, Selwen shouldn't have felt it all over her, like the heat of his body. "It wasn't simply that she was pretty. Though she was. She was staring up at a huge canvas and she looked almost reverent, and I asked her what on earth she saw in it." His lips curved, then, and there was something almost wry about it. And Selwen had the strangest notion that if she tried, she could almost reach out and touch the memory—but she didn't want to reach out. She clenched her fists tighter. "So she told me her thoughts and when I expressed my skepticism, she laughed, and I will tell you this."

He didn't lean forward. He didn't really seem to move at all, and yet suddenly it was as if he took over the whole of the Greek sky painted so bright and blue behind him. As if there was nothing left in the sky above or the sea all around but him and the way he was looking at her.

God help her, the way he was looking at her. He waited for her gaze to lock to his. "The world stopped. And when it started again, I was lost."

Selwen's heart was pounding so hard it made her worry it might break free. "I don't know what that means."

She didn't know if he could hear that she was scared. Or anxious. Or whatever it was, this carbonated thing inside her that kept bubbling and bubbling, but if he noticed, he didn't show it. "It means I asked her to let me take her out to dinner. She refused. But the next day, she met me for coffee and a walk through Borough Market. It was teeming with people. Perfectly safe."

"Because she was afraid of you?"

"Because she wasn't. But she thought she had better play it safe, all the same." He smiled again in that same way, and again, it was as if she could see his memory shimmering in the corners of her eyes. She didn't dare look.

"I was captivated," Thanasis said, though she thought he paused before that last word. As if he needed to be careful with it. "It took very little time for me to realize that I wanted her all to myself. And I'm a busy man." He looked down, and something almost self-deprecating moved over his face. "I do not say that with any false confidence or as a bid to convince you of my importance. I run a major corporation. It is a multinational concern and a large bulk of my time is spent handling the fires my father sets, making certain to put them all out. I have to attend business meetings all over the world, all the time. I wanted to make certain that I could see her in whatever free time I had."

Selwen couldn't breathe. His eyes were much too dark for that, and oh, the way he was watching her as he told these things. As if they were intimate. As if *this* was intimate, this conversation in the open air of a pretty morning.

"I asked her to be my mistress," Thanasis said. He inclined his head slightly. "And she agreed."

Her mouth was dry. Selwen licked her lips and then regretted it when his gaze tracked the movement. Or maybe, she amended, that was not quite *regret* she felt. "What does that mean? What an archaic word."

"How funny," Thanasis murmured, that gleam in his gaze seeming to move inside her, too. "That's what she said."

Selwen didn't like that. It made something seem to yawn open in the pit of her stomach. "When I think about *mistresses* I think about smutty historical novels where dukes pranced about, keeping their mistresses in London houses and their proper wives in the countryside."

"I am not a duke," Thanasis replied, mildly enough, though there was nothing mild about the way he was studying her. "I moved her into a flat in London. Not a house. If the distinction matters."

"Your flat?"

"Not my flat, no." Something in his gaze shifted. "I wanted to keep her far apart from the rest of my life. And yes, before you ask, this eventually became a source of tension."

Selwen was finding it difficult to breathe. It was like there was a band of something inflexible wound tight around her chest, and it kept cutting deeper into her. She thought it might cut her in half. "I don't understand any of this. Why couldn't you simply date her like a normal person? Why not simply have a girlfriend? And what was her life, that she could simply... become a kept woman?"

"She was a student. She was doing an art history master's program. She had graduated with distinction from her undergraduate program and spent the time that I wasn't with her studying. And as far as I know, she found that not having to worry about bills or money was a relief. Not having to concern herself with paying rent allowed her to focus on her studies."

"I suppose that is a benefit of being hidden away," Selwen said, a little too hotly. "Like something to be ashamed of. Or you would have simply called her your girlfriend, taking her out to dinner and squiring her about, wouldn't you?"

"I wouldn't," Thanasis said, another dark undercurrent in his voice. "I don't like public announcements, oblique or otherwise. I have a paparazzi problem, you see." His lips curved and this time, there was no trace of any humor in it. Nothing the slightest bit wry. "Perhaps you've met my family by now, like my charming half siblings, each one of them filled with bile and spite. They enjoy nothing more than planting stories about me in the press. It is their dearest wish that the stories might prevent me from doing my job. Not because they want the job, or any job, but because they know I enjoy it. And they do not wish me to have anything in this life that I enjoy."

"What that sounds like to me is a whole lot of main character syndrome," Selwen said with a sniff. "Has it ever occurred to you that some people don't think about you at all?"

"Many people do not think about me at all," he agreed, in that low, outrageously compelling voice of his. "But none of them are related to me. And as for Saskia, I think you're missing a key point in this."

He leaned forward then, as if he wanted to impress this part upon her. So much so that she was actually shocked he didn't reach out and put his hands on her body.

"She liked me," he said, and there was something quietly devastating about it. "She wanted to spend time with me as much as I wanted to spend time with her. I did not force her into my life. It was as if we collided, and once we did, the only way forward was with each other."

Her heart was slamming against her ribs. She kept thinking of *colliding*. Of *collisions*—two comets streaking across the sky and becoming one.

She kept thinking of that darkly beautiful face of his, and of his fingers thrusting deep inside of her, and the intense magic of his kiss—

Selwen wasn't sure when she'd last taken a breath. "You're saying that as if it should mean something to me, but I don't—"

"We met on Tuesday," he told her, his voice as intense as his gaze, as dark and as sure. "We had coffee on a Wednesday morning. By Wednesday night, I had already made her come apart some five times. Maybe more. By Saturday, we were like addicts, shambling about, sickened by the notion we might have to part. And so, we didn't." He didn't shift that gaze from her. "I found the flat. I moved her in. It took a week in total to sort these things out. When we did, we were together for two years."

"And then she ran away from you," Selwen managed to get out, though her voice was little more than a whisper. Something hoarse and strange and yet she couldn't seem to stop. "She ran away, or took a train, is that what you said? And you thought she was dead. Maybe, you didn't know her as well as you thought you did."

"I knew her," he shot back, and something blazed in

his dark eyes. "I know that everybody thinks that it's impossible for one person to know another. Everyone has a secret life, they say. No one can truly know their lover, they claim. But I'm telling you, whatever you call yourself now, there is not one part of me that Saskia did not know. Not one part of her I did not know in return. I am as sure of her as I am of myself."

"Then why did she leave?"

It was a stark question. It seemed to come from that pit inside of her that kept expanding with every word he said, and there was no small part of her that worried it would consume her whole.

Or maybe she was worried that she wanted it to do exactly that.

"I said I knew her, and she knew me. I didn't say we didn't have our troubles." Thanasis looked away for the first time in this conversation and Selwen felt something move over her, some prickle of foreboding. Especially when he rubbed his hand over his face. "As time went on, Saskia found the secrecy and privacy that I insisted upon grueling. It wasn't that she didn't enjoy what we had, but she did not wish to hide it." Selwen watched as his jaw tightened. "I didn't understand it at first. But she became convinced that I was ashamed of her." He shifted his gaze back to Selwen then, and once again she felt pinned into her seat. "Saskia was an orphan."

And there was no reason at all that those words, spoken about a woman Selwen didn't know or couldn't remember, should pierce her the way they did.

"Her parents died when she was very small," Thanasis told her, and she couldn't tell if there was something ruthless or sorrowed in his voice, then. "She was raised in care. A local vicar took an interest in her and helped her get a place at university. Sadly, he also died not long after. When I met Saskia, she was all alone in the world. And she believed that this meant I thought that she was not good enough for me." His nostrils flared slightly, the only sign of high emotion she could see. "She thought I was hiding her instead of protecting her."

Selwen felt her own chin rise again, as if she expected she might have to fight about this. Ancient history. A story about a woman she would never know. "What were you protecting her from?"

He leaned in again, his face stark and stripped down with something like temper—but nothing in her suggested she recoil.

Quite the opposite. The only word she could think of to describe how she felt was *exhilaration,* but that couldn't be right. She bit the inside of her mouth, hoping the pain might sort her out, but it didn't seem to do anything except hurt.

"This," he bit out. "I was saving you from *this*, Saskia. That terrible man you have decided to marry, the weight of his ego and his vanity and all his nasty little minions who will stop at nothing to drag you down to their level, tear you apart, and make you wish you'd never met any of them."

"I am not Saskia," Selwen managed to get out, though she could barely hear her own voice over the pounding of her blood in her veins. "And your father has never been anything but kind to me."

"I am pleased to hear that," Thanasis growled. "But he is not a kind man. And this is not a kind place. And you are spectacularly naïve if you imagine you have the tools to navigate it."

"I'm doing just fine, aren't I?" she shot back. "In point of fact, you're the only unkind person I've met on this island."

"My poor sweet *fos mou*," he said, with a dark laugh, "I have not even begun to be unkind. But I assure you, if you do not put a stop to this madness, that is the very least that I can promise you."

Selwen stood up then, in a rush. She felt flustered, and something far worse than that. There was that soft heat, betraying her. She could feel it between her legs, and everywhere else. Worse still, she had the strangest sensation that she was being torn apart. As if every word he said was a hook in her flesh, her bone—tearing her in a different direction.

She was surprised she was still in one piece.

It was possible she only hoped she was.

"Maybe," she said quietly, "this is exactly why she left you."

"She didn't believe me," he threw back at her, getting to his feet as well, and then they were too close, standing there on the porch where anyone could see them, but Selwen didn't back away. "We had a row. She told me she was going somewhere else to collect her thoughts and she didn't want me to know where. I didn't think she had a place in mind. She said she was going to take the train north and stop when she felt like it, and I would simply have to deal with that until she returned. But she never returned."

"Or maybe that's what she had to tell you so she could escape. Have you ever thought of that?"

"I think about that all the time," Thanasis growled at her. "But regardless of Saskia's intentions, what happened is that there was a train derailment. Her body was never found. It was five years ago. Where were you five years ago, Selwen? Where does your memory start?"

She couldn't speak. She couldn't *think*.

And then he made it worse by stepping forward and wrapping his hands over her upper arms, so he could put his face directly into hers.

"How did you end up in Wales, Saskia?" he asked her, his voice dark and rich, a threat and an invitation, all at once. "How did you stay hidden all this time?"

And everything inside of Selwen seemed to crash and burn. But she shook her head. She looked up at him and she could still feel too much. That longing for him that horrified her. This wild notion that she needed to touch him. The dizzying truth that his hands fit her shoulders perfectly.

She shook her head again. "I don't know if I'm your Saskia," she said.

"You are."

Selwen swallowed. Hard. "This is what I do know. When Ffion found me by the side of the road, I had no idea who I was. All I knew was that I wanted to hide."

She stepped back and without thinking, lifted a hand to her hair. "I cut off all my hair. I dressed in hoods and dark, loose clothing. I stayed close to home. I lived in that village for five years and I never made friends. I didn't *want* to make friends."

He whispered something beneath his breath, another Greek endearment or curse. She didn't want to know which.

She took another step back. "I have to assume that this picture you painted for me isn't true, even if you think it is. Because if I am your Saskia, Thanasis? Then I was running. *From you.*"

CHAPTER FIVE

THANASIS STAGGERED BACK.

It was as if she'd buried an axe in the center of his chest. Though he had to believe that an actual axe would have felt better than...whatever this was.

"What do you mean?" he demanded, his voice raw and strange because her words didn't make sense. They couldn't penetrate his brain, no matter how much his chest hurt. "Of course you weren't *running from me.* Why would you say such a thing?"

But Saskia, no matter what name she called herself now, did not take back her words. She crossed her arms. Her eyes were glinting with temper and despite his reaction to what she'd said, he recognized that. He remembered it. And he preferred it, if he was honest. It was better than the fear he'd seen in her eyes on the beach.

Their relationship had been wildly passionate. Their rows had been the same.

There had never been any *fear* between them. Seeing such a thing, then seeing her run, had made him feel as if he'd swallowed broken glass.

He couldn't believe she didn't remember these things. Or if she truly couldn't remember, if she had suffered some injury—something else he could not bear to think about—then he could not understand how she couldn't *feel* the truth inside her the way that he did. It was magnetic. It was impossible and bright and intoxicating, this string that he felt binding him to her.

It was the same inexorable pull that had been there between them since the start.

But the truth was, he also couldn't believe that she could jump to such a conclusion no matter what she could or couldn't feel. She wanted to marry a man like Pavlos and she thought *Thanasis* was the one to fear?

Was this how twisted she'd gotten over the past five years?

At least this helps explain why she disappeared, he told himself, but that failed to make him feel any better.

"Let's look at the facts as you lay them out," Saskia suggested. Her chin jutted out and she spoke, a telltale sign that she was not happy with him and only too pleased to fight about it.

He tried to take that as a good sign. Because at least this was a Saskia he knew.

"You claim you have no memory," he reminded her, and it felt almost too familiar, to stand before her and defend himself. *I have never hidden you,* he had said to her years ago, and more than once. *You are hardly locked away in a tower,* fos mou. *Is the dramatic language necessary?* Looking back, it was possible he had deliberately said such things because he liked the way their passions came to the boil. He could admit it. Now. "I'm the one, then, who knows all the facts. And they are as I presented them to you."

"You are a man," Saskia told him in a withering sort of tone that was…new.

And not, to his mind, any kind of improvement. He stood straighter, something igniting deep inside him as he recalled the way he'd handled her in the past, when she'd been a little more careful with her mouth and the way she spoke to him. Maybe they'd both been a little more careful, then. Tempestuous, yes, but more careful with the things they said.

"Indeed I am," Thanasis agreed, and he did not think that he was being quite as reckless as she was. Though the urge was there. It swelled in him like something much darker, much deeper. An incoming tide of too many memories of the ways they'd worked things out in the past.

The way he'd assumed they would have worked it out after that last night, too.

It had never crossed his mind that she might not come back.

"I don't know what you think you told me," Saskia was saying in the same too-hot tone. "Let me tell you what I heard. You, in all your Zacharias state—" she did something with her hand that he could only describe as lowering and dismissive "—came upon an orphan girl who was merely trying to look at art. Which is, by the way, generally free. So let us assume that she was poor as well. A poor, lonely, orphan girl, all alone in the world. And then you came in and seduced her by the following evening."

Thanasis laughed before he could think better of it. *"I did not seduce you.* That is not how that happened at all."

Quite the opposite, in fact. He had been captivated by her, as he'd said. He had never felt anything like it. If she had insisted on public coffees forever, he suspected he would have gone along with it. He had wanted to spend time with her. He had wanted to simply drink in her presence.

He had been turned inside out where she had been concerned, and he had spent years wondering how long he would have let that go on. How long he would have played that part.

But he hadn't had to find out.

She'd been the one to hold his hand on a dark street. She had interlaced their fingers and sighed at the sensation that had flooded them both. Then she had been the one to lean in, standing up on her toes to kiss him first.

Saskia had been the one to set them both on fire.

Thanasis had been burned through ever since.

"You seduced her and then you hid her away from the world," Saskia was saying, with great confidence. "I'm sure it's a nice flat you chucked her in, but did she ever leave it? You said you wanted to keep your relationship private but what it sounds like is that you kept her in jail. Locked up tight." In case he didn't get the implication, she leaned forward, slightly, her steeped tea gaze on him. *"Imprisoned."*

"I'm unaware of any jails that allow their inmates full and unfettered access to the entire city of London, a master's program in a university, and free rein to go wherever they might wish at a moment's notice—even an ill-fated train. That's not my impression about how incarceration generally goes in the United Kingdom. But perhaps you, lately of Wales and with no memory older than five years, have a different view. By all means, *Selwen,* share it."

He could see that she did not like the way he said that new name of hers. It was also possible she disliked his tone as much as he did hers, and he could not quite regret that.

"You imprisoned her." Saskia said it again, like she wanted it to land, and hard. "Yet you seem to think that she should have somehow known what your intentions were despite this. Did you tell her those intentions?"

He had.

Thanasis was certain that he had.

But as he thought that, he wondered. A ripple of doubt wound its way into him, then became something more like a flood. Had he truly chased away her fears? Or had he held her, knowing full well that when their hands were on each other, it only ever led to one place?

And it was a magical place, but had that only made it worse for her? Had he underscored the things she worried about when he'd meant to wash them away?

Had she truly believed that all he wanted from her was a convenient body?

The very notion made him feel something like sick.

"What happened that night?" Saskia demanded. "Did she finally stand up for herself? You wouldn't like that, would you. I can tell."

Thanasis had to breathe then. Deep.

"I don't know who you think you are," he said, very carefully, when he could speak again. "And I mean that literally. I've spent the past two days doing a great deal of research on what I presume was a head injury and the memory issues that can follow."

"I had no injuries," Saskia snapped at him. Defensively, he thought, and he wanted nothing more than to pull her into his arms. To kiss her, run his hands over her, and make certain she really was all right.

But he knew that this version of her would detest that.

"It could also be trauma," he said after a moment, when he could trust that he wouldn't reach out for her anyway. "The brain is a marvel. It is also fragile, like everything else that makes us human." He shrugged, though he felt anything but casual. "I thought she knew." He heard the way he said that, and shook his head. "I thought *you* knew, Saskia. You were the center of my world. I arranged my life around you. There was no shame in that. How could there be?"

"We are only talking about facts, not feelings," she told him, maybe a little too fiercely. She stood even straighter. Her dark hair was piled on her head today, and he liked it. It made him think about pulling out the pins he could see she still used and watching them scatter between them. It made him think of burying his face in the cloud of her hair as it came tumbling down. She looked as if she'd been on a long walk and the loose-fitting, flowy clothes she wore were nothing like the wardrobe she had preferred back in London. Then again, this was a Greek island like all the rest that dotted the Aegean, despite the presence of Pavlos. It was a place to flow about in linen and light colors.

But the loose, flowing clothing she was wearing today only made her eyes seem brighter. More intense.

"Ffion found me walking with great purpose down the side of a motorway where no one usually walked. And certainly not if they were dressed the way I was. She thought it felt off, so she picked me up." Those steeped tea eyes studied him for far too long. "I couldn't remember my name. Or where I was, much less why. And we did look. We both concluded I probably wasn't on the train, because I would have had to have walked miles from the derailment site. Besides, I was no worse for wear." Saskia frowned at him, possibly because he didn't react to that. "People died."

"Yes," he gritted out. "I am fully aware that people died, Saskia. I thought you were one of them."

He did not say, *I grieved you. I bargained with the heavens and lost. Again and again and again.*

He did not tell her that he had never slept again, not the way he had before. Not really.

"All I have of that night are my reactions afterward," Saskia said, her eyes narrowing as if she was seeing only monsters when she looked at him. "Cutting off my hair, dressing in drab, dark colors and trying to hide. What does that suggest to you?"

Thanasis wanted to move closer. He wanted to take her in his arms and kiss her until she came to her senses. Maybe she didn't remember him, but he knew from the other night that her body did, as clearly as he remembered her. But if he did that, no matter if she thrilled to his touch again, it would only prove this case she was trying to build.

This version of his relationship with her bore no resemblance to reality, but the fact that she might imagine it—and the possibility, however slight, that the Saskia who remembered him might see it that way too, if he could reach her again—well. He couldn't risk it.

He cared too much about what had actually happened between them. He wouldn't let memories, or the lack of them, change that.

Thanasis stayed where he was. "I would say that everything you're describing sounds a lot like a person who suffered a significant traumatic event," he said quietly. "And was likely depressed and confused in its aftermath."

"But what was that traumatic event?" she asked sharply. "The train derailment? Or you?"

And she would never know, no matter what she remembered, how deeply that wounded him.

"Saskia," he said, though it hurt to say her name, "I won't deny that I could easily have hurt your feelings, but I would never—"

"But you don't know, do you?" There was something hot in her gaze, a kind of knife's edge that matched her voice. "All this time, you've been mourning something you might have broken yourself."

And for what was, possibly, the first time his entire life, Thanasis was speechless. He could only stare at her—this woman back from the dead, the love of his life, who was treating him like some kind of criminal.

Who was suggesting things to him that made him want to howl and roar—

But he didn't.

He couldn't have said how long they stood there like that, staring at each other. Thanasis found himself playing the whole of their relationship over and over his head, and that was nothing new. What was new was the way he felt as if it was a forensic examination today, as if he was turning it all over, poking at it, looking for clues to prove that she was right.

Not only that she was right, but that he had deeply and fundamentally misunderstood the most important relationship of his life. The only important relationship in his life.

Until he'd met Saskia, he had not believed in love. Until he'd touched her, he hadn't understood how one person could connect to another like that.

He had grown up here, after all. In this circus, where everything was for show, nothing was ever as it appeared, and any sign of weakness was swiftly and ruthlessly punished.

Only with Saskia had he dared experiment with the notion that it was possible to feel, and deeply, and yet exhibit no weakness whatsoever—only strength.

But how could he explain this to this woman who lived in her body and wore her face, but was not Saskia, somehow? How could he convince her that the way she had decided to twist their relationship was not only wrong, but something like ruinous?

He couldn't. And he almost wished he'd never seen her again, he thought then, even though he knew that wasn't quite true.

What was true was that there was a part of him that would always regret, now, that she had so quickly and resolutely tarnished his memories of those two years they had shared.

Then again, perhaps the real loss was that he could no longer trust himself, or his own memories where those years were concerned.

"You have nothing to say, do you?" She made a face, as if she expected nothing else from him. But he remembered that it was this woman, not his memory, that had kissed him back like her life depended on it. It was *this* Saskia who had clung to him and rode his hand as if she had pulled it to her body herself.

That made him feel better.

To some degree.

Because it meant he wasn't going mad. There was some solace in that.

"I understand that you can't know," he said, perhaps more to himself than to her. "That you can't recall the things I can. That you feel you must make these things up."

"What I feel," she said, in that same edgy way, "is that I am marrying your father and it is just as well for the both of us that I can't remember any Zacharias but him."

Somehow—*somehow*—Thanasis did not reply to that the way he wished he could.

The way every atom within him demanded he should.

"My father is neither a good man nor kind man," he told her, as coolly as he was able. "I understand that you think I'm insulting him when I say this, but I'm not. Do not take my word for it. Ask anyone. His only virtue is that he knows it. He knows exactly who he is and he delights in seeing how far people will go to cozy up to him no matter how repugnant his behavior."

"I have seen no repugnant behavior," she replied, her chin tipping up again.

"You will," Thanasis assured her, his voice quiet. "I hope you do not, but you will."

He made himself move, then. He went over to the briefcase he'd stashed beside the bench and pulled out a business card. "I can't stand here and try to convince you that my memories are true, not when you're so determined to think the worst of a relationship you can't even remember. I won't."

"Convenient," she murmured, but there was something about the way she was looking at him. Something that made his heart kick a little harder.

"Ask yourself this. Why did you take nothing with you if you were running away from me? Not even a wallet. If that train hadn't derailed, you likely would have been tossed off at the next stop because I don't think you paid for your ticket." Saskia frowned, but she didn't argue. He kept going. "But none of that matters. What matters is that you are engaged to a man that everyone considers a monster, even the man himself. You should look into that. You should ask yourself what it is he plans to do with you, once you are his wife."

"He plans to let me paint," she told him, and he didn't think he was imagining the note of defensiveness in her tone, then. "He's given me an art studio where I will be free to do as I wish."

"Will you?" Thanasis shook his head. "I hope for your sake you're right."

He handed her his card, but she didn't take it. She stared at it as if it was a live snake. He felt his lips shift into some sort of curve, though it felt to him more like a grimace. He reached over and tucked the card beneath the strap of the bra he could see beneath her shirt. It sat there on her shoulder and he barely touched her as he did it.

But they both reacted as if he'd doused them in gasoline and then lit a match.

"Maybe," she got out, hoarsely, "she left you because you thought she was an object you could treat as you liked."

"She wasn't leaving me," he told her in the same voice, and even more intensely. "Someday, when you remember what actually happened that night, we will revisit it. But I'm not discussing it with you."

"Because you know you can't defend yourself."

"Because I know what happened, and you don't." He reached over and tapped the card he'd slid beneath her strap. "In the meantime, keep that card. Everything on this island belongs to my father in one way or another. There may very well come a time when you might like to leave. And if he would prefer that you stay, you'll need help."

He remembered trying to leave himself, when he was a child. He also remembered the precious few times his mother had tried to do the same, and had been turned back to the villa by every last villager with a boat.

Pavlos's power here was far too great.

But Saskia couldn't know that. "Are you so delusional that you think I would ask for help from the man who—"

"I would be very careful with any accusations, Saskia," he said, quietly. Much too quietly. "Because I know exactly what happened on that beach. I remember precisely how you responded."

"I wasn't…"

She looked lost, there for a minute. It made his chest hurt.

"You have already accused me of predatory behavior. Toward a woman you don't believe you ever knew."

She frowned again, and he wondered if any of this

was getting through to her. If somewhere, deep inside, there was even the faintest possibility that some memory of what it had actually been like between them was getting through—

But she shook her head, as if shoving it away. "You're right that I don't know what happened between you and your Saskia five years ago. But I do know that what happened between you and me the other night was wrong. I'm engaged to your father. That's the beginning and the end of anything that needs to be said between us."

It was the hardest thing he ever had to do—it felt as if he was tearing his own ribs out of his chest as he did it—but Thanasis nodded. "Agreed," he said curtly.

Somehow.

And it was as if Saskia had been standing there pushing with all her might against an immovable wall, only to see it crumble. Her body shifted as if the wall had given way. She looked something like crestfallen.

It was terrible to watch. All Thanasis wanted to do was to sweep her into his arms. He wanted to comfort her. There had been a time when he was the only thing that could ever comfort her, even if he was also the reason she had been upset in the first place.

She had told him so herself, a million times.

But this Saskia saw darkness where there had only been light, love, and arguments that had gone round and round because both of them were stubborn. Both of them were passionate. If they hadn't been, they wouldn't have gotten together in the first place.

There are words for women like me, she had shouted at him that night.

Yes, he had shouted back. *Mistress. I chose it deliberately. You used to like it.*

Because it had once been its own source of heat between them. It had lent itself to all manner of games that they'd played until they were sated and silly with it.

Because both of them found power dynamics particularly exciting.

One night he had only allowed her to say *yes, sir.*

One weekend, she had greeted him at the door naked and had stayed that way until Monday.

They had exulted in it, this archaic arrangement where he was in control—except she was the only thing on the planet that threatened that control. By her very existence.

They had been entwined with each other, irrevocably. She had told him she was leaving, but only to clear her head. *To see a sky that isn't yours,* she had told him. *If only for a little while.* He had known she was coming back.

There was no other option. Not for either of them.

Maybe it had been toxic, but it had been *theirs.*

How could he explain this to a woman who patently refused to believe it? Who wouldn't understand what he was telling her, because if she didn't remember anything that had happened before that night, she couldn't possibly remember the blaze of their connection or the ways they'd exulted in it, sinking just as deeply into the dark as into the light.

He couldn't explain it to anyone.

Having her back, but only a part of her, was an exquisite agony.

Thanasis was not certain he would ever recover.

"Whatever you think of me," he told her when he was certain he could speak, in as even a tone as possible, "know this. There is absolutely nothing I would not do to help you. And there is very little that is not within my power. All you have to do is call."

"I won't," she told him, but her eyes were wider than before, and glassier.

Most importantly, she made no move to take that card from the place where he had stashed it. If she meant what she said, surely she would have ripped it away from her body and thrown it on the ground.

So he did something he would have sworn was impossible. He took one last look at his Saskia, risen from the grave, and he soaked her in as best he could.

Then he walked away, into the cottage, and did not go out again until she was gone.

He made some excuse about business to his father, in a text, and was back in London before nightfall.

But he didn't go to his house on Hampstead Heath. He went to that flat in Chelsea instead. He let himself in with his key and then he stood there, drawing the scent of her that lingered there—or perhaps it was a phantom, but he didn't care, it was still the only part of her he had—deep into his body.

He stayed there until dawn, tortured by the ghost of the Saskia he'd lost.

And, worse, by the terrible loss of the Saskia he'd found.

CHAPTER SIX

Selwen heard that Thanasis was gone with everyone else, at the formal dinner that Pavlos called his *casual little supper table,* when, in fact, it was a formal affair.

One he insisted upon, each and every night.

That first night she sat there with all of those harsh words that she and Thanasis had spoken resonating in her like some kind of tuning fork, even though he was now, by all reports, back in London.

"Thanasis *rarely* tears himself away from the pleasures of the Big Smoke," one of Pavlos's illegitimate daughters told Selwen with a sniff and a sharp Eastern European accent. "It is unlikely that you will ever see him again."

This was said as an aside, and it was not an attempt to try to poke at Selwen about Thanasis. The suggestion was that Selwen's marriage to Pavlos would be brief at best, something all of his mistresses' children had been at pains to tell her—but it was the Thanasis part that made Selwen feel…strange.

She should have been delighted that he was rarely here. That dealing with him wasn't something she would have to worry about with any regularity.

Selwen should have been celebrating his departure.

Why aren't you jubilant that you chased him away? she asked herself, but she couldn't seem to get there.

It was that last expression on his face, she thought. It was the way he'd looked at her, as if she had shattered him as they stood out there in front of his cottage. She couldn't seem to get past it. She could feel it inside of her in the middle of another one of Pavlos's long dinners, like a melody she couldn't quite name playing endlessly around and around in her head.

By the time the dessert course came, she wanted to dig that haunting tune out of her head with her fingers. She wanted to get back to the person she had been before Thanasis had turned up and claimed to know her. Selwen wanted to be the woman who had been perfectly happy to sit at this table, lost in her own thoughts. The woman who had deliberately not learned the names of Pavlos's children, or these makeshift courtiers of his who laughed at the end of every sentence he uttered and were more than happy to debase themselves before him, if that would gain his favor.

But that woman had been concerned primarily with her own security, she realized as the days bled one into the next. That woman had thought that she'd finally found the very things that Ffion had always told her she needed. Safety. Her very own space. Art all around her, a soft place to land each night, and her heart's desire in all things.

The woman she was now found her heart significantly more complicated than it had been when she'd met Pavlos, and she hated it.

The art studio that Pavlos had prepared for her was one of those cottages down toward the olive groves.

In order to get to it, she had to pass the cottage where Thanasis had been staying—the one that the staff told her was his alone.

"It is kept ready for him always," her favorite maid told her one day when Selwen asked, trying her best not to appear *too* interested. "No one is allowed in it, no matter how many people come to one of Mr. Zacharias's parties." She leaned closer, her dark eyes gleaming. "I'm not supposed to tell anyone this, but only the housekeeper has a key. So that no one can slip in without the young Mr. Zacharias's knowledge."

Meaning, Selwen thought, Pavlos himself was barred from entry.

"Is that…normal?" she asked.

The maid made a face. "Before the young Mr. Zacharias insisted on this arrangement, his father would often…leave him all manner of presents in the cottage. Usually ones that were decidedly unwelcome, if you get my meaning."

Selwen did not get her meaning. What present wouldn't be welcome? But something in the way the woman said it kept her from asking. She had the strangest feeling that she didn't want to know.

"What I *want*," she muttered to herself after the maid took her leave, "is to stop thinking about that man."

About the way that kiss had seemed to alter the cells inside her body. About the way his fingers, deep inside of her, had made her feel as if she was once again a complete stranger to herself, only this time it was somehow less scary.

She wanted it all to *stop*.

And yet every day when she walked down to the studio to sketch and paint, or, more often, to stare out the window toward the sea while *thinking about* sketching or painting, she found herself thinking about Thanasis instead.

About the way his face had changed when she had thrown all those things at him. All her hot takes on a relationship she hadn't taken part in. Because even if she was his Saskia, even if that really was who she'd been once, she couldn't remember it now. So she might as well have been a stranger, dropping her opinions all over him with nothing to back them up but the worst possible interpretation of what he'd told her.

But he hadn't seemed *angry*, she reminded herself. Was that what she'd expected? For him to shout or threaten her?

And if she really had worried about that, why had she gone at him the way she had? Systematically dismantling a memory that was clearly precious to him...

"But I'm right," she told herself, every time she ended up in this particular circle of thought.

And as she was usually alone when that happened, she was the only one around to notice that she sounded weaker each time she said it.

Pavlos, on the other hand, was becoming more and more jovial. And perhaps more comfortable with Selwen, she supposed. There were no more respectful, careful walks amongst the olive trees. When she tried to tell him about her art, he would wave a hand. Dismissing her.

She told herself he was simply a very busy man, what with his work and his commitment to so much socializing.

"I have news for you, girl," he said one night, jolting her back from wherever her thoughts had taken her...off to a dark-eyed man who was far too beautiful and who only resembled his father *a little*. "There has been enough lolling about. There is a gala in Athens this weekend. I will take great pleasure in showing you off. It's about time."

Pavlos had gathered his faithful in one of his favorite solariums, and the music was loud. The laughter was piercing.

Selwen was certain she had misheard him. "I'm not going to any gala."

And maybe it was because Thanasis had planted all those stories in her head. Maybe it was the way all of Pavlos's minions always looked at her, always studying her, as if waiting for her to crack into pieces they could kick away with their well-shod feet.

Whatever it was, she saw it when it happened.

When this man who she had decided would keep her safe looked at her so coldly she felt as if she was suddenly back in the dark depths of a long Welsh winter.

"I beg your pardon?" His voice was mild enough. But it was the way he said it. It was the way he looked at her while he said it.

Like he hated her.

Selwen told herself she was being dramatic, even though she had never been anything of the sort before. She tried to make him understand.

"We agreed," she reminded him. "I am not built for public things." Though even as she said that, she wondered. Was that true? Or was that what she'd held onto from her life as a secret mistress? She swallowed and kept going. "A gala sounds very public, doesn't it?"

They had been officially engaged for weeks now. It had been the better part of a month, in fact, though she was certainly not counting days from Thanasis's departure because *that* would make no sense at all.

And yet something in her jumped—and not at all in the way it had on that dark beach that she absolutely did not spend any time thinking about—when Pavlos reached over and touched her face.

Everything in her seemed to screw itself tight, as if she wanted to armor herself against him.

You're being ridiculous, she told herself. *This man has never been anything but kind.*

"You will change your mind, of course," he told her, and there was something in the way his dark eyes moved over her that made her bite her tongue. Made her certain not to laugh the way she wanted to, because she could tell that it would not be received well. "I am Pavlos Zacharias. My wife will be on my arm when I wish it."

Something she hardly recognized inside of her seemed to rise, them. Selwen found herself smiling. She wanted to bat his fingers away from her face, but, instead, she made herself reach out and touch his arm.

"That settles it then," she said, channeling the light and air and sunshine of this place by day. Hoping it emanated from her. "I'm not your wife just yet, am I?"

For a moment, though she was aware that there was that music and all the usual laughter, it seemed very quiet, there between them. Intense, and not in the way it had been with Thanasis. That had seemed to come as much from inside her as from him. This was something completely different.

This was not an ache, but a weight.

Until, finally, Pavlos cracked a smile. Selwen felt something in her seem to release, too. "Not yet," he said, and though he was smiling, his gaze was still cold. "Not yet, my girl."

And when she slipped away from the party a little bit later, she stepped out into the cool night air, and felt how flushed her cheeks were. How hard her blood seemed to be pumping inside her body. How cold she felt, everywhere else, as if Pavlos had threatened her.

Why did it feel as if he had threatened her? Of course he hadn't.

But though she knew exactly where the card was that Thanasis had left her, that she hadn't thrown away, she didn't go to it. She didn't so much as pick it up.

She told herself that Pavlos was drunk, the way he often was. She'd imagined that they would have a perfectly civilized marriage where he would tend to his pursuits, she would handle hers, and they would meet when it suited the both of them for some kind of communal event. She had rather thought it would involve a nice walk. Perhaps a swim.

That night, she sat up late in her room and convinced herself that he'd simply forgotten. And she'd reminded him. And all was well.

Nothing had changed. She had made the right decision. He would respect it. Tonight was an anomaly, that was all.

"He has been nothing but kind to me," she repeated, again and again.

Another week went by, with Selwen clinging on hard to these fantasies of hers, before reality came crashing in.

She had just about convinced herself she'd imagined the whole thing.

It was a normal morning. She woke up in her bed, smiled at the sun that poured in through the windows, and took her time with her breakfast. She liked her tea. She liked a bit of toast and some proper jam. When she set out for her walk, it occurred to her that she really ought to go and see Pavlos about another strange thing he'd said at dinner the night before—though she was sure she was mistaken. He'd been obviously intoxicated and he'd slurred something at her about weddings and cathedrals and honeymoons in Paris, where everyone could see them.

Selwen had smiled and convinced herself it was the drink talking.

She picked her way through the maze of halls, quiet all around her in the early morning. She knew her way all over the labyrinth that was his villa now, because she liked to walk until she got lost and then find her way back. She had once asked her husband-to-be why he liked a house like this that so many people got lost in, disoriented, and bewildered.

Once you enter, I decide when you leave, he had replied, and then he'd laughed in that big, bold way of his and she'd assured herself that he was joking.

Because he had to be joking.

It was easy enough to find her way to Pavlos's vast suite at the highest point overlooking the ocean, with all of the various wings twisting off in different directions. She expected him to be up and working in the office he kept here, as he always claimed he did.

I work all morning so that I might play all night, he liked to say.

But when she let herself in to the atrium that contained his private pool, a set of hot tubs, and various other luxuries arranged on a terrace with the sea in the distance, so blue through all the archways and windows, she stopped dead.

Because Pavlos was up and awake all right, but he wasn't working.

And he wasn't alone.

Selwen felt as if she was having some kind of out-of-body experience.

She was standing there, watching the scene unfold before her, and she was also seemingly standing somewhere else, witnessing all of it. Herself, standing there. And then Pavlos and the woman she recognized as his massage therapist, neither one of them with a stitch of clothing on and a great deal of bucking and moaning and—

And she must have made some kind of noise. Selwen couldn't understand how, even if she had, they could possibly have heard her over the ruckus they were making, but they both turned and looked at her.

A great many things became clear in that terrible moment.

The massage therapist did not look in the least bit surprised, or in any way worried about being caught with Pavlos by his fiancée. That was a critical bit of information, certainly.

But even more clarifying was the fact that Pavlos... sighed.

"My darling girl," he said, making no attempt to... *untangle* himself, "if you do not knock, you cannot be surprised at the things you might find on the other side of a door."

And then, as she stood there with her mouth actually open, the two of them simply...continued.

As if they hadn't been interrupted in the first place.

It took Selwen much longer than it should have to realize that they weren't going to stop. That they didn't care that she was there. That, on the contrary, Pavlos might actually *like* the fact that she'd seen him. That she could no longer pretend he was someone else.

She staggered out of the villa and found herself wandering blindly about in the careless Greek sunshine with no idea how to process what she had just seen.

She felt sick.

And she felt something else that didn't make any sense. It teetered a little too close to some kind of sharp-edged relief and she clung to that, because it felt better. If she could have, she would have scrubbed her eyes out so that she could get those images out of her head.

Down on that beach she definitely did not dream about, she considered it a little too intently.

Eventually she found herself standing outside Thanasis's cottage and thought about the way she'd caught sight of him *just sitting there,* that morning. Just waiting, and watching. And how determined she'd been to find that predatory.

It occurred to her now that she'd been unpardonably naïve for entirely too long.

Ffion would not have approved.

Selwen stared at that chair where Thanasis had sat, scowling at it as if she could make his apparition appear if she concentrated hard enough.

She thought about all the men she had danced with on various islands. How she had somehow convinced herself, one dance at a time, that all anyone wanted from her was the dancing. She'd convinced herself that this thing with Pavlos was the same. A bit of a dance, that was all. That was all he wanted from her, she'd been sure of it.

"What a fool you are," she told herself, though the breeze stole her words away.

Because it had always been about sex. All of it.

Those men who had danced with her had wanted more. Pavlos had not showed her olive groves because he thought she had a particular interest in olives, but because part of the dancing *he* liked to do was showing off his wealth.

And here she was, heedlessly tripping face-first into situations she not only didn't understand, but had actively tried not to when the truth was really very simple, there at the bottom of it all.

She liked dancing. But she had absolutely no interest in all that bouncing and flopping around that Pavlos and his massage therapist had been doing. Selwen couldn't remember a single time she'd wanted anything like that, with any man, whether the men in the village back in Pembrokeshire or the men in the many island *tavernas*.

It was like she couldn't remember that part of herself either.

There was only one man who had ever seemed to

affect her body at all. Only one who had made her feel that if she didn't have some part of him inside her, she might die.

She had wanted to *die,* and she had, right there on his hand.

Selwen stared at Thanasis's cottage, and felt something like a shiver move through her, except it felt a good deal more like an earthquake. As if she was crisscrossed with fault lines and they were all tearing themselves apart, here and now.

When she stayed in one piece, somehow, she wheeled herself around and marched herself through the labyrinth of the house to her bedchamber so that she could start packing her things.

And that was where Pavlos found her, quite a long while later. He had certainly not *rushed* to come to her. To explain himself, or apologize—

Which was what Selwen thought he was going to do when he stood there in the doorway and regarded her, with eyes she suddenly couldn't fail to see were cold. And not at all kind, as she'd convinced herself they were.

"Where do you think you're going?" he asked, with what sounded like only the very mildest curiosity.

"Away," she said, and was surprised that she didn't sound particularly upset.

Surely she should have been crushed to a pulp.

But Pavlos laughed, and she found she felt even less upset. "I had no idea you were such a child," he told her. "What did you think? That I would become a monk simply because you behave like a nun? What foolishness."

If she cared about this man the way she should, surely she would have been more hurt than disgusted. Surely she ought to cry, throw things. Try to rip him apart, the way she had—

But she couldn't think about that just yet. How fired up she'd been to rip Thanasis apart, and while she was at it, rip into his memories too, when all he'd done was kiss her on a beach. And when she'd melted all over him, like molten fire in his hands.

She felt absolutely no need to do that now.

It was another dose of clarity. She was beginning to wonder if it was possible to overdose on the stuff.

"It's my fault," she said, and perhaps her voice was too light, too easy. Because his eyes narrowed and, if possible, grew colder. "I should have made it clear from the beginning that I cannot tolerate disloyalty."

"This is like a child trying to run away from home." Pavlos laughed again, and she could admit, now, that she hated all the laughter in this villa. It came with sharp-edged knives. "You cannot have been confused about who I am, Selwen. I have made no secret of it. You have been present at too many of my parties to imagine that I was a man who abstained from the pleasures of the flesh, or, indeed, any pleasures at all."

"It is one thing to drink too much. It is another to flagrantly sleep with another woman in the house where I'm staying. I think you know that, Pavlos."

She thought he would get angry. But he only sighed. Then shrugged. It was a great, theatrical sort of gesture.

"I wish you good luck with this tantrum of yours," he told her in that same patronizing tone. "You will not find it easy to get off this island, I am afraid. And when you are ready to have a conversation like adults, you can come and find me." He laughed again, long and mean. "Though I would suggest that in the future, you knock."

What she thought was, *Everything Thanasis told me was true.*

She felt herself vibrating with some great emotion she didn't understand. Temper, perhaps. Outrage. But it wasn't personal. She wasn't pleased with herself for putting herself in this position, but she wasn't *hurt,* either.

What she did not like was the fact that Pavlos did not seem to think that she could leave this island when she wanted.

She didn't like that at all.

Selwen thought of the things she'd suggested—maybe more than simply *suggested*—Thanasis had done to some version of her that was lost to her, and had to bite back a shudder. The truth was laid out here before her now, and starkly.

She could believe anything of Pavlos, in this moment. The scales had fallen from her eyes, but she hadn't been protecting herself from the reality of him. She had simply been invested in the story he'd spun for her about the life they could live.

Or her own blinders, more like.

But staring at a man who had probably not even showered since being with another woman, a woman he employed and had likely been sleeping with all along, made her realize that Thanasis was nothing like his father.

She simply knew it.

She felt it inside of her, the way she felt her ligaments

move when she did. The way she knew she breathed without checking in on the mechanics of the act.

She just *knew*.

"I'm not going to fight with you," she told this man, this fiancé of hers she had never bothered to get to know. Had she thought it wouldn't matter because she knew herself so little too?

But there was no time to dig into that, because Pavlos laughed again. When he moved further into the room she probably should have been alarmed.

Even if she was—and she refused to accept that she was—she held her ground. She lifted her chin up. She did not drop her gaze.

She refused to allow herself any hint of a reaction when he drew close enough to reach over and pinch her chin between his fingers.

Not all that gently.

"Don't worry," he told her, and there was something worse than simply *cold* in his gaze. "You'll learn."

And then he kissed her.

It was not a nice kiss.

It was clearly meant to show her who was boss here, and she had the distinct impression that he wouldn't mind too much if it made her cry, either.

All of that might have wrecked her, but it didn't. It couldn't.

Because something else was happening to her, like a great tide streaking across a sandy beach and washing it clean.

Though in this case, it was the opposite of clean.

Because this was the wrong mouth. This was the wrong man.

And when he finally pulled away, she clapped a hand over her mouth and did nothing but stare at him.

She could see that he was saying something, but she couldn't hear him. His mouth was moving, his gaze was cold and dark, but she didn't care.

Because she remembered.

She remembered *everything*.

She remembered who she was, at last, after all this time.

She remembered standing in that museum in London and being immediately aware of the man who came up beside her to stare at the same canvas that she'd already been baffled by.

Before he'd even spoken to her, she felt her entire body prickle into an awareness that she'd understood at once, even if she had never felt anything like it before.

My God, she remembered every single thing.

She remembered Thanasis, at last.

She remembered every single moment she'd spent with him, in vibrant, passionate detail—including the night she'd left.

Saskia, she whispered, if only in her own head. *I am Saskia Gordon.*

And he wasn't wrong. Everything he'd told her was true. Especially the fact that she had been madly, wildly, head over heels in love with him.

I was madly, wildly, head over heels in love with him.

But she bit all of those memories back as she watched Pavlos sneer at her before he left the room.

Once he was gone, she felt her body reject that unwanted kiss even more. She ran to the bathroom, brushed her teeth and spat. Then again. And again.

And only when there was no trace of that man in her mouth did she go to find the card Thanasis had given her in the place where she'd hidden it away, because some part of her must have known that nothing was safe here. She pulled it out and she let her fingers trace over his name.

Thanasis Zacharias. No corporate logo necessary. Just his name and a number, because everyone knew who he was.

And now she did, too.

She knew exactly who he was to her.

And when she called, he answered on the first ring.

"Are you all right?" he asked, and she could hear that undercurrent of urgency, that dark imagining, right there in his voice. She could feel him all over her, and inside her. *She knew who he was.* "Has something happened?"

Everything, she wanted to say, but she couldn't. She didn't.

"I would very much like to leave the island," she told him, sounding astonishingly prim when inside of her it was all fire and wonder and *him. Them.* "And I'm under the impression that that won't be possible."

On the other end of the line, she could hear Thanasis breathing, but he didn't speak.

Her eyes fell closed, because she remembered *all* of him now. His naked body, drenched in sunlight, as he stood there beside the bed they'd shared. As he pulled her to him to wrap her legs around his waist and thrust deep and sure inside of her.

All of him, like that first time, when she'd kissed him on the street and he'd had to keep her hands from going where they shouldn't, not out in public.

I don't want to rush this, he'd told her.

I do, she'd replied, and nipped his perfect lower lip.

He had checked them into the nearest hotel, carried her over the threshold of the suite he booked on the spot, and only when he'd laid her out on that bed and come down beside her had she smiled at him and brushed her hand over that impossibly beautiful face of his.

Like she was learning it by touch.

I want to do this a great many times, she told him quietly. Intently. *But you will have to be careful at first, because I've never done it before.*

He hadn't asked questions. He had gazed at her as if he could drink her down whole, or perhaps as if she was the answer to a prayer he hadn't known he'd sent up in the first place.

Fos mou, he had said quietly. *My light. I assure you, there will be nothing between us but pleasure.*

And for so long, that had been true. For so very long, it had been enough.

She heard him shift on the other end of this line and tried to imagine where he was sitting. In that office of his that she'd snuck into once, late at night, so she could do unspeakable things to him and make certain he thought of her while he sat there ever after.

He'd made certain to punish her for that.

Deliciously.

"I will have a plane there within the hour," he told her. "Meet it on the tarmac."

When he rang off, she looked around at the things that she was packing up. Things that belonged to a traumatized Welsh girl who didn't know who she was, who had picked a name that started with an *S* because that had felt right.

But she didn't need the things Selwen did. She wasn't the woman Selwen had been, lost but determined to do what her only friend had wanted her to do. In the end, she took only the things that Ffion had given her, tucking them away in her shoulder bag.

And then, unencumbered by the rest of the things Selwen had gathered, she walked out to meet her past.

Saskia again, at last.

CHAPTER SEVEN

BY THE TIME the plane landed in the United Kingdom, Saskia felt like herself again.

Not *completely* herself, of course. It was complicated. There were those five years in Wales to come to terms with, not to mention her remarkable decision to marry a man like Pavlos. It was going to take her some time to unpack that.

Maybe a lot of time.

But once she was back in London, she felt as if she could take a full, deep breath for the first time in a long, long while.

The funny thing was, she hadn't even realized that she wasn't doing that already. She would have sworn that she had never felt more relaxed than she had on Pavlos's island, but her body told her a different story now. She felt herself truly, deeply relax. She felt her shoulders creep down from her ears and her spine melt against the seat.

Like her body remembered London all on its own. And was happy to be home.

Thanasis's plane landed in the same private airfield he had always used when she'd flown with him all the time. Saskia braced herself as the plane taxied to a stop, expecting to see him now that she knew who he was to her…and then disappointed when he wasn't there.

"You need to get a hold of yourself, madam," she muttered to herself as she exited the plane and climbed down the steps to the tarmac.

She was beckoned into the back of a waiting town car and offered the usual refreshments, which she waved away. The car started moving and she sat back against another cozy leather seat, feeling her body relax even more. Like this car was a spa.

It was so easy, this life. The part of her that was still Selwen, who'd imagined herself a practical and deeply unfancy Welsh girl, was awed at the matter-of-fact luxury she'd already experienced. Unlike Pavlos's island, there was very little pressure here. No need to perform. No need to show up at endless dinners filled with glittering enemies. And yet she could now remember exactly how frustrated she'd become with it.

Just as she could remember the beautiful simplicity of her life as Selwen. It had been such a quiet life. Such a good one. Ffion had cared deeply for her and she had showed it every day. Selwen had been able to share her own affection in return. And it was only now, in full possession of all her faculties and memories, that she understood why this had been so important for her.

Because all the people she had loved had died, and usually while she wasn't around. Her parents. The vicar. They'd all died while she was off doing something else and none of them had ever been replaced. She been entirely on her own in the world until she met Thanasis.

Ffion had found her. Ffion had taken care of her. Ffion had made that lost child inside of Saskia whole.

She had been the family Saskia had always wanted.

And when the time had finally come, Saskia had sat at her bedside. She'd held Ffion's frail hand between hers and told her in every way she could that it was all right for her to go.

It's time now, she had told her dear friend. *You have places to be, Ffion. And lots of loves waiting for you, I warrant. I will be perfectly fine, this world will go on turning, and I will honor you with every breath. I promise.*

Ffion hadn't opened her eyes again. But Saskia could still remember the clasp of the hand she'd held in hers, how Ffion had gripped her just the slightest bit harder— one last goodbye—and then had slipped away.

It was a beautiful thing, Saskia thought as the town car navigated its way through the wet and crowded London streets. It was a beautiful, terrible, and lovely thing indeed to hold space for a loved one's death. To honor someone who had done so much for her by witnessing her departure on her last final journey.

She wouldn't take that back. Not for anything.

Those were sacred years, she thought as they sat in the usual London traffic. For all that she hadn't known who she was, she'd known that Ffion loved her. And that had been enough. And now that she knew the context of those years, and what had come before, she knew that she'd never felt she had an opportunity to simply… scrounge around in clothes that didn't make the most of her looks in any of her previous incarnations. She'd learned early on in care that she could use the fact the adults found her pretty to her advantage. It had been the same later, at university. It was amazing the things that people would do for her, or help her with, just for a smile.

When a person had nothing, she used the tools she had.

Then there been Thanasis, coming out of nowhere when she hadn't even been looking for a man, or anything resembling a man, because she'd had work to do. Saskia had never been in the slightest bit of doubt that he found her ravishingly beautiful. He'd told her so all the time.

What she hadn't known, as time went on, was whether or not that was the only thing he valued about her.

And she couldn't really say that experiencing him as Selwen had changed that much. Or at all. Because she'd been there when he'd first clapped eyes on her in the villa's grand hall. She'd seen the shock on his face, then the recognition, then all of that fire.

A familiar fire now, though she hadn't understood why it had affected her the way it had then.

Still, she'd been on that beach when he'd kissed her, and he certainly hadn't done it because of her personality, had he? He'd been kissing a memory. She had too, little as she'd realized it at the time.

So really, if she looked at it that way, they were back to square one.

The same square one that had put her on that fateful train.

The car pulled up to the private entrance of the lovely building in Chelsea, tucked away on a wide street within walking distance of the King's Road, that she knew all too well.

But his driver left nothing to chance. He didn't wait to see if she could find her way to the place where she'd lived for two years. He guided her inside, up the private stair to the old flat, and when she walked inside Saskia was surprised to find the place smelled exactly the same as she remembered it. No mustiness to indicate that it had sat just like this for five years.

Everything was exactly as she'd left it when she'd raced out the door that night, making sure to slam it with all her might behind her.

Suddenly she found that she wasn't breathing all that well after all.

Saskia swallowed hard. She walked further inside, not even tossing her bag on the table in the foyer the way she always had when she'd lived here, because she couldn't quite believe that this was happening.

And when she made it into the lounge, she found Thanasis standing there, waiting.

For a moment, they simply stood still on opposites sides of the room, their gazes locked together.

Saskia wanted to sob. She wanted to bawl her eyes out, sink down to her knees, and let all of the emotion that was charging around inside of her release at last.

She wanted to hold tight to Selwen and her memories of Ffion. She wanted to tell Thanasis everything that had happened since the last time she'd seen him as herself. She wanted to run to him, she wanted to run away, and she remembered everything now—

But she'd forgotten how it *felt*.

To be around him like this, fully aware that she loved him *so much* and so disastrously.

She had forgotten that it was possible to love like

this. *It's like a cancer,* she had shouted at him that last night. *Every day, it takes over more of me, and what will be left, Thanasis? What will become of me when there's nothing of* me *remaining?*

You know perfectly well I don't want that, he had replied, calmly, because he'd been playing the part of the rational, reasonable man that night.

A role they both knew he could not always claim.

You don't know what you want, she had thrown at him. *And in the meantime, while you flutter about in indecision, I am dying.*

The only deaths you suffer are the little ones, Thanasis had retorted, moving closer to her right here in this room. He'd gotten his hands on her and they'd both sighed a little, because that always led to the same place. *Over and over and over again,* fos mou. *And yet you complain?*

I knew that you could make me come the moment I met you, she'd told him, tipping her chin up and perfectly happy to stay belligerent. *What I didn't know was whether a man like you could love anything.* Then she'd leaned in close and bared her teeth at him. *I still don't.*

He had responded to that in typical fashion, right there on the soft rug that covered part of the polished wood floor. If she let herself think too closely about it, she could still feel the aftereffects of that wild claiming, charging through her. Making her feel, as always, that she would fight and kill and die to keep hold of this man no matter what he did or didn't do in return.

That was exactly why she left.

Standing here now, across from him in this hushed

room filled with so many memories, she could see that he was remembering the exact same thing.

"Welcome home," he said, in that low voice that never failed to take up residence in her bones.

She wanted to rip into him. She wanted to paint that archangel's face of his. She wanted to toss herself into the air with the full knowledge that he would catch her when gravity took hold.

God, the things she wanted. She thought they might tear her apart.

"I apologize, Selwen," he said after a moment, when all she did was stare back at him, her heart a rampaging beast inside her chest. "I forget that you would not remember having lived here."

Saskia opened up her mouth to tell him that it was fine, that she did remember, that she was finally herself again now. Not Selwen. Not that poor waif of a Welsh girl who, if she had to guess, she would have said had been unknowingly grieving this. *Him.*

Not because he had been terrible to her, because it wasn't as simple as that. But because that much love had nowhere to go. That was why it had sat in her like grief for five whole years.

No wonder she'd imagined she was in mourning. She had been.

But not for the reasons she'd imagined.

"I will give you a tour," Thanasis told her. He moved toward her stiffly, and really, this was the moment. It would be so easy. She would simply say, *I remember you.*

And then…

But that was trouble, wasn't it? She already knew what would happen next.

So she said nothing when he walked over to her, and indicated with a tilt of his head that she could put her bag down.

She didn't want to. She wanted to keep on clinging to it, and the remnants of her life in Wales were tucked inside of it, like they were some kind of talisman she could use against him. But she reminded herself that Selwen didn't know she needed to ward this man off. Selwen might have had a physical reaction to him, and she thought he was a villain, but she clearly wasn't *afraid* of him. Selwen thought her reaction to him was an anomaly.

Selwen had no idea what happened when he really touched her. When he didn't stop. When she wouldn't let him.

Saskia placed her bag, perhaps a little too heavily, on the arm of the couch that she knew every last square inch of. She and Thanasis had christened every surface in this flat.

Repeatedly.

And if they were not christening it, they were living here. Laughing here, talking here. Fighting here and loving each other here.

He had taught her all the ways that she could take his cock and all the way she could use it to drive him out of his mind, right here on this same couch. He had sprawled back, all of his clothes in disarray. And she had knelt there happily between his outstretched legs, held that thrillingly dark gaze with hers, and sucked him in deep.

She looked away now, because she was afraid that he would be able to see it on her face. That longing. That hunger.

"You liked this flat because it had character," he told her, and she thought he sounded a little stiff. Remote. Perhaps he had seen more on her face than she had intended. "I believe you said that living in a block of flats would only depress you."

"I can't imagine having opinions on blocks of flats," Saskia said, because she thought Selwen would have. When the truth was, what she'd wanted—what she had always wanted—was a home.

And despite all the years and everything that had happened, this flat still felt like home.

It was something about the light. It was the way the rooms seemed to flow one into the next, and the way that they'd put this place to rights together.

It was not until later that she had realized that in making this place the home that she'd always wanted, she had played directly into his hands. Because how could she leave this place? How could she walk away from it when she'd put so much of herself into it?

This flat had been his ace in the hole, she'd decided toward the end.

"You have lovely taste," she told him now.

Thanasis made a low noise. "I don't know that I have any real taste at all," he replied after a moment. "I default to minimalism, as I'm sure you can understand, having spent time amid the Baroque theatrics that my father considers decor. I'm not the one who found all the pieces that make this flat what it is."

Saskia remembered finding her way through Portobello Market, then letting Thanasis take her to far more exclusive shopping arenas, and that was why the flat reflected both of them. It was neither as Bohemian as she might have made it nor as minimalistic and corporate as he would have.

Every bit of it felt like *theirs*. It always had.

Until, that was, she had begun to obsess about the fact that he had a whole other house in London. A famous house that often turned up in magazines that he didn't want to sully with the likes of her, his downmarket mistress.

Those memories sat on her heavily. Saskia almost wished they hadn't come back to her like all the rest.

Thanasis was unaware where her head had gone, and showed her the small study that she'd made into a proper little library. "You liked to read here," he told her. "You studied here. You preferred it when there was a fire in the grate because you could pretend you weren't doing your coursework. I believe you once told me that you preferred to imagine you were an eighteenth-century heroine instead."

"How fanciful," Saskia murmured.

But the truth was, she adored this room. It got light in the morning and in the evenings, when she'd had work to do and he was off on one of his trips, she would often find herself in here. There was always reading to do and essays to work on, and she would pretend that she was something out of an Austen novel as she scribbled away, then curled up on the chaise with the fire crackling.

She had started her drawing and painting in earnest here, the artistic impulse inside of her no longer held hostage to the practicality that had governed her all her life.

It had been easier not to feel lonely that way, surrounded by art and study.

He led her down the hall to the guest bedroom that he'd used as an office sometimes, when he'd stayed here long enough that it required he check in with work. It was still set up that way, and her objection to that was simply that the room looked like it could be anywhere. There was nothing particularly noteworthy on the walls. There were no identifying characteristics.

So no one could tell, she had understood at some point, whether he was in London or across the planet.

That was how committed he was to keeping this thing between them private.

There were closets along the hallway and when she looked back over her shoulder, she could see the door that led into a bright and happy eating kitchen on the other end. She could remember cooking in there. He'd been absolute shit at it and she had taken great pleasure in teaching him some of the hallmarks of her university years. A quick Bolognese. Packet ramen. Omelets made of anything they might have on hand.

Over time, they'd developed a few easy dishes they could both make to feed each other when they didn't want the intrusion of the outside world, not even in the form of a food delivery.

She turned back around again, deliberately not thinking about how paranoid she'd originally become once she'd understood that he really did not intend to take her out, ever—unless costumes were involved—concentrating instead on that outrageously masculine back of his as he led her down to the final room. The bedroom.

God help her, but the things they had done in this bedroom.

The four-poster bed was made out of remarkably heavy wood, and she knew that because they had certainly done their best to send it skating this way and that across the floor. But it had always held firm.

It was a beautiful bedroom, and Saskia tried to focus on that. She supposed that what Selwen would notice was the seating area arranged around another fireplace. Not the bed. Not the expansive bathroom suite that took up more square footage than the whole of Ffion's little house in Pembrokeshire.

She moved for the doors that led outside to the narrow terrace that wrapped along the side of the flat, accessible from the bedroom and kitchen. She didn't have to look out to know that there was a whole outdoor dining and lounging area set down on the kitchen side, tucked beneath a hard canopy top to keep the weather out. There was a pergola a bit further along and she knew there was a hot tub tucked away beneath those vines. What she could see right now, without memory to help her, was the private seating area off the bedroom. It was enclosed in glass so that it was entirely possible to lie naked and tangled up with Thanasis, the rain coming down all around them, yet so warm and so loved that it was as if they'd become one.

With each other. With the weather.

"Lovely," she said again.

"Not very much like a prison, is it?"

She turned, slowly, and studied Thanasis as he stood

there. He was standing over by the bedroom door, giving the distinct impression that he did not wish to crowd her or to make her feel stuck back here with him in any way.

But he also didn't look particularly happy about it.

"A beautifully appointed prison is still a prison, Thanasis. It doesn't all have to be concrete cellblocks and metal doors."

"Forgive me," he said at once, though there was a fire in that dark gaze of his that she recognized. His temper. That temper had always exploded when he was with her, and she'd loved that. Because she'd been quite certain that she was the only creature on this earth who could make Thanasis Zacharias lose his shit.

But he wasn't losing it now. And she had to remind herself that Selwen wouldn't like it much if he did. Selwen would see that as evidence that she was right about him. "And what do you need to be forgiven for this time?" she asked.

"I did not bring you here to litigate a past you can't remember," Thanasis said after a moment, his voice calm. His gaze anything but. "Not only would that be churlish, it wouldn't get me anywhere. And you don't know this about me, Selwen, but I'm not a man who likes to tread water. I prefer a destination."

Saskia wanted to laugh at that. Selwen wouldn't know that she should. She settled on a sniff. "If that were true, I'm not sure why you bothered to answer your father's summons to attend his engagement party. Much less obey."

He leaned against the doorjamb, his dark eyes moving all over her, and he seemed to be in no hurry to conceal the fact that he was doing that. "You wanted to leave there in a hurry. And I'm guessing that he did not offer you any transportation options. Does that mean that the engagement is off?"

"As far as I'm concerned, it is." She pursed her lips, trying to decide how to go about talking about this. "You warned me. I didn't believe you. But it seemed that the longer we were engaged, the more he seemed to forget all of the things that we'd agreed on."

"My father has never met a boundary that he did not try to crash through at the first opportunity," Thanasis said. "I'm only sorry that you had to experience this yourself."

"You're not sorry at all. You're the one who told me what would happen."

"I told you what I thought would happen, yes. I'm sorry you had to experience it."

Standing this close to the very bed where they had worked out entirely too many issues in their relationship, over and over again and yet had never solved a thing, was not doing anything good for Saskia's head. It felt like she was lost between the past and the present, and the only real thing was him—

But she knew where that led.

She threw open the door to the terrace and stepped out, pleased that it was still raining. She could stand in the glass enclosure, ignoring the cozy couches and chaises that she also knew entirely too well, and watch the drops that hit the glass and the patterns they made. Back in the day, she'd painted those patterns.

Thanasis came up behind her, but he didn't put his hands on her. He moved to stand beside her instead, clasping his hands behind his back as he too gazed out at the rain. At the buildings across the way, bright white even on such a gloomy day.

"There isn't much rain in Greece," Saskia found herself saying when, surely, she hadn't meant to speak. "Or anyway, I didn't see much rain while I was there. I believe I actually missed it."

"The sun can make up for a lot of sins," Thanasis said, in what sounded like agreement. "But not all."

He was so close. Even when she hadn't known who he was to her, she had felt this compulsion between them. She had felt it the moment he'd stepped into the villa. He had done nothing to draw attention to himself and yet she'd found him there immediately, standing in the doorway as if he'd called her specifically.

Here, in this flat where they had built a life together, she could feel all of their history pressing in and yet still, none of that was as magnetic as he was.

She had never been any good at resisting him.

Please, she chided herself. *You never tried.*

It caused her actual, physical pain not to close the distance between them. She wanted more than anything to simply turn to him as she always would have in the past. Press herself into his side, slide her arms around his waist, *anything*.

She had only felt safe and whole right here, in his arms.

And she supposed that she ought to feel terribly sad that nothing had changed. That she had spent five years forgetting he existed, completely unaware of him or this place or the years that they'd spent together, and it was still the same.

She could feel her body changing when it was near him. She could feel herself ripening, softening, readying herself for any part of him he might wish to give her.

Saskia could feel herself heating up, from the inside out, and there was nothing the least bit sad about it.

"The flat is yours," he told her. Briskly, she thought. She had to think that meant she was getting to him, too. "Stay here as long as you like."

She studied him, though she could only do it from the corner of her eye or he would see it. From this angle, she had that particular view of his perfect jawline she had sometimes thought was responsible, entirely, for her inability to stay angry at him. Then there was the sooty brush of his lashes, far too long for a man, but they only made him seem hotter, somehow.

More dangerously ruthless.

This close to him, she was sure that she could almost smell him. If she leaned closer, she would surely be able to catch those hints of his scent that had used to drive her wild. Something spicy. A hint of citrus. The kind of musk that could as easily be vetiver or simply...*him*.

"That's very kind. You have already done too much." She sounded wooden. Probably because she felt wooden, because really, why was she letting this go on? She had returned to him. She could put her hands on him and tell him she remembered.

That she remembered everything.

Yet Saskia knew that if she did, he would be inside her almost before the words left her mouth. She knew that if she told him, all the dams would break and it would be a mad rush and she had no idea if they would ever come up for air again.

She wanted that so badly she could taste it.

But she still didn't say anything.

"You took nothing with you when you left." He turned toward her, that dark gaze something like assessing as it moved over her face. "I told you that already. What that means, however, is that all of your things are here. The closets are filled with your clothes. The study is filled with your books. And any trinkets you might see in this flat are entirely yours, picked up by you, sometimes with me and sometimes without. I will not taint that by telling you which is which."

"I can't possibly wear the clothes of another woman," she said, severely, because apparently she was really committing to this thing.

"Then you're more than welcome to open up your wallet, which you left right there on the bedside table, and help yourself to any of the numerous credit cards you find in there. Buy yourself a whole new wardrobe, Sas—" He caught himself. "*Selwen*. It is all yours. Do as you wish."

She wanted to cry, so she made herself huff a little bit instead. "I'm sure that I don't need that kind of charity. I'm sure that I don't—"

He leaned in, and there was something so stark on his face that it made her think that she really was going to cry, right then and there. And once she started, how would she stop?

"Selwen. You have no one in this world save for me. And I'm sorry for you, I am. But that does not change your circumstances. You have already told me what you think of me." His mouth curved into something too bitter to be a smile. "At length. And I am hoping that removing you from my father's clutches will go some way toward repairing that image you hold. But even if it doesn't, none of this matters to me without Saskia. You don't have to remember her to be her." His dark eyes were on her, all heat and longing, loss and grief. "All of this is yours. It always was."

"But—" she began.

And he reached over and put his finger on her lips.

Shushing her, she was aware.

But she was also aware of that great roar of fire that burned like a furnace deep within her. The way every part of her changed, and began to hum in that awareness. That reaction.

She saw twin flames of that same fire in his gaze.

And she was as sure as she could be without being inside his head that he could see it on her, too.

"I didn't bring you here to make things worse," he told her, though his voice was too low. The edge in it too deliciously rough. "And I won't. Suffering my presence doesn't go along with living here, Selwen. I promise you."

And it was a good thing that he had his finger over her lips, because otherwise she might have been tempted to tell him that *suffering his presence* wasn't what she was after at all. Everything inside of her was a mess, but one thing was clear.

It was impossible not to want him.

"If you need anything, you have the number to my personal mobile," he told her, his voice gravelly.

He took his finger away and she felt her lips part of

their own accord, though she didn't really think she was breathing.

She wasn't sure she *could*.

For a moment, they stood there, the rain beating against the glass as they made their own heat, and that fire between them that seemed to blaze higher and higher by the second—

And she really thought that with their faces so close, he could easily, simply, bend his head and—

But he didn't.

Thanasis simply looked at her like he had that same complicated ache inside him, and then he left her there.

All alone in this flat, as if the five years and whole other lives that had separated them had never happened at all.

CHAPTER EIGHT

THANASIS TRULY DID intend to leave Saskia alone. To allow her to settle into that flat again—without him this time—and build whatever kind of life she wanted back here in London. He thought that was the very least of the things she deserved after losing her memory and ending up engaged to a man she should never have met.

He waited for his father to call and announce that his fiancée had run off, but Pavlos never did anything of the sort. Whether he was hiding it or simply hadn't noticed yet, he didn't bring it up in their unavoidable business meetings and Thanasis certainly felt no particular compunction to reach out to him.

The truth was, as much as he might have tolerated his father's nonsense over the years, he didn't really think that he had it in him to be civil to a man who had done something to make Saskia bolt. And he had a hard enough time separating his business dealings from his father's. The last thing he needed to do was entertain the gutter press with a feud that would no doubt be reported widely, word for word.

He tended to his business. He haunted his office, jumping on things he normally left to his underlings, because he needed something to focus on that wasn't the Saskia of it all.

Not that it worked.

Besides, Saskia was one of the few who had access to his private mobile and when she called, he made certain that he was available.

The first few times, she asked him questions about London. About the neighborhood. About what she should do and where she should go like she didn't have access to the entire internet—

But then, the Saskia he knew had always been fiercely independent and capable. He had no idea what Selwen knew about London or how she felt about big, sprawling cities.

He answered her questions every time.

It was not until the third week of this that he began to wonder why it was she would call up a man she thought so little of for his thoughts on neighborhood eateries, shops, and nightspots.

"What sort of nightspots will you be frequenting?" he asked when she called the next time. He had walked out of a tedious meeting to take this call and he could look down the length of the office floor toward that meeting room, where he could see the tensions were rising.

But he didn't care.

"As you know," Saskia said into his ear, "I do like to dance."

Thanasis had spent a lot of time thinking about the accusations that she had levied at him on the island. He could not dismiss them all out of hand, and that was what concerned him the most.

She could not remember what happened between them and, as a result, he could not trust his recollections.

In the meantime, he was fully aware that she had danced and danced and danced her way across the Greek Islands. She had danced so much that she had somehow come to imagine that his father was an excellent dance partner, and he had found that he had no choice at all but to sit there and torture himself with images of this dancing—sometimes it was really dancing though, more often, it was a euphemism for other things he wanted to think about even less—until he was beside himself.

He would pace and pace into the small hours, wearing grooves into the hallways of his house on Hampstead Heath.

On the nights when he found himself in the flat, he would lie on the couch and drive himself insane with the memory of her. Right there with him. Lying on top of him. Fitting to him so perfectly that he had never felt quite right in his own body once she was gone.

He had wondered if he might truly go mad, for how could he possibly reconcile himself to this? Knowing that she lived, knowing where she was, and not having her?

How could he live with the knowledge that his father could, at any moment, have his debauched hands all over her?

Thanasis had begun to think that dying might have been easier than living without her, not that he intended to find out. In the meantime, he had resigned himself to the torture.

But now she wanted to go dancing some more.

"I have an idea," he told her, as it came to him in a flash. The perfect solution, with only slightly more torture than usual. "I will take you dancing, Selwen."

"Surely not," she replied, in such a smooth, deliberate way that it gave him pause. Because it made him think of Saskia. His Saskia. It made him wonder how much of her had come back to London, bubbling up inside Selwen after all. "What if we're seen? What if someone thinks we're together? Worse still, what if they know that I was recently engaged to your father?"

All valid concerns. Yet, "They won't," he said curtly.

And when they rang off, he sent his secretary a message, telling her to reach out to a client who had invited him to a masked ball in New York and tell them that although he had previously declined, he would now be coming. With a guest.

The next day he went by the flat for the first time since he'd foolishly greeted her here and ripped his own heart out with all he'd lost. Even though he had his own key, he buzzed up and waited for Saskia to let him in.

"Who is it?" she asked through the intercom.

"Who else knows you're here?" he replied.

She didn't reply. She only buzzed him in.

He took the stairs slowly, feeling the ghosts of all the other times he'd come here pressing in on him. Whispering him into states of nostalgia and need that could only cause trouble.

"She is not yours," he reminded himself beneath his breath. "She barely knows who you are."

But she opened the door at the top of the stairs before he made it there, and that felt the way it always had.

Like a homecoming.

Like he was finally where he was meant to be.

He got to the top and he watched her face closely as he drew nearer to her. He could have sworn that he saw that recognition again. He would have bet everything he had that it was there.

And everything in him sang out, but he didn't reach for her. Though he did see at once that she was no longer wearing the shapeless, flowing things she'd lived in on the island. She was dressed in her own clothes now. Even five years old, Saskia's wardrobe was timeless. She had an eye for the classics and always chose items of clothing because they flattered her shape, not because she wanted her shape to fit into them.

A critical difference that she had lectured him on at some length, many times.

Fashion is tyranny, she had told him. *Women are bludgeoned with messages about how they ought to look when half the time it's biologically impossible. It would be better by far to teach women to love any shape they find themselves in, and dress for that.*

I am fascinated, of course, he had told her, stretched out as he was beside her on their bed after a long and intense game of theirs that had involved experimenting with various bindings, and different ways to beg. She had done so, and so prettily, every time.

Not fascinated enough, she had retorted, grinning at him wickedly. Then she had started kissing her way down the length of his torso. She'd cupped him in her hands, and licked him, root to tip. *Why don't we experiment with fit, here and now?*

Now I am even more fascinated, he had gritted out.

But that was a long time ago. Today Saskia looked at him both as if she didn't recognize him and yet she did, and he had to order his cock to get control of itself as he followed her into the flat.

"Do you like coffee?" she asked, and slid him a look that he found…unreadable.

He was sure there were minefields here, but he couldn't see them. "I do."

"I thought you must. There's a rather dramatic espresso machine in the kitchen, and I can't imagine it would only be for me." She wrinkled her nose. "Besides, I like tea."

"You like tea all day and into the evening, yes," he corrected her. "But in the mornings, you enjoy a decent coffee, like all civilized people do."

"How very Greek of you."

He shrugged, and didn't quite smile, though it was the closest he'd come in some time. "I cannot deny it."

When they smiled at each other, he actually forgot what year this was. The only difference between this moment and any of the other ones they passed in this kitchen was that they weren't touching. And he almost forgot that too. He almost reached over, got his hands on her, and let himself—

But Saskia stopped him from doing it by simple virtue of turning away and applying herself to the espresso machine.

He did not tell her that he could remember when they'd installed it. When he'd taught her how to use it. Or how they'd competed, in those early days, to see who could make the better *freddo espresso* or *freddo cappuccino*. He remembered telling her that under no circumstances were any *ellinikós kafés,* traditional Greek coffees, to be made by anyone in the flat who was not Greek.

That almost feels a bit pointed, she had laughed.

It is a point, he'd agreed with intensity that was only partly feigned, *of honor. Greek coffee not made by Greeks tastes like the Ottoman Empire.* He'd shrugged when she'd laughed at that too. *No one likes oppressive coffee, Saskia.*

He could still hear her laughter. He could still see the smile she'd aimed at him, and the way she'd melted into him. What he didn't understand was how he could feel all these memories around them, pressing in from all sides, and she couldn't.

And when she slid him his coffee, perfectly made and precisely how he liked it, he wondered yet again just how much she really remembered.

"Tonight, we dance," he told her. "There will be a car for you at noon and we will fly to New York."

"New York," she echoed.

"I was uncertain if you would know what to wear to such an event, so I came to help you choose the appropriate gown."

"Gown," she repeated, her eyes narrowing.

"You have an extensive wardrobe of formal attire, Selwen," he told her, sipping at his coffee. "I don't know how you missed it." He inclined his head toward the clothes she was wearing today. It was nothing but a pair of jeans and one of those perfectly fitted T-shirts that look so simple and was thus exquisitely cut, in order to look so effortless. "I see you have found the rest of the wardrobe."

"Why would your Saskia have had a closet full of formalwear?" she asked, and though she'd made herself a coffee, she didn't drink it. "I thought you didn't take her anywhere."

"I didn't take her anywhere she could be photographed," he corrected her, mildly enough. "I didn't take her anywhere there would be pictures taken, paparazzi articles written, or anything like that. But there are other places in this world where a person can, if he's willing to pay for it, have his privacy."

"If you say so," she said, but something flickered in that dark tea gaze of hers.

He tossed his coffee back, watched her do the same, and he led her down the hallway to the bedroom again. This time he didn't spare a glance for that bed, or those stout posters that he had tested too many times to count. This time he simply marched himself into the closet. It was a large walk-in affair, with more than one room. Thanasis didn't point out that one of those rooms was his. He simply moved toward the back and found the area that held all of her gowns, and then he flipped through them until he found the one he wanted.

He laid it out on the center block and watched her stare at it as if she thought it might bite her.

"Do you not like the dress?" he asked mildly.

So very mildly, because the last time she'd worn this dress it had been their anniversary. Two years in. He had taken her to a private restaurant that could only be accessed through a series of tunnels and offered only private dining rooms. It had been a special night. Everything had been magical. They had felt *fated*. He had thought, *this life is so beautiful*.

It had been precious and he didn't think that either one of them, that night, had known that there would only be a few months before they would end so abruptly. She might have been nursing hurt feelings. She might have been annoyed with him. But she was also in love with him.

He'd known that as well as he knew himself.

He'd thought about that night often in the years since he'd lost her, and more again now that she was back and thought ill of him, because how could she have turned against them the way that she had? Where had the magic gone? He had never understood.

But he hadn't realized that today, he was testing her, until now. As he watched her face for clues as she stared at that dress.

"It's lovely," she said, which he was beginning to realize she always said. Because it was essentially meaningless. "If it fits as well as these jeans, it should look well enough on me too."

"I have no doubt that it will," Thanasis managed to say, remembering.

And when her gaze lifted to his, he was certain that she knew. That she remembered. That she knew exactly how he had helped her into this dress in the first place, and how he had left her shivering when he'd pulled her with him out to the car.

How they hadn't made it to the restaurant, but had burst into flame on the way there. He'd pulled her over his lap and hiked this very same dress up to her hips, because he couldn't bear not to thrust deep inside her. She couldn't bear to not take those thrusts.

Two years in and they'd still been wild for each other.

They hadn't made it out of that private dining room, either. That time, he'd leaned her over one of the chairs and hiked that dress up to her waist once more. Then he'd wrapped his hands around her hips and slammed his way into her again.

And when they'd made it home to the bed right there in the next room even now, he had her keep it on as he moved his way around her. Until he'd made her lie face down as he teased every bit of flesh that the crisscrossed back straps exposed.

With his mouth.

And only when she was writhing against him once more had he finally stripped her entirely, and then glutted himself.

Thanasis could have sworn that she was remembering all of those same things. He could feel it. He could *taste* it.

He was hard as hell, and he suspected she knew it.

There had never been a time in all the years he'd known her that he hadn't been absolutely right about what she was feeling, especially when it came to sex.

"Thanasis…" she began, and he knew he wasn't imagining the color on her cheeks. Or that understanding in her gaze.

"Twelve o'clock," he told her, with a coolness that cost him dearly. "Bring the dress. And whatever else you need for a weekend in Manhattan."

Then he made himself walk away. Before he didn't.

Before he couldn't.

And that night, he took her to a masked ball on a glittering Manhattan rooftop. They danced around and around, their identities hidden while flashbulbs went off all around them and far below, New York City gleamed and sparkled in all of its chaos and mystery.

Thanasis held her in his arms. He spun her around. And he thought even more that there was no possible way she could move with him like this—as if they were two parts of one whole—and still maintain that she did not know him.

He didn't see how it could be possible.

Later, they walked down a Manhattan street together, hand in hand. This was New York City. No one paid the slightest bit of attention to two people in formal attire, masks firmly in place, out on the street. No one cared if he had his hands on her. If their fingers were intertwined.

And if he didn't ask her why it was that Selwen from Wales would let a man she thought so little of touch her, well.

Maybe he didn't want to know if she remembered him or not. Maybe he wanted to bask in the notion that she might.

And that was what their weekend was like. A carved-out bit of space in a country off across an ocean where they could have been anyone.

The last time Thanasis had felt like this it had been in that flat in London, where he could simply be himself.

He took her out for dinner on the night they were leaving, in a crowded New York restaurant where no one would have cared who they were even if they knew.

"Why do you seem so much happier in New York?" she asked him.

The way Saskia might have, because she'd known him so well.

He smiled, tucked away in the corner of the loud, bustling restaurant, for he was completely unconcerned about anyone seeing them or knowing who they were in the first place. It was safe here. He did not have to worry about his half siblings or his father or even the European paparazzi who chased him—but never here.

"New York is anonymous," he told her. "We could be anyone here. No one is paying attention either way."

She was dressed like his Saskia. She was wearing the same effortlessly chic jeans she'd been wearing all day, in a dark gray shade. She'd changed from flats to heels and had dressed it all up with a black sweater and quietly elegant jewelry.

God help him, she was perfect. Still and ever, she was peerless and his.

His, something inside him insisted.

She studied him. "I don't understand."

Thanasis would have indulged her anything, particularly on a night like this. He reached across the small table and took her fingers in his again, and he felt her shiver, though she didn't look at him while she did it. But she didn't pull her hand away, either.

"What don't you understand?" he asked her, aware that his voice was rougher now. That was what touching her did to him.

"This. You. Your father has never met a single bit of space that wasn't a stage, because he is always only too happy to make it one."

"My father is a narcissist." He lifted a brow when she frowned at that. "I was raised by a narcissist, but that doesn't mean I am also one."

"Aren't you?"

And he could have taken offense to that. But he didn't think that was how it was meant. He toyed with her fingers, and chose not to let his temper lead the way.

Not in public. That was not how he preferred to vent it.

"I am not," he told her instead. "Perhaps to my detriment. All I wanted, ever, was something that was mine. Something that was not tainted by my father."

"Is that what I am?" she asked, those wise eyes of hers trained on him as if she was looking for clues the same way he was. "Am I tainted?"

"You will have to tell me." Thanasis still didn't like to think about his father anywhere near Saskia, but he pushed that aside, too. "You must understand, it wasn't simply that my father cheated. He did, and on an epic scale. Yet part of the joy in cheating, for him, was making certain that it hurt my mother. He went out of his way to make sure that it did. But she was a Greek woman, you see. As stubborn as the day is long and she would not let him see that she was affected. She would not react, and so he kept going, and they did this until she died."

"You say that as if you blame her," Saskia said softly.

And he forgot that this wasn't really his Saskia. That this was simply the woman who occupied her body now—and looked like her, and sounded like her, and hell, even smelled like her. Tasted like her. But she wasn't Saskia.

Yet tonight, hidden away in plain sight in this loud restaurant, he didn't care. He couldn't.

She was close enough.

And she was still the only one he trusted.

"I do," Thanasis confessed, though it hurt to say out loud when he'd avoided it all these years. He waited for her to recoil, but when she didn't, he took a breath. "I think about my mother all the time. What did her stubbornness get her? She was miserable. She made sure that I was miserable, too. If she couldn't leave him for herself, why couldn't she leave for her own child? I will never understand."

Saskia reached over and put her other hand on top of the place where their hands were already entwined.

"You were the child," she said, her voice soothing and her gaze intent on his. "She should have protected you above all things."

"I suppose it's possible she didn't know how," he allowed. "She was very young when they were married. And from what I can tell, remarkably naive."

"Then she should've figured it out," Saskia said, her voice getting stern. She gripped his hand tighter. "That's what mothers are supposed to do. It's supposed to stop being about them, because what matters is the child they brought into the world. The child who didn't ask to be married to an overbearing man. The child who didn't ask to be brought up in misery. That was her job. It's fair to say that she didn't do it well."

He wanted to ask her if she remembered her own tangled feelings about her young parents, who had adored her but had left her that night just the same, then had died on their way back to be there when she woke up. He wanted to ask her what mothers she recalled, as either version of her.

But instead he stared back at her for so long that he watched her flush, look down, then look away.

The food came then, which he thought probably saved her. She looked as if it was sent straight from heaven, and it made certain that she didn't have to answer what would probably be his very next question.

After dinner, they once again walked the dark, crowded streets, where they were entirely anonymous. He wrapped his arm around her shoulders and held her close, and maybe they were both pretending it was because it was cold.

But he knew better. Later, they would make their way out to his plane and head back to London. They would be there by morning.

They would be back in their usual reality.

Thanasis couldn't say he was in any rush.

First, then, there was this. Walking down Park Avenue with Saskia cuddled up tight beside him as if nothing had changed.

As if they were still connected the way they always had been.

As if she had never left and never would.

Thanasis vowed, there and then, that he would do what he needed to do to make Saskia fall in love with him.

Every version of her.

No matter what it took.

Because he did not intend to lose her again. He could not bear it.

CHAPTER NINE

LONDON WAS COLD and gray and as far Saskia could tell, completely missing the magic of Manhattan.

It had been painful to climb back onto the plane. To face the reminder she hadn't wanted that there was a reality to return to. That all these fingers intertwined and hands held weren't who they were.

That he still believed she couldn't remember him.

Saskia still couldn't seem to make herself tell him otherwise, and she tried. She kept trying. But she couldn't seem to make those words come out of her mouth.

She sat in the belly of the plane with him, pretending not to watch him as he rolled calls and answered emails, in that same resolutely competent fashion he did everything. This wasn't anything new to her. He had always worked, constantly, in all the time she'd known him. She had been the one with the schedule that was flexible, and she'd been only too happy to fit herself in around his.

Because it had seemed like what *they* had to do, *together,* to make sure they spent the most time together.

She had studied on this plane. She had painted and sketched on this plane. She had flown with him to far-off places and never exited the plane at all, waiting for him to finish his meetings and come meet her back here to fly some more.

Saskia was tired of these memories. She was tired of nostalgia. She was tired of second-guessing everything she said and everything she felt because she was still trying to pretend to be someone she wasn't.

When the truth was, she had taken great pride, back in the day, of always being entirely herself. Because she had never had the option to be anyone else. She had never *wanted* to be anyone else.

But then she had met Thanasis, and she had wanted so badly to be *his*.

And she realized then—as they sat in the back of another town car, driving through the listless, damp London streets—that the only reason she was still concealing the fact that she had her memory back was because, on some level, she wanted to hurt him.

Because he had hurt her, all those years ago.

She had been so deeply in love. And she would have sworn that he was, too—she'd been certain he was—but he'd never said it.

He'd never *said* he loved her. He'd never said those words.

Oh, he'd said a million other things, and often, but never that.

Saskia had let it fester inside of her, like a wound.

Until she'd come to the unpleasant conclusion that, in the end, their entire relationship could be looked at in two completely different ways at the same time. There was the story that they'd met and fallen for each other at first sight and had arranged their lives around that ever after, and she loved that story.

But there was also another way to look at it.

That Thanasis had seen her, claimed her, and then tucked her away where she could cause him no trouble at all. That he'd kept her meek, and a secret, so that he wouldn't ever feel embarrassed by the fact that he'd fallen for a no-name orphan girl he'd met more or less on the streets.

She'd veered back and forth between those two stories all the time, in those years, depending on how *kept* a woman she felt she was at any given time. And eventually, the bad one had got its teeth in her.

And now, all these years later, she really couldn't understand how she'd let that happen.

They'd walked through the streets of a foreign city and she'd felt that sheer, sweet joy in her chest, bubbling up like glory.

They had talked of nothing in particular and anything that occurred to them as they moved, and she'd forgotten that part. The way it felt to have his arm slung over her shoulders. The way it felt to move through the world with this man, constantly aware of him, and fascinated by him, and always attuned to his every movement, because that was how much she'd entangled herself with him.

She never knew what he might say next. She prized his smiles, and his rare laughter. And she didn't believe that she would have been able to throw herself so completely into him if he didn't feel the same way.

She'd seen the evidence in New York, hadn't she?

There had been the way he'd danced with her, there in the crush of a crowded rooftop ballroom. Around and around he'd spun her, but she had been close enough to see the intensity in his gaze. As if he would throw himself down and allow everyone in the ballroom to stomp all over him rather than let go of her for even a moment.

Then there had been the way he'd led her through the crowd, that possessive grip on the back of her neck or on her bicep, guiding her so easily that she didn't need to do anything but trust him.

There was even the way he'd walked her to the door of the rooms that had been set aside for her in the town house he kept in lower Manhattan. He'd stood outside her door and smiled down at her, and then he'd bowed, just slightly as he'd left her there.

I hope this nightspot met with your approval, he'd said.

It has a lot of potential, she'd managed to reply, feeling hot and flushed straight through. From the dancing. From the way they'd walked back together. From simply being close to him again.

And she hadn't moved from the door, so she'd seen it when he'd glanced back over his shoulder. She'd seen when his face was no longer the picture of courtesy, his eyes alight with a need that echoed in her, low and deep.

Then at dinner their last night, where he'd told her about his mother—something he'd never told her before. The way he'd played with her fingers, which wasn't the heat that she was sure he could feel as easily as she could. It was intimate, the way he touched her at that table. The way she touched him back. There was that deep intimacy, in all of it.

She thought that they'd walked away from that restaurant changed, somehow.

They'd smiled at each other as they'd walked back

downtown, weaving their way in and out of the crowds. A part of the bustle and roll of the New York streets.

But all she'd really been aware of was him.

Now, when they finally reached the right address in Chelsea in this gray city across the ocean from all that intimacy and light, she felt torn up inside from all these memories, all these sensations inside of her. She scowled at him when he made no move to get out.

"I think you'd better come up," she told him.

He looked at her for a long moment, those dark eyes of his as unreadable as ever.

He nodded, slowly.

She thought that was ominous. It made her stomach hurt.

Maybe because of that, she made a point of gathering her own luggage and carrying it in with her, because she knew he usually had his driver do such things. It seemed necessary that she do it herself.

She didn't want to ask herself why.

"Don't be ridiculous," he told her as he followed her into the building, and took the garment bag and her small case from her.

For some reason, maybe because she was completely unable to handle herself the way she should have been able to, she found that ominous too.

Saskia climbed the stairs, entirely too aware of him at her back. Particularly because he didn't seem to notice that he was heaving a case up the stairs with him. He was that fit. He always had been.

It set her teeth on edge, or maybe she just wished she could bite him a little—

She pushed that aside. It was unhelpful.

By the time they made it to the flat itself, Saskia was vibrating with a stress she couldn't entirely name. She felt as if she might explode. Her skin felt strange, stretched too tight around her body, as if someone had come and switched it in the night.

She couldn't help but think that if they'd stayed in New York, things would be different. Instead of walking back down to that town house and getting in a car to take them to the airport, would they have ended up in his bed?

Or hers?

Inside the flat, she crossed her arms tightly over her chest as if that could keep her heart in place, then she turned to face him.

"You were going to go back to your real house, weren't you?" she asked.

"That seems like rather a loaded question." One of his dark brows rose. "It is just a house. It is no more or less real than this one. The only difference I know of is that my house on the heath is—"

"Legitimate?" she interjected.

"Well-known," he corrected her, with a certain pointed patience. "Particularly by my father. And all of my half siblings. They send the paparazzi there themselves. I have always wanted to keep you safe from these things."

She felt strange again, this time as if something in her was ticking, like some bomb set to go off. "Your father promised me that I could stay private, but he was already talking about taking me to galas in Athens. Weddings in Paris cathedrals."

Thanasis stood taller at that and she watched his jaw

turn to granite. "That would make sense, of course. Everyone knows him to be an unapologetic womanizer. His trespasses against my mother were exhaustively covered in every paper there was. Of course he would wish to make a spectacle of his second wife, who everyone would assume is too naive to know better."

"I think maybe I was too naive," she said quietly. "I believed him."

"But not enough to marry him," Thanasis reminded her. "And in the end, really, this is what matters."

She opened her arms then and watched as his gaze moved, as if he couldn't help it, down the length of her body and up again.

"I'm dressed in all her clothes now," Saskia said, and she was aware of the dissonance in her own head. And the fact that she was still lying to him. "But she wouldn't have made the mistakes that I've made, would she?"

"She was very street-smart," Thanasis said, though he seemed to hesitate before he used that word. "She could read people at a glance. She never would have believed my father, but then, I would have told you that she never would have left me, either. Not even for a dramatic effect in the middle of a fight."

Saskia could hardly breathe. "And what if I can never be her again? What happens then?"

"You must be you." Thanasis was still standing there, facing her. He didn't shift his gaze from hers. "You are still you, Saskia." He didn't seem to notice that he said the wrong name. Saskia jolted, but he didn't. "It doesn't matter what you remember. It doesn't matter if you ever remember. Do I wish you could remember everything that happened between us? Of course I do. What we had was special. But I thought you were dead for five years. You alive is what matters. If your memory doesn't appear and never will, that is still all that matters."

He meant that. She could see it. She could *feel* it.

She looked at him, her heart pounding. "What if there's a way that I might remember?"

"I have studied this, a lot, since I walked into that villa and saw you there," he told her then, and he rubbed a hand over his face and that, too, told her how much he meant what he was saying. It made her whole body shake, deep inside. "It could be anything. A bit of music. Coming back to this apartment. Anything."

"Maybe you haven't tried the right thing," she suggested.

And then, because she was tired of punishing herself, she walked toward him. She watched his face change the way it had before.

Shock. A quick assessment. Then that long, slow burn.

She walked directly into him, wrapping her arms around his waist and arching herself into him. She tipped her head up, fully aware that doing so thrust her breasts into the wall of his chest.

It felt exactly as fantastic as she remembered.

"It sounds to me that the major way you and your Saskia communicated was sex," she said, and she didn't even stumble over the *your Saskia* part. "What if…?"

"You can't be serious." He shook his head, but his arms went around her and he held on tight. "You may have forgotten what happened on the beach, but I have not. I have no desire for you to look at me like that ever again. As if I could possibly…"

Thanasis shook his head.

"This is different," she said. When he scowled at her, she pushed back from him and waved her hand around at the flat they were standing in. "There are pictures of us everywhere here. Did you think I wouldn't notice that? You said that every trinket that was here was something I put here myself."

His scowl only deepened. "You did."

"I did this." She pointed to the frames on the mantel, on the side tables. "I went and put these pictures of us, everywhere."

It had been like being haunted all over again. Everywhere she turned, there was another picture. Candids. Posed shots. Funny little moments of them together.

It had been almost too much to bear.

No wonder she'd felt the need to call him about *dancing,* of all things.

"Saskia," he began.

But he heard it that time, and he shook his head as if he despaired of himself.

"Selwen," he corrected himself.

And she still did not tell him who she really was. Or what she remembered. There was something wrong with her, that much was perfectly clear to her.

But she couldn't bring herself to care about that.

Instead, standing slightly apart from him, she kicked off the flats she'd been wearing on the plane. She shrugged out of the duster she'd been wearing to keep the weather at bay. She let that fall to the floor, and made sure that he was looking at her as she peeled off the sweater beneath, then shimmied out of her jeans.

He looked as if she'd struck him over the head with one of the heavy vases in the foyer.

Then he looked something a lot more like haunted when she unhooked her bra and let it fall too. And then his expression darkened and went molten hot when she peeled off her panties.

When she straightened, she let her hair fall all around her and she watched the way that he swallowed, hard. She could see the tension in him, and how his hands were curled into fists he kept tight at his side.

"You said I know you," she said, standing there naked before him and somehow never feeling more powerful. "And I want to. I want to know you in every possible way. Maybe it will change my memory. Maybe it won't. But either way, Thanasis. I want you."

Then she turned and headed down the hallway toward their bed.

And her heart was pounding so hard that she wasn't sure she could manage to keep walking. But she also couldn't hear him, and that was the trouble.

She took one step, then another. She kept walking, and she didn't allow herself to look back. She passed the study. Then she passed the guestroom. And right up ahead, she could see the bedroom door—

But then she was in the air, because he was sweeping her into his arms and holding her high against his chest. Thanasis kicked his way into the bedroom, tossed her on the bed, then followed her down before she could bounce.

Then his mouth was on hers, his body was a heavy weight on top of her, and everything made sense again.

This was better than the beach, because she only felt she really bloomed when he was pressing himself against her like this. When he was holding her down so that she could wrap herself around him and press herself even closer.

Saskia realized belatedly that he had taken the time to remove his own clothes back in the living room. And wasn't that thoughtful, because now there was no barrier at all between them.

Finally, she thought. *Finally.*

He ate at her mouth in some kind of delicious fury and then his hands were joining him in the exploration, and he was muttering against her neck. Half in Greek, but half in English as well.

"Perfect," she heard him say, and low curse against her breast. "Still so fucking perfect."

And it thrilled her.

He took his time inspecting every last part of her, and making sure she was all in one piece. That she was *her*. He found every new scar and freckle.

He knew her body so well, and he remembered everything.

He checked the entire front part of her body, down to the soles of her feet, and then he turned her over and started up her backside.

And when he got to her neck, he set his teeth to her nape and he hauled her up onto her knees with an arm around her middle. She thought that he might take her like that. One smooth, thick trust—

She was pretty sure he considered it, but then he pulled her over to her back again, came down with her, and slammed himself home.

Saskia was lost, immediately. She arched up to take all of him, and that easily, shattered apart.

It was one thing to have fingers inside of her on a beach, but this was something else. Something much, much better. This was heaven. This was *hers*.

This was all of him, buried deep inside of her, and she had never wanted him more.

Not even that first time.

"I want to see you," he told her gruffly. "All this time, I've only seen you in my head. It's not enough, Saskia. It's never been enough."

As the orgasm faded, he began to play those dark and beautiful games of his, taking her from the heart of one fire and tossing her into the next. He slowed down when she tried to speed up. He laughed when she sobbed out her pleasure and her need.

And still he kept playing.

She didn't know how he had it in him, after all this time. But that was Thanasis.

He was methodical. He was ruthless.

He brought her to the edge and tossed her off the side of it again and again.

And only when she began to dig her nails into his shoulders, and had tears pouring down the sides of her face, did he relent.

He built up one more fire. He made sure that she burned first.

And then, only then, did he follow her.

For a while, everything was scorchingly hot and just as beautiful.

Saskia couldn't believe that she had finally made it back here, to this bed, with him.

When she felt him stir beside her, she rolled over and threw her leg over him so that she could straddle him, for a change. He smiled up at her, and so she took her time, sliding up and down his chest. Kissing him and biting him, and laying her own kind of claim all over that glorious body of his.

When he kept trying to grab her, she shook her head. She made herself frown at him.

"Place your fingers behind your head," she told him.

His arrogant brow rose, but he looked delighted. "And if I refuse?"

"Then there will be penalties."

"But what if I like the penalties?" he asked, with a laugh.

Then he stopped laughing, because she slid all the way down the length of his body and found her way between his legs. Then she smiled up at him, held his gaze, and sucked him deep into her mouth.

He didn't keep his hands where she told him to. But that wasn't surprising. They ended up in her hair, and though he let her play at first, as it went on, he began to guide her. He began to use her head as he liked, and it had the expected effect on her. Immediately.

She loved it. And if Saskia had any doubt that she loved it, her entire body broke out in goose bumps. She was slick between her thighs.

As he thrust into her mouth, she came close enough to her own cliff.

And then, when he threw back his head and flooded her, she came too.

He was hauling her up almost immediately, flipping her over and finding his way between her thighs, because he knew. He tossed her legs over his shoulders and settled in.

Saskia could feel him hum his approval, deep between her legs.

And then everything was the way he ate at her, the way he licked and sucked, and enjoyed himself so obviously that he had her bucking against him and crying out his name—so fast that it ought to have been embarrassing.

But it wasn't. It was Thanasis. It was the two of them. It was *this*.

Before she was done falling apart, he was pulling her to him once more. Then they were kissing again, deep and wild.

He pushed his way inside her once more with her legs wrapped tight around him, her heels encouraging him to go faster, harder, *forever*—

Because everything was blistering heat, and the glory of this thing was only theirs.

And this time, when they burned to ash, they did it together.

CHAPTER TEN

Thanasis didn't want to fall asleep. He wanted to marinate in every moment—but he must have drifted off anyway. Because when he woke, Saskia was pressed against his side with one hand flat over his heart.

He was surprised she didn't wake when he felt it kick. Hard.

But she kept sleeping.

And he stared up at the ceiling, the sweet weight of her nestled warm and tight beside him, and wondered what he had done.

When Saskia finally stirred, he operated purely on instinct and memory and pulled her into his arms. By the time he realized what he was doing, it was too late. He was kissing the top of her head, then her sleepy mouth. Then he carried her into the bathroom the way he'd always done in the past. He ran a bath and while it was filling, he brought her into the shower and rinsed her off thoroughly. Only then did he settle her into the bath and climb in across from her, so they could both soak.

They had spent long hours here, their legs tangled together and their gazes hot and sleepy. Sometimes the rain pattered against the window. Sometimes they would fog it up with the bath's heat. Sometimes the light from outside filtered in, making them glow. They would sit here in the warmth with the scent of lavender and sugar in the air and all around, and tell each other things that would have felt incidental or even pointless if they'd shared them over a meal. Things that were so tiny that they hardly mattered, and yet he could remember each and every one of them now. All these years later.

Her feelings about bananas. Her least favorite pop song and, conversely, her secret, shameful favorite. Her deep suspicion of men in khaki trousers, particularly with American accents. Her aversion to the word *moist*.

Thanasis could remember all of it.

Sitting here with her felt so easy, so natural, that it was tempting to tell himself that they had erased that stretch of lost time. That they had simply glossed over it.

But he had lived through every ghastly moment of it. He remembered it entirely too well.

Now, finally, he had been with her again. And it had been glorious in every possible way, as always—save for the one, small detail of her lost memory.

Because *he* remembered everything, but she didn't know who he was, no matter how many pictures of them were scattered about this flat. She didn't know who they were. So this might have been fantastic sex for her—and he knew that it had been—but that wasn't the same thing.

And he wasn't sure how he could reconcile the fact that *he* felt as if his soul had been turned inside out, that *he* had felt that deep and intimate connection with *his Saskia* as if they were *them* again while she had simply…

Had sex.

It made him feel hollow.

Only darker.

"What's the matter?" she asked him, tilting her head to one side as she regarded him.

Thanasis rose from the bath, because he couldn't bear to lounge about in the relaxing hot water while this was happening, mimicking the relationship he'd once had with her and now likely never would again.

He got out and dried himself off, and she followed. Then they were out in the bedroom again and he couldn't pretend that he wasn't...

Whatever this was. He didn't know how to name it.

"This shouldn't have happened," he told her. More sternly than necessary.

She frowned. "I wanted it to happen."

"You don't know who you are." That came out louder than he'd meant it to, but he didn't take it back. On the contrary, it was as if saying it loosened something in him. "You don't know who *I* am. This meant something to me and you don't even know why."

Saskia frowned at him. Then she looked away and he could have sworn that she looked something like guilty. But what could she have to feel guilty about?

"Thanasis..." she began, as if she was testing out his name in her mouth.

And he did not need to focus on that image.

"I've spent my whole life trying my very best to make certain that I am nothing like my father," he told her, and now he did fight to keep his voice even—but it was a losing battle. "The lengths I have gone to, in every regard, beggar belief. I have separated myself in every possible way I can. I go to that island as little as I can. I minimize all possible conversations, because I do not wish to entertain him and I am tired of running interference for him. Yet I am forever apologizing for him, cleaning up his messes, and soothing the feathers he ruffles all over Europe and beyond."

She made as if to speak, but he shook his head. "All this to discover, in the end, that I am the same. I might as well not have bothered to distance myself from him at all, for it turns out that despite all these efforts, I am no different from him at all. Where it counts, I am the same monster."

Saskia was frowning at him as if he'd lapsed off into Greek. "What are you talking about?"

"I know what sex between us is like, Saskia," he belted out. And he never lost his temper. He never lost his cool. Never, that was, unless it was Saskia. The only person on earth who had ever managed to get under his skin since he was a child. "I know exactly how it feels and what it does. And I know what it was like when we met, so I know exactly what you experienced tonight. But for me, it was so much more than that. And I knew it would be. *I knew it,* and I did it anyway."

"I don't know what that means."

But she did. He could see that she did.

"I knew what would happen," Thanasis said, again, to make certain he was facing this. That he was acknowledging what had happened here. "And how is that fair? You were so determined to think the worst of me and then, given the opportunity, I lived down to every expectation. At the end of the day, I'm as much a monster as my father ever was."

And he didn't know what he expected, but it wasn't that flash that seemed to go through her like an electric shock. "You are nothing like your father," she told him, her voice serious and her gaze grave. "Nothing at all."

"You don't know him either," Thanasis said.

"I do know him," Saskia retorted. She took a deep breath. Then another. "And more to the point, Thanasis, I...remember."

He couldn't move. He couldn't let that word make sense. He couldn't take it in.

Saskia gulped in more air. "I remember," she said again, even more deliberately this time. "I remember the stories you told about him back in the day. And so I remember how he treated you, now. And I know how he treated me, so you need to believe me when I tell you that you are not in the least bit like him. Not at all."

"You remember?" Thanasis concentrated on the only part that mattered. "You remember...before?"

He was staring down at her with an expression on his face that he could *feel*, and was certain he had never worn before. He felt *outside* himself, and something like dizzy, and he could not have looked away from her if his life depended on it.

He didn't try.

"I knew exactly who I was when I came back to London," Saskia told him, her gaze still wide and glued to his. And on the one hand, the confession was a relief. Thanasis hadn't been going mad, after all. He had seen that recognition all over her and he'd been right, she had known him. *She had known him.*

And those moments in New York that could only

have occurred between two people who'd loved each other for years were real. He hadn't made that up, either.

He stared at her, and neither one of them had clothes on, but that didn't seem to make a difference. He didn't even realize he was stalking toward her until she made a small noise of surprise when her back hit the bed.

"You knew," he said. "When you came back to London."

Her eyes widened even more, but she didn't look away. "Yes."

"And might I be given some explanation as to why it is you felt the need to lie to me?" he asked her.

With a frigid courtesy that felt a lot like a weapon. When she winced, he imagined she felt it that way too.

And the Saskia he knew had always charged face-first into any confrontation, but she didn't this time. She shook her head, a kind of anguish in her gaze. "I don't know," she said quietly. "I really don't. I can't defend it. I just… I felt that I had no choice but to do it."

"Maybe you do remember, after all," he suggested darkly, so close to her now but not touching her. Not again. Not even though she was his once again, the Saskia he had mourned and grieved, lost and found. "Maybe the monster is in the blood of the Zacharias family and that's always been obvious to you. Maybe you knew better than to throw yourself from the frying pan into the fire this time."

That anguish in her eyes faded, replaced by a spark he recognized.

It was her temper, kicking in the way it always had before, and he didn't know whether to celebrate that or mourn it, too.

"Do you want to know why I remember anything?" she demanded, her voice hot. "I'll tell you. I found your father and his massage therapist. I think I told you that, though to be honest, it's a blur. And I'm not even sure that I would have cared about that as much as I should have, if there had been any repentance. If he had promised me that I'd never see it again."

She made a face, and he had to wonder what was on his. Or maybe he had simply frozen solid at these details he certainly didn't want to know. He hadn't liked it when his father had regaled his mother with the squalid details of his trysts at the dinner table.

He certainly didn't like imagining *his Saskia* subject to a similar fate.

It made him want to fly directly to that godforsaken villa and burn it down with a match from his own hand.

Saskia squared her shoulders and kept her gaze direct. "If you want to know the truth, I didn't *want* to sleep with him myself. I don't know that I would have minded that much if he'd decided that other arrangements had to be made." She sighed. "I can't really access the part of me that was Selwen. But I know that all she wanted was a home. And safety. A place where she could simply rest. He made it sound like he would provide those things for her. He promised her that he would."

Thanasis had to unclench his jaw. "There is absolutely nothing safe about my father."

"Oh, he was making that clear," Saskia said, ruefully. "He certainly wanted me to see him in the act, or didn't much care if I did, anyway. It would have been easy enough for him to lock the door. He didn't." She eased herself back on the bed, hoisted herself up, and then shifted around so she was kneeling there before him. "What he did do was come in and say a lot of vaguely threatening things to me while I was packing to leave. Then he kissed me, not very nicely—I think so I would know he meant it."

Everything inside Thanasis simply…shattered.

As if he had been made of glass all along. And now he was smashed into dust.

That shattering, and smashing, went on and on—but it didn't hurt. Distantly, he thought perhaps it drew blood, but he didn't mind.

"I beg your pardon," he said, and he could hear his voice as if it came from far, far away, and barely sounded like his at all. "What did you just say?"

"He kissed me," Saskia said again, and her eyes widened with concern, but she still didn't look away from him. "And I didn't like it. Do you know what I thought?"

"I can only imagine." Once again, Thanasis thought that his voice sounded so far away that he could barely credit that it was his own. He no longer recognized it. Or himself. "Particularly if your thoughts in any way mirror mine."

She knelt up and then she put her hands on his chest, as if she couldn't feel the glass shards where his flesh had been. As if she didn't understand that he was no longer the man he'd been. That there was nothing left of him but dust and regret.

"No one has ever kissed me but you," she told him. Simple and devastating. "No one has ever touched me but you, and I hated it."

When he only stared down at her, somewhere between stricken and frozen and *shattered*, she hurried on. "I hated it, but it was a wonderful thing all the same, because it brought everything back. I knew everything about him was wrong and that was how I found me again. It all came flooding back while he was standing there, saying God knows what. I didn't care. I remembered *you,* Thanasis. I remembered *us.* I remembered everything."

"How could you have decided to marry him if you had never even kissed?" Thanasis demanded, when that was really very low on his list of concerns just then.

"Because I didn't care about him," she shot back. "I'm not sure I cared about anything, Thanasis. You don't understand, I don't think, what it was actually like to be Selwen. To be me, but cut off from everything I care about and everything I am. To make the best of it with what I have, yet always feel off. Lost. Especially after Ffion died. She was the only thing that made me feel *real*."

"You told me." Thanasis reached out to set her back on the bed, but he ended up holding her there instead, high against his chest. "You wore the equivalent of sackcloth and ash. You scuttled around the sodden streets of Wales. In a hood with downcast eyes, no less."

"Because somewhere, deep inside of me, I knew that everything was wrong," she said, very distinctly. Very clearly. "I didn't want anyone else looking at me. You're the only one I have ever wanted anywhere near me. You know that."

"Yet you somehow thought you could have a sexless marriage with a man so debauched that he is a cautionary tale often told to children on the Greek mainland?" He shook his head. His grip tightened on her arms, but only enough to remind him that she was real. That he wasn't dreaming this. That this was happening—for good and ill alike. "You believed this was not only possible, but desirable?"

"When I tell you that he was nothing but kind to me, what I mean is that he truly was nothing but kind to me. Until he wasn't." Saskia shook her head. "I'm not a complete idiot, Thanasis, and neither was Selwen. We took walks together in the olive groves. He seemed overwhelmingly respectful of my wishes in all things."

Thanasis snorted. "He's always playing a game. Perhaps the game this season was innocence. Virtue. Either way, his games have a way of ending badly."

"I saw who he was." Her expression was set, her gaze clear. "And I didn't like what I saw. That's why I called you."

That was not the only reason she'd called him, he thought. Not the only one, not if she was finally telling him the truth.

"But first there was a kiss."

"And thank God there was," Saskia said, with another blast of that temper of hers. He could see it light her up and something in him actually shook, because God help him, but he'd missed this. He'd missed *her*.

He'd missed the enduring joy of being in the presence of the one person in this life that he could be entirely himself with, no matter what was happening between them. Being shouted at by Saskia ranked better than all the obsequious boardroom interactions he'd ever had or ever will. Saskia furious with him was always better than any other alternative that didn't involve her.

He'd known that five years ago. Then he'd lived it.

"If he hadn't kissed me, I would still be there on that island," she was ranting at him now. "I would still not remember who the hell I am. And that would be a crying shame, Thanasis, because I liked Selwen. She took care of me. When I had nothing at all in this world, I had her. And Ffion loved her, which is reason enough to think the best of her all on its own." Her voice went ragged, then. "But I prefer *me*."

Thanasis reached over and slid his hand along the side of her face, so that his fingertips brushed her temples and he could run his thumb over her mouth.

She was back. She was his.

They still fit. They always would.

But that shattering inside him had stopped, now. And her return came with a terrible clarity that he couldn't ignore. It was as if the scales had finally fallen from his eyes, and now that they had, he saw the truth of things.

Maybe he shouldn't have been surprised that a clarity like that, cut-glass and dust, was painful.

"I must go," he told her abruptly, because he didn't want to leave.

He watched her mouth drop open. *"Go?"* she echoed.

But Thanasis couldn't explain this to her. There were too many shards of glass stuck deep in his chest, and he knew himself to be the real villain in all of this after all. He could see it now.

And there was only one way to fix it.

Only one thing that would, if not make this right, at least make it better.

He had to hope it would.

"You can't go," she whispered. "I've only just come back."

"Saskia," he said, and her name was the song it had always been in his mouth. In his heart. "You will never know how much you mean to me. You will never comprehend it."

And then he turned and walked away from her, because it was that or lose himself in her again. He couldn't let that happen.

He couldn't lose his momentum when he'd only just found it.

It was long past time for reckoning. And he knew he'd either do it now, or not at all.

Because he was already more monster than he liked to admit.

CHAPTER ELEVEN

IT WASN'T UNTIL she heard the front door of the flat shut that Saskia finally accepted the fact that he was gone. He was really gone when she'd kept thinking he'd turn back. She'd kept thinking he'd reconsider.

She stayed where she was, kneeling on that bed and feeling winded.

And she stayed there a long, long while.

Thanasis didn't come back that evening. He didn't come back for days.

She started to wonder if he planned to come back at all.

One night, Saskia sat in her study with the fire blazing, wrapped up in a sweatshirt she knew was his. She would have known it was his even if she hadn't found it in his part of the closet. She was sure she could smell that hint of vetiver in the fabric, that ghost of him that haunted her everywhere she turned in this flat.

Though there were worse ghosts. She stared around at the pictures of the two of them on every surface, laughing, smiling, *gazing* at each other. She remembered each and every one of the moments captured. It was like, having deserted her for so long, her memories were working overtime now.

That or her heart was in charge, making sure she knew exactly how broken she could feel.

Eventually, as the days passed her by with no sign of Thanasis, Saskia realized that she had never really considered the possibility that *he* might leave *her*.

Even that fateful night when she'd stormed out of the flat in high dudgeon but with no preparation, she'd expected him to be there when she got back. She had tucked a fistful of twenty-pound notes into her pocket and had taken off into the night. She'd bought her train ticket with cash just like she'd bought herself snacks off the trolley, too.

She'd sat there on the train as it left Paddington Station, telling herself bold stories about how she was going to break free of *that man* and start a whole new… *something*.

All the while secure in the knowledge that she would do nothing of the sort.

If she hadn't thumped her head and wandered off from that train, she likely would have found her way back to him much sooner. The actual details of the derailment were blurry to her even now, but she rather thought that she'd ended up on that roadside because she'd been trying to walk her way home.

Because Thanasis hadn't simply been her lover. She hadn't simply been his mistress. Maybe, she'd thought then, it was a special sort of foolishness to imagine that there had ever been anything simple about those descriptions—or those relationships—at any point in history. Because it was all people, wasn't it. And if those people were anything like her, they'd been doomed from the start.

Because that was the thing that there was no getting past, then or now.

Saskia had not only been in love with Thanasis since the moment she'd laid eyes on him in the Tate Modern, she had been equally in love with him—if significantly more horrified by it—from the moment she'd clapped eyes on him in his father's villa.

She'd wanted desperately to pretend otherwise, and she'd tried. She truly had. But she had been more engaged with Thanasis as Selwen—even while telling him all the terrible things she'd imagined he might've done to a version of her she couldn't remember—than she'd ever been about anything else in those five years.

She had kissed him on that beach. He had brought her alive, and she'd hated it. She'd pretended it wasn't happening, because she'd wanted to stay locked up inside herself. That was what she'd understood. That was *who she was*.

Or rather, that was who she'd become. That was why Ffion had given her that list, and some money, and had ordered Selwen to do what she'd asked. She might not have known who Selwen really was, but she'd understood the important bit.

That Selwen was hiding, whether she knew it or not.

She might have forgotten all the details, so little did the men she'd met impress her, but Selwen had danced her way across Greece. Just as Ffion had asked. She'd hit one island after the next, had flitted from one *taverna* to another, and the only man she'd looked twice at was the one who resembled Thanasis.

The one who sometimes looked a little bit like him around the eyes. And the mouth.

If she'd never run into a Zacharias, Selwen would likely still be dancing now, a mystery to herself and shut off from everyone else.

Instead, she'd come alive. She'd come *home.*

And now she sat about in this flat that she could remember decorating all too well, because each item that had come into it *meant something.* She had considered it nesting, and she knew he had, too.

This had been their *home,* a safe place for both of them.

It had been that for a long time.

Until, that was, she had decided that he must think less of her. Because if he didn't, why would he keep hiding her away?

But now that she had nothing but time and space to look back at those days—and how hurt she'd been, and how determined she'd been to hurt him too—Saskia realized that there had been a safety in it. Because even then, she'd had absolute faith in the fact that she could shout at him, throw things, act up in any way she liked. That they could roll all over that bed and seemingly never come up for air, and that he would never leave her.

And now he'd left her twice.

Once because she'd made up the very worst version of him and used it against him.

This time because she'd showed him the very worst version of herself.

Having been more versions of herself than she was comfortable with, Saskia couldn't say she enjoyed just...*sitting* with all that. But she did.

Because it was the least she could do. It was the bare minimum she owed this great love that had somehow gotten so twisted and torn. It was what she had to do, she understood, because once she was done looking inward after the tumult of regaining her memory and coming back here and New York, and then finally wrapping herself up in Thanasis again...

Once all the *sitting with it* was done, she would have to act.

And she needed to decide what that would look like, now that she knew everything.

Including her own failures, this time around. Because the Saskia she was now, the Saskia who had been Selwen, would never dream of wasting that much time with manufactured fights and hurt feelings.

This time—if there was a *this time*—she didn't intend to waste a single second.

All told, it was more than a week before she heard his keys in the door one evening. She didn't believe it at first. Saskia had dreamed this very thing too many times already, rushing out into the lounge to find herself completely alone—

But this time, when she heard the door open and then shut, she raced down the hall from the study the way she always did—

Then skidded to a stop when she saw him.

He looked different tonight. Taller, somehow. And sterner, as if every stray bit of emotion had been flayed from his bones.

She thought, *this is it. He's come to officially break up with me, tell me to get out of his flat, and carry on with my life.*

"Saskia," he began, in a voice that seemed dark and heavy.

And she couldn't bear it. She couldn't *take* it.

"Don't!" she cried out.

He stopped, looking startled.

Her chest hurt from all the wild breathing and her poor heart besides, but she understood that this was her chance. She had to take it—before he could say the things she didn't want to hear.

"I'm so sorry I lied to you," she said, swift and to the point. "I don't know why I did it. It was unfair, but then, so were all the things I said to you when I was Selwen. I didn't have to remember everything that happened between us to know—at an immediate glance—that you're not the kind of man who would do those things."

"That isn't—"

Saskia cut him off. "A man as scary as I made you sound doesn't stand around listening to a character assassination from a woman who claims she doesn't remember him. So I can tell you with total confidence that even when I was Selwen, I knew better than to claim you were that kind of man." He was scowling at her, so she took a breath and kept going. "I think, somewhere deep down I couldn't remember, that my feelings were hurt. I thought you'd been ashamed of me, back when we lived here together. Maybe I wanted you to be ashamed of yourself."

He stopped scowling. He sighed instead. "I don't think that this has any—"

"All of this is ridiculous," she said, cutting him off again, because maybe she was a little bit desperate. Or a lot. "Because the truth of the matter is what I told you before you left this time. You're the only man I've ever wanted. Only you, Thanasis. Only and ever you."

"Saskia," he said again, his voice even more intent this time.

She rushed toward him then. And when she got to him, she took his hands in hers and she held him tight, staring up at him as if her intensity alone could change this.

Because it had to. "Don't you understand?" she asked him, with all the urgency she felt inside of her. "I love you, Thanasis. I've always loved you. Even when I was lost to myself, I must have loved you just as fiercely, because I was clearly keeping a vigil all these years. I was mourning you all the while."

She couldn't read that look on his face, so she gripped him harder and she kept going. "And I do remember what happened that night. I'd worked myself up into a state and nothing you said or did could change it, because I wanted to be yours forever and you seemed perfectly happy to stay as we were. And the reality is, I was always coming back. I had no intention of really leaving you. How could I? I could no sooner leave you than I could leave myself. I had to *actually leave myself* to stay away from you."

Saskia thought there was moisture on her face, though she couldn't bring herself to check, because that would mean letting go of him. And she was tired of letting go of him.

"I just love you, Thanasis," she said, with all the love and sorrow, regret and hope she had inside of her. "I hope you know that. I love you so much."

Slowly, he switched their arms so he could take her hands in his, and then he was the one gazing at her. And she couldn't read a single thing on his face. He looked so stern. He looked so terribly forbidding.

She thought, *this is actually happening. He's going to end it after all of this and I have no one to blame but myself.*

"You loving me is convenient," he told her, in that dark, stirring way of his. "Because Saskia, I have loved you this whole time. I thought you knew. I loved you from my very first glimpse of you in front of that execrable painting. And every single thing I learned about you since then has made me love you more. There has never been a single moment that I have been the slightest bit ashamed of you, nor could there ever be. When I told you that I was trying to keep you safe, I meant it. *From Pavlos.*"

"I wish I never heard his name," she threw out, almost like she was in anguish, but her heart was doing cartwheels inside of her chest.

He loved her. He said he *loved* her.

"Did you think that I had left you?" he asked, studying her face. And to her surprise, when she nodded, he laughed. He laughed so hard that she found herself smiling too. He laughed and he laughed, and then when he sobered, he pulled her closer. "I did not spend five years disbelieving your death, then grieving your loss, to leave you simply because you did not choose to tell me every single facet of your new existence. You do not owe me any explanation about your memory, *fos mou*. My only concern was that I had taken advantage of you when I could remember what you could not."

"If you did, I can only hope that you'll do it again," Saskia said. She smiled. "And soon."

Thanasis smiled back. He pulled her closer and kissed her, on her forehead. On each cheek.

And then, finally her lips.

But not the way she wanted him to. Not that all-consuming fire.

He set her back from him once more, and smiled when she scowled up at him.

"I wanted to come before you the man I should always have been," he told her with all of that same ruthless intensity. "I spent all this time thinking that I could make this work. That I could spread myself between my father and myself and somehow be whole." He shook his head. "But what I cannot do, what I will not do, is leave you some kind of bargaining chip in the middle. He might not have known that you were mine first, but he will know you are mine forever. And I will not have him within a breath of you, Saskia. Not ever again."

"I don't care about him," she said at once.

"But I do," Thanasis replied, and his dark eyes glittered with that temper that she knew only she got to see. "That is where I have been. I have separated myself from that waste of a man, at last. I have severed our business relationship. As expected, he dramatically disowned me on the spot, and I'm delighted. I don't know why I didn't do it sooner. From this point forward, there is no relationship between us. He will never see either one of us again."

And he was holding her so tightly that she moved closer, and made sure she was holding him, too. That they were holding each other.

"Thanasis," she began, but he shook his head.

"That is not all," he told her. "I had to find a way to

forgive my mother, too. I have been so angry with her for staying. I have blamed her for putting up with him all those years when the truth is, I don't know why she did it. Maybe she thought she was protecting me."

Saskia thought her heart might burst. "Maybe," she said softly, "you should forgive yourself, too. You were a child. Maybe you were angry at her because it was easier than the fear you must have felt, growing up in such a volatile environment."

"I will become the man you deserve," he told her, his voice a raw vow. "I promise you, Saskia."

"I realized that the only reason I was interested in him is because he reminded me of you," she told him then, urgently. "Not his personality, of course, but there were glimpses. You come from him, after all. Every now and again, I would see the ghost of you and it kept me happy. Happy enough to overlook everything else."

"I do not wish you to have to overlook anything," Thanasis gritted out at her. "I do not intend for you to suffer through anything, for anyone. You deserve the world, Saskia. And I intend to give it to you."

"I love you," she said again, and it tasted so sweet that she said it once more.

She thought she could say it forever, over and over and over, and never get sick of it.

He smiled at her then, and it was a real, rare, beautiful smile. If she hadn't already been crying, she would have started then and there.

Then he stepped back.

And while she watched, not sure if she was shocked or delighted—or both at once—Thanasis dropped easily down to one knee. His eyes on her, he reached into the pocket of his coat and pulled out a small box.

Saskia held her breath. Her hands moved to cover her mouth.

He cracked open the box and nestled there within it was an exquisite ring, a gorgeous diamond set with smaller ones all around it, and it shined so bright it was impossible to look at it and *not* smile.

"Marry me," Thanasis said to her, and though his voice was deep it was a question, not a command. "Be my wife. The mother of my children. The light of my life. Because you are already the love of my life, Saskia. This is true when you lived, this is true when you died, and it is only more true now that you are mine again."

He did not shift. He kept his gaze trained on her, with all their lost futures bright and shining there between them. "I cannot imagine a day without you. I have already lived too many of them and I do not wish to do it again." His expression grew even more intense. "I am not ashamed of you. I do not want to hide you. And I will protect you from anyone who comes for you, whether it's my father, my silly half siblings, or anyone else who is foolish enough to imagine that I will not use every last thing in my power to keep you safe, happy, and filled with as much joy as you can bear."

"Yes," Saskia whispered. "With everything I am, everything I was, and everything I hope we will be, *yes*, Thanasis. I can't wait to marry you. I can't wait to grow old with you. I can't wait to live our whole lives together, the way we're supposed to do."

Then she sank down on her knees too, and cried

without restraint or the faintest shred of shame when he slipped that ring on her finger.

And when their mouths finally met again, she knew at last that she was home.

That *they* were home.

That this sweeping, life-altering, all-consuming kiss, made of fire and love and the rest of eternity, would always be the only home they needed.

CHAPTER TWELVE

THEY DID NOT stay in the flat, though they couldn't bear to part with it. They moved instead into Thanasis's beautiful house on Hampstead Heath, which reminded Saskia of a museum.

"Maybe a mausoleum," she murmured, when he walked her through the marble halls and echoing rooms.

"Something like that," he agreed, and then he showed her into a particular room that was all books and art, all arranged around one enormous canvas on the far wall.

Saskia recognized it at once. "It's that painting," she breathed, her hands over her mouth again, this time because she was laughing. "You went out and got that dreadful painting."

He came and stood beside her, pulling her into his side because they liked everything better when they fit together like puzzle pieces.

"It is dreadful," he agreed, gazing up at it. "I bought it shortly after we met, when that exhibition ended. It has not improved in all this time." He smiled down at her. "But I find I cannot bear to part with it."

She tipped her head back. "You've had it all this time."

"You might not have been here," he told her, his smile fading while the intensity in his gaze grew. "But there is no place I have ever been that you are not, *fos mou.*"

They married quietly and without fanfare, and spent that first night back in the flat, as if to finally christen the place with their legal union. As if that was the only way they could leave those rooms in Chelsea that had seen the whole span of their relationship.

Neither one of them wanted to get rid of the place even then, but they couldn't go back after that. They cleared it out of everything that was theirs and leased it out.

Then they set about making his mausoleum into their home.

And every time the sun was out over London, Saskia would find a reason to sit with him in the mornings in their well-tested bed, gaze out at the sunrise, and think about this life she'd almost lost twice.

She only wished that Ffion was here to see it.

But I think that you see just fine from where you are, she would think. *And I hope you know that I'm right where I belong.*

Thanasis turned a little-used greenhouse and shed into an art studio, and insisted that she use it. Saskia felt like a fraud, and expected that she would waste her time the way she had when she was on the island.

But instead, she found that when she picked up a brush or a pencil, the lines seemed to form of their own accord.

Maybe, all along, her interest in art had been an attempt to use beauty to find safety. And now she was safe, and her life was more beautiful by the day, and at last she could let the art in her free.

It was a magical, creative, fertile time. In more ways than one.

They had their first baby nine months from that first night back together in the flat. She was a chubby, smiley girl, filled with life and love, and they named her Selwen Ffion, because it only seemed right.

"And because," Saskia whispered to her daughter in the middle of the night, as the baby latched on and her husband lay beside her with his hand on her back so she wouldn't be alone, "I think Selwen deserves a better life. And you'll give her one, my darling girl. I know you will."

If there was nonsense in the tabloids about them, neither one of them cared. Every now and again, one of Thanasis's half siblings would turn up to cause trouble, but Saskia insisted that they treat them as if they didn't expect that trouble at all.

"You don't know what it's like to be alone in the world," she would remind her husband. "Not really alone. You might not have understood your mother, but at least you had her."

As she made his half siblings food. As she let them tell her their wild stories. As they proved themselves incapable of living up to the myths they tried to tell about who they were, time and again.

She would smile at Thanasis and tell him it was all for the best. It was all okay.

"The very least we can do is give them a soft place to land, for a while. Because you know they won't get that from Pavlos."

He was barely worth thinking about. They rarely did. Yet when he died, he clearly thought he'd got in the last laugh, because he had not disinherited Thanasis at all. He'd left it all to him—but had made certain to call Saskia *the tart* in his last will and testament.

"Charming as ever," Saskia said, and laughed so much that she thought she might actually pull something.

Thanasis did not bother to go back to the villa and sort things out, as Pavlos must have assumed he would do. He left it all to the others and let them sort it out themselves.

"It's your birthright," Saskia said. "Surely you must want something."

"I have everything I want," Thanasis told her.

"You have a right tart, apparently," she said, still laughing.

But he crawled into bed beside her, after she put the new baby down, and showed her precisely how he felt about the things he wanted—and how he preferred to receive them.

They got to four perfect children, two girls and two boys. And they had a very serious discussion about whether or not they should stop.

"I wanted a family and a home," she told him. "You have given me all of that and more. They have expanded my heart more than I ever imagined possible."

"And you have taught me, every day, that the only way to love is bigger," Thanasis replied. "Bigger. Wider. So that these children never have any idea that there's any other way."

"I love you so much," she whispered. "I can't believe that it's possible, but I love you more each day."

The passion between them only grew. Everyone said it would go the other way. Everyone promised them that it would fade, but it didn't. It grew and grew, becoming only more intimate, and more beautiful as they went.

Thanasis only expanded his business. Saskia showed her art in London galleries, and when she sold her first piece, they framed a print of it and put it next to that modern scribble, for posterity.

That was how they ended up with the fifth baby, then the sixth.

It was all that beautiful living. It was all that love.

And so it was after their seventh, with the house run over with all of that noise and light, laughter and feelings—a mausoleum no more—that they finally decided that they'd reached capacity.

"I love you pregnant," Thanasis told her. "But maybe, going forward, we can find other ways to enjoy that perfect body of yours."

And he was true to his word.

The children were not always happy, which was a good thing. Happiness alone meant little. Happiness tested led to joy. And so they had their joys, and their deep pains, but they also had their parents. Their champions in all things, their fiercest advocates, and the first to call them out when they were wrong.

But not the way Thanasis's father had done in his time.

They started with love. They led from love.

Love, in the end, was who they were.

And late in their life, when they were both old and

gray and their children talked around them as if they'd become the children themselves, they still held hands.

Like they were new.

* * * * *

*Did you fall in love with
Forbidden Greek Mistress?
Then you're sure to enjoy
these other dazzling stories
by Caitlin Crews!*

Greek's Christmas Heir
Greek's Enemy Bride
Carrying a Sicilian Secret
Kidnapped for His Revenge
Her Accidental Spanish Heir

Available now!

MILLS & BOON®

Coming next month

KING'S EMERGENCY WIFE
Lucy King

'I'd like you to draft an announcement regarding the imminent change to my marital status.'

If Sofia was startled by his request, she didn't show it. She barely even blinked. 'Have you finally made your choice?'

Ivo nodded shortly. 'I have.'

'I understood none of the current candidates were deemed to be suitable.'

'That's correct,' he said. 'I had to think laterally. Outside the box. It turned out to be an excellent move.'

'Then may I be the first to offer you my congratulations.'

'Thank you.'

'The palace will breathe a sigh of relief.'

'I can almost hear it now.'

'I'll draft the announcement immediately and email it to you for approval,' she said, glancing down briefly to jot something in her notebook. 'It will be sent to all major news outlets within the hour.'

'Good.'

'The people will be ecstatic.'

'I certainly hope so.'

'Just one thing…'

'Yes?'

She lifted her gaze back to his, her smile faint, her expression quizzical. 'Who's the lucky lady?'

'You are.'

Continue reading

KING'S EMERGENCY WIFE
Lucy King

Available next month
millsandboon.co.uk

Copyright ©2025 Lucy King

COMING SOON!

We really hope you enjoyed reading this book.
If you're looking for more romance
be sure to head to the shops when
new books are available on

Thursday 25th September

To see which titles are coming soon, please visit
millsandboon.co.uk/nextmonth

MILLS & BOON

MILLS & BOON TRUE LOVE IS HAVING A MAKEOVER!

Introducing

Love Always

Swoon-worthy romances, where love takes center stage. Same heartwarming stories, stylish new look!

Look out for our brand new look
COMING SEPTEMBER 2025

MILLS & BOON

OUT NOW!

THE TYCOON'S AFFAIR COLLECTION

CRAVING HIS LOVE

USA TODAY BESTSELLING AUTHOR
SHARON KENDRICK

Available at
millsandboon.co.uk

MILLS & BOON

FOUR BRAND NEW BOOKS FROM
MILLS & BOON MODERN

Indulge in desire, drama, and breathtaking romance – where passion knows no bounds!

OUT NOW

Eight Modern stories published every month, find them all at:

millsandboon.co.uk

afterglow BOOKS

Afterglow Books is a trend-led, trope-filled list of books with diverse, authentic and relatable characters, a wide array of voices and representations, plus real world trials and tribulations. Featuring all the tropes you could possibly want (think small-town settings, fake relationships, grumpy vs sunshine, enemies to lovers) and all with a generous dose of spice in every story.

♪ @millsandboonuk
◉ @millsandboonuk
afterglowbooks.co.uk
#AfterglowBooks

For all the latest book news, exclusive content and giveaways scan the QR code below to sign up to the Afterglow newsletter:

SCAN ME

afterglow BOOKS

She's grumpy. He's sunshine. Will love grow?

Let's Give 'Em **PUMPKIN** *to Talk About*

ISABELLE POPP

Could this be the start of a new chapter?

The Secret Crush Book Club

KARMEN LEE

- Grumpy/sunshine
- Small-town romance
- Spicy

- LGBTQ+
- Small-town romance
- Spicy

OUT NOW

Two stories published every month. Discover more at:
Afterglowbooks.co.uk

LET'S TALK
Romance

For exclusive extracts, competitions and special offers, find us online:

- **f** MillsandBoon
- **X** @MillsandBoon
- **◉** @MillsandBoonUK
- **♪** @MillsandBoonUK

Get in touch on 01413 063 232

> For all the latest titles coming soon, visit
> millsandboon.co.uk/nextmonth